reUNION

also by david daniel

NOVELS

The Marble Kite

Goofy Foot

White Rabbit

Murder at the Baseball Hall of Fame
(WITH CHRIS CARPENTER)

The Skelly Man

The Heaven Stone

The Tuesday Man

Ark

STORY COLLECTIONS

Coffin Dust

Six off 66

reUNION

david daniel

thomas dunne books
st. martin's press ≈ new york

This is a work of fiction. All of the characters, organizations, and events portrayed in this novel are either products of the author's imagination or are used fictitiously.

THOMAS DUNNE BOOKS.
An imprint of St. Martin's Press.

www.thomasdunnebooks.com
www.stmartins.com

Library of Congress Cataloging-in-Publication Data

Daniel, David, 1945–
    Reunion / David Daniel.—1st ed.
        p.   cm.
    ISBN-13: 978-0-312-36371-0
    ISBN-10: 0-312-36371-0
    1. Class reunions—Fiction.   2. City and town life—Fiction.
3. Massachusetts—Fiction.   4. Decision making—Fiction.   I. Title.
PS3554.A5383R48 2008
813'.54—dc22

                                                        2008005777

First Edition: May 2008

10 9 8 7 6 5 4 3 2 1

In memory of
my parents,
whose gifts to me
were a love of words
and a gypsy heart

acknowledgments

Many thanks to Joe Byrd, Helen Bray-Garretson, Tim Coats, Jim Cocoros, Kathy Duckett, Lee Duckett, Amy Farranto, Ed Ford, David Harrison, Byron Hoot, Karen Johnson, Claire Krasnow, Ed Krasnow, Judy Loose, Kathy Mackel, Beverly McCoy, Floyd Nease, Adam Robinson, Bob Sanchez, Arthur Seamans, Patricia Thorpe, Daniel Trask, Emily Trask, Jason Trask, Timothy Trask, David Tuells, and Gary Watkins. Special thanks to Ruth Cavin and Toni Plummer at St. Martin's Press. Thanks, too, to my student writers Keith and Kevin Carnevale, Scott Ellis, and Barbara Klain. Finally, for her continued love and support, my wife Stephanie.

There is one moment in childhood when
a door opens and lets the future in.

—Graham Greene, *The Power and the Glory*

What might have been and what has been
Point to one end, which is always present.

—T. S. Eliot, "Burnt Norton" *Four Quartets*

ONE

rock
breaks
scissors

i Tom

"First visit to Boston, sir?" The young woman at the airport kiosk slipped the picture postcards into a small bag.

"First in a long time," Tom Knowles said.

"Where are you from?"

"Los Angeles." Tom considered bouncing the question back, but why? *Brief* was the plan for this trip. In, out, gone.

At the car rental desk he upgraded to a Ford Escape for the extra cargo room and soon was creeping south in the Friday afternoon crush. In Adams Point, as he exited onto 3-A, he slowed to glance at a weathered sign. BOSTON 12, one arrow pointing in the direction he'd just come from, another pointing ahead: NO. WEY. 3. Some things didn't change. Was there a DPW shed somewhere, with a supply of such signs, plentiful as sharks' teeth? A car honked behind him and a BMW jerked past, the driver's mouth twisted in a snarl of words that definitely weren't "Welcome home, Pilgrim." Tom just grinned. In, out, gone.

Crossing the high bridge over the mouth of the river between Adams Point and North Weybridge there at the sea's edge, he glanced automatically to his right. Still mighty, even in abandonment,

3

huge gantry cranes looming, the shipyard dominated the landscape. The "Graveyard" he had come to call it, thinking of the ships built there as enormous steel coffins, thinking of Dad.

Along Bridge Street the Dari-Twirl ice cream stand remained, the tall marquee with the Eskimo girl in place, though she had age spots now; and at the Atlantic Diner a sign still claimed IF THE COL-ONEL MADE FRIED CHICKEN THIS GOOD HE'D BE A GENERAL; but most of the businesses were new.

Tom had timed his journey for a break between gigs: the ending of a schlocky sitcom he'd been a writer for, a stinker that had died the cancellation death it deserved, and the prospect of selling a screenplay that he had pitched at half a dozen meetings the week before. *Take five, brah,* his agent had advised (Randy was a misplaced surfer dude, twenty years younger than Tom): *Go get your past squared away; leave this to me. I smell blood on this one. Then you come back, go to work, and we drag race our new Porsches on Sunset.*

None of that would happen. A few days away Tom would begin to sense that something very strange had befallen him; and soon he would grasp the outlines of events that even his writer's mind, forced to its ragged limits, would be hard-pressed to imagine. But all that was yet to come, and now, with the wheel of gulls over the sun-spangled water and the mild late September air streaming through the Escape's windows, he focused his attention ahead in rising anticipation.

The neighborhood was little changed: sidewalks, fancier cars in the driveways, kids kicking a soccer ball where once they'd punted footballs, but mostly things remained, including the white Cape Cod house on Edgewater Road. His mother had resisted the trend toward vinyl siding, but the cedar shingles were holding up well, and the window sashes didn't look half bad under the pressed metal awnings that Dad had believed would be a good investment. "They'll last forever," he'd enthused; and he'd been right.

He pulled in behind the Dodge Aries K that was practically as old as the awnings and got out. The front grass was shaggy; ditto the privet hedge running along one side of the property. Farther back, where the lot gave way to a neighbor's backyard, the apple trees were spiky and untended now. Overall, though, the property looked all right.

The side door was locked. Knocking a second time, Tom peered through the pane into the kitchen, visited by the sudden thought that sometime between when he'd spoken with his mother by phone from LAX that morning and now something had happened to her. He dug his cellular telephone from his jacket pocket and was about to dial her number when she appeared, shuffling down the short hallway into the kitchen, pale and stooped and vaguely smiling, wearing a faded yellow housedress.

"I didn't hear you," she apologized when she'd opened the door. "I had the TV on." Still did; voices were booming in another room.

He hugged her, kissing the thin hair on the top of her head, then backed off as her hearing aid whistled shrilly. She adjusted it and stood looking up at him with watery eyes in the same sky blue Tom had inherited. "Are you still smoking?"

"Two cigarettes a day," he said, "that's it." He'd bought the pack that morning.

"Even after all these years, I can never smell tobacco without a craving." Raleigh had been her brand. She waved a frail hand, as if dispersing a smoky past. "You're thinner. Have you lost weight?"

His weight had been the same for years, since he got out of the army—175 pounds on his six-foot frame—but it was a mantra whenever she saw him, admittedly not often these days. What did it mean that she imagined change where none existed, yet made no note of what had altered indelibly? Could she have missed the lines that had etched deeper into his face, or the voice, roughened to a raspy baritone? And there was the gray threaded into his sandy hair, would have strayed down into his beard, but he'd shaved it off months ago. Without the beard, his face sometimes seemed too lean to him, his jaw set with a look of vague discontent (Tamara thought so), his eyes wary where once they'd been curious. Perhaps it was a parent's affliction (or blessing) to be blind to changes in a child.

She, however, had physically changed, and he didn't miss the ways. No longer the erect-postured, big-boned woman she had been, she was shrunken now, bent with the dowager's hump women of her generation sometimes developed late in life. Her hair was wispy, colorless, and her skin as crinkly as old crepe paper and mottled with bruises, like pink spiders on the loose flesh of her arms. Her eyes, which had always had a wide, almost startled quality, were pouchy and red-rimmed. All of which confirmed the purpose of his return. His mother had grown too old to take care of herself, let alone the house. She was ready for assisted living, but if he'd expected she'd be prepared to go, he was wrong. Nothing, he noted as they settled in, suggested any sense of readiness. "Have you spoken with a Realtor?" he asked.

She sighed. "I've been in this house forty-five years. Since your father and I bought it." Tom knew the story. His folks had moved from a tiny flat in East Boston to come here to a house smaller than they'd hoped for, closer to the bay than she liked ("the really run-down properties were right along the water, don't you know— shanty Irish"), but at ten thousand dollars, with a thirty-year GI loan, it was affordable. "When we'd signed all the papers, all the 'wherebys' and 'therefores,' and got the passkey, we looked at each other and we thought, *What on earth have we done?* It seemed an unbelievable sum."

"The price you'll get for it is going to seem pretty unbelievable, too," Tom said. "I'll call someone tomorrow."

"Maybe we should wait and think about this."

"We've been over this many times on the phone."

"Why couldn't you just keep the house and . . ."

"And *what*, Mom? I don't live here. I haven't lived here in years. I live in California. You could come out there, but you don't want to." Hearing the exaggerated singsong in his voice, the note of mild reproach one might use admonishing a child, he left off. His mother didn't seem to notice. Had she even heard?

"We'll discuss it," she said vaguely. "There's time."

That, too, was a Knowles family mantra. *Let's think on it. We'll see. There's time.* Dad, especially, had been famous for putting things on a back burner, where it was simple enough to forget them until they evaporated, or boiled over. Tomorrow. When my ship comes in. When the cows come home. All that futurity that never arrived, or sometimes (as with his father's illness) turned up with a vengeance. Tom sighed. He could have told her that change was like pulling off a Band-Aid—painful any way you did it, so best done fast—but why start his visit with a hassle? He'd call a real estate agent and get the house priced and listed. In, out, gone. He went to get his travel bag.

Later, when they had finished treading the safe ground of who was doing what, who still lived in town, who had died—not yet getting to anything truly personal—he and his mother sat in the den drinking tea. This had been his parents' bedroom in the early years, before they'd added two bedrooms upstairs. Now his mother had reverted to using this as her quarters, sleeping on a daybed. A housekeeper came in once a week, an Irish woman Tom spoke to on the phone from time to time and who seemed genuinely to care for his mother and gave him updates on Mom's condition, but the house smelled of Vicks and mothballs and dust. Issues of *Yankee* and *Time* and the day's *Herald* (the crossword puzzle and Word Jumble duly filled in) lay about. From among a stack of papers on a hassock Mom withdrew a page and squinted at it. "I saved this." She passed it to him. "In case you're interested."

The article was about his high school's homecoming celebration and reunion. His class was having its thirtieth. A postcard had come to the house, his last known whereabouts, although he hadn't lived there for decades. He had briefly considered attending his tenth reunion, back in '74. *Haven's End* had been published earlier that year, and he had entertained the idea that coming back as a novelist might be interesting. But he had let the notion fade and hadn't bothered with any subsequent events. For what? To sit around with old classmates, picking like buzzards at the entrails of the past? It'd make meager fare. He didn't voice any of this to his mother and simply laid the page aside, saying he would not have time. It was immaterial to her. "You must be hungry," she said. "Do they still feed you on airplanes? I forget."

At nine o'clock his mother went off to bed, and Tom retreated upstairs to the room that had been his. He turned on the duck decoy lamp his grandfather had made for Tom's tenth birthday. The room was smaller than he remembered, the sloped ceiling lower, but there was still the twin bed of walnut-finished pine, the desk with the duck lamp, the blue curtains with the ship's wheel motif, only slightly faded, those tacky aluminum awnings having done their job of muting the sun all these years. He unzipped his travel bag and removed slacks, shirts, a sport coat, some ties, and hung them in the closet, which was empty save for a few articles of clothing gathering dust in the back.

When he sat experimentally at the desk, his knees touched the underside. It was here that he'd done homework, crammed for tests, written his column for the high school newspaper. The little Olivetti was long gone. He'd carried it off to college and by second semester, well on his way to flunking out, he'd hocked it for beer money. Ironically, it was later, in the army, working as a clerk, where he'd finally learned to type using all of his fingers. After his discharge he'd bought a used IBM Selectric and on that machine he'd typed papers for his second and successful go at college. *Haven's End* had been written on it, too. These days he used a laptop, which he had considered bringing along with some vague intention of jotting notes for another screenplay but hadn't—frankly, he was a little light on ideas lately.

He had adjusted his watch in flight and did likewise now with a travel alarm clock, but his body was still on California time: barely 6:30. He knew he should sleep soon or he'd be fighting fatigue for days, but he wasn't tired. Remembering the postcards he'd bought, he took one out: GREETINGS FROM BEAN TOWN scrawled across the skyline in hokey yellow script. Tamara wouldn't mind; she'd never been east of Palm Springs. He wrote her East Hollywood address; then: *Home place smaller. Lots to do in a short time. I'm ticketed on a flight a week from Monday. Will let you know. No ghosts yet.* He hesitated the briefest moment, then wrote "Love" and signed it. He let himself out the back door.

Crickets shrilled in the September dark. He stood on the lawn and breathed. Moving through the night on an easy wind was the aroma of the sea, a few streets away. Unlike the Pacific, which rarely gave any olfactory sense of being there at all, the Atlantic wasn't shy about making itself known. Depending on tide and wind and season, it had a hundred formulations, from a fetid mud-flat stink to a metallic, heat-dazzled brine. Tonight a sweet iodine tang told him the tide was high. Without being conscious of deciding to, he set off down the road.

There was scarce light beyond the glow cast by occasional streetlamps, so the darkness seemed full, the streets enclosed by overlacing branches of maple and oak. These were the same streets he had roamed on foot and by bicycle with friends before any of them were old enough to drive. Remembered images whirled into focus: familiar houses, the brook where they used to catch eels, a tarp-covered shape alongside a garage (could Mr. Shanahan still have the Edsel?), the chestnut tree under which they'd gathered pails full of shiny brown horse chestnuts for use in third-grade arithmetic exercises and later in pitched battles with the kids from streets farther inland. The world seemed suddenly full of the past. Then Tom turned the corner and there was the sea.

Not the open ocean, the coast here was formed of bays and inlets and the snaking tidal estuaries that marked the boundaries of town, Adams Point to the north, Bingham and Standish to the south. On his left he could see the jut of the wooded headland that rose to the Crow's Nest. Were lovers parked up there now? Below the hill was the beach. Far out a silver blanket of fog shimmered. He stood for a while and let his mind fray out. On the way back to Edgewater Road he remembered to mail the postcard.

Upstairs in his old room he got ready for bed, although he still wasn't tired. He lay in the dark, arms crossed behind him, head nestled in his palms, watching the shadows of wind-stirred leaves on the ceiling, listening to the whisper of the gently blowing curtains, and wondering: Had he ever really belonged in this house, this town, this life?

Tom woke Saturday morning surprised at how deeply he'd slept. After coffee with his mother, followed by a walk-around survey of the house to determine what would need to be done, he sat at the antique secretary desk in the living room and made phone calls. He arranged for a local real estate agent to do a market analysis, peppered managers at three assisted living complexes with questions about their services, then scheduled to meet with one on the following Monday. Next was donating his mother's car to a charity ("You know the one about the little old lady who drives only on Sundays?" he joked with the woman he spoke to). By noon he felt on top of things. Why was it always easier to deal with someone else's life than with your own?

Jacobs' Hardware in Picknell Square had seemed old even when young Tom went with his father on Saturday mornings to get mortar mix, marine screws, the odd-but-essential tool for one of the many do-it-yourself projects Dad always had going. The store appeared to have more clerks than customers at the moment, yet somehow it was holding its own in a world of hardware superstores. He had a few repairs to make to get the house ready for sale, and he selected the dozen or so items he needed. When he got out he found a sheet of paper under one of the Escape's wiper blades.

WHS HOMECOMING GAME TODAY!!
ALL WELCOME!!

At the intersection where he would normally turn for home, a procession of cars and vans flying crepe streamers passed through, horns blowing. He hesitated. He wanted to go through the house, cellar to attic to garage, get the job done; but there *was* time, he reasoned. Look at all he'd accomplished in just half a day. Pausing only a moment longer, he swung right and followed the procession.

Tom had gone out for football his first two years of high school, powerhouse seasons when the team ran deep with talent and held state rankings, which pretty much consigned him to second string; but he'd loved the game and stayed with it, making almost a fetish of conditioning, and senior year was going to be his year. In the preseason he played well, and in the final scrimmage he shone with a long touchdown run. Then, just before the opening game, he quit the team. He pushed the memory away.

At the crest of Elm Hill, traffic slowed and he heard the muted drums and brass. Ahead, before a sweep of playing fields and courts, stood the old high school building, a vast brick relic with its looming bell tower and clock, the hours marked in Roman numerals. Beyond, in a leafy, self-contained campus, was the facility that had replaced it—long, low sweeps of prestressed concrete, plate glass, and steel.

The old stadium, at least, remained. A hulking stone structure with arches and gateways, it had a look of permanence. For Tom the stadium had always possessed a mystique, even back when, on bright yellow weekday afternoons in September, through the lengthening shadows of October and into gusty November, he and his teammates had played football. On Saturdays, before large, noisily partisan crowds, they had thrown themselves against their opponents as though repulsing enemy invaders as from the sidelines pretty girls waving pompoms cheered them on. Feeling a visceral pull of the past, Tom found a parking spot and made his way to the ticket window.

Immediately upon entering the stadium, he felt the illusion fall apart. The outer structure was only a shell, the original banked seating gone, replaced by tiers of aluminum and plastic benches that held a scattered crowd. On the field, the players looked surprisingly small, garbed in uniforms that didn't have so much as a smear of dirt or a grass stain on them, and he realized this was because the turf wasn't real. He almost left right then.

But the scoreboard stopped him. He'd have to have been blind for it not to have. A digital wonder, it was mounted at the home-town end of the field, although it was gaudily visible from every-where, busy with a succession of sight and sound effects, instant replays, players' mug shots, stats. When Weybridge accomplished something—held the line on fourth and short, sacked the quarter-back, or as they managed finally to do late in the first quarter, scored a field goal—the scoreboard exploded with electronic fire-works. But form can never overcome a lack of substance, and the game proved dull for Tom. As the quarter ended, he rose to leave. What happened next was something he would not think about right away. When he did have occasion to reflect on it some days later, he was given to wonder if it had been the first link in a chain.

As he reached an exit tunnel, he turned to look back. At that moment, the scoreboard flashed, WELCOME HOME WHS '64! Tom's class. The words vanished and new words appeared, a thousand lit-tle lights bright against the backdrop of September trees: AMONG THE MISSING. And: IF YOU KNOW THE WHEREABOUTS OF THE FOLLOW-ING, PLEASE CONTACT A CLASS REP! Names of alums began to appear, one after another. He was startled to see his own.

TK was *rushing. Something had held him up at home, causing his delay, and he was going to be late. This prospect filled him with a jittery discom-fort, a sensation that he'd have thought that by senior year he would've been rid of, but not so. If anything, he was scrutinized more closely now than ever, made to feel that the school administration still ruled, and he was powerless to change it. He jogged partway, slowing from time to time to walk; he didn't want to arrive sweaty. The tie, which under the unwritten rules each male student was "urged" to wear, pinched at his throat where his pulse pounded. As he rushed along Commerce Street, the school in view* *now, the tower clock tolling the half hour, he broke into an all-out run, and so he was sweating anyway when he entered the main lobby. With luck, he could slip past the . . .*

Pop Sterns was waiting.

TK's heart sank.

"You're late, Knowles," the vice principal said, glancing needlessly at his watch.

Sterns (no one had missed the irony in the name) backed him into the wall of trophy cases. He was a lean man of medium height, with close-cropped gray hair, flinty, deep-set eyes, and a military bearing. It was his job, he liked to say, to find the "miscreants" (a word TK had picked up from one of Mr. Longchamp's Word Wealth *lessons) at Weybridge High and "mete out"(another vocabulary gem) discipline.*

"I know," TK said. "I'm sorry."

"Sorry? This is the third time this month."

Second time, wasn't it? But TK kept silent. You didn't argue with Pop Sterns. There were other students now, tardier even than he was, slipping in through the side door from the student parking lot, quick dark shapes in silhouette against the bright morning outside. They ducked behind the vice principal's back on quiet feet, scooting past the way guilty drivers do when a cop has pulled over a speeder. Sterns was oblivious to them, having drawn down on his target. "And you know the dress code. Doesn't your mother iron your shirts?"

She doesn't do much of anything *anymore, TK thought; she was asleep when I left for school, and I didn't have time to iron it myself. But he said, "I'm sorry, sir," aware that he was repeating himself.*

Sterns seemed not to notice or to care. "Room three-oh-nine after school."

"Is there any way I can serve it tomorrow? There's a newspaper meet—"

"Out of the question. Maybe tomorrow you'll get here on time."

TK made no further appeal. Detention trumped all extracurricular activities. Just then, something caught his eye. In the room behind Sterns's back, through the pane of pebbled glass in the door, with VICE PRINCIPAL *painted on it, he noticed movement. A face appeared—there for just an instant, blurred by the glass—then, quick as a silverfish, gone. Inexplicably, a shiver darted along Tom's spine.*

Sterns tore a pink detention slip from his pad. "Three-oh-nine. Move it."

It was the Westminster chime in the old high school tower clock, Tom realized. That's what had prompted the memory. 7:30—P.M. this time. He released a pent-up breath and laughed. *Okay, so I'm late now, too.* He found a space in the parking lot, and as the last peal faded away, in its place came the strains of rock 'n' roll.

The VFW hall was a wood-frame building situated behind a stand of trees in back of the old high school. It had been there as long as Tom could remember, though he'd never been inside. The fathers of kids he'd known had belonged to the Veterans of Foreign Wars club, and he'd once asked his own father why he didn't belong, he had been a soldier, after all, but all Dad said was he wasn't a joiner.

As he started for the building, where a group of people dressed for an evening out were climbing the steps, a surprising churn of nervousness made him pause. But why? These were just people he had spent a few long-past years with. Okay, some of them had been important then: friends and rivals, kids he had sat beside in classrooms, eaten cafeteria lunches with, girls he'd had the hots for, guys he'd snapped locker-room towels with—but for all that, they were strangers with whom he'd had no contact since leaving Weybridge's ivied walls thirty years ago. Yet wasn't that what reunions were? Attempts to bridge the chasm of years with flimsy ropes of memory? With a tingle of anticipation, he climbed the steps to the covered porch and went into the hall.

A banner was strung above the entrance to the function room on the left: WELCOME BACK CLASS OF 64! Rows of enlarged black and white photographs from the days of yore flanked the entry, forming a gauntlet for anyone coming in. A hundred or so people were already gathered in the function room. Stifling one more wobble of indecision, Tom peered into a smaller room on the other side of the lobby. Amid a drift of cigarette smoke a scattering of VFW club members sat at card tables or perched on stools along a bar. A TV mounted in a corner featured candlepin bowling. One drink, he thought; get his bearings. He *was* a veteran, after all.

The patrons were men, in small groups or alone. Sports trophies and signs occupied the back bar—GOD BLESS THE USA and sentiments to that effect. This was where the proper business of club member-ship went down: the poker games and the talk and the drinking. Beer and shots seemed to be what the bartender was serving. Tom ordered Cutty on the rocks. He drew out the pack of Winstons he'd bought before leaving L.A., lit one, and drew deeply, shutting his eyes to savor the rush. Scotch and a cigarette was still one of those marriages made in heaven. In the other room, Tom Jones was singing "What's New Pussycat?"

Tom made imaginary conversation with the bartender, playing it in his head the way he wrote dialogue, building one line, then another and another on that, like LEGO blocks, tension holding them together.

What year was it?

The song?

Your high school class.

1964.

Long time gone.

Thirty years.

All those freaks, huh? Runnin' around, hair down to their ass and—

That came a bit later.

—smokin' wacky weed. I remember—

We were on the cusp. High school felt like it was still the fifties.

—kids pissin' on the flag, when we had brave guys dyin' for a cause. You know what I'm sayin'. You were in, right?

Drafted. Served a year, then got out as a conscientious objector.

Yeah, Tom thought. How would that play? It was true enough (he still had the honorable discharge with Richard M. Nixon's signature printed right on it), but explaining took time, finesse. And who was asking, anyhow? The barman was down at the other end chatting with some regulars. Tom forked out another butt (last of the night, he told himself), drank, and scanned the room again. Some of the men were younger than he, some older, a few in their late forties, like him. The TV had Doppler radar showing thunderstorms approaching greater Boston. "Don't you want to take a raincoat?" his mother had asked. "We may get a thumper." He said he wasn't going to be outside. Anyway, he didn't own a raincoat; there weren't many thumpers in Los Angeles. "Well, be sure to have fun. That's what reunions are for."

His chief recollection of high school was how restless he'd been to get out. Ditto for the army; his had been a generation of draftees. Long ago that was. Long time gone indeed. Yet some of the same ones who couldn't wait to get out, give them a while, a wife, kids, time payments, a crappy job, it never failed, they joined organizations like this. Any port in a storm, shipmate. Drop anchor for a while and get a cargo on with people who damn well understood. He got another drink. Places like this were mad with ghosts.

They had to number in the millions by now, the ghosts. Fifty-eight thousand from his war, some of whom had once been members of that class gathering across the lobby there, shaking their booties, as clueless to what was going on as they were to what the words to "Louie Louie" were really saying. And as messed up a war as Nam had been (and it *was* one colossally messed-up war, the bungle in the jungle), even in bad wars, people did courageous things.

"One more?"

"Yes," came easily to his lips, "*but*," he told the bartender, "I should go next door instead and check out the action."

He gave the gauntlet of photographs a passing glance and stepped up to a reception table where an attractive woman with gray threaded into her tawny mane smiled expectantly. She wore a large round button wreathed with curlicues of green and white ribbon and sporting a photo and the name Lorie Paige. He vaguely recalled her. "Name please?" she asked.

She consulted a list, evidently not finding him. "Class of 'sixty-four, right?"

"But I've had extensive surgery to make me look this good."

She glanced at him quickly before realizing it was a joke. "You're among the missing," she chided. She knew what to do though. From a sheaf of pages of headshots photocopied from the class yearbook she snipped out his photo, pressed it onto a sticky tag, printed his name underneath with a marker, and handed it over. The photo was poorly reproduced. His head looked wide, capped with crisp brown hair, his nose turned up slightly at the end. "I think you gave me Wally Cleaver's by mistake."

Frowning, the woman reached for it.

"You know, the Beav's brother?"

"No, that's you," she insisted dryly. "Would you like to sign up for the raffle drawing? First prize is dinner for two at Hugo's Lighthouse."

What had he been expecting, a nostalgic hug?

The room was low-ceilinged, dimly lit, the floor ringed with tables and chairs, with one small area left open for dancing. He judged that about 120 classmates and guests had turned out. Along the far wall a deejay was in action, playing "Sherry" at the moment. At the cash bar a guy in a gold vest was serving beer and jug wine. That didn't augur well; an evening of seeing ghosts would seem to call for stronger spirits. Taking an option on the idea that he could always slip back to the VFW bar next door if need arose, Tom bought a Bud and drifted toward the wall.

"TK?" someone said behind him.

It took a moment to recognize the vastly bearded man squinting at him with a look of uncertain wonder. Tom extended his hand to shake, but Paul "Brain" Mclain ignored it and gave him a hug, clapping Tom's back.

"Holy crow!" Brain marveled, stepping away. "TK! Or should I say Thomas Knowles Jr., author. I read that novel you wrote."

"So you're the other one. I knew my mom bought a copy."

"I said 'read,' not bought. I haven't bought a hardback since *The Exorcist*. I liked yours though. But do you think I can remember the plot?" He waved fingers in a vague gesture at his head. "The hard drive's kinda sketchy."

As was his hair. Once a crisp copper red, it had made a retreat from his wide brow halfway back across his scalp where it grew in twists, the same rust color as the unkempt beard. The big change, however, the most obvious alteration time had wrought, was that Brain Mclain wasn't the chubby kid that Tom had known. He was lean to the point of gauntness, which exaggerated his shapeless corduroy sport coat, wrinkled shirt, and dark chinos that bagged at the knees and rode three inches above lime green Chucks. Looney Tunes characters smiled from his yellow tie.

"Man, I thought about you when we put this thing together," Brain enthused. "I'm on the committee, but we had no current address, so I said, 'Let's send a notice to his mother.' You still talk to your mom, don't you?"

Tom gave a brief account of his return from California, admitting that he hadn't considered being here tonight until a few hours ago at the football game. "It's a crime what they did to the stadium, but they've got this scoreboard straight from *Star Wars*. It flashed 'Where have you gone, Miss Mutterperl?' And then I saw *my* name, and that was it. An inner voice said, 'Get thee to the reunion.' What're you drinking?"

Brain raised his palms. "I'm good."

"What became of her?"

"Who?" Brain looked momentarily confused.

"Miss Mutterperl. Audrey. Wasn't that her name?"

"I've no idea. The scoreboard, though. You really dug it?"

"Have you seen it? It's like—" Tom stopped. Brain was rubbing his hands together and grinning expectantly. "*You* built it? I should've known. It's incredible. When did—?"

"Wait'll you see what I've got cooked up for later." Brain gripped Tom's shoulder and gave him a quarter turn. Beyond the

18

deejay, against the wall, stood a long table covered with red sheets that draped several humped forms.

"What is it?" Tom asked.

"Hold your horses. You'll see."

Tom smiled, a memory occurring. "Has it got four speeds?"

Silently Brain mouthed the words, looking mystified a moment, then his eyes widened and danced. "Oh, man! The A-BOM! I haven't thought of that in years."

"Whatever became of it?"

"Who knows?" Brain laughed. "It ought to be in a museum."

"Alongside the guillotine. Remember the grand unveiling?"

"When Croz almost lost his—" Brain broke off, his grin vanishing. "Yeah, well, jeez. You heard about Croz, right?"

Tom had. It hadn't been all that many years after high school. Mom had sent him the obituary. Brain said, "If he *had* lost his . . . you know, that day in the garage . . . he might not have had to go to that damned senseless . . ." He cleared his throat. He was rubbing his hands together again.

"It wouldn't have mattered," Tom said. "Not having one wouldn't be enough. It's *handy*, of course, but you don't need one to squeeze a trigger. Or play guitar. Croz wanted to be . . . was it Link Wray?"

"Duane Eddy." Brain's smile made a partial return. He lifted a hand, fingers curled. "To the class of 'sixty-four—members here, there, and departed."

"Let's put something in that imaginary glass," said Tom.

"No, gotta keep my head straight for later."

"Ah, for your show. No hints? Even for a pal?"

"*Former* pal." And that was true. After graduation Tom never saw him or any of their classmates again. "Anyway, all will be clear in the fullness of time," Brain said.

They talked awhile longer, Tom learning that his old friend had taken a couple of degrees from MIT (no surprise there), worked in research for a time, and was back in Weybridge now working for the school department. Soon Tom saw some other people making their way over—Kippy something, and a kid he remembered from Latin class, Roger Hascomb, whom they'd called Roger the Dodger, though Tom had no idea why. Roger the Codger worked now; with his snow-white hair and humped shoulders he looked grandfatherly. He wasn't acting it, though. He and Kippy were whooping like a pair of frat pledges, while the women they were with wore the frozen smiles of people attending a reunion that was not their own. "Mclain!" Kippy bugled. "You old brainiac weird-beard! And TK? They're crawling out of the trees tonight!" Tom slipped away at the first opportunity. In the VFW bar he asked the bartender to run a tab.

At nine o'clock a dinner buffet was served. Tom found himself at a table with a dozen people, some of them classmates, such as Mary Agnes Kinney (née Blanchard), Judy Carini, and Stan Jarvis, a three-letter jock in his day, still looking fit as he passed out business cards identifying him as president of Jarvis and Easton Real Estate. Tom made a mental note to call him about selling his mother's house. Jack Grogan was there, a tall, once-slender basketball player, now sporting a paunch that pushed at his white patent leather belt. Russ Rigden talked in a monotone about his impending early retirement from an Omaha medical practice to the Sun Belt, where he would golf in perpetuity. A thin, beak-nosed man set about asking each of his classmates to make a statement for posterity, which he captured with a camcorder; Tom seemed to remember he'd been one of the kids (Larry something) responsible for setting up and troubleshooting A/V equipment. When Rigden's turn came, he stood, straightened his bow tie, and declaimed with studied indifference, "Russell Rigden, physician, presently living and practicing in Omaha."

"Is this for a class archives?" Stan Jarvis wondered aloud.

Larry (was it Black? Blane? *Blake*, that was it) grinned good-naturedly. "I promised my grandkids I'd show them a reunion."

"Well, come by the field tomorrow afternoon," Stan said.

"We're getting a softball game together. There's no saying for sure if all of us will be alive for the next one."

"Cheery thought," murmured Rigden.

"Actually," Mary Agnes Kinney said, "death is one of the two great themes underlying all reunions. I read that somewhere."

"What's the other?"

"Mmm . . . you would ask."

"Nostalgia," offered a dark-haired woman wearing glossy pink lipstick.

"I'd say friendship," said the former Judy Carini.

"It's golf," said Rigden. "God's game."

Speaking up for the first time, Tom said, "It's sex."

The others looked his way. "Sex and death are the two great themes of literature and life, so that must include reunions. Golf may be third. I wouldn't know; I never play. With a show of hands"—he was improvising now—"how many of us got through high school with our honor intact?" He raised his own hand.

"How are you using 'honor'?" the woman with pink lipstick asked.

"In the quaintest way possible. Anybody?"

There were sidelong looks, a few evasive grins. No one else raised a hand. Tom lowered his. "So it's as I always feared. *Worse* than I feared. I was the only virgin."

"Wait . . . wait," the woman in pink lipstick said. "Are you asking . . . ?"

"Let me rephrase it. How many of us were getting laid?"

"You've been drinking, guy," said Dr. Rigden reproachfully.

"It's a fair question," Stan Jarvis intervened.

This time there were looks of amused acknowledgment. All hands stayed right on the table. Tom sighed.

"Proving what?" Rigden grumped. "That 'end of innocence' pap I overheard you peddling earlier?" For someone who'd spent most of his career in the Midwest he didn't appear to have acquired much of the region's fabled friendliness.

"Proving that truth gets less painful with time. Because we see that *first* great theme looming ever nearer. We hear the hoof-beats . . ." Tom drummed a little tattoo on the tabletop. He was feeling the booze.

"Come on," Judy Carini said, "we're supposed to be having fun. Who's up for dancing? Do you think the deejay's got Michael Jackson?"

Coffee was served. Mary Agnes Kinney asked Tom, "Are you working on another book?"

How did she know about his writing? Before Tom could reply, Jack Grogan was pawing at his shoulder. "What's this about a book?"

"*Haven's End*," Mary Agnes said. "It's a novel about growing up—some of it in a town much like this one."

"Oh. So what else do you do, Tom?" Grogan went on, still probing. "I mean, do you make a *living* doing that?"

"He also writes for television." Mary Agnes rattled off a list of shows Tom had written for; defunct now, all of them. Thankfully, she didn't mention the screenplays he'd sold; after every second assistant line producer got done adding his two cents, the resultant films hadn't been much to be proud of. He remembered Mary Agnes (then Blanchard) as a girl whose stock in trade had been gossip, and she'd maintained a large inventory. "Your book *was* about here, wasn't it?" she asked Tom. "That first part?"

"In some ways. Suitably disguised, I hope."

"To protect the innocent?"

"To protect me from getting strung up on the nearest lamp-post."

"It was pretty edgy," she allowed. "Would you classify it as magical realism?"

"I was just trying to tell a story."

"I've gotten a lot of mileage out of telling patrons that Tom Knowles and I took classes together."

"Patrons . . ."

"I'm the town library director. So, you see? We both ended up in books."

"We had Mr. Longchamp together, right? I recall that."

"He gave me fits with all that vocab he made us learn. Remember *Word Wealth*?"

Tom laughed. "I use 'bucolic' all the time. And I never say the 'g' in 'poignant.'"

"He's gone, you know. Heart attack last year. I saw the obituary."

"One of life's two big themes. I'm sorry to hear it."

She was looking at him speculatively, as if trying to square this persona with who he had been in high school. "*Are* you writing another novel?"

"I've made stabs at a few. They sit in drawers, bleeding. Maybe I had my say with that first one. But Longchamp, wow. There's a blast from the past. And Miss Mutterperl. What became of her?"

"I've lost track. She gave up teaching. Couldn't take the grief is what I heard."

"I liked her," he said. "I learned from her."

Mary Agnes had other stories about their teachers and classmates; but gossip works only if you feel some kinship with the people talked about, however tenuous. Tom felt none. The Hollywood stars trashed in the tabloids were more real to him than most of the people here. At the first chance, he excused himself and slipped away.

When the deejay wasn't spinning musical nostalgia, he was trafficking in trivia that harkened back to the early 1960s. What was the price of a gallon of gas? A car? A house? Who were the hot movie stars? He had to supply most of the answers himself, which didn't say much for the collective memory of the class of '64. The music was good though—no one could screw that up—and it began drawing some of the women to the dance floor. Tom saw Brain Mclain standing by watching them and went over. "Go ahead," he said.

"Huh?"

"Whoever the fantasy girl is. Ask her to dance."

Brain's face colored. "I was just thinking. About how time seems to level things out. Yesterday's BMOC or worst social retard—*moi!*—ain't much difference anymore."

"So prove it."

"Nah. But am I right? Isn't time the great leveler?"

"Women are dancing with each other because we're still too chicken to go out there. And the old caste system is alive and well." Tom nodded at a table where for most of the evening a handful of their classmates had been sitting. They had been the ruling social elite back in the day, and they had found each other again. There was Dennis Daley, one of the biggest snobs in school, buttoned up in a brown three-piece suit, looking as plump and self-satisfied as an October woodchuck. There were Barry Higgins, Janet Brown, and one of the O'Leary twins (the unfriendly one). It took Tom a moment to recognize Niki DiLorenzo, and another moment to realize what was different about her. In high school she'd been almost skeletally thin, throwing up her food in the girls' room; now she swelled out of her low-cut top. "Silicone Valley," Brain said when Tom mentioned this.

In the folks here tonight there seemed to be a seesaw between loss and gain. While there was definitely less hair, there was certainly more weight. One who had kept her figure was Diana Richards, who just then stopped dancing and went to the special table and sat down. Dee, as she was known, hadn't been part of the in-crowd, though she had a popularity of her own: a minister's daughter with a hint of sin. She still had an aura of heat, sitting there in a short black dress, black hose, and high heels. Tom suddenly knew whom Brain had been watching.

"Man, I would love to dance with Dee, just once in my life," Brain said.

Another song had started, a slow one. "'In the Still of the Night,'" Brain murmured. "The Five Satins." It was a habit for as

24

long as Tom had known him; they'd sit in the Atlantic Diner, nursing vanilla Cokes, and Brain would name every song spinning out of the Rock-Ola in the corner. Brain shook his head now. "No, you're right. It's a drag, but that's the script."

"Forget what I said. Let's go dance with her and Niki. Let's rewrite the script."

"Too late; I'm cast. Have been for thirty years." His shoulders slumped. "See you later, TK." He wandered off. For a moment Tom debated asking one of the women to dance, but he couldn't decide between Dee Richards and Niki DiLorenzo, so he did nothing. Then he spotted Mike Burke.

Mike was sitting in a far corner, his back to the wall, his tie loose, his hands parked on top of a cane. Several guys with their wives or their dates were clustered near him as he held court.

"Man, I used to love watching you pitch," one of them was saying as Tom went over. "You could hang a sinking curve on a batter, guy'd be standing there getting Biked and not even know it."

Getting *Biked*. Tom hadn't thought of that expression in years. Bike was the brand name stitched into the elastic band of every jockstrap in those days.

"Could *still* throw," Mike Burke growled.

"Sure, I didn't mean—"

"If it weren't for this goddamn cane and the bum liver and bad eyes—never mind practically getting my balls shot off trying to stop a bank robbery." At Mike's bark of laughter his listeners got that spooked look that comes from being in proximity of a loose cannon that may abruptly swing your way. Muttering hasty good-byes, they fled. When Mike looked up and saw Tom, the smile returned. "Thought that was you."

"Let me buy you a drink."

"Siddown." Mike flashed a pint of Black & White he had secreted under a sport coat that lay on the table. He poured a knock into Tom's cup, added some to his own. "Someone asked me a couple months back, would I be on the reunion committee. I told 'em my one suggestion is go top shelf on the hooch and make it free. Obviously they paid no attention. But they didn't stint on the green and white streamers, or these buttons, no sir." In Mike's yearbook photo, a flattop and jug ears gave him an eager, boyish look. There was nothing boyish in his face now. It was hard-weathered, his hair a faded brown, worn in a comb-over, and his teeth were certainly capped. The hands perched atop his cane were leathery and chapped.

"The sinking curve stands pristine in the collective memory, apparently," said Tom, "so I won't comment on it except to tell you I did get a piece of one once."

"*How* much've you had to drink?"

"It was at the park, the summer before senior year."

Mike blinked, maybe computing time, and then pursed his mouth morosely. "Nineteen sixty-three, a fateful season if ever there was one."

"Ah, sorry," Tom said, realizing his gaffe.

"Why? Because I had more brass than brains? Screw it. To the Brockton game. To our heedless youth."

"Better days."

Mike drained his cup, wiped his mouth with the back of his hand. "Where you living now?" Tom told him. "L.A. and you're not carrying a pocketbook?"

"Yeah, it's great. How about you?"

"Still on the old sod. Same house."

"Is Mo here?"

Mike sagged, and Tom knew the answer before he spoke. "Vegas last I heard, learning to deal blackjack. Ain't that some shit? This is just since July, but it's looking more permanent every day."

"So you're the one who requested 'Achy Breaky Heart.'"

Mike's grin was sardonic. "I suppose by most standards she passed the upper limit for a cop's wife. She put up with my drama for twenty-six years."

Maureen (*Hickey* had been her surname, and didn't *that* cause some kidding) and Mike had been high school sweethearts, and among their classmates it was a matter of faith that they'd mated for life. Mike told the story, different in the particulars from others, but the same in its general weave: people together, then drifting apart. Their two kids were grown and flown. "Still . . . twenty-six years," Tom said. "My marriage didn't last five."

"Writers've gotta be as tough on partners as cops, spend all that time chasing words around in your mind."

"I never got shot."

"I won't bore you with a replay of that. I'm bored to death with it myself. But with this third leg"—he stumped the cane on the floor—"I can't make a clean getaway and get the hell home where I can drink in peace."

"Is that what you want? I'll go out with you."

"Soon, buddy. Schmooze a bit. I'll flash you the bunt sign when I'm ready."

By 11:00 P.M. Tom had schmoozed all he cared to. He was among people he'd known only marginally ages ago, and he felt no impetus to be part of their lives now. The motivating force that had driven friendship then had been chiefly geographical, based on living in the same town, but that link was long gone, as were the social needs that had accompanied it. Russ Rigden, the gaunt doctor from Omaha, waiting for retirement; Mary Agnes, the town librarian, whose backyard fence had become the Internet; Mike Burke, Brain Mclain; even Larry Blake preserving the evening on videotape (would anyone ever watch it?): they were all just middle-aged strangers, inhabitants of scattered worlds. Tom wasn't so naïve as to have expected to find that youth endured, but it occurred to him that he had been seeking *some*thing, some reconciliation of then with now. Was lasting friendship possible? Meaningful work? Undying love? Not according to anything he had seen tonight; and while this was an unhappy knowledge, it more or less confirmed what he had come to accept over the years.

Time to bounce.

Mike Burke was in his corner, ringed by new listeners. He seemed content enough; let him be. At the door, Tom glanced around for someone to say a formal good-bye to, but the members of the organizing committee who had greeted arrivals were nowhere in sight. If he owed a farewell to anyone, it was to the VFW bartender, which he offered along with a ten-dollar tip as he settled his tab.

Outside, the night was close and still, swollen with impending rain. He fished out a cigarette and discovered it was his last. Had he smoked the entire pack? His tongue felt scorched. A white-haired man stood by the deck railing, the tip of his cigar brightening and fading in the dark. Glancing Tom's way, he exhaled a balloon of smoke. "Part of the enslaved one-fifth?"

"Excuse me?" He was older, sixty-five perhaps, raspy voiced. Was he with the VFW, asking about an old military unit?

"Hooked on tobacco. Twenty percent of the adult population smokes, down from fifty percent thirty years ago." The man nodded and went back inside.

The weather forecast had been right. Trees at the edge of the parking lot tossed in a rising wind, and bruise-colored clouds were massing, lit by occasional flickers of energy. The silhouette of the old high school bell tower was visible beyond. As Tom made his way toward where he'd parked, someone called his name. He turned to see a woman coming across the parking lot toward him.

"Tom." Vivid just then in a flash of lightning, she was small and trim. "Are you leaving?"

Penny? "Penny."

She smiled, and it was both acknowledgment and revelation. Penny Griffin. Or that had been her name in school. "It's good to see you, Tom."

"It's good to see *you*." Her hand was firm as he shook it. "Have you been here all along?" He hadn't seen her till now.

"I came late. I had to work."

"On the night of your class reunion?"

"Yeah, well. Hey, I know you're a writer. That's so great. It must be difficult though. Everyone says writing is hard."

He laughed. "Everyone's right, for once." Suddenly he had a reason to stay. He wanted to talk to her, tell her about things, learn what she'd been up to. She looked just as she had in high school. Not *exactly*, of course; who could?—and yet of all the people he'd seen tonight she seemed the least changed. She was petite and pretty, her hair done up in a French braid. She was wearing a simple white blouse and a gold chain necklace, a dark skirt . . . and no glasses; *that* was different. They both glanced up at a rolling peal of thunder. "It's going to come down," he said. "We should get back inside."

"I'm just leaving."

"So soon?" he said disappointedly. He didn't offer that that's what he'd been about to do.

"You stay though. See what Brain's got cooked up. It's going to be exciting."

Brain's show. Tom had forgotten about it. A searing crackle of electricity burst, sharper now, closer. There was ozone in the air. "Come back in and dance with me."

Penny clutched her arms across her chest, as though in response to the temperature, which was cooling with the coming storm. "It's late."

"One dance," he said.

"I can't. Really. Bye, Tom." And she hurried away.

"Hey," he called after her, "is it still 'Griffin'?"

But she was gone. A few days later, he would wonder if it had been curiosity or something else (the storm? a moment's blindness? fate?) that prompted his next decision. Whatever the case, he changed his mind about leaving and went back to the reunion.

The deejay was gone. His spot was occupied by Brain Mclain, who had drawn over a second table to make one long unit covered with an impressive clutter of electronic equipment. Brain stood behind it wearing headphones as he worked a mouse and studied three monitors. He seemed oblivious to anything else in the room around him. After a moment, he signaled for the lights to be lowered, and the hall was given over to semidarkness.

On the wall to the right of where Brain stood, movie images appeared: people in caps and gowns, moving in slow march-step to the unheard strains of Elgar. On the wall to Tom's left, scenes of a basketball game flickered into view. It was footage from their time at school, and like the commencement ceremony, the people moved in a jerky, home-movie rhythm. On the wall directly behind Brain a static shot of the stadium emerged, and there was the old scoreboard showing a tally of Home 42, Visitors 0, and another—in washed-out color this time—that had Weybridge over Standish 14 to 6. Apparently Brain had gathered archival films and spliced scenes. The graduation march dimmed and here came the members of the football team, running out from one of the stadium arches to take the field, lining up like young gods of autumn. Was this the big show then? Grainy old glories of yesteryear? It smacked of anticlimax.

Then, simultaneously, the images on the walls dimmed, flickered blurrily, and were gone. More overhead lights winked out, and music rose, school pep songs, the inevitable "Cheer, cheer for old Weybridge High," to the tune of the Notre Dame Fight Song . . . "Uncork the whiskey, drink up the rye!" and the irreverent and eternal refrain: "Send the sophomores out for beer, and don't let a sober junior near . . ."

A new set of film images took form . . . 1950s and early 1960s cars arriving in the school parking lot, the old high school gymnasium, then pastel images of teenagers dancing—the pep song fading as rock-and-roll music rose over it, the distinctive stair-step harmonies of "At the Hop." The remaining hall lights went out. Suddenly, effortlessly—astonishingly!—the dancers came off the walls and moved right into the room. Tom's heart gave a staggering leap of surprise.

It was an eye-popping illusion. The reunion crowd drew a collective breath and released it in a drawn-out "awwww." The translucent forms appeared to enter the dim interzone of the VFW hall dance floor, where they began to occupy three-dimensional space. That portion of the hall between where the crowd stood and where Brain Mclain was set up was suddenly alive with semitransparent dancers gyrating to the infectious, driving beat. Tom and the people standing near him actually backed up to give the spectral dancers room.

Tunes changed ("Teenager in Love"), rhythms shifted ("Lonely Teardrops"). The images sharpened, and there on an easel stood a placard announcing a WELCOME BACK hop with the date September 21. Tom realized that the dance had been thirty-one years ago, almost to the day—*would* be thirty-one years ten minutes from now, he saw with a glance at his watch. It was nearing midnight.

"Jeez," a woman behind him whispered, "some of 'em are here tonight!"

It was true. Some of the same people there in the holographic display were gathered for the reunion. People began calling out names as they watched the dancers spin by. There was Kippy and Lorie Page, and Jack Grogan, minus the gut. There was Mike Burke and Maureen Hickey, he awkward, she graceful, but moving together in what would become the steps of their dance as husband and wife. Tom searched the images for his own.

The volume sank, allowing the sheer spectacle of the holograms to take over. Despite the function room's low ceiling, there was an illusion of enormous gymnasium space overhead, up where climbing ropes might be coiled and flying rings tied off in a shadowy firmament.

The source of the images, Tom realized, had to be the old films, and yet Brain had somehow added clarity and vibrancy. Gossamer curtains of tobacco smoke that had been drifting into the room from the adjoining VFW bar all evening now created shimmering cones of light as the lasers projecting the holograms penetrated them. People were still calling out names as they recognized themselves and others. There were groans, too, and disbelieving laughter. Songs gave way to other songs, dancers changed partners.

Having gotten over their initial awe, the crowd began to edge closer to the images moving there in the glistening light, and soon people were dancing alongside the projections of their younger selves, dancing to the same music, then and now.

A young Dennis Daley appeared, wearing a madras shirt and a tie that dangled to his crotch, and even then he'd had a narcissist's glow. "Hey, Dennis, move up there," hooted a voice. "Let the camera guy get you with you. The way it's always been." But middle-aged Daley needed no encouragement. He brushed at his thinning hair, tugged the hem of his vest, and went forward. He was smitten. Larry Blake didn't need to be prompted, either; he was recording it all.

Niki DiLorenzo materialized, girlishly thin, in a polka dot dress and a pair of falsies that looked like missile nose cones. "There were grooves in a record," someone stage-whispered behind Tom, "that were deeper than her cleavage."

"Deeper than her mind, too," someone else added.

The Beach Boys' voices rose in "Surfer Girl."

"Whoa, check out Dee."

Adult whistles greeted a young Diana Richards gliding into view. She was radiant in a green dress and a bouffant that sparkled like spun gold in the gymnasium lights. Leading her was Ray Sevigny, looking cool and a bit dangerous in pegged pants and a pale sport coat with skinny black lapels. He had his palm against the small of her back and she was arched prettily against him. You could feel their heat.

The entire spectacle was strange and wondrous. There was no telling for sure what songs might have been playing then (the source film wouldn't have had a sound track, certainly), and yet Brain had matched music and motion so deftly it was hard to imagine that his choices weren't the same records that had been clocking 45 rpms on that night in the early fall of 1963. The music became the raunchy sax and slinky guitar of "The Stroll," and the kids moved into two lines, girls here, boys there, and pair by pair they stepped together, joining hands and doing the funky walk through the clapping gauntlet of their classmates, all moving to the sinewy rhythm: Teddy Simon with Niki D., Jack Grogan with Judy Carini . . . even bulky jocks like Stan Jarvis and Mike Burke managing a passable Stroll. There were kids who weren't here tonight, Dave Cole, Sally Horne . . . Tom, still searching in the mix for himself, looked again at Ray Sevigny (his hair Brylcreemed to dark perfection, from the pompadour prow to the badass D.A.) with Dee Richards, the minister's daughter, who, if things went as planned, would be parked up at the Crow's Nest in Ray's '49 Merc before the night was over.

There they all were, just kids again, and if the passage of years distorted memory, amplifying the good things and muting the bad, then that was as it should be. Tom was genuinely moved.

If he'd thought of the school dances at all over the years, it was as shams, ersatz mating rituals, school certified and PTA approved, overseen by teacher-chaperones doing their level best not to appear bored, when the kids would've preferred something more primal. All at once, however, he saw differently. With a tender feeling that surprised him, he looked on girls who had dressed with care, had thought long about their dresses, had labored over their hair and nails, the touch of Ambush or Emeraude behind the ear, primped again before the girls' room mirrors—nothing haphazard or accidental, no; this was too important for anything to be left to chance, the stakes being romance and deep emotion. The boys, with their pressed slacks and Thom McAns and slim ties, the dab of Clearasil, the splash of Canoe; and the songs, which Brain had synchronized perfectly to the action, songs that Tom had considered sappy, such that when one came on the car radio now, he would reflexively change stations, weren't sappy at all. They were imponderably romantic.

All around, others in the VFW hall appeared to be moved, too. The joking stage whispers had subsided. People were edging closer, as if wanting to touch their own images, or just touch *them* collectively, connect with what all of them had been. Tom thought of Brain's question about time, and he was stung by his own snide reply, because he was wrong, and Brain was right—time *was* the great leveler. For suddenly the distinctions faded. It wasn't us and them, the cool and the uncool, the jocks and the nerds, the babes, the scabs, jds, brown-nosers, grinds, grubs, or any of those superficial categories that they once had used to armor themselves against their fears; no, it was just a group of kids on the brink of their final season together, there in their innocence, whose deepest desire was nothing more than to hold someone close and move under the soft lights, and perhaps, later, to kiss soft lips and murmur soulful declarations of love. Naïve? Yes, but there in the shimmery columns of light, with spinning pixels of color, what they once had been was made manifest again, given dimension, given *life*. Tom experienced an unexpected wave of affection for them.

On the heels of this thought came an almost paternal wish to shelter and protect them, for Tom recognized that they were utterly unaware of what awaited them in the coming twists of time, oblivious to the perils that were soon to drain away their youthful energies, and ultimately to exhaust their hopes, shatter their dreams, and to send some of their very number to death.

"Ooohs" and "Awwws" continued from the crowd in the VFW hall. Brain hunched at his panel, headphones on. He ought to have been beaming with triumph, for it *was* a triumph, a feat of imagination and technical virtuosity and bold daring, but in the faint gleam of the monitors, his face was knit with concentration.

Jack Scott began to sing "My Own True Love," his baritone stepping slowly into the words. Not without a churn of envy, Tom watched Judy Carini and Jack Grogan snuggle closer, saw Pete Cameron and Tammy Muldoon do the same, Anita O'Hare and Roger Hascomb: longtime sweethearts and new pairings, couples likely and unlikely. From where he stood at the fringe of the crowd Tom found himself scanning the long ago images, looking for . . .

There—at the faraway edge, in a gray sport jacket, too padded in the shoulders, too wide in the lapels to be anything other than a hand-me-down, but with the dark tie and white shirt, passable, stood TK Knowles . . . and, by God, he *did* look like Wally Cleaver. He wasn't dancing. He was on the sideline with some other stags, the basketball net overhead stuffed with balloons, the steel rim fringed with crepe streamers that wavered in unseen currents. Tom felt a stab of sympathy for the shy boy standing there affecting an awkward nonchalance.

The Platters began to sing. *"They-yy, asked me how I knew . . . my true love was true . . ."* Kids there in the festive gymnasium and people here in this drab function hall began moving in slow rhythm, kids whose only reaction to time was to welcome it, and adults unable to dispel the dark awareness of time as more enemy now than friend . . . they were, Tom understood, in some paradoxical way, one and the same. Distinctions of past, of present disappeared, reconciled in a state of reunion.

TK stepped away from the sidelines, looking at once resolute and afraid. With slow but determined strides he started across the gymnasium floor, sidestepping between dancers, moving toward a cluster of girls. TK went to one girl, pausing to speak to her. Who was she? The faces were blurry, indistinct. In a moment, TK was leading her to the dance floor, though he still could not see who she was. Other dancers—then, and now—intervened, cutting off a clear view.

Lightning flickered outside, followed almost immediately by a long, rolling crackle of thunder. The images broke up briefly and then re-formed. Protectively, Tom pushed closer to the holograms. Who was the girl he was leading to the floor? Larry Blake continued to bustle about with his camcorder. Another boom of thunder sounded, audible over the song, and *felt* as the building shook. It broke the spell. Tom glanced at Brain, who was frowning at his monitors, scanning data that gleamed in miniature on his eyeglasses. He looked troubled. Tom went over. Brain was hunched at his keyboard, headphones on, oblivious. "Aw, God, no," he muttered.

"What is it?"

No response. Tom reached and touched his shoulder. Brain jerked up his head. He plucked off the headphones, leaving them to dangle around his neck. The storm," he said in an odd, colorless voice.

"Is that a problem?"

"The wiring in this place is crap. You know how expensive this gear is? If there's a surge . . . Damn!" He began flipping switches, poking keys. The Platters went on singing "Smoke Gets in Your Eyes."

The music ceased midphrase. Even though the holograms held form, the abrupt cessation of sound shattered the illusion, brought people up short.

"Show's over!" Brain's voice cracked with tension. "I'm shutting down." He waved his arms. His Looney Tunes tie hung askew. "Everyone back!"

From what? From where? Bewilderment. Unnervingly, the shimmering light-people danced on, silently now; but something else had changed. It was as though the images, the laser projections, had become suddenly dangerous. People withdrew from them, herding back toward the ring of tables, to the more solid world of half-gone drinks, of suit jackets and pocketbooks slung on chair backs. A gust of wind flung open a door, which crashed back against the wall. Women shrieked. Raffle tickets and empty drink cups swooshed across the floor. Then, as if a dam had burst, the downpour drummed the windows, ran in turbulent sheets down the glass, blew through the open doorway.

Overcoming his paralysis, Brain rushed toward the power supply outlet. But he had neglected to remove the headphones, which were still clamped around his neck. As the cord tightened, the headphones were yanked off. He tried to grab them, but he slipped on the wet floor. He did a pirouette, at once awkward and graceful, and doomed as an attempt to stay upright. His feet skated out from under him and he went down hard.

Tom got to him as Brain rolled onto his side, sputtering something about tripping, breaking. *Did he break a leg?* Tom motioned for him to lie still, but Brain was flailing his arms like a man trying to shoo away something terrible. *"Trip the circuit breaker!"*

Tom understood. But when he looked around for an electrical box, a master switch, *some*thing to cut off the power, all he saw was a bewildering tangle of cords and cables. He moved around to the back of Brain's equipment, stepping carefully on the wet floor. Snaking from the back panel was a thick red power cord. He followed it to a wall outlet. He reached to take hold of the plug end, ready to yank it loose, when a stupendous thunderclap exploded outside. He recoiled. In the hall there was a crackle-*zap!*—like a small bird might make hitting an electric insect killer. Someone shrieked.

The power faltered again.

"Do it!" Brain's voice was a breathy wail.

Tom bent toward the plug, taking firm hold. Outside, directly overhead, there was a deafening explosion. Sparks spat from the wall plate. He was flung backward and landed on his side and smacked his head on the floor. Mist swarmed across his vision. He struggled to stay conscious. He could make out people crouching near, reaching as he had done to Brain, as if to help him up—but they didn't. They stood frozen, as though afraid to touch him, worried that he might be electrified somehow. *He* wondered that, too, but then he realized that something else had seized their attention, something off to the left of where he lay.

Tom squinted.

A swirl of sputtering yellow light was arcing slowly along the wire, moving his way. He lay there and watched with a detached wonder. He had the faraway thought that he should get up and move—but he didn't. Like a ball of fuzzy electric yarn being unwound, the light approached with hypnotic stealth. He could hear the spitting sound it made, like bacon cooking on a hot griddle. More insistently now he had the thought: get to your feet, run!

But the time for fleeing was gone. The crackling glow reached him and there was an awesome Sizz-*ZAP!* For an instant, white sparks seemed to hang frozen and beautiful, like the pendants of a crystal chandelier, and then they engulfed him. Vague shrieks came from the dimness beyond, but his awareness was there inside the burst of light, which covered him like a fiery shroud. His back arched rigidly, the muscles along his spine spasmed and cramped. He had the sensation as of hands seizing him, taking hold of limbs, hair and clothing . . . and then he was yanked sharply into blackness.

2̄ TK

june 1963

With a grunt, the Clam Man hefted the last of the racks and set it atop the others arranged in the rear of the mud-caked panel truck. Wiping his hands on the gray denim work apron tied around his stout waist, he turned to TK, who was the only digger out this overcast morning. From his pants pocket Clam Man drew his cash, which he always carried in a wad, the bills folded and secured by a rubber band. TK knew the routine; he held out his hand, palm up, as the Clam Man licked a thumb and counted out a ten dollar bill, two fives, and two ones. He dug in his pocket for the fifty cents, and not finding it, dealt out another dollar.

"I have change in my car," TK said.

"Keep it. You done well."

TK thanked him. Half a rock would buy a couple gallons of gas.

The Clam Man pulled down the overhead door with a clatter. The truck's meager refrigeration would be just enough to get the load up north. He drew a faded bandanna from a back pocket and mopped it across his high forehead and glanced out at the mudflats where the tide was rising. "Your comrades didn't make it this morning." The Clam Man often used the word "comrades" referring to the diggers. It made TK think of those Pottsylvanian spies from *Rocky and Bullwinkle*, Boris Badenov and Natasha Fatale. "I don't think they got the fire."

"It was raining pretty hard earlier," TK said, offering the others a defense.

The older man smiled thinly. His name was Sid Yarrow, but everyone called him the Clam Man. He knew the tides in his head and would show up each day at various coves along the South Shore, his ungainly little truck arriving as the loose-knit crew of diggers finished, never too soon or too late. Nobody worked *for* him—as a digger you worked for yourself—but he was the middleman, and his cash-on-delivery five-dollars-a-rack was the best price along the shore. From here, he would drive the day's haul to a plant on Plum Island, north of Boston, where the shellfish would be purified before being sold to restaurants and fish markets. One of the things TK liked, aside from the cash, was that he could go into any seafood restaurant in eastern Mass and eat clams that he may well have dug. Not that he did that; he didn't have money to spend on fancy dinners, but the point was he *could* do it.

"You've got the Sweat Bug, boy."

TK checked to see if a horsefly had landed on him, though somehow he didn't think that's what the Clam Man meant.

"People you can divide into two kinds, snap just as neat as a matzoh cracker. Those who're willing to work hard and sweat, and those who ain't. You stack 'em up, the second pile's always gonna be a lot higher than the first."

TK figured the Clam Man to be somewhere around sixty-five, and although he drove the beat-up truck and dressed in worn-out clothes, diggers who'd been selling to him for years said Sid was a wealthy man. "Guy's worth a million clams," a digger named Artie Dewitt joked, "and he lives over in Germantown in a shack I wouldn't park my T-Bird in." TK didn't know about that, but he liked the Clam Man, liked that he was reliable, and that whatever the time of day, whatever the weather, if there were six diggers or only one, as today, he never kept them waiting around once a dig had ended. The Clam Man seemed to know about all kinds of stuff, and he was sometimes willing to share.

But he was fussy about certain things.

On the day TK got his permit and began serving his apprenticeship, he'd toiled away, matching the other diggers for effort, yet yielding only a fraction of their results. The Clam Man arrived a few hours later, as the tide was rising. Giving TK only the briefest nod of acknowledgment as they were introduced, he went about his job: opened the truck and removed some wooden boxes with screen bottoms—the "racks"—each digger taking a sufficient number to hold the clams he had in burlap sacks. TK quickly poured his harvest into a single rack, barely enough to reach the brim. Eager to avoid comparisons with what the others had dug TK lifted his rack, which was surprisingly heavy, into the truck. Without a word, the Clam Man took it out and set it back on the ground. TK sensed he'd done something wrong, though he didn't know what, and no one said a word. Afterward, when the Clam Man had gone, one of the veteran diggers croaked, "Kid, we dig 'em, the Clam Man handles 'em. Don't pull that shit again." TK never did.

In time he learned about *honkers* (clams that were too big and likely to be tough) and *seeds* (too small and needing more time to mature) and, of course, *stinkers* (clams that were dead). Of the crew of six to eight guys that assembled most days in one or another of the coves along the Weybridge shore, the others all were older than TK. They were shift workers at the shipyard digging for extra cash, or college students earning tuition, but age wasn't a measure of anything; it all got down to how you produced, and over the course of three summers, beginning when he was fifteen, TK had grown into a reliable crew member. There were others who dug more clams on a given day, including the legendary Artie Dewitt, who sometimes would arrive for an early low tide, sleep off a big night in his T-Bird, then arise, howl his trademark "*Dig* for the money! *Dig* for the money! Ah-*wooo!*" and trot down the beach on spindly legs and outdig everyone. TK had developed an eye for reading the mudflats, spotting the areas that were likely to be productive, and working efficiently for the several hours before the tide turned.

"You're in shape, boy," the Clam Man said. "You don't get these muscles in a gym, lifting barbells. This is the muscle you get from sweat work."

TK wasn't sure what the distinction was, and the Clam Man didn't seem inclined to elaborate. "See you tomorrow," he said.

At his car TK pulled off hip boots and put on sneakers. He set the boots, clam fork, burlap bags, galvanized pail, and thick rubber gloves into the trunk to be hosed with fresh water when he got home. He put on an old washed-out Boston Braves cap of his dad's and sat on the hood of the Rambler and gazed out to where the furrows of his recent digging were being erased by the slow, gray-green lapping of waves. A few seagulls trolled for leftovers.

Rolling out of bed in the dark for an early tide, sometimes even before Dad was up, was always a struggle. Once he was out, however, and headed toward the sea, inhaling the smells of morning, sometimes his breath smoking in the chill dawn, TK always wondered why everyone wasn't up. It was the best part of the day.

The horizon was clearing to the east and the Boston skyline rose miragelike, atint with rosy light. The tallest building was the new Prudential tower, where there was supposedly an observation deck from which you could see all of greater Boston. Be a nice place to take a girl, TK thought, though at the moment he wasn't sure who that girl might be.

He felt the $23 in his pocket. It would go into the sock drawer of his dresser until Saturday morning, and then the week's total would get deposited in his account, the transaction hand-entered by the pretty red-haired teller at Weybridge Savings Bank, minus the five bucks he allowed himself each week for gas money and summer fun. Seventeen was the best age he'd known yet; better even than sixteen had been. Would it always be like this, each year trumping the one before it, life getting better all the time? He'd have to ask his parents about that; they'd each had over forty years of living. Meanwhile, it was time for a stack of pancakes at the Atlantic Diner, and then he'd see what the June morning brought.

Days when he wasn't clamming, TK would sometimes go over to Legion Field. Football camp didn't formally start until mid-August, but Mr. Mosher, the coach, was a fanatic about fitness, a product of his days as a Marine D.I. during the Korean War. If you were out of shape when camp opened, he about killed you with conditioning drills. At 155 pounds soaking wet, TK wasn't one of the bigger kids on the squad, even for a back, but he was fast, and he knew it was essential to be fit. At the field one morning he found Mike Burke playing three-flies-six-grounders with some of the little kids in the summer rec program. An ice cream truck had just arrived, so Mike had the kids round up the balls and then sent them off to spend their money on Popsicles. "Hey, Knowles," Mike called, "take a few swings?"

TK was game. From an assortment of bats in the grass near home plate he chose a black thirty-two-inch Adirondack with friction tape wrap. He gripped it all the way down, the knob jammed tight against the heel of his left hand, and took a stance. With no catcher in place, Mike threw to the backstop, using the rubber-coated practice balls. He tossed a dozen or so pitches at medium speed. TK got wood on several and stroked them into shallow outfield. Soon, in his casual way, Mike said, "Ready?"

TK felt a thrill of adrenaline. He considered putting on one of the batting helmets that lay nearby, but most would be sized for ten- and twelve-year-olds, and also he knew that such a move would be saying that he was afraid. He had played Little League and JV ball in junior high, but he hadn't stuck with the game. Mike, on the other hand, was a pitcher of uncommon skill. He had grown into a big kid, with a powerful sidearm delivery and a fierce fastball. He wore a deep-pocketed Whitey Ford model glove, so dark with neat's-foot oil that TK thought of it as a witch's cauldron where Mike brewed up his stuff. But Mike's weapon, the pitch that from as early as ninth grade had local sports reporters writing about it, was his hanging curve.

"Whenever," TK said.

He chopped at several pitches, hearing the ball *thunk* against the backstop wire before he was even halfway around. Mike wound up and threw again. The pitch came straight at him, and TK knew he'd been stupid not to wear a helmet, that the ball was going to bean him, probably crack his skull, and he was letting go of the bat, dropping backward in panic when the pitch broke and went over the plate waist-high and he was sitting in the dirt like a jerk. *Biked!*

"Wow," he croaked, dusting off the seat of his dungarees. Mike laughed.

TK dug in. Again the fastballs zipped past, and the curves had him guessing, and even if he read a pitch right, he was late and was dandling the bat out there as the ball struck the wire. Sweat was streaming on his brow when Mike called, "One more?"

TK had had enough; he wanted to run some laps and do some wind sprints on the track before the day got too hot. Mike saw his hesitation. "For an easy out?" he needled.

"Okay," TK yelled back. "One more."

Mike began his windup, his six-three body coiling with grace, and then uncoiling with no grace at all, just power, and the ball was steaming at TK's head. But this time he didn't panic. He stood his ground, watching, waiting. He began his stroke a fraction of an instant sooner, pivoting from the waist, shoulders solid, and he felt the Adirondack and the Spalding connect, felt the collision of ash and horsehide, and he lofted the pitch long and deep, Mike turning on the mound to watch, too, as the ball floated far down to drop onto the grass and roll all the way to the tennis court fence. TK felt a wild rush of elation and an eager desire to run the bases (which he resisted). Mike whistled with real appreciation. "Sweet."

"Lucky," TK said.

After, they sat in the shade enjoying Popsicles. Offhandedly, Mike said, "I'm being bird-dogged." TK looked at him, puzzled. Mike took off his cap and hooked a forearm across his suntanned brow, which was streaming sweat below his flattop haircut. "Scouted," he explained. "The Senators are looking at me."

He said it casually, but TK jumped on the words. "The *Washington* Senators?"

"Uh huh."

"You *serious*?"

"I got a letter."

"That's wicked pisser!" TK actually looked around, as if he might spy unfamiliar men sitting in the bleachers, peering from under the brims of fedora hats and scribbling on steno pads. In truth, he had no idea how baseball scouts looked or what they did. All he saw were a few of the playground kids playing rock, paper, scissors.

"But like my old man says," Mike added, "he'll believe it when we sign on the dotted line."

When they'd walked back to the diamond, where the younger kids were ready for more action, TK got set to take his run. "Next time I'll join you," Mike said. "Or Mosher's gonna kill me with drills."

"You're still going out?"

Mike mirrored his surprise. "Why not?"

"Is that a good idea? I mean, with the Senators looking at you?"

"You sound like my old man."

"But what if—?"

"I get hurt?"

"I don't know . . . or—"

"I won't. Besides, you don't win the girls with a baseball."

"You've already got a steady." Mike had been going with a girl named Maureen Hickey since the end of sophomore year. She wore his ring on a chain around her neck.

"One of these days she might wake up and wonder what she's doing with a guy whose ears stick out. Nope, gotta be a football hero. See ya."

That evening, before supper, TK overheard his parents talking in the kitchen.

"And you've been insisting it was a cold."

"Oh, for the love of Pete. *Probably* a cold, I said." His dad gave an exasperated spurt of laughter. "There's cold in them thar hulls."

Mom was not amused. "Honestly, Tom, I don't like the idea of waiting. When some ache or pain's bothering a person, you give it a little while, to see if it goes away on its own, then you see a doctor."

"But there isn't any ache or pain."

"You know what I mean. That cough's been going on for two months."

"Oh, it hasn't been that long."

"It's been *at least* that. At the Shanahans' party you were coughing."

"What's wrong?" TK asked.

They turned then and saw him standing there. "Hey, son," his dad said, giving a grin. "Nothing's wrong. We're just yakking. Grown-up talk."

Mom cast a firm look Dad's way, and then addressed herself to TK. "Dr. McGowan found something on your father's lungs. On an X-ray film."

TK frowned, stepping into the kitchen. "What do you mean? What did he find?"

"A blurry patch. Dad's going for more tests. It could be pneumonia."

Pneumonia? TK was trying to make sense of this. "That's not good, is it?"

"Dr. McGowan wants to examine it."

"I still say I'm fighting a summer cold," Dad insisted.

"But it doesn't mean like . . ." TK heard a quiver of uncertainty in his voice, "anything *really* bad, though, right?"

"Hush," said his mother.

"Oh, come on now, Champ." Dad looped an arm around TK's neck, scrubbing playfully at his scalp with the work-roughened knuckles of his free hand. "Ever since I mended my ways and gave up my four-pack-a-day habit? Don't be silly. *I* couldn't see anything when the doctor showed us the film. I think they spot things even if there's nothing there. They got to justify charging an arm and a leg."

TK slipped free of the hold. His dad didn't sound worried, or look worried, either, his broad, sun-browned face opening up with its grin, and this reassured TK. He felt reason return. The idea of anything bad *was* silly. Dad was kidding about the cigarette habit. He had never smoked in his life. He did have that dry cough, but that could just be a cold, sure. It *was* damp inside the ships. TK hugged his dad, feeling the hard strength there under his work shirt; and after dinner, with a big wedge of strawberry rhubarb pie for dessert, he told his folks about getting hold of Mike Burke's curveball and whacking that sucker way out onto the grass, and about the pro scouts who were "bird-dogging" Mike, and about how he'd dug almost five racks of clams that morning. Only later, as he was folding his money into a sock in his dresser drawer, did he remember he'd forgotten to ask them if every year life got better.

Further tests revealed that Thomas Knowles Sr., had cancer in his lungs, and in the second week of July he took medical leave from his job as a rigger at the shipyard and began treatment to destroy the cells creating mutiny in his body. That was how TK understood it from the explanation given by Keystone Steel's specialist, who had taken over the case from Dr. McGowan. After each visit to the hospital, Dad was even weaker, though at least he was at home where TK and Mom could tend to him. Overall Dad was uncomplaining, even cheerful. TK overheard him on the telephone one evening telling his brother, TK's Uncle Matt, "I'll show the sneaky son of a bitch who's boss." Mom, when she spoke of the disease at all, refused to give it a name or, if pressed, referred to it only as "the C," as though she were hanging on to the original diagnosis of a cold. TK understood that these were just word tricks, and yet he drew hope from them.

The other thing he had hopes for that summer, when he wasn't worrying about Dad, was finding a girlfriend. The girl who had more or less occupied that role, Janine Brewer, a sophomore he had dated a handful of times the previous spring, had gone away right after school let out, to work as a counselor at a kids' camp in Maine. Her second week there she had written to tell him that she was "in love" with another counselor, a boy from Ohio named Craig. TK's reaction to her letter, written on crisp white stationery bearing the camp's pinecone logo and a whiff of Janine's lavender scent (though for what purpose, he wondered fleetingly, if the letter was a brush-off?), was, surprisingly, indifference. The one twinge he felt wasn't so much about the mysterious Craig (though he did wonder about that, trying to picture him) but rather that Janine had called it "love," a word that she and TK had certainly never used with each other. In fact, he had never used it with anyone. Love seemed such a big emotion, and while perhaps it was just that *writing* something was often easier than *saying* it ("cancer" anyone?), nevertheless, there it was. The letter gave him a vague desire for something other than just a replacement for Janine, for something more involved, more . . . connected. The letter also rekindled a conversation that he'd been having for years with his friend Brain.

Growing up, when the rest of the kids were playing with chintzy toys you sent away for to Kellogg's (navy frogmen powered by baking soda, balsa-wood gliders) Brain was onto bigger things. By sixth grade he had already won a *Popular Mechanics* contest with a design for a drill bit that could bore triangular holes (as he demonstrated cutting eye-holes for jack-o'-lanterns), but his nickname had come earlier.

One day some neighborhood boys were using a magnifying glass to fry ants. Initially, Brain was interested in how the lens concentrated sunlight to generate heat, but soon he began to speculate on the ants themselves. How did they organize their labors? What made them work so hard? Was it possible to harness their energy? His science fair project that year proposed to find out. From cast-off windowpanes he built an ant farm and set it up in his bedroom. As he compiled pages of notes and drawings of his observations, excitement grew among his classmates; his teacher called him the brightest student she had ever had and said he was on the brink of discovery. Then, before any conclusion could be reached, disaster occurred. His kid brother cracked the glass, and ants overran the Mclain household, earning both boys a whipping from their father, and Paul the rhyming nickname from his friends (which owed as much to irony as to truth). Then, sometime in seventh grade, when he was a chubby, prepubescent kid having sticky dreams about Annette Funicello, Brain veered off the path of simple science.

Sex was a taboo topic in Weybridge: practiced certainly (the booming birthrate among the largely Roman Catholic population left no doubt about that), but talked about, if at all, only in private, as on the weekend retreats from which the Holy Name kids would return tittering with misinformation at the nuns' cautionary tales about the dangers of heavy petting and self-pollution (incidents of failing vision and ravaging acne were bleakly reported to have occurred). Brain dismissed such stories. At the town library after school he would search dictionaries and encyclopedias, tracking down the words he'd seen scribbled on the walls of boys' bathrooms or overheard being used by the older guys who hung around the soda fountain at Kresge's. He would learn the meanings (if not always the pronunciation; he went around for months talking about the "gun*eetals*"—a term his disciples adopted unquestioningly, until someone finally figured out the correct way to say "genitals"), and then share his findings with others.

Late in the spring when he was thirteen he claimed that he'd developed a device that combined the labor-saving potential of an automatic dishwasher, the entertainment value of a hi-fi record player, and the educational benefit of one of those white-coated "doctors" you saw pushing Doan's Pills, Preparation H, and Serutan ("That's 'Natures' spelled backward!") on TV. To dramatize the impact that he believed his device would have—and no doubt with a wry nod at the fact that students practiced air-raid drills at school in the event that the Russians carried out the treachery that everyone feared they would—Brain dubbed his invention the "A-BOM."

That was the year that boys in their grade lived in cringing fear of betrayal by their own hormone-driven bodies, dread of being called upon in class, as when Old Ma Casey seeing their odd, hunched posture when they rose in her Latin class, would crow, "Stand up *straight!*" to which Bob Crosley joked one day at recess, "That's the trouble; we *are!*" But it was one thing to laugh about it outside; in class each of them had his moments of gut-clutching as he waited to be asked to recite, desperately trying to keep the Latin in mind ("*amo, amas, amat*") and nothing else. So when Brain boasted that his invention would put an end to "kamikaze boners" . . . well, they were intrigued.

Even after unveiling the A-BOM one afternoon, with its near tragic consequences, he persisted over the next few years in his mission of shining light on the shadowy mysteries of sex. In spite of his broad knowledge of the topic, however, Brain had no direct experience, and therefore he spoke with limited authority. By the time TK was fifteen, the summer he first dug clams, he was ready for a new teacher.

On the crew of licensed diggers who worked the tidal coves was a lanky, long-faced man named Artie Dewitt. He would show up in his two-tone black and white '57 Thunderbird convertible, which led the others of the crew, who were around Dewitt's age of twenty-two, to jokingly refer to him as "Don Juan in a T-Bird." It was clear, though, that they looked up to him as a man of the world. After work TK usually biked straight home, but sometimes after a late-afternoon tide, the older diggers would punch open cans of beer, and TK would find reason to dawdle. The others would urge Dewitt to tell a story, and after a little feigned reluctance he would, invariably beginning, "You shoulda seen the babe I was with last night."

In no hurry, aware that his listeners were hanging on his every word, he would recount a casual meeting with a gorgeous woman that led in due course to a pickup and, unfailingly, to a steamy session in his car parked by the moonlit sea. Here his telling would grow quite graphic, and as far-fetched as some of the tales seemed, no one challenged them. On the contrary, the others would claim to have seen the T-Bird at the Crow's Nest, or parked down along the beach till all hours. "He gets more ass than a bathhouse bench," they agreed. "He's got more rubber in his glove box than on his Goodyears."

As TK worked that first summer he earned gradual acceptance from the other diggers—all except for Artie Dewitt, who paid him no attention whatsoever; and in an odd way this increased the man's appeal. TK retold Dewitt's stories to his friends, who became fascinated as well. One night late in August, TK and Brain sat on a curb at Dari-Twirl, their bicycles leaning on the kickstands nearby, when TK saw the T-Bird pull out of traffic on Bridge Street and wheel into the parking lot, top down, neon flickering on the spinner hubcaps and on the golden hair of a woman riding shotgun. TK hopped to his feet. "That's him!" he whispered excitedly. "That's Dewitt."

"Don Juan?" Brain rose, too.

Avoiding the rows of cars slotted in haphazardly around the ice cream stand, Dewitt found a corner of the lot, under the tall Dari-Twirl sign, near where several members of the local surfing fraternity were parked, boards strapped to the roof of a Country Squire wagon. As Dewitt climbed out, he bent to say something to the blonde, then headed for the service windows. He wore pressed white jeans, a short-sleeved madras shirt with matching belt, and loafers, and TK and Brain took in the details with interest. *Was the uniform part of Dewitt's success?* They watched him chat up the suntanned brunette at the service window, saw her smile, maybe even blush, and soon, carrying a soft-serve cone with a cherry red dip, no doubt intended for his date, Dewitt started for the T-Bird.

"Talk to him," Brain urged.

"And say what?"

"*Any*thing."

"Like what?"

"Who cares?"

TK fumbled forward. "Hi," he said. "Nice night, huh?"

If Dewitt was surprised to see him, it didn't show. He wore only a look of bland disinterest.

"Um . . . this is my friend Paul Mclain."

Dewitt paid Brain no attention. His manner was that of someone with more important things on his mind than a pair of kids whose idea of kicks was hanging around Dari-Twirl. "Well, carry on," he sniffed and started past, would've left them there, but Brain jabbed TK in the ribs.

"Uh . . . can I, uh . . . ask you something?" stammered TK.

"What is it, kid?"

And TK blurted, "How can we find some girls?"

Dewitt stopped. "What? Here?"

"In general, I mean. *Any*where."

Dewitt waved at a mosquito. "What am I, a pimp?"

TK's cheeks warmed, but he pressed on. "I figured if anyone knows, it's you."

Dewitt appeared to think this over. He was nothing if not vain about his reputation as an operator. Then, as though deciding something, he motioned them away from the cluster of other patrons, led them over by the tall sign that depicted a smiling Eskimo girl. "Half a rock each," he said. At their confusion, he made a "gimme" gesture with his free hand. "I don't *give* this stuff away. These are trade secrets. You're getting a discount only on account of I know you, Knowles."

TK hesitated, then took out a dollar, one of the five he allowed himself each week for spending money, and handed it over. Dewitt stuffed the bill into a pocket of his white jeans. "Okay, one question apiece."

A question? TK felt cheated. Though what had he been expecting? That Dewitt would fix them up with the brunette at the service window? Coax the blonde in his T-Bird to spend the rest of the evening with two virgins on bicycles? Melted ice cream was pearling at the bottom rim of the waxy red dip on the cone in Dewitt's hand. TK's mind was blank. He sent a helpless look at Brain, who always had questions—and did now. Brain cleared his throat. "I was wondering . . . how do you know when . . . when you're in?"

Dewitt frowned. "What?"

The tall neon sign made zigzag reflections in Brain's glasses. "You know, like . . . *in*, and not just between the girl's thighs? Say maybe you're making out on the beach, how do you know your pecker's not just stuck in wet sand?"

Dewitt gave him an are-you-for-real look, but it was clear that Brain was all *too* for real. "Trust me, you'll know."

Brain exhaled loudly and stood a little straighter, as if a hod of psychological bricks had fallen from his shoulders. He beamed. "Wow—neat."

Dewitt rolled his eyes. "Okay, Casanova, you're up," he told TK, "but quick. I don't wanna be *wear*ing this cone."

This time TK didn't falter. "I'd like to get a girl," he said.

Artie Dewitt narrowed his eyes. "*Nail* one, you mean. Bag one."

"Just meet one."

"Meet one. A chick. You're joking me, right?"

"No."

"That's your question? How?"

"Yeah."

"Jeezus, it ain't about *meet*ing one. It's knowin' how to *scoop* 'em." He gestured up at the lighted sign. "If I wanted to, I could make that *Eskimo* chick. It's technique, it's finesse, it's—"

"I mean, how do I find a girlfriend?"

Dewitt's mouth opened, then closed. He looked even more exasperated than he had with Brain. Ice cream was oozing over his fingers in pale streams. "I got no time for this. Get lost."

"I paid for one question," TK said, strangely emboldened by having voiced the question he'd asked himself often but had yet to answer. "That's mine."

Dewitt glanced at the cone in his hand, and with a sigh he tossed it aside. It made a soft *splat* on the asphalt. He began wiping his fingers on a napkin. "A girlfriend. Not a chick, a broad, some snatch, a piece of tail . . . a girlfriend. I got that right?"

"Yes."

"No wonder you're a loser."

TK was silent.

"You obviously don't know squat about the Four-F club."

"The what?"

"Case closed."

"Wait," Brain spoke up. "That's when you can't go into the army on account of medical reasons, right?"

"Jesus, you two." Dewitt dropped the crumpled napkin. "Four-F. *Find* 'em! *Feel* 'em!" He ticked off the words emphatically on his fingers. "Please tell me I don't gotta give you the third F."

Brain mustered a grin. "I guess we know number three all right."

"That's the goal of one and two, but it ain't the most important. If you want to be in the club, it's F number four that—"

He broke off, his attention caught by something off to their left. TK and Brain turned. The blonde had climbed out of Dewitt's car and was mincing across the parking lot on high heels. She was thin in tight jeans that stretched over her round behind and was pretty in a tough, Adams Point housing project kind of way. Brain's mouth hung open with naked lust. TK stared, too. Unaware of the three of them there, the girl walked around the outside of Dari-Twirl and into the ladies' room.

Dewitt was first to speak. "Come with me." He started toward his car, paused, and said over his shoulder, "C'mon, I ain't got all night."

The surfers had gone, and the T-Bird sat alone, gleaming pristinely under the glow of the tall sign. "Lean in," Dewitt said. "Go on, put your heads in. Both of you."

They did. TK looked at the bucket seats, the chrome console, the automatic floor shifter. There were even seat belts.

"Take a whiff," Dewitt ordered, demonstrating.

They breathed the mingled aromas of car wax, leather upholstery, the spicy scent from the little Playboy bunny air-freshener dangling from the rearview mirror, and something more . . . a faint tang of perfume and tobacco smoke and, even fainter, an animal musk that was unmistakably female. Brain gave a soft groan, as if he were inhaling ambrosia. TK felt his pecker stir. Dewitt said, "You think the fox that left that smell in there is my girlfriend? You think the parade of babes that climb into this scarf wagon are *girl*friends? You two are hopeless. Scrape off."

He opened the driver's side door and climbed in. They were dismissed. There was nothing to say. The blonde would be back in a moment and they'd be standing there playing pocket pool. They turned to go. Then, suddenly, Brain stopped. "The last one."

Artie Dewitt's gaze fogged. "What?"

"F number four. We know one, two, and three. What's four?"

"Only the most important of all. For*get* 'em."

A few years later, Brain's awe for Artie Dewitt would curdle when Dewitt began dating Dee Richards, toppling the preacher's daughter from the pedestal that Brain had constructed for her in his imagining. But that was still some time away, and on that warm August night at Dari-Twirl, Brain was convinced that he had found a teacher. For his part, TK sensed that what he had gained was well worth what he'd paid, because now he realized that when it came to learning anything about romance, sex, or even love, he was on his own.

3 Tom

He opened his eyes to a world blurring slowly
into focus. Emergency lights had come on, giving everything a
yolky yellow glow. An alarm was sounding somewhere, distant, like
a bell buoy clanging in dense fog. There was a smell, too, a tart
smoke-stink that prickled his nostrils and reminded him vaguely
of . . . *some*thing. His dominant impression, however, was of a murmur of voices. Faces surrounded him, like images out of Rod Serling's *Night Gallery*, at once comical and grotesque, and—at the
moment—as though glimpsed through opaque glass. They were
familiar, and yet he was sure he had never seen them before. The
voices grew more distinct, and he realized they were coming from
the mouths of the faces:

He's alive!

How do you feel?

Is there someone to call?

What the hell was going on? Words were bogged down inside
him, unable to rise out of the mire of images and indistinct impres-
sions. A bearded man was squatting beside him, holding his wrist.
The man's bow tie was askew and perspiration glistened on the
dome of his head. Now something did float from his mind to his
tongue. "What's . . . happening?"

"You tell me," the man said.

"I guess . . ." Piecing it together now. More words untangled
themselves. ". . . I flaked out."

"You lost consciousness for a moment. Do you know me?"

"Mmm . . . not sure."

"What's *your* name?"

"TK."

"Maybe it's a concussion," a woman crouching nearby whispered. "From when he fell."

The surrounding faces became more like normal faces now, not as interesting as their *Night Gallery* counterparts, but familiar and reassuring. He squinted and his vision cleared sufficiently to see his inquisitor was the dry Cornhusker, Russ Rigden, M.D., apparently taking his pulse.

"We're at our high school reunion, class of 'sixty-four. The big three-oh. I'm Tom Knowles."

There were puffs of relief. Rigden rose. "He'll be okay."

People were eager to explain what had occurred. Apparently, Tom had gotten an electric shock, though for the life of him he couldn't remember it happening. He sat at one of the round tables with a mug of coffee. The power had come back on, and the crowd cleared out quickly once they were assured Tom hadn't died. Soon only Tom and Brain Mclain remained in the hall.

"Did you see it happen?" Tom asked.

"Jeezum crow," Brain murmured, "when I saw that flash, I thought . . . whoa. Y'sure you're all right?"

Was he? He *felt* okay. Rigden had declared that his pulse and respiration were normal.

"Is my hair all frizzed up and standing on end?"

Brain grinned. "That would be my hair."

Several members of the VFW post had stuck around awhile, looking by degrees anxious and self-important, but Tom reassured them, too, and they drifted away to the bar in the other room. Tom and Brain wandered over to where the electronic equipment sat.

"There're some fried circuits, I think, but the lasers seem fine," Brain said. "That was quick thinking on your part—pulling the plug. I'm grateful."

"Anytime. But not again tonight."

"So, how'd you like it?"

"Like what?"

"The show, dimwit." Brain seemed eager. "What did you think?"

"Ah, the show," Tom deadpanned. "You mean aside from reminding us how badly we used to dress?" He clapped Brain's shoulder. "You saw the way we all reacted. It was incredible. The old football films and school dance footage, the music, and especially the holograms—*all* of it," he elaborated. Brain was fairly bouncing with happiness. Tom offered to help bring the gear back to wherever he kept it, but Brain said he would come get it tomorrow. He was too jazzed right now.

What time was it? Tom realized he had no idea.

"After midnight. Some people are going out for a nightcap. You game?"

"I need sleep. I'm still on California time."

"Aw, man, don't poop out now. We'll go to the Monkey Bar. There's no telling when any of us'll see each other again."

"No, I better—"

"Dee Richards is going to be there," Brain blurted.

"Ah ha. So this isn't all about Brain bonding with his old ex-buddy TK."

Brain shrugged. Well, Tom wasn't feeling any the worse for his experience. In fact, as he thought about it, he found himself getting a second wind. "I don't even know where the Monkey Bar is."

Brain smiled. "I do."

The storm had passed. As they crossed the parking lot, which was all but deserted now, puddled from the rain, Tom stopped, recalling something. "For just one moment there, before I came around, there was a scorched smell."

"Electronic circuits," Brain said.

"No, this was . . . remember when we used to play in your dad's workshop, and he'd use a soldering iron? That's what I smelled."

"Solder?" Brain shook his head. "Sorry, man. Nothing like that here."

Tom shrugged. "If you say so." But he was sure.

Don't . . .

A slow sensation of ascent . . . the world beyond the windows a pale nothingness.

Stop . . .

Stirrings in the dimness, something soft-bodied, with clasping limbs. *Don't . . .*

A moan that is distinctly human and female. *Stop . . .*

The fog swirls back in.

Tom cracked open his eyes to weak daylight. He lay on his back. He did not move. He imagined booze still sloshing around in his system, like bilge in the hull of a boat. So what would it be? The thumping throb of a headache; the dizzy queasy awfulness? Incredibly, aside from a sandpaper tongue, he felt . . . fine. Keeping the rest of his body still, he rolled his head to the left. Daylight seeped through a gap between window drapes. Someone lay beside him. He pushed up on one elbow and squinted at a mass of tousled bottle blond hair. This did not augur well. He peered around the unfamiliar room: sturdy furniture in dark fabrics, TV on an industrial wall mount. Motel room. Wonderful. He lay back. He had a shrouded recollection of a wrestling match with a bra.

Don't you ever stop? Don't . . . stop. Dooon't . . . stop . . .

He rubbed his eyes. *Oh, God, who plugged the coin into you? You're insatiable. Where were you when we were in high school?*

Dee Richards? He sat up abruptly. It was Dee Richards, all right. The slow rise and fall of her breathing told him she was in a deep sleep. He hesitated a moment, indecisive, then rose, found his shorts on the carpet beside the bed, and drew them on. He opened the drapes just enough to illuminate the room with soft light.

In the bathroom he peeled the wrapper off a tumbler and drank two glasses of chlorine-tasting water before, finally, he leaned close to the mirror. His hair was a horror, one side of his face sleep-scarred, but overall he didn't look half bad. The fact that he couldn't remember much of last night told him he should look a lot worse.

Dee Richards hadn't stirred. He sat on his own side of the bed and studied her: the lines webbing her eyes stained with mascara, the sag in her cheeks and under her chin, her lips parted as she puffed soft breaths. He tried to superimpose on this the woman she'd been as recently as last night (it was last night, wasn't it?), the woman in the short black dress and high heels and shining hair. As if subliminally aware of his scrutiny, Dee stirred, moaning softly.

Where were you when we were in high school?

And where were you, thought Tom. But he could imagine where young Diana Richards had been. Parked up at the Crow's Nest or in the back row of the drive-in theater, with any of a succession of heavy-breathing hot-rodders and jocks—the minister's daughter got around.

As if prodded by his thoughts, Dee groaned and sat suddenly, heavily up, the sheet falling away from her breasts, which, without the push-up bra, sagged some, though they were still full, freckled on top above the tan line, the nipples rosy. She cast a narrowed look his way, recoiling slightly, then without haste drew the sheet up around her. Her face relaxed again. "Timezit?" she murmured.

"Getting on to checkout time, I imagine." He watched for a reaction, but she only blinked contentedly a few times, then rose, wrapped the bedsheet around her toga style, and walked flat-footed to the wall mirror. She tipped her head to one side, then the other, and finally said huskily, "Did I survive the train wreck?"

The question might have been rhetorical; beyond the initial blurred glance, she hadn't given him any sense that she even knew he was there. Still, he said, "You look fine." Not a lie. What did she expect? They weren't kids. And the way they'd been pouring the sauce . . .

"Not that. I look great. I always look great." She said it without a speck of irony. "I mean last night. Whose idea was that, anyway?"

Whose idea was what? The reunion? After? (*Doonnn't . . .*) What *did* happen? (S*top . . .*) He had no idea; but right now, deep thinking seemed beyond both of them. She went on studying her reflection. He picked up a booklet of matches from the bed table. Printed on the flap was the grinning cartoon face of a chimp and the name Monkey Bar. A fragmented version was coming to him. A place by the beach— hanging party lanterns, surf foaming palely in the dark beyond a deck. Dee ended her inspection and turned from the mirror, regarding him directly for the first time. "We were the last ones dancing."

"We were?"

"We closed the place. Mary Agnes Kinney was still there . . . a few others. You wanted to keep the party going. Mary Agnes has never missed a chance to keep yapping, so she was game. Mclain, too."

"Brain was there?"

"With ill designs on jumping my bones. I told the others I'd ride with you and show you an after-hours bar down on Nantasket."

"Is that where we are now?"

"You really are clueless, aren't you? We ditched them." She came over and patted his cheek. "I chose you as the better of evils. And it *was* evil. But I'll tell you . . . I wasn't disappointed."

Tom frowned. He remembered almost nothing of what she'd recounted. *Other than the electrical storm that had fritzed Brain's media show.* Hmm. "Was Brain okay?"

"Why do you call him that?"

"We always did."

"It's stupid."

"How many kids in our class went to MIT?"

"Or wanted to." She made a face. "Being smart is overrated."

"Depends who's doing the rating."

"So being a school janitor is a big deal?"

"Brain? Yeah, right."

"I'm going to take a shower. Be a good boy and bring us some coffee."

"Why don't we go out for breakfast?"

She ignored him. Unwinding the sheet and dropping it on the bed, she padded naked to the bathroom, her ass broader than it had been in high school, but still shapely and firm. Tom watched appreciatively till she shut the door. He located the rest of his clothes and put them on. When he got back with two paper cups of coffee, the air in the room had the stirring scent of freshly washed hair and lightly perfumed female flesh. Dee was wearing the black dress she'd had on last night, slightly the worse for wear, but still displaying her amplitude. She had a towel around her hair, and a few damp tendrils hung loose. She was sitting prettily before the wall mirror, applying eyeliner, her lips pursed.

"What?" she said.

"Just looking."

"Don't."

He shrugged. The yearbook lay on the coffee table. "You brought this?" He picked it up.

"It's Mary Agnes's. I took it for safekeeping."

He ran his fingers over the pebbled black cover and the raised silver writing. *Kaleidoscope 1964.*

"*Yech,*" Dee spat. "Where'd you get this coffee?"

"Vending machine. Let me take you out for breakfast."

"I already told you."

"But you didn't."

"N-O."

He opened the yearbook and began turning pages. In the class portraits section he found Diana Richards's photo, and he remembered the look with absolute recall. Her hair in a bouffant, a smile that even then, in the summer before their senior year, had a definite quality of allure, lips that made one want to kiss them. " 'Dee,' " he read aloud, " 'our glamour girl! Watch out Hollywood! Fashion Club, 10, 11, 12. Jr. Party Committee. Loves *Come a Little Bit Closer*, drive-ins, and hot rods.' " He looked over. "Do you still like Jay and the Americans?"

"I still like hot rods. Let me see that." She gazed at her photograph as though peering out of a tiny windowpane into time. "You can read that?"

"Well . . . actually, yeah." The print was surprisingly clear.

Dee fished in her pocketbook and drew out a pair of glasses and put them on. He thought she'd say, "Let's see *you* now," but apparently she had other ideas. She turned pages to a succession of people she'd known: girls in white Peter Pan collar blouses and confident smiles, boys in blazers and ties, hair shiny with oil. Most hadn't been in Tom's circle of friends, and yet many of the faces came back with a clarity that surprised him, considering that thirty years had intervened since he had last seen any of them. He had the thought that in high school Dee had been way out of his league, but the evidence suggested that was no longer true. "I'm going to be around a week or so. Why don't I take you out for dinner or something?"

Dee clapped the yearbook shut matter-of-factly, took off her glasses, and returned to the mirror.

"So what about it?"

Dee gave her reflection a final appraisal, then began tossing makeup items into her pocketbook. "About what?"

"A date. I'm not sure we were at our best here."

"Oh, you were at your very best. I've got no complaints." She turned to look at him directly. "What, are you going to bring flowers and call at my door?"

"Why not?"

She laughed, as though at some joke he wasn't in on. "Look out the window. Go ahead."

He parted the drape liner. The parking lot was wet from overnight rain. Beyond rose a sign, alight in the overcast morning. THE 3-A INN. On the other side of the road was the familiar: BOSTON 12, NO. WEY. 3. One question answered. They were in Adams Point. "Brain told you his theory?"

"What?" She came over to stand beside him. "The Cadillac."

A pearl gray Escalade stood live-parked near the motel office. Through the tinted windshield he could just make out a driver. A thought occurred. "Are you married?"

"Twice. Both ex."

"So who's that, your father?"

"Soon to be hubby number three. I phoned him when you were getting coffee."

Tom dropped the drape liner. "Odd you didn't remember him last night."

"Fun makes me forgetful."

"Should we invite him in for coffee?"

"I don't think he'd go for that."

"Why? Is he the jealous type?"

"Mmm . . . more the suspicious type. He's the district attorney."

She picked up her handbag, patted his cheek once more, and headed for the door. "Oh, the motel bill is on your MasterCard. Hope you don't mind." Partway down the corridor she turned and tossed him a set of keys. His. Back at the window he saw Dee appear outside after a moment, pausing to smooth her black dress over her hips, then open the Escalade's passenger side door and vanish into the smoked glass interior. The vehicle stayed put, giving Tom over to imagining what was going on inside (a kiss hello? probing questions?), then it drew slowly away. When he reached for his cigarettes on the table he discovered that Dee had left the yearbook behind.

The house was adrift with the lemon and ammonia scents of cleaning and the warm fragrance of tomato soup his mother had on the stove. He'd phoned her from the motel to let her know where he was (no mention of Dee Richards), then had eaten breakfast at a pancake house on 3-A. Customer receipts in his wallet showed that he had indeed paid for the motel room, along with a $160 bar bill. He hoped others could remember the high times better than he did.

He spent a couple of hours in the cellar, sorting what was there. Some of the more serviceable items would go to Goodwill; the rest was for his mother to decide what to keep and what to toss, though he was an advocate for the latter. Tackling the attic next, he opened the overhead trapdoor in the upstairs hallway, swung down the folding steps, and climbed up. Stooping under the rafters, in the weak glow of a hanging lightbulb, he looked on an array of cardboard cartons, discarded furniture, and housewares.

Within twenty minutes, working amid cobwebs and the pervasive smell of mothballs, he had inventoried most of what was there. In one of the last cartons he came upon issues of the high school weekly newspaper, the *Echo*. The newsprint gave off a faint must. Gingerly, because the paper was brittle with age, he opened one issue and saw his column, "Curb Feelers," the name as dated as the title of the particular column, "Lady's Choice." He read the lead. "Your phone rings one evening and it's a girl asking, 'Would you like to go out Saturday night?'"

He drew over a cane chair, dumped some shopping bags from the seat, sat, and read on.

Your heart beats faster. You thought she'd never ask. "Sh-sure!" you stammer. Or maybe: "Gee, I'd like to, but . . ." because you've already said yes to another girl, who happens to have her own car and spending money.

Far-fetched? How about when the deejay at a school dance announces "Lady's choice." Girls step away from their girlfriends and walk across the gym floor and go straight to boys and ask, "Do you want to dance?"

This sometimes happens twice in one night. And maybe there's a snowball dance, too, and both partners get to go and each ask another person to dance. So maybe three times on a Friday night, girls do the asking. Three times. While us guys can ask thirty or three hundred times.

Us guys. The piece went on in that vein for another half column, concluding with a series of rhetorical questions. What if girls could ask boys for a date anytime? Drive to their homes to pick them up? Choose the movie? Buy the popcorn? Venture a good-night kiss? It was mildly amusing stuff as a peek into another time, but prize-winning journalism it wasn't.

Tom shuffled through several more issues, the newsprint as dry and yellowed as antique lace. One column, titled "Black Hole"—about girls' pocketbooks—began: "What is really in that mysterious dark place which every girl knows and every boy can only imagine?" How Freudian was that?

Well, in the interests of advancing knowledge, this reporter has conducted some research. His findings are as follows. Inside the Black Hole you might find a fat wallet, stuffed with snapshots of kids in school, but also of Pat Boone and Ricky Nelson. Three shades of lipstick. One laminated, slightly tattered school bus ticket. Nail file. Kleenex. Hair spray. Compact mirror. Assorted gum wrappers . . .

The column amounted to little more than a list with occasional asides ("An eyelash curler?!"). There wasn't a whisper about cigarettes or Tampons—forget Trojans—but a thought stirred as he read, a vague, unremembered something . . . Related to pocketbooks? He couldn't put his finger on what it might be, and he laid the issue of the *Echo* back into the box, which he set alongside a carton of Christmas decorations in the "dispose" pile, and went on with the culling.

By two o'clock he had amassed a heap of bags and boxes, which he lugged downstairs and brought out to the side porch. He'd take a break and tackle the garage next. Curbside pick up was on Friday. If he managed things right, he'd have a goodly heap on the sidewalk by then, have the house under agreement for sale, his mother settled into new quarters, and a few days after that, with luck, he'd be on a flight to L.A.

The copy of the *Kaleidoscope* with "Mary Agnes Blanchard '64" inscribed inside the front cover was on the kitchen table. He wished now that he'd left it at the motel desk with a note for someone to call Dee Richards to claim it. It was just one more thing to deal with. He sat down to soup and opened the yearbook. He turned to the section of senior portraits, flipped pages, and there was his. There *was* something of Wally Cleaver in it, or Tony Dow, the actor who'd played him. "Thomas Knowles," the entry began, "TK . . . *sincere*." And that came back with a nudge of amusement. Though it hadn't been like that the first time he saw the word, the day when the 1964 yearbook had been handed out. Not even close.

Sincere? TK stared at the word next to his name. What kind of a thing was that to say about someone? At lunch he tracked down Brain in the cafeteria sucking a half pint of milk through a flavor straw. TK clumped the yearbook onto the table, opened it, and pressed a finger to the page. Brain glanced at the page, then looked up quizzically, the May sunshine outside making his eyeglasses gleam like baby moon hubcaps.

"Who wrote these quotes?" TK asked.

"Everyone on the staff got some to do."

"Who did mine?"

"Dunno. It was random who got whose. We had to come up with hundreds of them. Friendly, ambitious, *adorable*. That's what Niki DiLorenzo got. We couldn't say 'flat as Kansas.' "

"But 'sincere'?"

"If it's any consolation, I'm not crazy about mine, either. Did you see it?"

TK hadn't. Was it 'eccentric'? Who else brought flavor straws to school? Brain frowned. " '$E=mc^2$.' I mean, who even knows what that means?"

"They know it means smart, at least."

Brain looked solemnly at TK. "What would you have preferred?"

Sighing, TK slumped into a chair. What *would* he have preferred?

Handsome? Ha. Great athlete? Tough? *No, I'm not tough. Or a star athlete.* He didn't know. Something else though, for goodness' sake. Not "sincere."

Now, all this time later, Tom could only smile. Whatever emotional load the adjective had carried then was long gone. It was just a word, no worse than any other, better than some—about as insightful as anything ever is in a high school annual. He turned more pages, moving through a gallery of young faces, coming to the S's. He looked at Ray Sevigny, who gazed out of the picture from skeptical eyes in a lean, handsome face, his dark hair pulled down in a little twist, *à la* Tony Curtis (not Tony Dow). He wore a black sport coat, a string tie. *Raymond Sevigny. "Ray." Sheet metal program. Track 10. Boss wheels! Ambition: to have his own auto body shop.* Across the top of the picture, in a small neat cursive, someone had written "Deceased."

Tom felt like the air had been sucked from his chest.

Ray Sevigny dead? He was shaken by the thought. Sevigny had seemed too wily, too tough, too . . . *cool* for death somehow. When? How? There was nothing else there to give a clue. He flipped more yearbook pages, back through club photos, team shots, candids, back to the portraits, and realized that whoever had written "deceased" over Ray Sevigny's had done so for a number of other pictures, including Bob Crosley's—a dozen of Tom's classmates at least, gone to their final reward.

He stood in a steamy shower a long time, scrubbing off the attic dust and whatever remained of last night, then put on fresh jeans, Nikes, and a blue work shirt. The garage would have to wait.

The number of celebrants had dwindled; still, a dozen people were there, dressed for action, when Tom got to the playground field. Stan Jarvis, out of his Rotarian suit and looking massive in a blue sweatshirt emblazoned with Jarvis and Easton Real Estate, had brought an assortment of bats and gloves. Tom begged off playing;

he wanted to speak with Mary Agnes Kinney and ask about her yearbook, but no one had seen her. "Come on," Stan encouraged. Tom wasn't eager, he had a lot to do, but he agreed to play at least until more people arrived. Sides were chosen, and he was teamed with Roger Hascomb, Kippy Morse, and some spouses. No sign of Brain. He wasn't disappointed that Dee Richards hadn't come.

Softball was a clumsy game. Everything always felt too heavy. You flailed at the ball, trying to bash it, and more often than not ended up looking feeble. The fielding for the most part was worse, and the scores for both teams were soon in double figures. Larry Blake shot video and conducted interviews as though he were reporting for *Wide World of Sports*. The matchup was pretty even, though it was clear that whatever their former skills had or hadn't been, a lot of years had passed. By the fifth inning they quit keeping score. As Tom took his position in center field, his attention had wandered. So what was the big deal about the notes in the yearbook? Some people kept track of things; and in any class—especially thirty years on—stuff happened. People died. And yet, for some reason (one that made no sense, since he was eager just to get out of Weybridge and back to his life), he felt a desire to learn more.

The cries seemed to sprout from the air. Tom came alert. At the plate, Stan Jarvis was twisted around in the follow-through of a mighty swing. Tom saw the ball soaring in a high arc. Jarvis had tagged it good, and it would drop deep, far to Tom's right and roll a mile. Let it, he thought; there was nothing riding on the game.

But he started to run. He felt his feet hitting the ground, knees pumping high. At the edge of his vision, Kippy Morse was a blur in left field. Tom ran faster. As the ball neared the end of its flight, just about to hit the ground, he lunged, glove outstretched. He knew he'd fall, and at the last instant he turned it into a headlong dive. He hit the grass flat out, rolled on his shoulder, came up on his feet, and managed a halfway graceful stop. Puffing, only beginning to be aware of what he'd done, he turned to face home plate and raised the glove, the ball nested snugly in the webbing. Everybody cheered.

And that was the game. He was jokingly named MVP, interviewed by the earnest Larry Blake. Stan Jarvis harrumphed dramatically about being robbed, but it was clear that he took joy in the catch, too. People produced beer and soda, chips and pretzels, and everyone sat on the grass or on tailgates, talking. Briefly, Tom huddled with Stan Jarvis about his plan to put his mother's house on the market, and Stan promised to follow up.

Shortly, Tom saw Penny Griffin loping across the grass, wearing jeans, a pink blouse, and sneakers so white they looked like patches of chalk on the grass. Her auburn hair was brushed and shining. "How do you feel?" she asked him.

"Like someone ought to step on those sneakers."

"Seriously, how are you?" Was she asking about the night of carousing, of his having been with Dee Richards? No, she hadn't been with the crew of nightcappers. "I heard you got a shock. You scared people."

"How'd you find out?"

"Brain came by the diner this morning. I'm on shift, but I got someone to spell me for an hour."

"You missed the action, girl," Kippy Morse said, punching Tom's shoulder. "He was party central—not to mention the star today."

Tom was still amazed. By all rights, after a night like he'd reportedly had he should've been dialing up Ralph on the big white phone. "All you've gotta do is stick your finger in a light socket," he deadpanned. "Why didn't I know that in high school?"

"It's true, dude. At the Monkey Bar we were all getting our buzz from you."

And your drinks, Tom thought; but Kippy said it with such admiration, Tom could only shrug and try to look modest. "You were smart to leave," he told Penny. "Things got a little foggy."

"I'm sure it was fun," she said, with unintended irony.

In truth, he felt a little tickle of . . . oh, remorse might be going too far—let's say, mild disappointment, a locker-room flavor of adolescent bravado: *How did it go afterward?* (Nudge, nudge.) *Oh, it* went. (Wink, wink.) *After I ditched you slugs I ended up in the sack with one of the all-time hotties of yore.* It smacked of an Artie Dewitt escapade . . . pretty drab these long years later. Maybe if he'd remembered the experience, or felt some shared tenderness, but he didn't. The encounter with Dee Richards, whatever it had been, was a haze. To change the subject, he took the yearbook, which he'd brought along to return. "I want to see your picture," he said.

Penny groaned, but didn't try to snatch the book away. They sat on the grass and he opened it. In her portrait she was as he remembered her. Her hair in a pixie cut that framed her slender face, she gazed through horn-rim glasses that might have given her a sober, studious look, except for her smile. It wasn't the kind of smile that most of them—Tom himself—wore, tricked up for the occasion, coaxed by some word from the photographer. Hers was real, linked to the sparkle in her eyes, and ultimately, he sensed, looking at her now back through three decades, inseparable from who she was inside. This, more than anything else, made her pretty by a set of standards all her own, a set that, unfortunately, he and most of his classmates had not been ready for. "Penelope Griffin . . . 'Penny,'" the text read.

"Has the last name changed?" Tom asked. He saw a wedding ring on her finger.

"I kept it. Ours was the first generation that could."

Her list of high school activities and achievements included pep club, tennis, prom committee, honor roll, and candy striper at South Shore Hospital. Penny, he realized now, had flown under his radar in those days. And that was one more thing that bummed him about the weekend, as if he was in some kind of weird samsara, having to relive all of his old missteps. He needed to get out of there, to get back to L.A. as soon as possible. He asked Penny if she would return the yearbook to its owner, then said he had to be going. On an impulse he offered Penny a ride back to work. They said good-byes to the others. As they headed for the Ford, he mentioned the notes over the portraits in Mary Agnes Kinney's copy of the yearbook.

"She feels someone's got to keep track. The war was a big cause. Four of our classmates were killed there."

He whistled softly. "I didn't realize it was that many."

"There've been other deaths since—from many causes—but those were the earliest." As they reached the car, she paused. "We should go look at the war memorial. Are you up for that? It's just over there." The wooded hill overlooked the town hall and the old high school.

She was probably ten inches shorter than he, but she matched his pace. When they reached the top of the hill, however, she was winded. From here the bell tower jutting above the yellowing maples was the dominant view. The memorial consisted of several granite boulders with their facing sides cut and polished, carved into which were the names of people from town who'd served in various military campaigns, going back to the Revolutionary War and continuing through the Civil War (all of those names lichen-claimed now) and on to the bloodbaths of the twentieth century. They moved to the Vietnam era, and there were listed the people they'd known. Penny pointed to his name.

From the moment he'd reported for the draft and endured the humiliating rituals of induction and training, until the day he got out, he'd been a reluctant soldier. And yet here was his name on a stone with the names of others who'd served, including some who had not survived the experience. Their names stood apart, in a Vietnam roll of honor, eleven from Weybridge, each marked with a star and a date. Chris Ahern was there, and Robert Crosley, William Lennox, Raymond Sevigny.

"Remember when time was on our side?" Penny said it so softly she might have been talking to herself. "Or, at least, we thought so." She was bent close to the stone, tracing each name with her fingertips, as though inscribing them in memory. "So young, all of them. Think of what they missed."

"Like the rest of the war?" Tom asked, hearing the edge in his voice, "Johnson? Nixon? Agnew?" *Tasting* the names almost, like rue on his tongue, but not wanting it there; not now.

"What about the war *ending* because we helped make it end?" Penny said, rising, still speaking quietly. "Or those leaders being forced out?"

Was it worth the trade? Is it ever? It was always arrogant men— men who'd never heard a shot fired in fear or anger, and yet who felt a righteous zeal in consigning the young to death, bestowing hurt upon others, for causes that no one ever truly believed in. And then some of the young grew up and forgot, and they did the same to a new generation. He thought this, but it was a tired, bitter argument even for him, and he didn't give it words. And anyway, Penny wasn't his enemy. "You're definitely the glass half full type," he said, smiling to lighten the moment.

"I don't know. Sometimes. You always were."

"Me?"

"TK Knowles. 'Sincere.' "

He looked at her, surprised. "Now how did you remember that?"

"I dug out *my* yearbook when I got home last night."

"We ought to take the damn things and burn them."

She seemed shocked by the idea.

"It isn't reality anymore," he pressed. "I'm not sure it ever was. We were living in a dream, as if this town was important somehow." He stopped, struck by how he must sound. He thought she would object; he wished she would. But she didn't. She glanced at her watch and said she should get back to work. They started down the hill, scuffing through the first fallen leaves that lay on the path.

"I'm surprised Brain didn't show up today," she said. "He's been looking forward to this weekend for months."

"He said something about working on his media show," Tom remembered.

"How was it last night? Pretty amazing?"

The ironies again. "Yeah, amazing," he agreed.

"Did you get to see Mike Burke?"

"I saw him. He's still in town, huh?"

"Still here. Did he mention . . . ?" Discreetly, she let it hang.

"About Mo leaving?"

"I worry about him. But I think she'll be back. They're still in love."

"You worry about a lot of people."

"Do I?"

"Brain, for instance. Mike. Mo."

"Friends do, don't they?"

"I guess I'm measuring differently these days." He laughed. "Where I live, friendship has a whole other set of rituals."

Her cheeks had patches of color. "I've never been to Los Angeles. Tell me."

"Well, for one thing, friends are kept in compartments. You might make social plans with three or four different sets. Then you decide which are going to be best for your career right then—your A-list—and those are the folks you hook up with."

"You're joking."

"Not really."

"Isn't it awkward to call the others last minute to cancel?"

"Who calls?"

She gave him an astonished look, and he shrugged. "Monday you might phone and say, 'Sorry, I flaked,' and that's cool. They understand. Everyone does it."

"That would take some getting used to. This must feel strange to you. Being back here. You'll be heading home to California soon?"

"As soon as I get my mom settled."

He drove her to the Atlantic Diner, where she tied her hair in a bun, prior to finishing her shift, but she didn't hurry inside. They sat in the car, updating: she was married to a man named Alan; no children; her parents were in Florida. "I worked in an office for years, but I came back to waitressing. And I volunteer at the hospital." All at once, her mouth quivered and he saw that her eyes had filled.

"Hey," he said gently, "what's wrong?"

She shook her head. "I guess it's seeing those names back there just now. And it's also . . . this weekend. The reunion."

"Is that it?"

She dabbed at her eyes with a crumpled tissue. "I'm feeling a little vulnerable."

Impulsively, he put an arm around her shoulder. For an instant she relaxed, then he felt her stiffen. He withdrew his arm and sat back.

"Sorry," she said, clearing her throat. "It's seeing all you people. All that promise realized. And soon you're going back to other places, to your real lives. And I stay here, and Brain and Mary Agnes and Mike . . . We're the ones who never managed to reach escape velocity, I guess."

He arched an eyebrow. "Escape velocity?"

She sniffled and smiled. "Brain's influence."

"He was a rocket scientist before people even used the term."

"He's told me about how you two used to run around together."

"Long time ago—as he reminded me last night. I don't think early friendships are meant to go the distance. They serve their purpose." She looked at him questioningly. "To use his metaphor," Tom expanded, "they're booster rockets, to help launch us, then they fall away and we're on our own."

"Is that what you think? It sounds rather grim."

"Be honest. Was last night about deep, undying bonds?" She didn't have a ready reply, and he didn't want to be argumentative. "Ah, let's drop it. It's too nice out." And it was a glorious September day. The air was mild and the trees hinted at the colors to come, but he couldn't shake the knowledge that soon enough the world would be stripped bare for winter. He was suddenly thinking of the

74

implacable movement of time, like a canoe gliding through still water, leaving slipstreams in its passing, small eddies into which people's separate lives were drawn before being pulled slowly, inexorably away, connected only in the vaguest sense of all being part of some vast, formless whole.

"Thanks for the ride, Tom—and the talk." Penny's smile had returned, if a little tentatively. She shook his hand. "Have a great trip back."

4 TK

The Thing.

The Sneaky Sonofabitch.

The Big C.

Neither of his parents, TK began to realize, ever spoke the actual word. It was as if, by their refusal, the disease would go away. The word was there, of course (in the diagnosis, in the lab reports, even in church one Sunday when someone had offered up Tom Knowles's name in prayer), but in the house at 21 Edgewater Road, it was as though a ghost dwelt among them, felt but unseen, imagined but never named, as if to do so would invite it permanently into their lives. Yet wouldn't speaking of it be better than pretending it didn't exist? Could that give them a chance to exorcise it? Or did it matter either way? Did they really have any power to control Dad's illness? Such were the questions TK dwelt on during the weeks of waiting and watching as the treatments went on.

In English class in TK's junior year, Mr. Longchamp had introduced a poem by Robert Browning. A strange work titled "Caliban upon Setebos," it was about a crude beast contentedly sprawling in the mud outside its seaside cave. After having several students stumble through a recitation of it, Longchamp had halted them, taken, apparently, with an inspiration. Without a word, he clambered onto the desk at the front of the hall and lay stomach down. Titters rustled among the class.

Mr. Longchamp—"Longwind," as he was known behind his back—had left a position at a prep school in Maine to become chair of English at Weybridge High. A rotund, wavy-haired man of about forty, he had a flair for the dramatic, which included wearing a paisley silk scarf tucked softly around his throat in place of a necktie. This alone would have set him apart, but he also insisted on holding his classes in a cavernous lecture hall that went otherwise unused, and he had a penchant for poetry that none of his colleagues in the sullen halls of WHS shared. In class he had students read aloud— "to hear the *music*" in the language, he said, and "feel the shape" of the words. Now, lying on his ample belly on the desktop, he enacted the beast Caliban.

Poet Browning, Longwind had already explained, borrowed the storyline from Shakespeare's *The Tempest*, a play about seeking a better world. With a chubby fist cocked under his chin, Longwind (as Caliban) gazed around—in "*fear*," Longwind suggested, "that for even *thinking* what he was thinking, he might be struck dead!"

TK sat up a little straighter, as did other kids in the rows beside him.

"Because," Longwind went on, scrambling to a kneeling position, "Caliban has been warned by his dam—remember 'dam'? Who else that we've seen had a dam?"

"Who gives a damn?" whispered Bob Crosley from his seat behind TK.

In the front row a hand shot up. "That monster guy in *Beowulf*. Grendel."

"Yes. And who else?"

Silence.

"Trick question," Longwind prompted.

Still, it took a moment. TK raised his hand. "All of us?"

"Correct. Even I have a mother."

Laughter. Longwind was a goofball—and maybe a fairy, some kids believed—but he got them interested. "So this Caliban, he's been warned. Told never to take a cookie from the cookie jar. Never pick his nose in public."

"Never touch his pee-pee," Croz murmured under his breath.

"And never, *ever* to utter the name of God," said Longwind, and then stage-whispered, "Setebos."

A pin dropping would've sounded like a car crash in the hush of the lecture hall. Longwind, in character as the beast, peered around a little more confidently. "Setebos?"

Then, wonderment slowly overcoming fear: "Setebos." Nothing. And now a new idea seemed to root in the creature's brain, taking hold, until, with a final noisy clatter, he cried, "Setebos! *Setebos!* SETEBOS!"

As the echoes died in the hall, Caliban (for Longchamp had *become* Caliban) peered up wonderingly at the shadowed ceiling, as though it were the heavens. No bolt shot from the blue. No tiles fell. The lights didn't sizzle and flash. Even the most reluctant classroom scholar (and there were plenty at WHS) sat attentive, eyes forward. They got it, got what Browning, and the teacher, too, had been after. So when Longwind climbed off the desk, a smile quirking his lips, and asked were there any questions, who should raise a tentative hand but Crosley?

"So it seems like that—" Croz cleared his throat, "that guy . . ."

"Guy?"

"Uh, that . . . monster thingy. Caliban. It's like he's saying the word people always told him not to say."

"Go on."

"The words everyone's always been too chicken to say."

"Which is . . . ?" Longwind prompted.

" 'Setebos'?"

"And that is . . . ?"

Crosley puffed a breath, his brow clenching toward further understanding; but finally he shook his head.

"Anyone?"

TK spoke. "The unsayable."

"Yes!" Longwind clapped his palms together, his round face beaming shrewdly. "And we must each ask ourselves—What is the unsayable thing in *our* life?"

He went on about Caliban setting himself up as a minor god, and spying a line of crabs scurrying along the sand, letting twenty pass before stoning the twenty-first, suggesting something about the randomness of the universe. This last part got a little abstract and sailed past a lot of heads, TK's included; yet overall the moment was a triumphant one. But on a morning in late July, when TK went out onto the clam flats before dawn, he wasn't consciously thinking of Mr. Longchamp's class. He was thinking about his dad, and when he finally stopped his labors and looked around and there in the distance the first rosy glow of the Boston skyline was materializing out of the ground fog, TK whispered, "Cancer."

And again. "Cancer."

Then, with growing vehemence, swinging the clam fork down into the mud, speaking in a choked voice, "Cancer! Cancer!" shouting finally, "Goshdamn stupid stinking idiotic *cancer!*"

It would have made a bizarre spectacle had anyone been there to observe it: a teenage kid hammering at the mud with angry blows and crying out strangled words. The lone witnesses, however, some seagulls waiting patiently nearby for any overlooked morsels, were unfazed.

As July moved into August, Dad grew weak and pale. The doctors insisted that these were common reactions to chemotherapy, and they remained soberly optimistic. To keep his mind occupied, TK threw himself into conditioning. With the loss to graduation of several of last year's starters, he had a shot at a halfback spot. Now, with Coach Mosher's rigorous twice-a-day workouts only a few weeks off, TK hoped that his fitness would give him an edge. In the self-contained world of WHS, it was the athletes who got the prettiest girlfriends, and football players were at the top. Though he had dated a few girls, and Janine Brewer had been the closest to a steady, he had yet to find someone really special. He wanted to change that. Football, he hoped, would make it happen.

One evening in August, he set out to run a couple miles, as was his habit, and then he planned to catch the Red Sox on the radio with his dad. When he got back from his run and showered, Dad was sleeping, and Mom said they should let him rest, so when Brain called after supper and said that he and Croz were going to the drive-in theater and did TK want to join them, TK agreed.

There always came a point in the dog days of summer when you felt the first faint stir of interest, more curiosity than anticipation, about school. Who would be in your homeroom? What classes would you have, which teachers? It was a topic of conversation on the seawall at the beach, or at Varsity Pizza, or wherever kids got together. For TK and his friends the drive-in theater on 3-A was such a spot. At two dollars a carload, it was affordable entertainment, though sometimes, by habit dating from junior high, they simply walked in. The drive-in abutted a small farm not far from their neighborhood, and they were able to slip into the theater lot through a gap in the board fence that stretched across the back.

That night's feature was *X—The Man with the X-ray Eyes*, with Ray Milland, which Brain, especially, was hot to see. For TK it was mainly a chance to spend time with his friends; opportunities had been scarce since Dad got sick. They sat three-quarters of the way back, on the concrete stoops that formed the footings for speaker poles. Cars containing families would fill in the area ahead of them, and down in front, between the concession stand and the screen, was a playground where kids already in pajamas played under the soft eyes of parents. The rows farthest back from the screen, which would be the darkest reaches of the drive-in once night fell, were where couples on dates parked. As daylight waned and spotlights played over the blank screen and music issued from the PA system,

TK and his friends sat talking. At the first notes of each new song, Brain would quietly interrupt whoever was speaking, and addressing no one in particular would name song, singer, and date ("Jimmy Clanton, 'Venus in Blue Jeans,' 1962"; " 'Get a Job,' The Silhouettes, 1958"). Someone hearing him do this for the first time might ask how he knew that stuff, and Brain would shrug and say that he listened to Arnie Ginsburg's *Night Train* show on WMEX. But *all* of them listened to Woo Woo Ginsburg, and yet *they* didn't know every song and pop group, especially those from the 1950s. It was just one of the things Brain did, like conducting odd experiments in his father's garage, and exploring a fascination with sex. "We're *all* fascinated with sex," TK had once noted, "but you're the only one who actually reads books about it!" and Brain had merely shrugged about that, too. In his view, there was a big world out there; how were you going to know anything about it if you didn't look?

The topic turned to Mike Burke, who had just left for a week at a Washington Senators farm camp.

"If he plays against the Sox, we should all go to Fenway and boo him," Croz said, but he was clearly impressed that someone they knew was a prospect for the majors.

Brain, who didn't care about sports, was philosophical. "Mike'll get away from here. And he deserves to. Me, I don't know if I ever will."

"You could go along to sniff jockstraps," Croz said. It got no reaction. "I still don't get you." He seemed genuinely perplexed. "Why would you want to leave? Everything you need is right here." He swept a hand as if it were evident there before them, as real as the scratchy Elvis song echoing across the filling parking lot, and the scent of exhaust fumes. Brain appeared unconvinced.

"Here we know what to expect, at least," TK said, advancing Croz's case. "And how life's going to go on being. How's that a bad deal?"

But uncharacteristically, Brain wasn't quick to speak. His face was clouded, and for a moment TK saw bleakness in his eyes, and it occurred to him that things as they are weren't always that great for Brain. Mr. Mclain had a TV repair service and spent most of his time working, like everyone's dad; but when he wasn't working, he tended to drink a lot and could get a nasty temper. He wasn't above knocking his sons around. Not that Brain or his brother complained, but TK knew it happened. Brain sometimes turned up with bruises and unconvincing explanations of how he got them. Now, hesitantly, he said, "There's this idea I've been developing."

"Not another A-BOM?" Croz whined.

"You remember that, huh?"

Croz cupped his crotch protectively. "I'm gonna forget?"

In sixth grade Brain had persisted in his mission of shining light on the unspoken mysteries. He continued to pore over encyclopedias, even discovered a magazine called *Sexology*, a medical journal founded by a doctor named Wilhelm Reich (mostly it was long boring articles about glands and secretions, though occasionally there were cool pictures of gross diseases or freakish sex organs). He sent away for a pair of "X-ray specs" advertised in the back of comic books, which promised to allow the wearer to see through clothes, but he quickly declared the device a fraud. To really make something like that work, he said, would require a headset as big as a table model TV—quite impossible!—never mind that it would expose the wearer to doses of radiation that would soon kill him. Brain's breakthrough, however, (developed with all the secrecy of a Pentagon weapon and unveiled with nearly as much hoopla as Ford Motors had used the previous year to announce the Edsel) came when he was thirteen.

The day of the unveiling there were eight boys gathered in Brain's father's garage workshop. On a little TV stand near the back, cloaked with a vinyl picnic tablecloth in a red-and-white checked pattern, sat Brain's device. He had draped a strand of colored Christmas bubble lights over it.

"What is it?" kids wanted to know, crowding closer. "What's it do?"

"What every good machine does. Frees the user."

"Yeah? From what?"

"Manual labor. I call it the A-BOM." He spelled it. "Now, I need a volunteer."

It was understood that Croz would be the lab rat. Not only was he physically the smallest of them, it was his role. Hadn't he once agreed to a spin in an industrial clothes dryer at the coin-op laundry in Picknell Square (meant to simulate free fall in a space capsule, Brain had persuaded him)? He stepped forward. "What're we gonna blow up?"

"You, actually. Here, look." Brain opened up one of his old man's *Playboy* magazines and spread the centerfold for Crosley to see. "Feast your eyes." Croz didn't need encouragement. "Now, I'm going to draw this privacy screen and ask you to step behind it and drop your pants."

Croz blinked. "Whaa?"

"Just do it. You'll be glad." Croz shrugged and obeyed. "And now," Brain said, removing the bubble lights, "I give you the genuine, fully functional, four-speed, soft-pad A-BOM!" He snatched off the vinyl tablecloth. "The Automatic Beat-Off Machine!"

On the table sat a portable record player. Brain pointed out that the tone arm had been removed and the turntable fitted with a lamb's wool buffing pad of the kind used on an electric floor polisher. Croz, half concealed by the screen, was frowning along with the others. "How's it . . . I mean, where do you . . . ahem . . . do I stick . . . ?"

"Your member!" someone called.

"Your pud!"

"Your half-incher!"

"Your gun*ee*tals."

Brain shushed them. "You don't stick anything anywhere. I'm gonna draw the screen, and you just *rest* it." He patted the lamb's wool pad. "Here."

When the privacy screen was in place, Croz, only his head and shoulders visible above the top, evidently did as instructed. Standing discreetly to the side, Brain fingered the record player's power switch. "Ready?"

Croz nodded. With no further fanfare, Brain turned on the record player. "Sixteen revolutions per minute," he announced.

Bob Crosley looked down, looked up, blinked.

Silence fell on the group of boys in the garage. Brain advanced the speed knob. "Thirty-three and a third rpms. You okay?"

Behind the screen, Croz nodded. His uncertain expression had melted away.

"Forty-five rpms."

Tension drained from Croz's face. His eyes, under half-shut lids, took on a dreamy glaze. Brain moved the selector one last time. "Seventy-eight rpms."

Croz's lips curled gently upward. One moment he looked transported. The next, his mouth flew open in a chilling scream. He flailed his arms, hitting the folding screen, which collapsed. He stood there, gaping down, his dungarees and BVDs bunched around his Keds. It took another moment for everyone else to realize what had happened. At the highest speed, the buffer pad had slipped loose and an edge of the metal turntable protruded like a saw blade. The cut was minor, no blood, even; though to hear Croz's scream, he was all but an amputee.

"I can still hear that cry," TK said, laughing quietly now.

"Yeah, nice move, Bowels. I could've become a pecker-palegic!"

"Sorry," Brain murmured. "I should've secured the pad better. Anyway, my new idea isn't an invention. It's more like a . . . theory."

Clustered around the drive-in speaker pole, TK and Croz exchanged a look, interested now.

The part in Brain's wiry copper red hair zigzagged across his scalp like a geological fault line. Even clipped short the hair was impossible to manage, seeming to corkscrew out of his head. Brain scratched at it now and began to lay out his theory, according to which, in all of Weybridge's history, no one important had ever come from the town. Even the first settlers, he said, had been out-casts from the Plimoth Colony farther south, and like those Pil-grims they all would have perished from cold and starvation if they hadn't been bailed out by the local Indians—though not from any sense of universal brotherhood so much as an exchange for rum, and given the first chance, the settlers had sent the natives packing. Brain's interest was in more recent generations of Wey-bridgers. "Maybe it's the coastal fog," he speculated. "It gets into us and clouds our minds, and no one questions it because no one's aware of what's happened. Which is exactly what they want you to think."

"Wait, wait." TK was confused. "Who?"

"Us."

"But who're 'they'?"

Brain waved a vague hand. "The powers. As for the rest . . . what do the townspeople do? For a living, I mean. What jobs? Remember when the *Kaleidoscope* sent around the questionnaire, and that question about future plans? What did kids put?"

"You're on the yearbook staff," said Croz, "you tell us."

"They wrote teacher, office clerk, bookkeeper . . ."

"Yeah, so?"

"Sew buttons on ice cream. I'm just telling you. They put mechanic, fireman, shipyard worker . . ."

TK and Croz pinched their tongues and chorused, "My father works at the shipyard," (which came out, "*shit*yard") and laughed.

Brain stayed serious. "You had cop, telephone and electrical lineman, hairdresser, bus driver, DPW crew. TV repair."

"When's the sex part of this coming?" Croz asked.

"So the list of careers is pretty short. You want to be a yardbird, or a nurse, fine; but a secret agent, or an explorer? Forget it. Not that it would've mattered a squirt hole in snow if anyone *had* written those, because they still couldn't be them. The point is no one did write anything like that."

TK forced a little spurt of laughter. "Yeah, those are realistic."

"Or astronomer, sculptor."

"Has this got a point?" Croz objected. " 'Cause the show's gonna begin soon, and I wanna go get some eats."

"The point *is* no one writes anything that isn't on the 'approved' list"— Brain supplied quotation marks with his fingers—"because it doesn't occur to anyone that they *can*. The powers want it that way."

"Doggonit. *What* powers? Can I find 'em in the phone book? Are they on—"

"The ones that keep us from opening our eyes, from seeing what's really going on. Who hold us back from getting where we might really wanna be. *If* we could ever find out where the heck that is. But we won't. And our parents, and teachers, and guidance counselors—the ones who should help us—they're in the fog, too."

"That's it," Croz declared, exasperated, "I'm gonna get some food."

"Wait. What'd you put down on the questionnaire, Bob?"

"Who remembers?"

"Come on, try."

Croz sighed; he seemed convinced this was just another of Brain's rambling mind leaks. "A barber, I guess. How do I know what I'm going to be? It's stupid. This whole thing is."

"How about musician? I get the idea you'd like that."

Croz was frowning. "I might. So?"

"Yet no one wrote it on the questionnaire."

"It's crossed my mind. If I get a band together."

"And what? You think you're gonna be Duane Eddy? Look, I don't mean you're not talented. You play fine, but this has nothing to do with that. It's . . . more. It's as if around here the question is, 'What *don't* you want to be when you grow up?' "

TK had been following the exchange, but just then he spied a girl walking along between the speaker stands. She was carrying a cardboard tray from the refreshment stand, piled high with popcorn, hot dogs, and cold drinks. She wore Bermuda shorts and a striped jersey and had horn-rimmed glasses. Croz spotted her now, too. "Heads up," he murmured. "Four-in-the-face alert."

TK recognized Penny Griffin. She'd been in his art class last year, and he knew her as one of the girls who sometimes came over to the beach from the south side of town. He stood and she saw him and angled their way.

"Tom? Hi."

"Hi, Penny."

She greeted Brain and Bob Crosley, too, but her attention went back to TK. "Where's your car?" she asked.

"Oh, well, we're on foot tonight."

"You walked?" She seemed intrigued with the idea.

"It's not far. Us North Weybridge guys . . . you know. Kind of a tradition."

"That sounds fun."

"How about you? Are you with someone?"

"My family. We're parked over there somewhere." She squinted toward the rows of cars, rounded shapes in the gathering dusk.

"There must be a lot of you," Croz said.

"Only my folks and my younger brother and—Oh, all this food?" She blushed slightly, or maybe it was a brush of sunburn TK was just noticing. "How's the summer going for you guys? You haven't been at the beach much, Tom."

He was surprised she'd noticed. "Working," he said. "And getting ready for football. How about you?"

"I'm working, too. Well . . . volunteering at the hospital."

"You're a candy striper?"

"Uh huh." Penny Griffin was short and perky, with a pretty enough face, even with the horn rims, he thought. "Well . . . see you guys in a few weeks, I guess. Bye."

When she'd gone, Croz slugged TK's arm. " 'Hiiii, Tommy,' " he teased, " 'whatcha doin', Tommy? Haven't seen you at the beach, Tommy.' And you—'Are you with someone, Penny?' Jeez, she had enough food there for ten people. Maybe she's a secret chowhound—though she definitely ain't fat. Am I right, Brain?"

"She likes you, TK."

"Yeah, right."

"She blushed when you talked to her."

So he hadn't been imagining it.

"Penny," said Crosley. "Nobody's named Penny."

"Sky King's niece is," Brain said.

"I used to *love* that show."

"I used to love *her*. I'd dream about me and her in the *Songbird*."

"Yeah, as if Sky would let you make out with his niece."

"Make out, French kiss, touch her silk panties . . . I'm serious."

"The only silk you'd get is a parachute. Sky would chuck you out so fast your skuzzy little balls'd float."

"Be worth it," Brain insisted. "You agree, TK?"

"Huh?"

"Sky's niece. You could get Kathy from *Father Knows Best*, we could double."

"Yeah?" Croz growing serious now. "How 'bout me? Who would I get?"

"I don't think there's room in the *Songbird* for a triple. You think there is, TK?"

"I dunno."

"You could bring Lassie, Croz. Though I read that dog was really a boy."

"I'll bring Annette."

"Like fun. She's mine, too."

But TK wasn't really listening to them. Funny, he was thinking: this girl that he'd first seen in elementary school, a pigtailed little kid in a Dale Evans skirt (she was *still* small, as far as that went; what, five-two?), singing "I'm an old cowhand, from the Rio Grande" in a school variety show—the same show, as it happened, that had featured a pudgy Paul Mclain on accordion, just his whiffle showing above the bellowsing instrument, his pink ears visible around the sides as he squeezed painfully away at the inevitable "Lady of Spain, I adore you" (in their private version it continued, "I'll pull down your pants and explore you . . ."). The Griffins must've moved across town later, because Penny grew up on the more affluent south side. She faded from TK's awareness until high school brought the various reaches of town together. She'd been in a few of his classes, and he'd occasionally seen her on the beach, usually in the company of some of her more classically pretty girl-friends, but he'd never really thought twice about her. Until now. Hmm . . . funny. He looked in the direction she'd gone and had a sudden thought to go find her parents' car and invite himself in to watch the movie. Sure, and have her old man do what Sky King would do to Brain for invading his world.

The three friends settled again on the cement stoops and were quiet for a time, listening to music, swatting mosquitoes, and watching the slow twilight fade. TK picked up several bottle caps that lay in the gravel at his feet and examined them absently. "Look at us," Croz said, leaning back, knitting his fingers behind his head. "What could be more pisser than this?"

"Yeah, it's pisser," said Brain. "Friday night, summer's almost over, we're gonna be seniors, and we're sitting here like this is the height of . . . whatever."

"What's wrong with this?" Croz seemed honestly bewildered by Brain's attitude.

TK suddenly remembered what he'd been about to say before he'd spotted Penny Griffin—how last spring when he was filling out the questionnaire for the yearbook, for one instant, as quick as a dart of flame, a thought had come to him and he had been tempted to put "author." And then the flame had flickered out and he had written "teacher" instead. But the thought had been there. He'd *imagined* the possibility.

"We're on vacation," Croz went on, "what're we supposed to question?"

"Everything. The *mean*ings of things. Why we're here, where we're going . . . what the heck it all adds up to." Brain glanced appealingly at TK, but TK didn't want to get drawn into it, and his friend seemed to sense it. Brain turned back to Croz. "Your *mind* isn't on vacation. We should be thinking about stuff that *matters*. Planning."

Croz rose. "I'm gonna take a leak and get some food. You guys want anything?"

"I want you to wash your hands," TK said.

" 'Want anything?' " Brain mimicked when Croz had wandered off to the refreshment stand. "As if the answers to all one could ever need were there. Croz and his simple pleasures—take a leak, get a hot dog and a soda. Ignorance is bliss."

"Ignorance is a piss."

"A piss is bliss."

They chuckled. Around them the sky continued to deepen.

"He has a point, though," TK said. "We've got it pretty good, y'know?" It came out more question than he'd intended, as if suddenly he wasn't sure.

"I guess. But how do we really *know* if we've got nothing to compare it to? For Croz, okay, I catch what he means. He likes music, but is he gonna get discovered farting around with an old guitar in his basement? He probably will be a barber, he'll get a chair at DeSantis's, and he'll stay here and have his bachelor pad, or find a girl. Maybe he'll put a little band together and play weekends, and he'll cut hair till all of us are old and gray. For him, that's cool, but . . ." He let the thought hang.

"But not for you," TK finished.

Brain shook his head.

"You'll go away and become a scientist and ask your big questions and you won't look back." TK realized that Brain had really thought about things, and he wanted out. With encouragement from Blinky Keenan, their guidance counselor, he was applying to Caltech and MIT.

"I hope so," Brain said darkly. "But I can't help thinking about . . . those powers."

"And the fog."

Brain forced a grin. "Yeah, the fog. And what about you?"

What *about* him? "I don't know if I'll go to college," TK said.

"Since when? I thought you were?"

"I'm just not sure."

"Well, you're going to have to get on the ball. You have to apply."

"There's time."

And there was. It was still summer, after all. Not one of the leisured, barefoot summers of the past, but still . . . He sat there, shaking the bottle caps in a loose fist as though he were preparing to cast the dice of his fate. Should he tell Brain about the little flame-flicker idea he'd had when he was filling out the yearbook question-naire? But he hadn't followed the impulse, so what did it prove other than Brain's point? Instead, he said, "I don't know. But if it means staying in Weybridge, so be it."

Brain sighed. "Things happen. Plans change. Look at your dad."

"That's only temporary. When he's well again, life'll be just the way it was."

"Will it?"

Brain must have read the sharpness in TK's glance. "Look, I hope so," he said, twisting around on the concrete stoop, "I really do. Your dad's a great guy—worth ten of my old man—but I'm just saying. You can't always just hold down the middle. Comes a time when you need to choose a side."

TK could have asked what "side" his friend was talking about, and what choosing involved—and who *"they"* really were—but he was confused. He and Brain sat there in the growing dusk, with an orchestra of insects chirring from the weeds, and the spotlights playing across the blank drive-in screen like UFOs on radar. TK flipped the bottle caps away one by one, hearing them tinkle softly in the gravel, and soon Croz returned with a tub of popcorn and the three friends settled in to eat.

Just before the show began, Ray Sevigny's midnight black '49

Merc cruised by and stopped, its glass-pack mufflers burbling, V8 engine rumbling under the louvered hood. Ray parked a leanly muscled arm on the window frame and looked at them. Sitting as close beside him as the Hurst floor shifter would allow was Dee Richards. She wore a white halter top that displayed her deep tan, and her eye-catching gold hair was teased out. Drifting from the car's radio was Arnie Ginsburg's *Night Train* show on WMEX. Ray Sevigny gave them a nod, neither friendly nor unfriendly, just an acknowledgment, but it made TK feel good. He and Ray had known each other casually in junior high, when both were on the track team. Sevigny had been a handsome, whip-fast kid who consistently won the fifty-yard dash, despite that fact that he smoked like a chimney. Ray gave the engine a rev, and then, in the unhurried way that he did everything (*including unsnapping Dee Richards's bra?* TK wondered), he shifted into first and rumbled off toward the farthest row back, up where family cars never ventured, and where nobody ever bothered to ask how someone could possibly watch the movie through a fogged windshield.

"D'you hear about the couple found frozen to death at a drive-in?" Croz asked when Ray and Dee had gone. "They went to a show called *Closed for Season.*"

"Yuk yuk," said Brain.

"I'll tell you one thing, Ray Sevigny don't need no A-BOM. And you can bet he won't leave town. Why would he? Lucky duck's got it made in the shade right here."

As the coming attractions began, TK slapped absently at a mosquito. All this talk about leaving . . . What was wrong with being here? Was there something he was missing? Okay, he had his longings, his frustrations, but wasn't he mostly happy with this world, with his friends, even his routines? And Brain was mistaken. TK could choose. When it was important to, he could take a stand. He knew that when Dad got better, all would be great again.

As the American International Pictures logo came up on the screen and music rose, he cast a glance back in the direction where

Penny Griffin had gone, wondering if she'd be scared by the movie. What would it be like to be with her on a double date in the backseat of Ray Sevigny's Merc? Would she be in any of his classes in September? Even with the glasses, she was kind of cute.

On the last Saturday before school was due to start, TK went down to Picknell Square. It was his habit on Saturday mornings to go to Weybridge Savings to deposit clam money, and then to O'Keefe's Pharmacy, where he would treat himself to a vanilla Coke. Once a month or so he went to the barbershop, where the three DeSantis brothers could be found in their neat white smocks, snip-snipping away. Today the customers were mostly kids getting ready to go back to school, and the clipped hair was piling up on the worn brown linoleum around the base of each chair. In the last chair a man reclined with a hot towel over his face as Vito DeSantis stropped a razor on the long leather strap suspended from the chair arm. TK would have to wait, but that was fine with him because there were lots of magazines on the table by the waiting chairs: well-thumbed issues of *Argosy*, *Post*, *Sports Afield*, all of which he bypassed now, turning instead to magazines he never saw at home, like *Peril* and *All Male* ("boner books" Croz called them). These featured sexily posed women with unbuttoned blouses, their ample breasts threatening to spill out. Sometimes TK took these women home with him in his mind. What he also liked about these magazines were the stories, action tales of wounded GIs on islands in the South Pacific or in bombed-out villages in France, single-handedly fighting off squadrons of Japs or Krauts, amid hails of enemy machine-gun fire. Today he chose a copy of *Real Man* and flipped through the pulp pages till he found a story about a sailor from a sunken destroyer battling man-eating tiger sharks.

One by one, the other customers' turns came until TK was alone in the waiting chair. As Vito DeSantis swung the sheet off his customer and the man rose, TK glanced up and recognized him as

Frank Ripley. Instinctively, TK drew back behind the magazine. Ripley was a town cop whose chief duty was serving as truant officer. He was a real SOB. Kids all over town had tales of Ripley tracking down school-skippers and hauling them in to the school authorities, but not before (it was said) he would rough them up, finishing with a threat of worse if they breathed a word to anyone. Some of the stories were probably exaggerated, but not all, and they spoke to the kind of fear Ripley instilled. TK felt it even now, doing nothing more than waiting for a haircut.

As Vito DeSantis stepped over to the antique cash register to ring up $1.50, Ripley took his cap off the hat rack, and as he did, his glance fell on TK. It should have been the fleeting look between any two strangers, but it wasn't. The truant officer's dark glance lingered, and in it TK felt a sudden weight, not of simple curiosity, but of something more probing. A shiver passed along his spine. Then Ripley drew on his cap, called good-bye to the barbers, and as he turned to go, he bent and laid something on the magazine table. When the man had gone, TK saw that what he'd left was a pamphlet. The cover bore an image of a large eyeball and the text: SOMEONE'S WATCHING YOU. With a stir of curiosity, TK picked it up; and just then Vito DeSantis called, "You a-next, son." Hastily he stuffed the pamphlet in his pocket, went over, and climbed into the chair.

Penny Griffin wasn't in any of his classes, though beyond noting this and feeling a small tug of disappointment, TK barely had time to think about her or Brain's theories or much of anything else, for that matter. He was taking six courses, each with a ton of homework. It was as though the teachers had gathered one day in the staff room and plotted torments designed to make the seniors' final year hell.

Each day when he got home from football practice, he would go to the living room, where Dad lay on the sofa watching TV. If a ball game was on, the two of them might watch a few innings together. Ordinarily Dad was hot for the Red Sox and carried on a dialogue with the TV, jeering the umpires and opposing players—especially if they wore pinstripes!—singing along with the Narragansett beer jingle ("Hey, neighbor . . . have a 'Gansett"); now he mostly was quiet, and while he didn't complain about feeling sick, he clearly wasn't himself. Often, he would fall asleep. TK would go upstairs and try to concentrate on *Tess of the d'Urbervilles*, or on factoring polynomials, or the impact of Boss Tweed and the Tammany Hall years, but he'd find that he couldn't keep his mind on schoolwork for long.

On some nights during the first weeks of September, Brain would come by and they'd go to the town library. Lately, Brain was preoccupied with college applications, which was something TK ought to be thinking about, too, Brain urged, along with setting up an appointment with a guidance counselor; and while TK knew this was so, he couldn't seem to muster much enthusiasm.

"If you're planning to win a football scholarship, you might want to think again. You don't even know if you're going to be a starter."

That was true, also. Coach Mosher hadn't said anything about TK's status, though he was playing well in the preseason and he remained optimistic.

"And why not join a club? The more stuff you can put on college aps, the better."

"Like what? Join you in the chess club? The rocket club?"

"Yeah, as if we'd let you in. I don't know, just something. As a backup."

TK wasn't even sure he was going to apply to college. The idea of yet more schooling was starting to seem pretty grim. Mostly he tried not to think about the future, or much else for that matter, besides football and his dad's recovery. He ground out his homework and managed still to dig clams on weekends, finding in the work an outlet for his restless energy and glad for the money.

And yet, the second week of school, when he saw a sign posted in the hall announcing a meeting for the *Echo*, the school newspaper, he decided to go.

The meeting was held during activity block, last period of the day, and by the time he located the room, cramped quarters on the second floor that the *Echo* shared with the *Kaleidoscope*, fifteen or so other students had already gathered, most in chattering little cliques. People turned to look at him, and he felt suddenly awkward and almost left, but just then a student called the meeting to order and he took a seat in back. Cathy O'Toole, a senior who'd been assistant editor last year, had taken over the editor's post. She spoke about how enthusiastic she was for the new school year and what some of her plans were, none of which sounded very exciting to TK. When she finished, she introduced the new faculty adviser.

The woman was tall, with cat's-eye glasses and listless brown hair in a bun. She was wide in the hips, and narrow in the shoulders, and she reminded TK of a duckpin. She wasn't young, exactly, though among a staff of battle-axes, many of whom had probably swigged their first liquor out of a hip flask, jitterbugging to Rudy Vallee records, she wasn't old, either. Twenty-eight, maybe? With a soft clicking of chalk, she printed her name on the blackboard—"Audrey Mutterperl"—stepped back, looking at it as though proofreading it for mistakes, then turned and addressed the group.

She was new to teaching, she told them, and she had volunteered for the post of faculty adviser to the *Echo* and was very much looking forward to working with them. She alluded to her own stint as a journalist after college, but she didn't go on and on, wanting to give time to the students. "So," she said, "questions?"

There were a few—stuff about meeting times and staff elections—that were quickly answered. "Anything else?" Miss Mutterperl asked, and waited. "Well, I'll ask one of myself," she said. "What will my role be? I want to get to know you, to serve as a coach if I can—and to be your cheerleader." The image struck TK as amusing, given her bowling-pin shape. "But I'm going to leave it up to you to set and meet deadlines. I want you to write the stories that you and your editor feel you should write. I spoke with Mr. Sterns about going from mimeograph to offset printing, and he approved it. Right away that will give the *Echo* a more professional look."

"What's wrong with the way it is?" one of the staffers from last year asked.

"It's a fine school paper, but I think we can make it even better. We can make it a showcase for your talents."

"How're we supposed to do that?" asked a frizzy-haired kid.

"Well, you'll still want to cover the school news—social activities, student government. That's the *Echo*'s main purpose. But I'm going to encourage you to go deeper and explore what the news *means*. I'd also like to have more columns and editorial space, where you can express personal opinions."

"Opinions about what?" Cathy O'Toole asked sharply.

"Anything. What being students at Weybridge High means to you."

"About teachers? The principal?"

They were challenging her because she was new. The teacher stayed calm. She folded her hands under her sizable boobs and looked around the room. The overhead fluorescents glinted on her glasses, turning them to hazy smears. "Absolutely. Now, are there any other questions?" There were none; the bell was about to ring; people began gathering their books. "Well, then, you can call me—" She hesitated, and for an instant TK thought she was going to invite them to call her by her first name, still printed there on the chalkboard, "Audrey"; but she said: "naïve. I think Vice Principal Sterns believes I am. But I have great expectations of you this year, and faith that with hard work, each of you will rise to them. This is a proving ground for who you'll become. I look forward to our journey."

Filing out afterward, the frizzy-haired kid rolled his eyes and murmured at TK, "Hard work? Journey? I joined this to get out of last period study hall."

And why did I come? TK wondered. At his locker he gathered his belongings and got ready to head over to the gym for football practice. When he looked up he saw Penny coming his way. "Hi," he said.

"Hi." Afternoon sunlight was thick and yellow in the corridor. Her hair glowed like a halo. "I was just at the Pep Club meeting," she said. "I wrote your name on a poster."

"Oh, yeah? How's the club going?"

"Well . . . we've got a lot of pep."

"I'll bet." At the far end of the hallway a custodian was working a buffer back and forth across the old terrazzo.

"How's school this term?" Penny asked. "I haven't seen you around."

"It's going good."

"I still can't believe we're seniors. How about you?"

"Yeah, same." He hesitated, and then said, "I went to a meeting for the *Echo*."

"Are you joining?"

"Thought about it, but I don't guess I will. I'm pretty busy with football." He considered explaining that he'd gone to the meeting at Brain's urging him to branch out, but why would she care. "Mostly I was just kicking tires."

"You'd be good at writing. I remember some stories you once wrote in class."

That night, his homework done, he sat in the circle of light cast by the duck decoy lamp his grandpa had made and took the dust cover off the little Olivetti portable typewriter. He'd gotten it in eighth grade, supposedly for typing papers, though he rarely used it. Now, sitting there without its cover, it seemed poised and ready, waiting only for his inspiration and his fingers to give it life. He drew a slow breath, paused a moment, letting his mind clear, then typed:

Private, says the sign on the teachers' lounge door. No Students Allowed. So I have to imagine them huddled in the smoky room, rubbing their hands and cackling with mischievous glee as they hatch plans to make our senior year m-i-s-e-r-a-b-l-e.

That was how he began his first article for the school newspaper.

At night sometimes, or early in the morning, TK would see his mom praying. His dad sat on the sofa, his big, calloused hands cupped together, eyes half-shut. Maybe he was praying, too, but what TK saw mostly was this powerful man being whittled down. When TK was young, he liked to watch his grandpa carving wooden ducks, marveling at a block of pine being transformed as his grandpa's tools—first the planes and the spokeshaves, then the knives and wood rasps, and finally sandpaper—were applied, the bulk of raw wood changing contours and something new emerging. This was what TK hoped was somehow happening with his dad on the cancer treatments: that a new, heartier man was in the process of being formed. But with each passing week, TK grew more doubtful. It was as though the tools—the medicines, the radiation—were too sharp, being wielded with too much force, and the block was being whittled down to nothing. He began to be afraid.

TK turned the mixer handle the last half inch and braced as the cold water gushed over him like icy needles. When he shut the water off, the rest of the showers were silent. Most of his teammates would already be dressed and gone for the day. Before leaving, several had stuck their heads into the shower room and called out, "Way to go!" Even Coach had come to him right after the scrimmage and clapped TK's shoulder pads, which was about as demonstrative as Mosher ever got.

TK dressed slowly, then sat on the locker-room bench awhile, basking in the moment, and when he got home his hair was still wet and his body still warm with the glow of that afternoon's play. Mom was in the kitchen in her housedress and apron, but she hadn't even started dinner. A brandy bottle stood on the counter and a glass nearby, with dissolving ice cubes. "What's going on?" TK asked.

Her gaze was unsteady. "What's that s'posed to mean? What do you think's goin' on?"

"But why? You've never . . ."

"I never what?"

He meant to say that she never drank (maybe a glass of beer at a neighborhood party, but nothing more, and certainly not in the afternoon and not alone) but he was alarmed at the quaver he felt in his voice, so he kept quiet.

"You're off playin' with your pals," she railed, "havin' the time of your life. I'm here alone to worry about your father. And every day he gets weaker . . . and more dependent. Well I can't do it all, and he doesn't *want* me to." With a brittle motion, she untied the apron and flung it on the table and broke down, her face clenched with a sudden storm of tears. TK hesitated, uncertain of what to do for a moment, then he went to her and put his arms around her.

When she regained herself, apologizing profusely, he got her settled in the living room, where Dad was asleep, and put one of her albums (Roger Williams at the piano) on the phonograph to relax her. He got a few dollars from his dresser drawer, said he'd go out and bring home pizza, and stepped out into the dark.

The punt came tumbling out of the murk, and he took it deep, felt the ball settle into his cupped arms. For an instant, it almost squirted free, but he clutched it and started to move. The turf was sodden after a night of rain, and the afternoon's scrimmaging had churned the midfield to mud. All practice long, both sides had been slipping and sliding and now in what would likely be the last set of plays because the daylight was fading, there was still no score.

He moved to his right where several of his linemen had opened a corridor, but not for long, as a number of red jerseys swarmed in. Cutting farther right, he was just able to get past a few defenders who were moving gingerly in the muck. Maybe it was all that walking in the tidal mud of the clam flats, or because the sides of the field weren't so chewed up, but TK felt sure-footed. Ahead, Mike Burke was moving doggedly downfield. TK ran right up on him, using Mike as a moving screen. When a red shirt appeared, Mike threw a block, and TK cut inside, passed Mike, who yelled encouragement, then angled wide right, hitting the gas as he turned, and then it was goal to go—except for one last defender. The kid came alongside puffing hard, arms pumping, and TK saw it was Animal Johnston, a rawboned junior who liked to hit dirty, who'd been kicked out of games for it, and behind his faceguard he was wearing a bad grin. "You're fucked," he panted and launched himself. TK braked, skidding, almost lost his footing, and Johnston flailed past (later, Mike Burke said that Johnston's face when TK faked him looked like "a fresh-wiped ass").

TK ran to the goal line, sixty-one yards he learned afterward, for the day's only score. It was just an intra-squad scrimmage, the last before the season would open away against Standish on Saturday, but it was a "take notice" play, and when practice ended, and Mosher clapped his shoulder, TK realized that he would start on Saturday.

Now TK knew with a sudden, crushing hopelessness what he had to do. The next morning he went to the training room and told Mosher that he was quitting the team.

The following Saturday TK drove over to the Mclains' house to pick up Brain. The ride to the game in Standish would take a half hour. He found his friend in the garage, sitting on a stool at his father's workbench, soldering. Mr. Mclain was self-employed as a television repairman, and the workbench was aclutter with TV chassis and cathode-ray tubes, awaiting repair. The facing wall, paneled with perforated Masonite board, was hung with the tools of his trade, along with an assortment of vacuum tubes in little cardboard boxes. TK had once heard Mr. Mclain at a neighborhood Fourth of July party telling the other guests that whereas the family doctor carrying his black bag to a house call was an occasion of fear for kids, his own arrival with his repair kit when the family TV was sick was greeted with glee. He was the most welcomed visitor to a household, he claimed, after Santa Claus.

"We should leave soon," TK said.

"Why don't you go ahead without me." Brain turned then and TK saw one eye was blackened and swollen nearly shut.

TK understood why Brain wouldn't want to be at the game. He settled onto an adjoining stool. "What happened?"

"A little mishap," Brain murmured. "I don't want to talk about it."

TK waited. Brain continued working for a moment before letting his shoulders sag. "I told the old man where I was applying for colleges, asked him to fill out the financial aid forms—he got mad."

"Jeez, why? Doesn't he *want* you to go to college? He went, didn't he?"

"He took night courses in Boston, had some idea of becoming an electrical engineer, but the commute, and having a family, and working . . ." Brain shrugged. On one shelf, gathering dust, were several big three-ring binders with "Franklin Tech" printed on them. TK could remember Brain's kid brother once pointing them out proudly, saying they were his dad's "college books." This put Mr. Mclain in a whole different league than TK's dad or other fathers in the neighborhood. Most were veterans who had come back from the war, married, bought small homes in town, and gone straight to work at the shipyard or the soap factory or some other place that was hiring. Brain's dad had started college, though for reasons TK hadn't thought about before he had given up. Did he now harbor some grudge against his son's ambitions?

"Why don't you go to the game," Brain said. "You can still see the kickoff."

All at once, TK didn't care. He wished his teammates well, but seeing them play ball without him, and seeing the cheerleaders, none of whom he'd end up dating now . . . how would that make him feel? "Maybe next week," he said. He drew a stool over to the bench next to where Brain was soldering wires. "That night at the drive-in, back in August . . . you said something about powers and what's really going on in Weybridge. What did you mean?"

"Why?"

"I'm curious." TK had begun to wonder if it had anything to do with the shipyard and what his dad was experiencing.

Brain continued working for a moment, the distinctive smell of hot solder drifting to TK's nostrils. Finally, he said, "What do you think I meant?"

"Come on, if I knew, I wouldn't be asking."

Brain set down the iron and unplugged it. He turned to TK. "It occurred to me one day when I was on the bus coming back from Adams Point. The bus stopped at the intersection where the artery comes in, and I happened to glance out and there's that road sign—you know the one?"

"North Weybridge, three miles."

"That's the sign, but that isn't quite what it says."

"I've seen the thing a thousand times," TK protested.

"You have. We've all seen it a thousand times, and it *is* three miles. But what it actually says is 'NO. WEY.' three miles."

"Large charge, it's the same diff."

"Maybe." And Brain began to talk about an article he'd read in *Popular Science* about a device called a tachistoscope. It was used in learning and memory experiments to flash visual information—words and images—at a rate and duration too brief to be detected by the human eye. "It's a kind of subliminal signaling."

"I don't know what you're talking about," TK said, though he was interested nevertheless.

"Say a company's trying to sell you a product, but you don't know if you even want it, so they plant the idea that you *do*."

"Wait—is this where they flashed 'Drink Coke' on a movie screen?"

"It was Pepsi, but yeah, that was one experiment; and supposedly sales at the concession stand went up."

"That sounds fishy. If you can't even see it . . ."

"The mind registers the signal below the threshold of seeing, and sometimes acts accordingly. I'm just telling you what I've read. But back to the sign in Adams Point. It's on a main route into town, so everyone passes it. Everyone's gotten the message."

"North Weybri—" TK caught himself. "No Wey, three miles. Hold it . . . you mean as in 'no w-*a*-y'?"

"Think about it. Reinforced each time we drive past. Preached to us all through school, and from the pulpit of Holy Name or Pilgrim Congregational, from Weybridge Savings to DeSantis's barbershop. No way. It's subtle and insidious and it's there, saying, forget about anything bigger, grander, *more*. Keep your ambitions small. Stay close to shore. No frickin' way. So the fog sets in and wraps you up, swallows you whole, and no one questions it. Ever," he concluded with a puff of breath.

TK twisted free of a sudden nagging thought. "And you're the blind carpenter, who picked up his hammer and saw."

"It was right in front of me, and it suddenly made sense." Brain shrugged, perhaps waiting for a rebuttal.

But TK hadn't shed his nagging thought after all. It was still there—about how last spring, in filling out the yearbook form, before he had written "Teacher," he had, for one brief moment, been tempted to put "Author."

5 Tom

Tom wasn't sure if it was sound that woke him or sensation. There was a low, heavy throbbing that seemed to make the very dark vibrate. He looked at the lighted face of the travel alarm clock. Almost midnight. The shade of the duck decoy lamp was ticking softly. Had the oil burner come on? No, the air was too mild for that; whatever this was, it wasn't in the house. He lay still and listened. His mother wouldn't hear it; she took out her hearing aids at night. After a moment, he rose and, wearing only his pajama bottoms, crept downstairs.

The sound was fading by the time he stepped onto the porch, the pine boards cool under his bare feet. It was mostly a trembling in the ground now. A train? Not a commuter run surely, not in early-to-bed-early-to-rise New England where the sidewalks were rolled up after dark. Then, all at once, he knew the sound.

In his youth there had always been noises from the shipyard, though it was a mile away: the clangor of hammers and riveters on steel, the rumble of enormous cranes moving slabs of hull and deck plating, air horns signaling the starts and ends of shifts. Tom listened awhile longer, but the vibrations had faded away, and he stood there in the aftermath of silence and surprise. Did that kind of work still go on there?

Back in the house, he took a carton of milk from the refrigerator, sniffed at the spout (his mother's standards of freshness were somewhat lax), and poured a glass. By the glow of the light in the vent hood over the stove he looked at the "to do" list he'd made. In the morning he had an appointment at the Elm Hill Estate assisted living facility. And Stan Jarvis had promised to come by to do a market analysis on the house. At the bottom of the page—more a footnote than a real item—he now wrote, "Shipyard?" He rinsed the glass and set it in the drainer. Upstairs, he lay in the dark, and a thought went skittering across the screen of blackness. Something from the night of the reunion . . . something he'd heard, or seen . . .

But whatever it had been had slipped away, like the cast of a car's headlights across a ceiling. Soon he was yawning, a great jaw-creaking yawn, followed by a second even bigger yawn, and then, like an elevator going down, he was dropping toward sleep. Once, just before he tumbled all the way, he heard shipyard sounds again—the dull clanging, the baying of a shift whistle—very far off now, a distant wind-whisper in the night, and then he was gone.

On a rolling stretch of wooded acres, Elm Hill Estate Elder Residence had its campus (that's what the woman Tom had spoken to on the phone had called it, a campus). The woman suggested that he might wish to come without his mother for an initial visit, but he'd decided, why add a step, so he'd brought her. The first glimpse was impressive. Elm Hill was ablaze with autumn maples and oaks and sycamores, though none of the trees that had given this highest point in Weybridge its name, the elms having long ago succumbed to blight. The buildings were sparkling colonial white.

Tom and his mother were greeted by a smiling Southeast Asian woman in a business suit the same tan color as the suit Tom had put on. Her name was Monica Kim and she ushered them into a paneled office, offered coffee and a brief account of the facility, then gave them a tour.

Tom found his initial impression confirmed. Elm Hill Estate was spacious and well kept, the old women and the few old men they encountered moving along ably enough on canes and walkers. In his weaker moments, when he'd first contemplated moving Mom into assisted living, Tom had dreaded finding dingy institutional quarters where the aromas of medicine and disinfectant hid the subtler odors of sickness and decay; but this was nothing like that. The rooms were spacious and bright. Even the employees they met, from medical staff to members of the housekeeping team, were friendly. Nor did he miss that they addressed the residents as "Ma'am" and "Mrs."

Earlier, Stan Jarvis had come to the house as promised and walked around, part of the time reminiscing, but also taking notes. He said that removing the pressed metal awnings would be a good idea, to give the property more curb appeal, but said they wouldn't be a deal breaker. Tom expressed his desire to get the house listed as quickly as possible, and Stan promised to get back in touch soon. So things were in motion and that felt good. Tom became aware of the music—it seemed to drizzle in from concealed speakers, wall-to-wall violin arrangements of pop songs—"Mack the Knife," "Michelle," and, honest to God, "We've Only Just Begun." With some pride, Ms. Kim pointed out a small room off the day lounge, which was set up with several computer workstations, where residents could, if they wished, keep in touch with family by e-mail. Not very likely in our case, Tom thought.

"We can visit the dining hall now," Ms. Kim said.

Later, as he and his mother walked out to the car, they passed a terrace where a score or more of residents were taking in the mellow September sun. A young woman in jeans and a tie-dyed shirt was teaching some craft, holding up a piece of cloth, and Tom had his image again of a college campus: a geriatric student body, with varsity Nerf bowling teams, and bingo contests and seminar classes of old folks speculating on the meaning of being . . . well, old.

"So," he ventured when they had driven out of the gates, "what did you think?"

Mom was silent and he thought maybe she hadn't heard him. Then she looked over. "You could have the house. I know it's worn, but you could fix it up, make it the way you want. The ocean is nearby, and Boston . . . and you've still got friends."

"Mom—"

"But now I know why you came home. Oh, you'll say this isn't your home, that it's merely where you grew up."

He sighed, frustrated. "My life is in California now—and I've told you, you'd be welcome to come out there to live."

"And *my* life is still here. This is where I live. So, I guess we both know what that means." After a pause, she said, "In answer to your question, that place is nice enough, and the people seem okay. That music, though, was awful."

Late that afternoon Tom called his agent in L.A. It had been only a few days and it was reasonable to expect that Randy hadn't heard anything about the film deal yet (these things took a while; and despite his talk, Randy Wilson wasn't exactly the Type A deal-shark he liked to pretend to be) though when he and Tom had left last week's pitch meetings, it seemed that a deal was close. "I smell it," Randy said. Tom might have been patient for a few more days, but in the business, out of sight was out of mind. At the least, a little "yoo-hoo" would remind Randy that there was a time difference between coasts.

"Synchronicity, dude. Just thinking of you." The phone connection sounded iffy and Tom pictured his agent tooling along the freeway en route to the Pacific Coast Highway to scope out the surf. "I'm on the horn with those villains at Warner. Give me your number; I'll get back to you in *uno momento*."

It was more like *diez minutos* before the phone rang. A woman speaking in a formal manner said, "After extensive polling, you've been voted the best-looking guy at your reunion."

For a moment Tom was convinced it was a secretary at the agency, put up to a prank by Randy; it was something he'd do. But that bit about the reunion—where'd that come from? Tom hadn't mentioned attending. "Best-looking, huh? I think you've got the wrong number. You obviously want an eye doctor."

Following muffled sounds, there was faint female laughter, and a new voice: "Doctor? Should I get granny glasses?"

Tom hesitated. "Penny?"

"I put poor Judy up to it."

"I should've known. Still haven't graduated beyond juvenile phone pranks, huh?"

Penny laughed, and he discovered he was pleased and surprised to hear from her. He walked out onto the porch, to the length of the stretch cord of his mother's phone, wanting privacy for the call—not that his mother could hear a word over the blare of *Murder, She Wrote*. "Where are you?"

Penny and several girlfriends who still lived in town had gathered at Judy Carini's house, as they did from time to time for a sleepover.

"A pajama party?" He was intrigued by the concept. "What do you talk about?"

"Diet, cellulite, the looming specter of hot flashes. Important things like that. This time we've got the reunion to hash over. We're going to go out for a little bite first. So far it's only us, and possibly Mike Burke. Nothing fancy, probably Szechuan, but . . . you're welcome to join us."

Was there a note of hesitant hopefulness in her voice?

"I'd like to, but I'm expecting a call from my agent and with the different time zones, it's tricky."

"Oh, Tom, that's exciting. A big movie deal, I bet."

"Well . . . we'll see."

"That is so fantastic. I just can't imagine that whole world." Her enthusiasm was real; Penny hadn't changed a bit. "Well, it was a shot in the dark, and you probably eat out all the time."

"Granny glasses," he said. "I just got that."

"You remember? Senior year?"

"I still think they would've looked cool on you. You'd have been a trendsetter."

She laughed. "Well, I realize how busy you are. I just wanted to say good-bye before you went back. Good luck, Tom."

"You, too."

Randy called back a little later. Zero action on the screenplay so far.

On Wednesday, Stan Jarvis phoned to propose an asking price that he believed would make the house sale attractive. "If you were willing to play a waiting game, we could start higher, but I know you want to get the place sold." An hour later, a woman from Jarvis and Easton Real Estate showed up with papers to sign. Then Tom and his mother stood at the window, peering out to watch as the woman drove a FOR SALE sign into the front lawn. He thought that his mother's eyes held a quality of bleak terror, as though the sign were a stake being pegged into her heart.

That night Tom awoke to the shipyard noises again—or he thought he awoke; part of it, at least, was a dream. In it, he was a kid, nine, maybe ten, and on a summer afternoon of doing nothing much (too hot for baseball or even the beach), he and Brain stirred out of sheer boredom, climbed on their bicycles (TK's twenty-six-inch Huffy was "Fleetwing"; Brain called his J. C. Higgins twenty-four-inch "Wilhelm," after someone named Wilhelm Reich, who he'd said had made a scientific study of sex) and rode over to the salt marsh cove on the Adams River. They sat in the shade and looked across the water to the shipyard, fascinated by the slow movement of the gantry cranes and by the occasional klaxon horn's deep *blaaat!* (and didn't *that* draw yuks and set them to making squeaky armpit farts!). Next morning, as Tom and his mother had coffee together, he mentioned the night sounds.

"No, all that's long gone," she said wistfully.

"All of it? I heard *some*thing. *Thought* I did anyway."

She shook her head. "Gone."

He wanted to protest. He'd stood on the lawn the other night, fully awake, and had felt the vibrations. Perhaps there was more activity at the old shipyard than she knew about; she didn't get out much, after all. But what did it matter? There were issues much closer at hand to deal with, and he needed to get them resolved over the next few days.

With some reluctance, Tom sensed, Brain had agreed to meet him. He'd suggested the place and was waiting outside as Tom parked in the small lot in back. They walked around to the entrance on Bridge Street in a tangible silence.

The Sand Trap had been old when they were kids. There had been a ring of such places tucked away on side streets, small taprooms and cafés that filled each day after a shift at the shipyard ended. Even 7:00 A.M., when the graveyard shift knocked off, used to see a small but dedicated cadre of men for whom some mood alteration was needed. Most of the bars had died once the yard closed; the few that survived limped along on a reduced clientele. The Sand Trap remained. The name suggested golf, though nothing in the decor echoed this: the interior was strictly functional, Tom saw. He got a Coke for Brain and Black Jack for himself, and they moved to a small corner table.

"My prediction was right," Brain said, practically the first words he'd uttered.

"What prediction was that?"

"That a lot of our classmates would wind up at the yard. Many of 'em would be here yet if U.S. shipbuilding hadn't gone belly-up. By the seventies, ships were being built in Japan, Europe—practically anywhere but here. Too expensive. Keystone Steel made a go of it for a while as a repair yard, taking in ailing tankers, coastal freighters, but it's a tough racket. And to handle the really big ships, the super-tankers, the warships? Forget it. Would've meant a new drawbridge, deepening the harbor—bucks that no one was willing or able to spend."

"What goes on there now?"

"A skeleton crew maintains the heavy equipment, but it's a losing battle with rust. Periodically you hear talk—usually in joints like this—about some of the old yardbirds scraping together a grubstake and starting fresh. Nothing comes of it. Talk's cheap, especially after a few boilermakers."

"Keystone still owns the place?"

"They never did. They lease the space from the adjoining towns, but who knows for how much longer. Even with the write-off, it's a loser, and that's got our mayor sweating. Weybridge isn't the hot-shot burg you remember. But," he said, giving Tom a sullen look, "you didn't call me for nostalgia."

When Tom finished telling about the sounds he'd been hearing,

Brain was scratching his beard. "Take your mom's word. The shipyard is dead. You were dreaming."

"I don't think so."

"Well, think again." Brain set down his empty glass with a bang and slid toward the edge of the booth.

"Whoa, what's up?"

"I don't know what you mean."

"You angry about something? The temperature in here feels as if it dropped ten degrees."

"Nonsense."

"Maybe I'm wrong, but does it have anything to do with the reunion?"

Brain scowled. "Why would it?"

"Okay. Forget it."

But the storm cloud hanging stubbornly over Brain didn't lift. "Okay. You honor us with a visit and you expect things are going to be the way they once were? Doesn't happen like that," he said at last. "It's stupid, but yeah. I was a little torqued when you took off with Dee Richards."

"That wasn't planned. I was just . . ." What? Operating on L.A. mode? You snooze, you lose. What did he owe anybody back here? It was everyone for himself. You sleep, you weep . . . But that didn't wash. "I'm sorry. If I'd known . . ."

"Ah, forget it," Brain said with an air of surrender. "I was kidding myself. Maybe it was the high of doing the hologram show. I thought it might earn me something with Dee. I think I fell in love with who she *was*, back when. Even that wasn't real. She was just fantasy fodder for a horny kid with an itchy hand. Not her fault. But the truth is she doesn't give two hoots about who I was or am."

"She's got a fiancé," Tom said.

"The D.A., Grasso. So maybe you kept me from making trouble for myself."

"Maybe. Will there be trouble for me?"

"You'll be gone soon."

"Yeah. Well, you weren't the only one falling for the past. Your show put us all right back there. That was really something."

Brain brightened some. "It was, right?"

"Has anyone else seen it?"

"Just the group of us there that night."

"Seriously? What about the school committee? The superintendent?"

Brain's frown returned. He reached for his glass, found it empty, and withdrew his hand. He declined a refill. He was fidgety. "What is it you think I do for the town?"

"Tech services? Media director?" Tom realized he didn't know. Brain mumbled something he didn't catch. "Sorry?"

"Jan-i-tor." Brain gave it an exaggerated enunciation.

"Yeah, right. Funny."

But there was no humor in Brain's expression. "Custodial maintenance engineer, if you prefer the candy coating. Lord of the key rings. The 'Viper'—here to vipe the floor. I'm the guy who pushes the big dust mop around the hallways after all the teachers and kids have gone for the day. The guy who fumigates the jock-strappy smelling lockers and swamps out the toilets and—"

"Whoa, hey—"

"—scrubs off the graffiti . . . and I gotta tell you, the joke lines don't get any funnier. 'Flush twice, it's a long way to the cafeteria' was old when *we* were kids. And how about the guy who scrapes the crud off the undersides of desks, sprinkles sawdust into the puddles of puke when a kid loses her lunch, okay?" But it clearly wasn't okay. A strident, aggrieved note had invaded Brain's voice. "I'm the gray man no one ever really sees. You gettin' the picture? Because *some*body's gotta do it, right? There's somebody's gotta do *every*thing. Way of the world. And all work is ennobling, as we sons and daughters of North Weybridge are taught at our mothers' knees. Work's the only thing that really counts, doesn't matter what kind. Can be cutting hair or making donuts or toiling in the hulls of ships—what matters is how *well* you do it, and the *spirit* you do it in. No idle minds for the devil's work. Happy heart and cheerful hands. Kilroy was *here!* Flush twice!"

"Brain—"

"And if it isn't done with joy, then it's *all* shit!"

Tom was frightened.

"But you and me, ol' *buddy*, we've got serene souls. We've been en*light*ened. I can see it on your face and hear it in your voice. Not everyone's lucky as we are. No frickin' way." He reached for the empty glass again, and this time he took hold with both hands and squeezed so hard Tom thought the glass would implode. He gritted his eyes shut, and Tom had the strong impression of him mentally straining to pull thoughts back into his head. Tom had grown peripherally aware of people at nearby tables.

"Why don't we go," he said in a low voice.

But Brain had begun to grin. "I've got this allergist I see, and he's got this busy practice—*every*body's allergic to *some*thing, right? He has this big staff, with associates, and pretty nurses, cash flowing in, new car every year . . . and I swear the guy's miserable. He's got ex-wives, and his kids don't know him. He tells me jokes that didn't get laughs when he first told 'em years ago, and I think, the poor sorry SOB. I want to hug the guy and tell him it's okay, but he's already disappeared back into the machine, on the treadmill, and it's moving so fast he's scared to death of trying to get off. And he's just one person!" Brain's grin had stretched so wide it looked like a rip in his beard. His gaze was unfocused. "Think of all the people, day in day out . . . same office, same little washroom, peeing in the same toilet four, five times a day, five days a week, eleven months a year. Man, I am so glad I got free. So . . . god . . . damn . . . glad."

He was hyperventilating when Tom went around to his side and put hands on his shoulders. He felt like a bundle of steel springs. Tom expected Brain to yank away, but he sat frozen; and after a moment the tension drained out of him and he went slack. "Come on," Tom said gently, "let's take a ride."

Brain didn't have a car; he had walked there. In the Escape he asked if they could just drive for a while. Tom headed toward the beach.

"Paranoid schizophrenia is what they tagged it at first," Brain said when they were under way. He whirled a finger in a small circle by his temple. "Eventually they scaled down the diagnosis to Schizo Affective Disorder. I guess the brain cells don't get smoked as bad, and the recovery rate is better. I landed in Met State, affectionately known as Slap Happy Valley. I was in a lock-down ward for seven weeks."

"I didn't know any of this," Tom said.

"How would you? We haven't seen each other in a dog's age. But rewind a bit. Before all that I was a class act. I was poster boy for 'life after Weybridge.'"

And he told it. From high school he had gone to MIT on scholarship (though not to become the world's foremost sexologist); he'd double majored in math and physics, then stayed on for grad work. Although it hadn't been his aim, he said, staying in school kept him out of the military draft. "That bothered me at first, knowing there were people getting sucked into this big black hole of a war. You and I had lost touch by then, but I gather that's what happened to you, didn't it?"

"I got drafted," Tom confirmed but didn't elaborate. His old friend's predicament had begun to engulf him with a feeling of helplessness. They were near the beach now. He drew to the curb, and they got out. Beyond the dark strip of sand, the darker water sparkled with reflected lights from the Germantown section of Adams Point across the channel. Again Tom had a sense of Brain having to pull his mind back, but after a moment, he resumed:

"I got a master's degree, could've continued, but frankly I was tapped out on school by then. Eighteen straight years is enough for anyone. But even after my deferment lapsed, it seems I still had on these magnetic boots that kept me safely clamped to the mother ship. I got a job that was listed as 'important to national security,' whatever that means. I figured I better do the work because maybe someday it'd lead to no wars, no one ever again having to make that choice. A rationalization, no doubt, but hell, we were all naïve in those days. On the job though, mostly I was just running. I ate, slept, and drank the work. I guess I was good at it, because after a few months I got picked for this research project. *Way* theoretical. And I was like, they want *me* for *that*? Somebody pinch me, I'm dreaming."

What "*that*" turned out to be was a program cosponsored by MIT and the federal government, and the director, who had been one of his instructors, wanted Brain on the team. "To work with Solomon Buckley. He's *Sir* Solomon now. He was one of the bright young minds in quantum mechanics back in the forties. Cambridge, England, you know? And by the late sixties he was getting into the stuff that would revolutionize physics. You know about the strings?" At Tom's puzzled look, Brain added, "Super string theory."

"I don't know much about it," Tom said.

"Almost no one does, really. Anyway, I made the cut, got the assignment. There were layers of reporting, and I was on a low rung, but I was in the game. I was working with Dr. Buckley. What we were about was trying to find proof of the theory—the legs to hold up the head. I was bunkered in a lab in Kendall Square for twelve, fifteen hours a day, six days a week with a big IBM computer for companionship. Mainly it was running numbers, producing scads of data, which we then had to correlate with parallel streams from elsewhere. Once a month or so I'd shuttle down to D.C. or out to Caltech. Did that for a couple years, then things started getting a little . . ." He trailed off.

"I'm listening," Tom said encouragingly. They were still standing by the Ford.

"The math had anomalies in it that we couldn't resolve, but it began to be clear that the equations pointed to other dimensions beyond the three or four we normally think of. Eleven . . . thirteen. Sometimes more. It was during that period when stuff began to go a bit cuckoo on me, personally. Not all at once. By degrees. I became—" Brain sought a word, "*entranced* with the fact of nothingness. It'd started in a small way back when I was traveling. I'd take a night flight, and soaring along up there at thirty thousand feet, thoughts would come. *Odd* thoughts. I'm not referring to, you know, 'What if we crash and end up as ground pizza?' Everyone thinks about that. No, this was more . . . existential. Here we are on this little planet, millions of miles from nothing. I wasn't sorry when the travel part of the job ended and the project moved to the next phase."

Brain puffed a breath, like someone bracing for conflict.

"But the thoughts didn't end. Like the notion that almost all of what we perceive as the physical world is just vacant space. I'd get to pondering that, and it was like I couldn't get my mind around it. It began to get pretty sketchy. I was . . . hey, you've written for the movies. What's the average length of one?"

Jarred by the transition, Tom frowned. "The running time of a feature film?"

"How long?"

"Two hours," Tom said warily, "give or take."

"And the script? How many pages?"

"The usual metric is one page per minute of screen time."

"So, a hundred twenty pages for a two-hour flick."

"About that. Are you planning to write one?"

"Okay, you go to the theater, sit in the dark and the feature starts—two-hour movie. How long is there something up on the screen?"

"How much of that time are there images on the screen?"

"How long?"

"I know I'm being set up here. Okay, two hours."

"The whole time, that what you're saying?"

"Sure."

A faint, unhappy grin curled Brain's mouth. "The 'motion' in a motion picture is illusion, a conspiracy of mind and eye. A film is a long acetate strip of tiny stills, right? So as not to make a hopeless blur as the film runs through the projector, the machine's got to stop for each frame, close a shutter while the film ratchets to the next frame, open the shutter to let light pass through, then repeat the process again and again, twenty-four times per second. And in between each frame, too quick for the eye to detect, is blackness. Roughly half the time there you're sitting in total dark while your nervous system constructs a world up there, life happening as if you're watching it occur, duped by your brain into faith, when it's all a mind trip in two dimensions, tricked up out of light and sound and pretty faces. The rest, the in-between, is emptiness. *Nada y pues nada*. Like what we take for this too, too solid world." His grin had grown ragged and desperate. "And therein lay my problem. Because my mind couldn't fill all that space."

"Hey—"

"I'd be walking, you know? Boston, wherever . . . and I'd get nervous about sidewalk grates. I'd spot one ahead and I'd detour around it, the way a woman in high heels will. The difference is a heel can get stuck, but I've got these size twelve gunboats. Yet I'd skirt *way* around. Why? Because I'd begun to worry that I'd fall through.

"Wait." He raised his palm to halt any interruption. "It gets better. One day I'm with some visiting scientists from England, we're up in a high-rise and the elevator arrives, door opens, and I know— I frickin' *know*—if I get on, I'll go right through the floor and on down the shaft and I won't stop. I'll keep falling for eternity. I had all I could do to keep from bolting. I babbled some excuse about having left my keys in the lab and said I'd meet them in the lobby. I took the stairs." Again the forced smile. "Sidewalk grates, the elevator . . . just symbolic, of course. What I was *really* scared of—" He broke off and looked around. Out in the channel, the running lights of a boat were visible, doubled in the dark water. With a whimper, Brain leaned closer, speaking so softly Tom had to lean forward, too. "—was that I could fall through the spaces in *atoms*."

Tom grinned, convinced it was hyperbole; but Brain's forehead was clenched tight. "Wig city, right? But there's nothing more rational. Physics. Go to the quantum level, to the stuff of matter, and ninety-nine-point-nine percent is just empty space. You've got the electrons spinning around the nucleus, and the distance between particles is like that between earth and the moon, and in between is . . ." he whispered the final word, "*nothing.*"

Believing he was truly doomed, Brain resigned. "Probably just ahead of being sacked. My quirks had started to draw attention. Ha, not easy to do in that crowd. But quitting wasn't simple. My supervisor said not till I'd undergone a psychiatric evaluation, and they raised the specter of 'security risk,' like maybe I'd end up on a street corner, babbling classified secrets to any and all. Fortunately, Dr. Buckley recognized the symptoms. He'd seen similar cases. It's kind of like that thing first-year med students go through, where they're convinced they've got every disease in the textbook—though this was rarer. He said I should take a leave and rest. So"—he spread his arms—"guess where I returned to?"

" 'When you have to go there, they have to take you in.' Good old Weybridge. And you got the school job?"

"Not just yet. I had a ways to free-fall yet."

There was a whole range to the manifestation of his anxieties, he explained, from vague disquiet to full-tilt, mind-warping terror that would raise the hair on his neck and make his brain creak like a flight of old steps. "Then—and this is going to sound truly whacked—I grew convinced that dreams were a gateway to other dimensions."

"Dreams."

"I kid you not. There wasn't even any science behind my obsessions by this point. At night I'd tie myself in bed with rope. Logical, right? But then you want a drink of water, so you untie the rope and go into the kitchen, turn on the light, and the sink is crawling with bugs. Roaches start scurrying and you're smacking them . . . roaches that aren't really there, of course, and some rational part of you *knows* this, but they keep scurrying, and you keep smacking . . . and that's when . . . when . . ." With a shudder he quit talking. He'd resumed the restless clasping and unclasping of his hands. "I'm getting antsy. Can we go?"

They headed back toward the center, moving past darkened houses, and Brain was silent for a time; then he said, " 'There were more tics than a clock shop.' " He turned to look at Tom. "Remember that?"

"Say it again?"

" 'People took him to be seriously zenned, but it was veneer, as crazed as crackalure, and under the feigned informality, there were more tics than a clock shop.' You wrote it. It's in *Haven's End*."

Tom didn't remember; he had written the novel a long time ago. He glanced at Brain with new surprise.

"Know when I read your book? When I was in Met State. I read a hundred books there. I needed *some*thing to fill the waking hours. This volunteer—nice old woman with orange hair and a wooden crucifix around her neck—she used to come through the ward wheeling a book cart. Nothing very appealing, but I wasn't fussy. I read whatever she had. One day I noticed a book by Thomas Knowles Jr. I didn't see your smiling mug on the dust jacket, and there was no mention of fair Weybridge, but the flap did say the author had grown up 'near Boston' and I thought . . . could it be? Once I started reading, I knew it was you.

"The way I judged a book in those days was to ask if reading it made my life a little less frantic. I went through yours in one night, pushed right on past the meds they were dosing me with. Then I crashed, and when I woke up I read it again. I pestered the volunteer to find some more Thomas Knowles opuses."

"There weren't any," Tom said. "Aren't."

"That's what she said."

"And the results of the litmus test?"

Brain's brow crinkled.

"Life. Did it get less frantic?"

"A little, I think. The book stuck with me. That line, about the tics—I thought that character could've been me. He was older, and he's a teacher; but he fooled people with appearances. For a time, anyway. Till it was too late. When he wigged, no one knew how to help him. Not all the king's horses or all the king's men."

Tom was silent. He hadn't consciously modeled the character on anyone real; and certainly whatever had happened to Brain had come years after Tom had left New England (*abandoned*, some would say, or *fled*, depending on whom you listened to). But that wasn't the point; people would respond to a character in ways that made sense to them. The important fact for Tom was that that character had made sense to *him*.

"The thing about madness," Brain went on, "afterward, when you've had the 'cure,' you find you're not crazy anymore, but you're not who you once were, either. Partly it's the drugs, but the circuit board's been rewired, too, and what you discover is a whole strange, new place, with strange new people, and hold on, brother. Most of us long for the strange from time to time. Usually the best we're able to get is the scramble provided by a smoke or strong coffee or a stiff drink. Or"—he sent Tom a glance—"a new bedmate." Tom let it alone; he wasn't here for amateur psychoanalysis.

"But none of that lasts. This is more . . . It's like your fly is down. Everybody knows, but no one says 'boo.' And that can be worse than somebody just telling you. So sometimes my opening gambit is, 'When I was in the bughouse . . .' or 'After my bout with madness . . .' It's freeing to come right out with it," he said, his voice coursing with emotion, "but it's like those kids Penny works with. People see them and it gets awkward. You know about Penny, right?"

"I thought she worked at the diner?"

"That's a paycheck. Her real life, the one that matters to her, is her volunteer gig at the hospital. She works with kids with bad cancers. I mean the worst."

"She didn't mention that."

"Oh, there're things about Penny few people know. *I* know because we've become close. We've helped each other cope."

"What does Penny cope with?"

Brain hesitated. "She's got things. Those kids, for one. A husband who doesn't like her out of his sight, for two."

All at once Tom recalled the urgency of her leaving the reunion, and the ride waiting to pick her up. "Is he abusive?"

"Let's say Alan's overly protective. Which she insists is for love. Anyhow," Brain added quickly, as though not wanting to violate confidences, "tell someone you've been hospitalized with a heart attack, they're all over you with caring, but if they know it was mental, they tiptoe around you in pity and fear, as if any second you might snap and grab a meat ax. Ah, I'm exaggerating. People are mostly cool, but it's like with those kids Penny works with . . . folks see the bald heads and the yellow skin and the wide, staring eyes, they get uncomfortable. Anyway, I did my time in Slap Happy Valley. I'm cured. Don't rope myself in bed at night, or worry about falling between the cracks—unless it might be to disappear into the canyon between Dee Richards's breasts. That's an oblivion I'd willingly chance." He gave it a weak grin. "No, I'm fine."

"Well that's good, then, right?"

Brain nodded, though he didn't look quite sure. "But along with the high anxiety, I . . . guess I lost a little mental sharpness. Like you take a scalpel to a rock . . . your edge is gone. Dr. Buckley had returned to England and won the Nobel by then. I tried to get another research post, but it was always, 'You're overqualified,' or 'We'll keep your résumé on file.' Now, being a janitor feels about right, in terms of dealing with stuff. And I get to tinker. That new scoreboard? I drew up the specs, worked out the electronics, and the town took it from there. My part's unofficial, and I do it on my own time, and I've got the school department's okay, if not their full blessing." He let out a breath. "Sorry for the little wig out."

"No sweat. You want a ride home?"

"Actually, you can drop me right here."

They were passing the old high school, which loomed vast and monolithic beyond the ghostly maples lining the drive. "*Here?*"

"There's a storage room in the basement that I use as my workshop. It's where I have the holodeck."

"You're going to work at this hour?"

"Why not? There's no one waiting up for me at home." Brain shook Tom's hand and climbed out. "I'm kind of a night owl," he said. "Whooo . . ."

6 TK

One day during lunch period TK went to Miss Mutterperl's homeroom. A handful of her students were there, goofing off noisily. The teacher looked exasperated. TK almost took off, but she saw him and waved him in. She dismissed the others and they fled.

TK had heard through the grapevine that some kids were giving her a hard time, which wasn't uncommon with new teachers. Students were territorial, and some felt threatened by any change. He thought about offering suggestions for dealing with the rowdies, but he decided he wasn't on that level of openness with her. He knew her mainly in her role as adviser to the *Echo*, and he liked her way of starting each meeting talking about journalism and writing technique and then letting the staff go to whatever they were working on. He told her that he had come up with an idea for a weekly column and wanted to see what she thought. "I might call it Curb Feelers." He hesitated. "You know what those are?" He felt disappointment when she shook her head. "Bad name, then. I'll find something else."

"Hold on," she said encouragingly. "I like to learn, too."

So he explained about the little spring rods you could install that stuck out from beside a car's wheels to let you know when you were at the curb. "That way you don't scrape your whitewalls."

Her eyes sparked with enthusiasm behind her cat's-eye glasses.

"So your column might be a place where you try out ideas, let them scrape against people's minds, and the readers' reactions will tell you if you're close."

Wow, had he meant that? Maybe on some level, without actually thinking it, he had. "That's the other thing," he said with growing confidence. "Ideas. I've got a few. I'm not sure if they're any good . . ."

Miss Mutterperl opened the top drawer of her desk and took out a magazine, with the irrepressible Alfred E. Newman smiling his gap-toothed grin.

"You read *MAD*?" TK was amazed.

"It's good to read a lot of things, but actually I confiscated this from a student who was reading it behind *Hamlet*." They shared a smile. She flipped through to one of the Don Martin pages. "I don't know for a fact, but I'll bet that when Mr. Martin sits down to work on a cartoon, he looks at his own world, and when he finds something there that interests him, he sinks his teeth into it."

"And doesn't let go?"

"Like a dog with a bone."

"So I should start reading *MAD* again?"

"I was thinking you could look at your life, do a little digging there. That's often where the best ideas are. What's going on these days, Tom?"

Well, I quit football because my dad is sick, and my mom has been drinking, my love life is a big zero, and I have no clue about college. But . . . as Alfred E. Newman says, "What, me worry?" He cleared his throat. "Nothing much."

Her expression said she wasn't quite convinced, but she didn't pry, for which he was grateful. She glanced at her bookshelf a moment, selected a book, and handed it to him. It was called *In Our Time* by Ernest Hemingway. "Do you know it?"

He said he knew of Hemingway, but not this book.

"You might like it. He was a young newspaperman, but he was also writing fiction that came out of his own life."

123

That night TK read several of the stories in the book that Miss Mutterperl had lent him. He especially liked one called "Up in Michigan," which the foreword revealed Hemingway had written when he was scarcely older than TK. It struck him as honest and direct. Another story he read was good, too, though it left him feeling uneasy. It was called "My Old Man" and was told by a boy whose dad had just died.

On a Wednesday afternoon in early October, as TK was coming out of the office of the *Echo*, a girl said, "Were you creating your latest literary offering?"

He had to squint across a large rectangle of sunlight shining on the buffed hallway floor. A girl and a tall, thin guy were standing by the row of lockers. TK laughed. "If you can call it that."

They stepped through the pool of sunshine to come nearer. The girl, he realized, was familiar, though he didn't know her name. She was holding a clipboard. "I'm TK, by the way. You're—?"

She moved her head to flick back her shoulder-length blond hair. "We know."

"In fact, we were just talking about you at our meeting," said the guy. "The Junior American Values Association. You know about JAVA?"

He'd heard of it; it was a new club this year.

"You were on the agenda."

"*I* was?"

"Your column," said the girl. "Some of the club members want to send a letter to the principal."

"Really?" TK thought he was pleased, though wasn't sure.

"A protest letter," she added. "Or maybe start a petition."

He looked at them incredulously. Was this a joke?

"But others of us argued that we should give you a chance first," the guy said. "Because you're a student just like we are. We hoped we could talk."

His heart was beating a drum pulse in his throat, and he was sure it gave his words a quaver. "What don't you like about Curb Feelers?"

"Some of the subjects you write about."

Later it would occur to him that he should have asked them to be specific, but at the moment he was confused. He didn't know what to say. "It's just words. I didn't think anyone took it seriously. It's for laughs."

"Well, that's good to hear." The guy was smiling now, looking relieved. "That you don't take it seriously. It shows we're in agreement." He turned to the girl, as though seeking confirmation of this.

But she was looking at TK with a cool, unwavering gaze. "If you feel that way, then maybe you won't write it anymore. But I don't think that's what you really feel. Listen to this." She raised the clipboard and read. " 'Does Father Really Know Best? Maybe TV wisdom needs to be taken with a grain of salt. Maybe the best kind of family is one where every member is heard, not only Dad or Mom, but Brother and Sister also. Where all opinions are treated with respect.' "

It was the last paragraph of his column from two issues back, and there it was on her clipboard, sentences underlined with red marking pencil like an essay being returned by a teacher.

"Or this." The girl flipped the sheet and there was his column from last week, which he'd titled, "I Like Ike, But Not Eich." He'd written about the Adolf Eichmann trial, which had taken place not long ago but hadn't been talked about much in school. The girl flicked back her hair and again read TK's words: " 'We should pay more attention to what's going on in the world. If we don't know about hatred, what's to stop us from hating, too?' "

She lowered the clipboard, still poised, still speaking calmly. "That's just a couple of examples. I don't think your column is only for laughs, as you say. I don't think that at all, and I don't believe you do, either."

He was flustered. "Well, no, you're right. I didn't mean—"

"That's pushing your opinions on the rest of us."

Pushing opinions? Where'd she get that? Fault him for trite ideas or his lame jokes, but how was he pushing anyone? He wasn't all that sure how he really felt about some of those topics himself. Writing about them was a way he was trying to find out.

The angle of sunlight had changed, falling fully on him now, and the heat made his face feel like it would combust. But he didn't move. The two students were in the edge of shadow, and he could see them more clearly. Blond and blue-eyed, in a gray, ribbed sweater and dark skirt, the girl had a cool beauty . . . stuck up, TK thought. The guy, who was his age or a little younger, was tall and thin, with a pronounced Adam's apple. Most of the after-school activities had let out, and except for the occasional slam of a locker somewhere, silence had fallen on the building. From far down the hall came a faint, stale-fart stench of burnt sulfur. TK had the random idea that Brain and his rocket club friends might be in the chem lab making gunpowder.

"So," the girl said, "what do you want to do? Will you consider changing your column? Or better yet, discontinue it?"

TK's mouth had gone dust dry, and despite the blaze of warmth in his cheeks, his hands were cold. "I didn't get your names," he managed.

"I'm Regina St. Claire, this is Chad Long."

He swallowed to open his throat. "Well, Regina and Chad," he said, trying to hold his voice steady, "thank you for coming to me. Because you've made me realize that I'm wrong."

Chad Long jumped on it. "Great. That's all we—"

"Wrong in thinking it's just a dumb column that nobody takes seriously. The fact is I guess I *do* hope kids read it, and think about it, and if they disagree, that's okay. They can write their own ideas. So can you. The *Echo*'s always looking for students to help out. As for forcing my opinions, aren't you the ones who're being silly? Or worse, maybe? Stupid." He turned to walk away.

"Wait," Chad Long called. "Let's—"

But Regina St. Claire cut him off. "We gave you a chance, Knowles. We'd hoped we wouldn't need a petition. Now we know better."

When he reached his locker, he was trembling. It took three tries before he got the combination lock open. He grabbed books, snatched his jacket from a hook, slammed the door with a bang. A short distance to his left, he was peripherally aware of another student getting something from a locker.

"Hey."

He spun, ready to tell Regina St. Claire to get lost . . . and was brought up short. It was Penny. "You okay?" she asked.

"Hi. Yeah . . . sorry. It's been a strange day." He was still shaky as he tried to replace the lock.

"Here, let me hold those." She took his books, freeing his hands to reapply the lock and spin the dial. In turn, he held her books and she got a sweater from her own locker and drew it on, a dark green cardigan with white reindeer parading across the front.

"What are you still doing here?" he asked.

"Detention," she said.

"*What?*"

"For masterminding a food fight in the caf. Or was it the cheating scandal?"

He narrowed his eyes. "You've never been on detention in your life."

Her grin was her admission. "Sad, huh?" Then he was smiling, too; his encounter with the JAVA kids forgotten for the moment. Penny's green eyes had a sparkle, even there in the lengthening shadows of the corridor. "Actually, I was practicing dictation," she said.

"You want to be a dictator?"

"Ha ha. Medical secretary. If I can get in. There's a lot to learn."

The idea of her actually knowing what she wanted, and what she needed to do to achieve it, intrigued him. They fell into step walking down the corridor. "How about you?" she asked. "Do you want to be a writer?"

The question surprised him. No one had ever asked it. He didn't have a good answer, so he simply said he didn't know what he wanted to be. He did mention that the aptitude test Blinky Keenan had given in guidance suggested he'd make a good truck driver. They laughed. Outside, they strolled together to the late bus waiting area.

"I love Curb Feelers," Penny said.

He was pleased by this; a little embarrassed, too. He told her about the column he'd just finished, about the football team and how the weights of the players listed in the program were often exaggerated.

"Is that true? I didn't know that."

"Mike Burke weighs one-eighty and the program has him ten pounds heavier. Stan Jarvis, too. It's meant to freak out the other team."

"To what?"

"Freak—you know, blow their minds . . ."

Penny looked confused. *What am I saying?* he thought. He was making up phrases. "It's a psychological tactic," he tried again, "to worry the opposition."

"I get it now. And what does Coach Mosher think about your story?"

"He doesn't know yet."

Penny smiled. "So he'll probably freak out when he sees it."

TK laughed.

"You're becoming our crusading journalist," Penny said with a note of admiration, and he suddenly wondered: Was that how his classmates viewed him? Was JAVA right? Did students think he was trying to convince them of things? But a more basic question occurred: *Was* he? He didn't think so; the idea of journalistic crusader put him in mind of that New York *Post* reporter, Victor Riesel, whose exposés of organized crime in labor unions had led an enemy to hurl sulfuric acid in his face, burning his eyes out. With a shudder, TK pushed the image aside. Ideas just came to him, as Miss Mutterperl said they would once you started to look for them. Right? He hesitated a moment, then told Penny about his encounter with Chad Long and Regina St. Claire. The green of Penny's eyes darkened. "That's stupid," she said. "They should mind their own business. I've met her. She seems snobby, if you ask me."

"Did she form the JAVA club?"

"I don't know. It's popular with some kids. A certain amount of that stuff's okay, I think. About not smoking and drinking, and being patriotic. But do we need classmates telling us which books are okay to read and which aren't? Or what movies? We're practically grown-ups."

Penny lived inland, on the west side of town. His distance home was shorter and generally he walked, but today he decided to wait for a late bus. Outside other students were milling in the mellow autumn sunshine, waiting, too. It was the season of leaves; they gathered in bright drifts alongside roads and swirled in the wakes of passing cars, and when the wind blew, the air was full of them. He and Penny stood by the curb when suddenly, with no sense of having intended to, he said, "Lately I've got this feeling that . . . a change is coming . . ."

Penny shut her eyes and drew a deep breath. "Don't you love it? The first smell of fall in the air? This morning was so cool I wore this." She meant the reindeer cardigan—not something that Dee Richards would wear, showing off her rack, but it was nice, and it didn't hide the soft rounds of Penny's breasts.

But that wasn't what he'd meant. There *was* that: the cool of the mornings, the changing leaves, the slant of sunlight, the smells, the mostly empty beach in the afternoons now—but this was like . . . Penny was looking at him, her eyes more softly green now, expectant. He took in a slow breath. "It's a feeling there's something . . . out there. Something . . ." He felt awkward all of a sudden. "I . . . can't explain it. It's . . ."

"You're a writer," she said gently, "try."

He wasn't sure he could; but her attentive waiting was encouragement. He thought of a movie that Janine Brewer had insisted he take her to the previous summer: *West Side Story*. It was a little dumb—the idea of gang kids singing and dancing in the streets—but the music was good, one song in particular, about something coming. But he didn't say this. He said, "It's like a storm approaching . . ." He actually glanced toward the horizon, but there was only golden light on the maple trees that lined the school drive, orange streaks just beginning to show in the green of the leaves. Farther along the sidewalk, some kids were horsing around. They had snatched a younger kid's lunch box and were tossing it back and forth, playing keep-away.

Penny's attention hadn't left TK; she was waiting. And now he was thinking of how several years back, right around this time, there had been a hurricane coming, and how Don Kent on Channel 4 kept talking about it, charting the storm's approach on a big isobar map in the TV studio. People went about their lives, but there was this impending feeling that things were about to change. The trees were already starting to toss in the wind as TK hurried home from school. Dad was going to be tied up indefinitely at the shipyard, so Mom asked TK to round up the lawn furniture and tape the windows, and as he hastily worked, he watched the sky go the oddest coppery green. "Something . . ." What was the word? Brooding? Unforeseen?

"Good?" urged Penny. "Bad?"

"Heavy," he said at last.

"Heavy?"

He felt stupid, wishing all of a sudden that he'd never brought it up. The truth was he didn't know what he meant. There was just a lurking sense he'd begun to have over the past several weeks. Like he would find himself in class, half listening as the teacher talked, and this sensation would come over him and he'd glance out a window as though being drawn there, though whatever it was he was supposed to see lay beyond view. Then, catching his mind wandering, he would

130

focus that much harder on the lesson . . . until, soon, he was drifting again. Senioritis, Brain had diagnosed when TK told him about it. But wasn't it too early for that? It was only October, after all.

And what about the dreams?

In them (only fragments of which he recalled) TK was running through narrow, unfamiliar streets that turned, without warning, into long white hallways, so bright they made his eyes hurt; or they became dank, shadowy tunnels, where he had to grope along half-blind. Sometimes, from behind doors in the walls, he'd hear the ragged scratching of something frantically trying to get out . . . *or in.* Other times he was being pursued. By whom or for what reason wasn't clear, but he understood with absolute certainty that he could not stop to confront the pursuers, that to do so would bring danger, perhaps even death. "And sometimes," he told Brain, "there's all this swirling color, like an explosion of sparks—like you'd get if you stuck a fork into a light socket."

Brain smirked. "I get dreams like that! I wake up and have to change my pajama bottoms."

TK didn't mention the dreams to Penny, or say anything more about his feeling of something looming. Why give her the impression he was weird (though she probably already had it)? Instead, he nudged the conversation to another topic.

"The Harvest Hop," she said enthusiastically. "Definitely. Are you going?"

The dance was still a few weeks away, and actually he hadn't given it much thought; a poster they'd passed in the lobby just now reminded him. "Probably," he said.

Penny nodded but kept silent, and he wondered: Was she waiting for him to ask her to go to the dance with him? *He'd* brought it up, after all. Did he want to ask her? Should he? Then the moment passed, and she said, "I'm on the committee. If you want to join us, we're meeting Friday afternoon to put up decorations."

TK was looking for some way to steer the conversation back so that he *could* invite her, but he didn't see how. And anyway, Penny had her own circle of friends, most likely already had plans, maybe even a date, and then it would be awkward. He was relieved to see the late buses arriving.

That Thursday they took his dad to the hospital.

7 Tom

On Friday morning, Tom went to the Elm Hill Estate campus again, without his mother this time. There were details to work out, papers to sign. On the way back, he stopped at the Atlantic Diner (IF THE COLONEL MADE FRIED CHICKEN THIS GOOD HE'D BE A GENERAL). Business was in a midmorning lull, and he found Penny stocking napkin dispensers. She looked tired, as if she'd been on her feet for hours, but she brightened when she saw him. There was a dab of red lipstick on one of her front teeth when she smiled. "I thought maybe you'd left to go back to California already."

"Soon." He gave her a nutshell account of the past few days. "I felt bad I couldn't join you gals the other night."

"Oh, don't." Penny swiped a damp cloth across the counter in front of him.

"Still, I'd like to continue our chat. What are you doing after your shift here?"

"I'm pretty much committed all day."

"You don't stop, do you?"

She shrugged.

"When then? You name a time."

"I don't think . . ." She hesitated. "Well, are you free this afternoon at four?"

At noon Stan Jarvis called. "We've got an offer." He gave the details: a young couple had seen the house, really liked it and, knowing the market, had offered close to the asking price.

"We'll take it," Tom said.

"Think about it. You may want to counter. There's some wiggle room, and my hunch is they'll come up a bit." They talked about a comeback offer, Tom insisting that he didn't want it to be a long, drawn-out business. "I'm working for you, remember? Let me call them and say we've talked, and make our counter. Look at it this way, Tom: it's money in your mother's pocket."

And yours, Tom thought. Ten minutes later, Stan Jarvis called back. "It's a deal, they'll pay it. They're thrilled to be in the neighborhood. Oh, and they want the aluminum awnings; they're into retro." He explained the details and the probable time frame for the sale to go through. "Don't crack the champagne yet, not till their financing clears, but have it ready. I'll be in touch."

Penny was in jeans and a work shirt, her hair still tied back, though in a ponytail now, not the bun she'd worn in her waitress persona that morning, and no red lipstick. With her were six kids who appeared to be between ages twelve and fifteen, several with Down syndrome; all, Penny had explained, were developmentally disabled. She put Tom to work helping her escort them out to where a van and driver were waiting in the hospital parking lot. "Where to?" Tom asked. All Penny had told him that morning was where to meet her, and to dress casually.

"We're going apple picking," several of the kids chorused.

They drove south through Bingham and Standish. The kids were chatty and eager; all were curious about Tom and full of questions for Penny, which she responded to with patience and humor. "You handle this crew alone?" Tom asked her. The young man at the wheel worked for the van rental company and was strictly a driver.

"Usually I have an aide, but I told her I'd drafted you. I hope you don't mind."

He didn't. At the apple farm, there was a tractor-drawn wagon to take pickers out into the orchards. The wagon was already half full of people, and as Tom started to lead the kids aboard, he was aware of people staring at them, some quite consciously keeping a distance, as though whatever these poor kids had might be catching. One mother got a little strange, and the man she was with told Penny there was another wagon on the way. Tom stepped forward, about to insist that they make room, but Penny said, "It's okay. We'll take the next cart."

Up in the orchard the kids had fun picking fruit, and when they'd filled their sacks, they played in the tall grass among the trees. When an apple fell nearby Tom asked if anyone knew about Isaac Newton and his discovery. The smallest girl, who wore a stocking cap pulled down over what was apparently a bare scalp, and had a sweet little face, made a raspberry. "Of course," she said. "We're not dummies."

"No, Vivian," one of the Down syndrome kids said, grinning crookedly at her, "we just look it."

They all laughed. "Throw one really high, mister," the little girl challenged, "see if you can break the law."

Tom was game. He tossed up an apple, and they watched as it dropped back into the grass with a soft thud. "That's not very high," the kids chorused.

This time he cranked it and was surprised at the power in his arm. The apple went up, up, as the kids and Penny all watched. When it finally fell back, Tom reacted with mock exasperation, and everyone broke into gales of laughter. Vivian gave him a shrewd look. "I think *you* just discovered gravity."

When the children were safely returned to the hospital, Tom sat outside in a meditation garden, waiting for Penny to complete her paperwork. She came out looking tired but happy, her face burnished from being outdoors, and sat on the other end of the stone bench. "The kids liked you," she said.

"It's mutual. That little Vivian is a sweetheart. Are they all— sick?"

Penny nodded. "With various things. Vivian's the most serious. Brain cancer."

"Oh."

"They enjoy being out doing things in ways few of us ever do. I'm glad you came."

"Thanks for keeping me from being a jerk with those folks on the cart."

"People are basically okay, they're just not sure how to react. I sometimes think it's too strong a whiff of frailty or something. If the situation were reversed, if they were the ones with these children, I'm not sure I'd act any differently than they do. But given half a chance, people tend to do the right thing."

"You are a sweet small-town girl."

"Small-town? I guess I have to plead guilty on that one. Not as sweet as you might think—and definitely not a girl," she said with a wistful smile.

She had undone her hair and brushed it out, and it shone a rich reddish gold in the dying sunlight. "You didn't tell me about this part of your life," he said. "Brain did."

"I don't always mention it. I figured your time here is short." She glanced at her watch. A couple of times during the outing she'd moved aside to take a call on her cell phone. "I guess I should be getting home," she said, but she didn't rise.

"Or your husband might worry?" The words were out before he thought to stop them.

For a moment, Penny was silent; then: "How much *did* Brain tell you?"

"About his troubles. And that the two of you are close."

"He has been a good friend. We've had occasion to lean on each other. I don't know if he told you, but Alan and I lost our daughter. In fifth grade Christina had a seizure and died. She was our only child." Tom expressed sympathy. From beyond the garden and the hospital parking lot came the soft sweep of evening traffic. "It goes so totally against any fathomable logic," Penny went on, "any sense of rightness. You feel there's nothing in the world that can replace what's been taken away. You want to find someone or something to blame. Alan stayed angry, and after he'd run through all the logical targets—me, God, the doctors who'd prescribed her medications—he found his best target was himself. Which was just as unfair. Tina had a condition; no one *caused* it."

Penny's eyes had taken on a faraway stare. "Remember a game we all used to play when we were kids," she said, "you whirled someone around by the arm and spun them loose, and they had to freeze in that position and hold it?"

"Statues," Tom said.

"It was like that. We'd try different things. Couples counseling for a while. Individual therapy. We sold the house and bought a condo. But each time, we seemed to freeze into people we didn't really want to be. I was a basket case for a long while, weepy and lost. Alan froze into guilt. It was in his face, his body . . . he just went around rigid with it. He felt that the fault was his, somehow. And over time it became—if he couldn't protect his child . . ."

"He'd protect you," Tom said quietly.

"He insists on driving me places, picking me up. He worries. He wants me to be safe. It's why I have a cell phone. He checks in if I'm gone for even a few hours. It took a long while for him to be okay with the occasional girls' night out. But he's always gentle, and he's been a good provider."

"How about today, you taking the kids? He's okay with that?"

"That's not negotiable. You can't really fight something like the loss of a child. You surrender to it. *I* did, anyhow. In a way, though, the experience of Tina's illness, and seeing what the doctors could do and not do gave me new direction. Working with those kids is how I've finally made sense of things since Tina died. I've been taking night courses in nursing. I'd like to quit the diner and do it full-time." She paused. "Being with those kids is one thing that doesn't change. Whenever I'm there, they need me right *now*. They're all about living. Philosophers could learn from them. They keep me from thinking too much about . . ."

She turned to him with a glance of surprise, then laughed. "I'm chattering away."

"No . . . it's been a long time since we've seen each other."

"You wouldn't believe how many times I heard at the reunion, 'You're still *here*?' Sometimes I feel I'm reversing a trend. Most of our peers are at the heights of their careers . . . some even starting to check out."

"Like Doc Rigden. He can't wait to hit the golf links permanently."

She smiled. "I'm glad he was around the other night when you—"

Tom winced in reaction to a sudden pain in the back of his head.

Penny frowned. "Are you okay?"

As quickly as it had come, the pain was gone, replaced now with a sensation of pins and needles, which branched into his arms and hands. He shook his hands, as if trying to rid them of the tingling.

"Tom." She'd risen from the bench, apprehension in her voice. "What's going on? Something is. Tell me."

Then that sensation, too, was gone. He told her, trying to make light of it. It wasn't an unpleasant sensation, he said. In fact, lately, he'd experienced a number of odd sensations. Sometimes they were as subtle as what one might feel passing through an unseen strand of spiderweb, the softest brush of something. Other times, like right now, he felt a tingling. Penny looked concerned. "Have you had any dizziness or nausea?"

"No."

"Shortness of breath? Blurry vision?"

"No, Nurse Griffin," he said, amused by her intentness. "I did misplace my glasses, but I find I can read fine without them."

She didn't seem reassured, but she sat down again. "After you got that shock, you were never fully examined. Maybe you should be. I know a great doctor here."

"Do *you* think there's a problem?"

"If you've got tingling, and you say it's been since that night, maybe you want to get it looked at, just to be sure."

But he didn't see the need. If the sensations continued, he'd consult a doctor when he got back to L.A. He didn't speak of the dreams. She glanced at her watch, and he knew her ride would be waiting. They both rose.

That night he had his most disturbing dream yet.

In his novel *Haven's End* Tom had written of a young man from a small Massachusetts town. His early life there, with its crises and growing pains and eventual escape to college, occupies the first half of the novel. Following graduation the protagonist is drafted, trained as an information specialist, and sent to Vietnam, flush with the idea of writing hard-hitting news amid the stenches of cordite and death. There, however, assigned to an admin unit in Saigon, required to type interoffice memos and press releases about the humdrum of military routine, all the while hearing tales of the growing antiwar sentiment at home, his disillusionment becomes total. Upon his return to the states, he declares himself a conscientious objector, and now must wait in limbo until his application for discharge is acted upon. It finally comes, and the last scene in that section is of him in his strange-feeling civvies (flared jeans, a flowery shirt, suede boots—no headband yet, not with a half inch of hair) as he wanders away from the barracks where The Who's "I'm Free" is blasting on someone's hi-fi. With just the clothes on his gypsy back, a lid of grass, and a sheaf of poems he's written, he makes his way west through the last third of the novel.

Classic artist-hero stuff. In fact, when the book appeared, one reviewer called the main character "kin to Stephen Daedalus and Holden Caulfield, with a pinch of Sal Paradise thrown in."

"Regrettably, your character's discoveries have become *every*one's discoveries these days," Tom's editor told him later, after the book had sold its way to a third printing and to the brink of paperback reprint before stalling. "Now, if you'd written it six months earlier . . ." Tom didn't bother to point out that he'd written it two *years* earlier, that it had taken most of that time for the novel to find a home. But he wasn't disappointed with the book or its sales. On the contrary; when it was your first outing, what was there to compare? Let the critics make the judgments. Joyce? Salinger? Kerouac? He would beam with pride and take it. Certainly he was optimistic; he'd written one, he could write another.

But he didn't. Nor, after brief consideration that it might be a triumphant return (Local Boy Hits It Big!), did he go back to Weybridge later that year for his high school class's tenth reunion.

In going to Los Angeles after college and the service, Tom set himself a new course, choosing to hold on to some romantic faith in life's possibilities. He'd written short stories and a novel, maybe he'd try his hand at a screenplay. There was a pay phone in the minimart around the corner from his dumpy apartment in West Hollywood, so he was able to call home when he wanted to talk, but no one from back east could reach *him*. Eventually, when it became necessary if he wanted to be in the "business," he got a telephone and an answering machine, but by then he had a small A-frame house in Laurel Canyon, and he was no longer so careful about who got the number, especially women.

"The reunion committee has never been able to find you," Brain said irritably. "You've cut yourself off."

"Correct me if I'm wrong, but wasn't that the original Brain Mclain plan? To achieve escape velocity?"

There was no reply. They stood in the backyard. Brain had come by to help load some furniture that was going to Goodwill. Tom looked up at the sky. Only a few weak stars shone through the misty scrim of clouds. "See?" Brain said. "No shipyard sounds." It was true. Except for crickets, the surrounding night was quiet. "Take my word, there's nothing there anymore. If you want, we can ride over and you'll see for yourself." But Tom didn't need that. He acknowledged that the sounds must have been in his dreams.

"Say more about the dreams," Brain invited.

So he did. Each dream was different, yet they were variations on a theme: he was young, lost, and on the run. Sometimes the setting was L.A., but it could be here, too. The things that didn't change were the feelings of panic, of needing to do something and being late and unprepared. "And pursued," he said.

"You began having them when you got here?"

"Since the reunion."

Brain mulled this for a moment. "Dreams generally aren't *about* anything. They're symbolic . . . suggestive. Those sound like anxiety coming out."

"Thanks, Sigmund."

"Maybe about the screenplay you're waiting to hear on, or getting your mom settled. Plus your being here, seeing people. How young are you in them?"

"A teenager."

"While you're here, where do you sleep?"

Tom nodded up at the window of his old bedroom. He saw what Brain was getting at. "It could be that, right?" he said, seizing this. "Stirring up memories."

"You wouldn't be normal if you didn't feel *some*thing."

"I'm no nostalgia buff."

"Maybe you want to relive an experience, or have another go at something you didn't get right the first time."

"Old scores to settle? I'm not sure about that."

Brain shrugged. "Well, I'm no shrink. But if you're worried, see Penny's doctor friend at the hospital. Dave Simkin. I've met him. He talks to you like you're human."

But Tom wasn't sold. Maybe the dreams were connected to some of the things Brain mentioned. He'd be heading back west soon. They'd pass. And for the next two days, Tom was so occupied by the final arrangements for moving his mother into Elm Hill Estate and closing on the house that he slept like a stone, undisturbed by dreams or sounds or physical sensations.

On the third night that changed.

8 TK

In the hospital Dad had *looked* different. The sun-weathered glow of health had paled to where there was so little contrast with the bed linen that he seemed at times to have faded away. His eyes, when he was not struggling against the downward tug of the medicines being pumped into him, had a glassy intensity. Sometimes, with TK or Mom sitting by, holding his hand and talking quietly, the look would go away and it became possible to reassure themselves that the treatment was taking its course, difficult though it was, and that he would be all right. In fact, the doctors' decision to release him in the first week of October seemed to confirm this. But it didn't take long to realize that Dad had changed.

His voice was a wisp, like the faint movement of water across barnacled rocks. And here was a man who would work a full shift at the shipyard, and after supper spend an hour with TK, tossing a football or a baseball, then perhaps mow the lawn or work on one of the many handyman projects he always had going, like the installation of a gas grill in the Knowleses' backyard lanai. Now, lying there on the davenport, with an oxygen tank nearby, he would nap in the afternoons, which was no more natural for him than tuning in soap operas on television was; but he did that, too.

One day when TK came home from school, Dad was there, watching *Days of Our Lives*. Seeing TK, he struggled to sit up. He nodded at the TV set. "Turn that off."

From the end table, he picked up a fold of glossy paper. "Mom found this in the laundry," he said, his voice rising with a gust of its former strength. "Where'd you get it?"

TK saw that it was the pamphlet he had taken from the barbershop (the big eyeball and the words SOMEONE IS WATCHING YOU), which he'd stuffed into a pocket of his dungarees and forgotten about. He explained this now.

"D'you know anything about the John Birch Society?" Dad asked.

"No," TK said truthfully.

Dad's face tightened, and TK anticipated he'd rip up the pamphlet, end of discussion. Encounters had ended that abruptly before. Dad was a man of few words when it came to some things. But this time, instead of clamming up, Dad drew his lower lip in, running his teeth over the stubble sprouting there, and then he began to tell a story. In it, TK's parents invited a soldier home to dinner one Sunday after church. The soldier was from South Carolina and was stationed out on the neck at the Nike base there. The man loved to sing, had a good voice apparently, and remarked to TK's parents that he'd like to join the church choir. He asked how he might go about it. It had been an awkward moment, Dad said, because both he and Mom knew that the man never would be invited to join.

The story wasn't a long one, but the telling took time because Dad had to pause often to catch his breath, and TK sat impatiently, wanting him just to get to the point, though he didn't dare interrupt. He saw that Dad wanted to tell it his way.

"You might've been three years old at the time. It was a simple Sunday dinner with a guest, the sort of thing that happened in those days, people having folks to dinner—and a man in uniform serving his country, why, of course, you invited him, the way if you saw a sailor with his sea bag hitching a lift back to the Navy Yard, you gave him a lift, and that was that. But our guest that day . . . he was a Negro; and it must've gotten around and been of particular interest to someone. Next day at work, when it was time for lunch . . ." Dad paused again to breathe. "We used to keep our lunch boxes in the hull of whatever ship we were building, because it was cool down there. I opened mine, ready for the liverwurst sandwich your mother used to pack me." He paused. "I'd one time commented that I liked liverwurst, and isn't that what I got every day for the first few years of our marriage?"

TK was sitting in a wing chair, wanting to flap his knees together like a second-grader who needs to pee, but he made himself keep still.

"I opened my lunch box, and there was a piece of paper. A note. And it said . . ." TK saw his dad go even paler, his voice coursing with emotion. "It said, 'Nigger's pal.' "

"Aw, no," TK breathed.

" 'Nigger's pal.' That's what it said." A pause. "No name on it. It was just paper torn from a notebook. I stared at it and I felt like someone'd poked a red-hot rivet into me. For what it said, sure; that was bad, but also because someone'd gone into my lunch box, in there with the food my wife had packed."

"What did you do?"

"Didn't know *what* to do. Part of me wanted to crush that note and start shouting, start swinging fists if it came to that. I was that angry. 'Course, I didn't know who to shout at or swing at. And I wouldn't have anyhow. It's not my way." He began to cough. TK glanced toward the green oxygen tank, waiting to see if Dad needed it; but after a moment the coughing subsided. Dad drew a labored breath and went on. "If I blew my top, then whoever stuck that note in there would've won. They'd have gotten my goat, which is what they wanted. What I finally did . . . I don't know if it was the right thing or not, still don't. I did nothing. Just played on like maybe it was a love note your mom had put in my lunch box. Might even have smiled; I don't remember. I stuck the note in my pocket, took out a sandwich, opened the wax paper, hoping my hands didn't shake too bad, and I bit into that liverwurst. And it was like chewing dirt. I snuck glances at those men, guys I'd worked alongside for years, trying to figure who might've done it. Was it him? Or him?" He coughed again and broke off.

"Did you ever find out?"

"Never did. Might not even've been one of them. Someone else could've got down there and put that note in, though it would've meant they knew my lunch box. Anyways . . ." He trailed off, looking momentarily confused. "Why'm I telling you this?"

"That pamphlet from . . . wait. You think *that*'s who did that to your lunch box?"

"I don't know. Prob'ly not. Their method is passing out stuff like this." He waved the pamphlet. "All printed up neat and official and sounding halfway smart. But it's just a piece of junk, like a dirty picture, that takes something good and twists it and makes it ugly. In a way, son, what that kind of thing is about is some lack in that person. A man who's too weak, too cowardly to treat others as equals, so he acts out of being scared. I'll tell you this, you meet up with folks like that—and I hope to God you don't—you give 'em a wide berth, because that kind of scared can get dangerous. If one person's bad connects up with another person's bad, and then someone else's . . . before long it can add up to a whole lot of bad, even though each person has put in only a little. I think that's what happens sometimes, even here . . . and what happened in Germany in the war."

Now his dad did what TK had imagined he would have done right at the first. He ripped up the brochure, his hands trembling as he tore the glossy paper, and that was that. "One more point," Dad said as TK headed for the stairs to go study, "if any good can come out of a mostly bad thing?" Dad managed a thin smile. "I never ate another liverwurst sandwich."

TK, too, found some good. Or at least he found a topic for his next Curb Feelers column.

9 Tom

At the liquor store in Picknell Square Tom picked up several more cardboard boxes for packing. As he put them into the back of the Escape, he happened to glance across Bridge Street, where he noticed a woman standing by a green pickup truck. She seemed familiar, and suddenly he was startled to realize he knew her. He closed the cargo hatch and crossed the busy street.

The pickup truck was still there, and pedestrians went by on the sidewalk, but there was no sign of the woman, whom he was sure was Audrey Mutterperl. Yet, was that possible? She looked the same as she had thirty years ago.

At home he checked the telephone directory but found no listing for his former teacher. That evening, as he was replacing a washer in the kitchen faucet, the phone rang. A man's voice said, "What's up, guy? I seen you looking."

"Excuse me?" Tom said.

"At my truck. What say we chew on some history?"

The voice sounded thick with alcohol. "Who is this?"

From the other end, laughter. "And you said I couldn't throw a curve past you."

Tom had never been to the Burkes' house, though he knew the neighborhood. Called the Cove, it was an area of narrow lanes and wood-frame cottages that had once housed shipyard workers. At the address Mike had given, the green pickup he'd seen downtown was in the driveway. An old push mower stood up to its wheels in grass. A building permit was tacked beside the door for what appeared to be an addition that evidently awaited completion; fading Tyvec wrap showed at the edges of the sheathing where trim boards had yet to be applied. Tom knocked on the screen door.

"It's open," boomed the familiar voice. Tom stepped inside, suddenly half-blind in the gloom. "So's the bar." Mike Burke's limping bulk emerged from the shadowy interior. "This way." They went through to a kitchen, where further signs of stalled renovation were evident. With the crook of his cane, Mike pulled out a chair for Tom. "Y'ready to do some damage?"

A beer can and some kind of liquor in a glass sat on the table. Tom had no thirst, but he understood there were rituals of hospitality and trust being enacted here. "Whatever you're having."

The decor was spartan. The only thing that gave the room a hint of character was an array of family photographs hanging in frames—Mike, Maureen, and their kids.

Mike set down a glass. It didn't look quite clean, but the Black & White erased any worry about germs and cut the freezer smell of the ice cubes. Mike popped the tab on a can of beer and set that down, too. He wore old chinos and an inside-out sweatshirt, the sleeves hacked off at the shoulder. His arms were still big, though the muscles sagged. "You're smart," he said. "Gettin' out from under. Damn things're never done."

"Sorry?"

"A house. Always something yapping for your attention. *This* ridiculousness." He waved a hand, indicating the space around them. "I built it 'cause Mo was forever saying we hadn't freshened up the place in years. I always figured, when the walls start closing in, you take a vacation. We'd go to Atlantic City, but she'd say, what about the fifty-one other weeks, stuck here with the same walls to stare at? She had a point. So I put on the addition. But it wasn't about that, because she split before I got it done. Anyways, it's all water under the dam now."

Under the *bridge*, he meant; *over* the dam. Mike raised his glass. "Under the dam."

In high school Mike had applied everything imaginable to a

baseball, including the curve that no teenage batter should have to face; but his hands, Tom saw, were startlingly small. It was as if he'd gotten the hands Brain Mclain might've worn, and Brain had been given the pair intended for Mike.

"Boy, the reunion, huh?" said Mike. "It reminded me there's a lot of water gone under the dam. Thirty years. Little did we know it then, but America lost its cherry big time after that."

"I'm curious about your call," Tom said.

"We'll get there, but indulge an old bud for a bit." Mike seemed to be nursing a buzz that had started well before Tom's arrival. "JFK, then King and Bobby and others. Bam, bam, bam." Mike clopped the back of one hand into the palm of the other in quick staccato. "Civil rights marches and burning bras . . . But the war, that's what really shook the screws till everything started falling apart. Seems nobody could get their head around that mother. You go in?"

"Drafted, but I got out early. I became a C.O."

"No lie, you could do that?"

"Maybe I listened to Phil Ochs too many times."

"Wish I'd had the balls."

"It wasn't about balls. I made the case, the army agreed. I don't think they had the stomach for a hassle. Those were tough times, like you say." Tom wanted to get to why Mike had phoned him, why he'd come; but his host was in no hurry, apparently.

"I enlisted. Something to do, I guess. I knew Topps wasn't going to be rolling out my rookie card. Not after that Brockton game. What the hell was I doing still playing football? I had scouts from the Show looking to sign me. I should've got my head examined."

"That's hindsight."

"Oh, I've got hindsight in spades. Too bad I didn't have smarts like Brain, or that knack you've got with words."

"That last bit's open to debate," Tom said, and he wasn't certain how being a wordsmith would have kept Mike from injuring his shoulder or from joining the Marines.

"When I got out, I went over to Adams Point to the JC for a while, but I'll tell you, being in the bush and then coming back and trying to sit down and do algebra and write essays? I didn't last a term. So, I figured if I was gonna earn a living, it'd have to be in another uniform. Only not a town gumball. That's where I drew the line. I still remembered Roper. Remember him?"

Tom didn't. Mike looked uncertain now, too. "Frank Roper? The truant officer."

"Ripley?"

"Frank *Ripley*. Who's Roper?" Mike gave it a second's worth of frown. "What a pisser Ripley was. Anyway . . . why'm I talking about this?"

"Something about you being a cop?" Tom suggested, his interest waning.

"How I got on the staties. Mostly it was my size, I think, plus the tour in 'nam. It was a good gig. I put in twenty-one years till some squirrelly little prick with a Saturday night special put lead in my leg." He drew a long sigh and looked momentarily befuddled. "But the big hit I took was long before that."

Tom knew what was coming. He took a sip of the whisky.

"Last game of the year, it turned out. Kennedy got shot that next Friday. A torn rotator cuff, then a dead president."

"Bad times, those."

"I don't know which vanished faster, hope in this country or the baseball scouts. Both gone quicker than crows from poisoned road-kill. Ah, well, could've been worse, right? I could've been a yardbird like the old man." He pinched his tongue: "My dad works at the shityard. 'Member that?" He hoisted his glass. "Under the dam."

"To the dam," said Tom, clicking the glass.

"Damn straight. My advice, ol' buddy—and I'm giving it now while I think of it: You sell the house, take the money, and haul ass. Ain't nothing here. The only ones of us left are stuck some way. Mortgage or family or a shitass job that you got to hang on to till pension." He belched softly. "At the reunion, you know how many times

I heard about what a great curveball I had?" His smile was more gri-
mace than grin, and Tom was struck by how deep the lines in his face
were, how sunken the eyes (cops and ballplayers looked old beyond
their years). "Anyway, I saw you in town today. Figured you probably'll be heading west again soon, so I better strike while I can."

"Where were you?"

"The bank. I'm a rent-a-cop." Mike reached the bottle from the
counter and gestured with it. Tom declined and Mike helped himself. "Queer as this sounds," Mike went on, "I got this notion about
the yard."

"The shipyard?"

"Maybe from Brain, I dunno. It's kind of a hobby. I'm sick of
sitting around with all this stuff undone, sick of finding reasons not
to do it. I'm up to here with waiting for the phone to ring and Mo
on the line from Vegas to say she's giving up this cracked notion of
being a dealer and is on her way home."

"What about the yard?" Tom asked.

Mike didn't answer right away. He lit a cigarette, lit Tom's with
the same match, and for a few minutes they sat there like a pair of
throwbacks, ice cubes clinking in the glasses, thin ribbons of
tobacco smoke unfurling in the afternoon light. Take away thirty
years and they might've been sitting in the park, sucking Popsicles
and talking baseball and girls. For some reason Tom thought of
Brain's holograms, the illusion of time and of youth they had created. Finally, Mike picked a fleck of tobacco off his tongue. "In a lot
of ways, when the yard died, this town did, too."

"That's news?"

"I've done some poking around, spent the odd afternoon at the
library reading microfilm. Mary Agnes is always eager to help, to
get her nose into anything with gossip potential." He nodded at a
nearby telephone table, where a tattered manila folder lay.

"You going to write a book?"

"Just curious. But there's something . . . I dunno, funny, about
how all that went down."

Now, in spite of himself, Tom was interested. "Go on."

"I'm not sure. It's like the company was facing some big trouble."

"Such as what?"

"Dunno. Hiding something maybe? I'm just spinning out questions, and I wonder about that, too. Is this just another kind of rock, paper, scissors? You know, me bumping around here in an empty house, avoiding stuff I oughta be doing? I'm good at avoiding the shit outta things. I guess I gotta ask myself, if Mo was here would I even care about any of this."

Tom still wasn't sure what "this" was, but his own curiosity was flagging. Mike's eyes gleamed with possibilities, but whisky wasn't fuel for sustained focus, and the gleam soon dimmed. "Ah, this is just one old gimp leg rambling along in the twilight, when I should be on the phone to Vegas begging Mo to come home. In fact, I aim to. That ice cube in your glass looks lonesome." This time Tom didn't resist.

The talk shifted to other things and went on a while longer, but it was desultory, about a past and a present that wouldn't quite connect, as though an essential middle piece were missing. Mike Burke walked him outside. As Tom reached his car, he thought of something. Mike was still standing bulkily in the doorway. "I meant to ask—was that Miss Mutterperl I saw in town today?"

"Say what?"

"Audrey Mutterperl. It's how I noticed your truck."

"The teacher?" Mike said, pulling at memory. "With the tits and that odd shape? Man, you *are* slumming in the past. I ain't glimpsed her in thirty years."

10 TK

On a Wednesday morning at 10:17, TK knocked on the frosted glass pane of his guidance counselor's door for his 10:20 appointment. "Always arrive early," Mr. Keenan was fond of telling his students. "It shows the person you're there to see that you mean business." TK didn't know if he meant business today or not.

"Ah, Knowles." Mr. Keenan ("Blinky" as students secretly referred to him, for his habit of closing his eyes, as if in deep thought, then suddenly popping them wide, like a surprised owl) waved him in. He had on his customary navy blazer, white shirt, and bow tie. "Have any trouble finding me?"

It was a joke. TK hadn't been to the guidance office since last fall; wouldn't be here now except that each of the seniors was scheduled for a session with his or her counselor to talk about the future. If experience held, it would be the same old deal as it had been since sixth grade: sit with a bored former classroom teacher who'd fled into the guidance ranks and talk in vague generalities about nothing very much for ten minutes, thank you, see you next year.

An array of college catalogues was spread on the desk, facing TK as he sat. Several were for schools he had never heard of, though that didn't mean anything; he didn't know much about colleges. In addition to the catalogues was an open file folder with TK's transcript and something from Educational Testing Service.

"Well, Knowles, your SAT scores seem in line with what we'd expect—pretty average—though there's been a decline in your academic performance in recent months."

TK wasn't sure if there was a question hidden in that, and Mr. Keenan didn't look up from his perusal, so TK kept silent. "You no longer participate in interscholastic sports . . . though I see you've joined the newspaper staff. So"—now he did look up—"what are your thoughts about college?"

Did he mean college in general or what TK considered his own ambitions to be? TK decided the latter. Keenan did have a shelf of his bookcase devoted to catalogues from schools TK *had* heard of— Princeton, Yale, MIT—evidently reserved for students who were likely to be accepted to such schools. On the bottom shelf were a dozen or so brochures for schools such as the junior college in Adams Point and vocational/technical institutes, along with a stack of flyers from the military recruiters. As with the majority of WHS students, TK's choices fell in a middle range: a mishmash of New England state schools, some universities like B.U. and Northeastern, as well as small private colleges, some with religious affiliations (including the Jesuit college that Blinky Keenan himself had attended several decades ago according to the framed diploma that hung on the wall behind him).

"I've thought about it a little," TK ventured. *Very* little, in fact. Given the situation at home, he no longer knew whether college was possible for him. "I don't know what I'd want to study."

"Hmm, well, a starting point is to consider the things that give you distinction."

"Distinction . . ."

"And make a list. For instance, what sets you apart? What do you like to do?"

"Well . . . I dig clams."

"Clams. You have an interest in mollusks?"

"With a clam fork." TK mimed the thrusting action. "It's a part-time job."

"I see." The counselor examined TK's transcript for a moment.

TK knew what it would show: that his generally okay performance had slipped in the past term, especially in math and chemistry. "I'm not sure I can afford college," he offered in an effort to distract Keenan's scrutiny.

It seemed to work. "That shouldn't discourage you. College is costly, it's true, but there are some well-endowed institutions." The man leaned closer, near enough that TK could see that the bow tie was a clip-on. "Do you know what well endowed means?"

Yeah, it means a girl like Dee Richards. Or what Niki DiLorenzo would kill for. "Isn't that a college that has a lot of money?"

"They do an evaluation of an applicant's finances, and often there's aid based on need." Blinky began jotting on paper—probably the names of some institutions that he felt were well endowed. "Now at *my* alma mater"—he cleared his throat softly and sent a glance at the framed diploma—"well, I was fortunate enough to receive some scholarships. Education was my major, of course, but my minor, the subject I really fell for—probably would've pursued if I'd seen any career in it—was psych. Know what that is?"

"Psychology?"

"The study of personality and human behavior. Fascinating. Freud, all that." Keenan cleared his throat again. "It isn't too early for you to be thinking about a major, Knowles. Have you got anything in mind?"

TK didn't. Majors and minors suggested baseball to him. In college wasn't everyone in the same courses, the way it was here? Some history, math? He had no clue. "Um, would it be okay if we talked about something else?"

"Oh?"

TK swallowed. "Something more . . . personal?"

Keenan sat back and gave his slow, round-eyed blink, and suddenly TK regretted having spoken. He hadn't planned to. He was almost ready to abandon the whole idea, say that he wondered about English as a major . . . but this other thing was in his head and the words had just popped out. Keenan wasn't squirming. In fact, he looked interested. He closed the file folder, moved it aside, and took off his glasses, squinting at TK with eyes that appeared weak and watery without them. "What've you got in mind?"

What *did* he have in mind? He wasn't sure if this was the time or place for this, or if Blinky Keenan was the person, but he *was* a guidance counselor, and TK didn't know anyone else whose job even remotely dealt with listening. He thought briefly about Brain's "No Way" idea, and how that might apply, but it was too weird. He needed something practical, advice he could apply to *his* situation, and that was a good question in itself: What *was* his situation? He exhaled. "I've been thinking about things and . . . uh . . . I don't know what's real and what isn't."

A small V of perplexity creased Keenan's brow.

"Like . . . *me* for instance." TK gave a hollow laugh and clumsied on, committed to trying to find words, even if it meant sounding foolish. "I mean, am I real?"

Keenan blinked and while he didn't look any less puzzled, he seemed alert, as if back in his training, in one of those "psych" courses he'd have been challenged by a real question, something with gristle and meat to it. Still, TK imagined the man might quip, "Well, you certainly seem real to me, ha ha." But he didn't. He cleared his throat (it seemed to be the thing to do) and said, "Is it something specific that makes you ask that, Tom?"

Tom. The last name formality was gone. TK swallowed again. The man hadn't pushed him away. "You know that feeling of 'I've been here before,' that 'this has happened already'?"

"You're talking about 'déjà vu.'"

"I've been getting it a lot lately. Like I've been through this before. But I don't know when or where, and there's also a sense that . . . I'm not really here. Or I'm not . . . not really *me*."

"Who do you imagine you are?"

"Maybe no one."

"No one."

"Or just . . . some energy moving along." He thought hard a moment more, and then shook his head in surrender. He didn't like to give up; in his writing he considered it his duty to find words—to say the unsayable, as Longchamp might put it; but right now he wasn't sure what he felt. Brain had said these odd ideas could just be senioritis, or brought on by TK's finally realizing that Brain's No

Way theory was real. He considered telling Blinky Keenan about the idea, but he didn't. Too bizarre. He even thought about sharing his dream in which odd, three-padded hands, or paws of some kind, were trying to push through a door, as if groping to find a way in, but what would Keenan think? TK could imagine the man shaking his head sadly and declaring, "Three-padded hands, huh? You know what Freud would say, don't you, Bozo? Or Alfred E. Newman? He'd say you're sick, sick, sick!"

Blinky was silent. He put on his glasses, and TK was reminded that there would be another student waiting, probably someone not mixed up, someone who knew what college to go to and what to major in. He predicted Keenan would say: *I'm pretty sure it's just a phase you're going through, this questioning of things. It's quite normal in a young . . .* "Is there anything going on at home?"

And TK thought: *Only my father dying and my mother coping badly;* and certainly those were factors, but they weren't the real issue, he was somehow convinced. But neither could he grasp what that issue might be, and after another few seconds he said, "Nothing I can think of." He was mightily relieved when there was a brisk knock on the door: the next appointment, arriving early, announcing that he or she meant business.

One afternoon when he had driven to school, TK saw a girl waiting for a town bus at the stop outside the schoolyard, and as he neared he saw it was Penny. He pulled over. "Miss your ride?" he called.

Penny shook her head. "I have to go to Central Square to pick out new glasses."

"I can take you."

"It's out of your way, isn't it?"

He was going to dig clams later, but he didn't say it; he'd have driven her to Boston if that's where she'd been going. "C'mon, hop in."

Turned around and headed west, he inhaled the fragrance Penny bore: a sweet, subtle mingling of wool, shampoo, and perfume. He stole a look at her. "What's wrong with those glasses?"

"Not strong enough anymore. I have a new prescription."

"How's that work?" He knew nothing about eyeglasses.

"The doctor tests you and writes down numbers, and the optician knows what they mean. Today I'll just pick out frames, and he'll fit them and call me when they're ready. It's pretty simple. Thank you for the ride, by the way."

They went into the optician's shop together. A woman got Penny seated at a mirror and brought over several cards of eyeglass frames, then retreated to let Penny choose. TK sat beside her, happy to be there. There was something . . . intimate in it, he thought. He watched in silence as she tried on pairs of plastic rims similar to the glasses she already had, but she rejected each pair. Tentatively, he spoke up. "Since you're changing prescription, maybe you should try a different look."

Penny met his gaze in the mirror. He hunted among the displays—and there were lots of choices: many of the cat's-eye style that people wore, and the thick dark horn rims that he associated with the brainy kids. Then, from a small selection of wire frames, he picked a pair that had an oblong shape. Penny's reaction was surprise; but she put them on and gazed into the mirror. "I look like an old granny," she declared.

They did make her appear older it was true, but certainly not grandmotherly. More like a college girl you might see in a coffee house in Boston, one of those who wore black turtleneck sweaters and smoked French cigarettes. She searched awhile longer and decided on round wire frames, with a larger eyepiece. The optician said he'd have them ready in a few days. TK offered her a lift home and she accepted.

Riding to South Weybridge, where she lived, they talked randomly about school, and he found himself studying her profile, wishing she would slide over closer to him, but he contented himself with the thought. After a short silence, Penny said, "I've been meaning to speak to you."

He glanced over. Was she going to mention the upcoming dance?

"I like your column in the *Echo*. It's refreshing. But, maybe you should . . . I don't know, choose other things to write about?"

"If this is about JAVA's petition, I didn't sign," he kidded. "But I hear they weren't thrilled by my last effort." In Curb Feelers he'd reprinted the club's charter (it turned out JAVA was a national organization) and listed some ideas from John Birch Society literature, just offering both for comparison, without comment—but there were similarities. He told Penny about the note he'd found poked through the vent on his locker door, calling him a "commie stooge."

Her expression showed her distaste. "That's just someone's ignorance. But I didn't mean JAVA." She seemed hesitant, on the verge of deciding whether to go on. "I went to the office during lunch period yesterday. I was supposed to get a list of chaperones for the dance, but the secretary wasn't at the desk. I overheard voices from Mr. Sterns's office. It was none of my business, and I was going to go, I *meant* to, but then I heard your name."

TK glanced at Penny, then back to the road.

"I couldn't see who was with him. His door was shut."

Pop Sterns had his name on a brass plate on the outer door, and beyond was the inner sanctum. TK had been there once—the office large, with bookshelves and framed certificates and a thick carpet on the floor—a Bigelow, no doubt ("a name on the door rates a Bigelow on the floor" according to the magazine ads).

"I tiptoed closer, till I could hear them clearly, especially Sterns, and I realized they were arguing. About you. The other voice, I recognized then, was Miss Mutterperl's." A little breathless, Penny recalled the conversation she had overheard:

"I've been seeing this growing attitude of rebellion."

"Oh, come on, Mr. Sterns. He's a good kid."

"He's become rebellious. He told Coach Mosher he was quitting football

the day before the season began, no explanation. And he's starting to be truant."

"You make it sound as though he's out stealing hubcaps or breaking windows."

"That'd be simpler to deal with, I'm afraid. No, this is more troubling."

"I'm sure there's an explanation. Have you—?"

"And then there's that so-called opinion column he's been writing."

"Has someone complained? Beyond that misguided petition?"

"I get information from many sources, Miss Mutterperl."

"I understand. But has anyone specifically—"

"This is your first year with us. I appreciate that you volunteered to serve as faculty adviser for the newspaper, and you seem to take it seriously, judging by the hours you put in—and that's something you may want to reconsider."

"I don't follow you, sir."

"What I'm saying is we're not running the Herald Traveler here. The Echo is meant to be a nice little outlet for the students."

"I agree. I'm trying to encourage students to be creative, imaginative."

"The point is it might be better not to let them be too imaginative."

"But if it's to be a student newspaper, we have to give them some—"

"What's wrong with 'kid in the hallway' surveys—'Who do you think'll win Saturday's game?' 'Who'll be crowned king and queen of the harvest dance?'—that sort of thing. Harmless. Neutral. Perhaps, Miss Mutterperl, we should have a more seasoned member of the staff take over."

"A more seasoned member was serving as adviser. There were three issues last year. We've doubled that in a month and a half. With due respect, sir, you said yourself that the Echo is more visible. Students are reading it, talking about it. It helps create spirit, conveys information. I think that Tom Knowles's column is a big part of that."

"Visibility among the student body is one thing, but the Echo has become visible to people beyond these halls."

"Oh?"

"I've had several worried phone calls from parents, and a note from Father McBride at St. Theresa's complaining specifically about articles Knowles has written."

"This is the first I've heard that. May I see the note?"

"Look, the point is—"

"What did the good reverend object to?"

"Now don't get high-hat with me, Miss Mutterperl."

"Sir, it's just that—"

"Enough. If this kid's such a talent, get him to write about . . . I don't know, the World Series or . . . President Kennedy. But I want you to handle this matter, understood? Or resign as faculty adviser."

Listening to Penny tell it, TK felt as stunned as Miss Mutterperl apparently had been. He drove as though on automatic pilot.

"Mr. Sterns told her he was going to keep an eye on the next few issues. I scooted, before they came out." Penny looked at him. "I don't usually eavesdrop, but when I heard your name . . . I hope I'm not upsetting you."

"It *is* a little upsetting," TK admitted, "but I'm glad you told me. You were brave to stay there. It sounds like Miss Mutterperl was, too."

"She sounded nervous. *I* was nervous just being there."

"Sterns has a way of making people feel uptight."

"And you have a way of expressing things. *Uptight.* That's interesting. So, what do you think you'll do?"

He couldn't bring this up to either Sterns or Miss Mutterperl because they'd ask how he knew. "I don't know."

"Is changing your column an option? Picking safer topics?"

"Like the king and queen of homecoming?"

"Or President Kennedy?"

"I suppose. It's just that lately I've been . . . on fire with ideas."

She scooched around to face him. "Tell me."

"We go to school, day in day out, and it's like, big deal. The three years we've been here . . . it's one-sixth of our life, but we just drift blindly along. For what? So we can take our place on the

159

assembly line and join the rat race? All at once I feel like this stuff we've been learning—the math, history, even poetry—it matters. I know, crazy. I can't believe this is me talking. Yet look what's going on out there."

Penny glanced outside, her smooth forehead wrinkling becomingly, and then turned back. "You're not talking about Commerce Street or Weybridge."

"In Washington, D.C. In Mississippi and Alabama . . . all over. There're people raising big, clumsy questions. Questions no one's had the courage to ask so openly before. It's important somehow. Maybe life and death important. This town, it's so small and . . . tight. It really is like the sign says."

She was still frowning, maybe struggling to push past her bewilderment. He briefly shared Brain's "No Way" theory, and the road sign's unconscious effects. "I'm not saying he's right. It's probably just coincidental, but it has a poetic truth, and Brain has been smart enough to see it. Forget about any ambition or plan that's bigger than this place, because there isn't any way it can happen. I mean, have you ever really seen a politician? Or a writer? Somebody who actually creates stories? I only realized recently that there are some who're still alive and not just names on the covers of books."

Penny looked troubled by what he was saying, but she listened without comment. When he concluded, they rode the last stretch of the journey in silence, and soon she announced simply, "The next street on the right is mine."

The Griffins' house was a tidy white Colonial with a two-car garage. Like many of the homes on this side of town, it was larger than his family's, though still modest, with a white fence in front and a gated arch on which a vine, speckled with tiny pink blossoms, climbed. In the driveway a kid of about twelve was shooting hoops. Her kid brother probably. He retrieved a rebound, paused a moment to glance their way, as though dimly curious to see who was driving his big sister home, then went back to his game. TK got out to walk around and open the door for Penny, but she was already out. He felt a need to add some kind of a point to his rant, but he couldn't focus his ideas. His face was hot, and he had the flickering thought that Artie Dewitt was right: *You can't be a friend to a girl you like.* Wouldn't it be much easier to join the Four-F club? Wasn't that what it was all about anyhow? Was he just laying down a smoke-screen because what he really wanted from Penny Griffin was beneath her sweater, under her skirt?

She was at the trellis gate, and he felt her gaze was cooler, not as welcoming as earlier. Though why should it be? He was challenging her most cherished ideas: that adults knew best, that Weybridge was an ideal place to live, that all their diligence and hard work would pay off and lead to some bright future. Penny swung open the gate. "All I meant to say was for you to be careful. You want to get through and graduate and go to college."

Do I? he thought hollowly. He wasn't sure anymore. Still, he wanted to respond, to say something to lift the downbeat mood he'd brought on, to tell her that he was just babbling, that he didn't really know anything . . . but he couldn't find a single word. He picked one of the pink blossoms on the trellis arch and offered it, but Penny had already turned and was hurrying up the walk to her house.

"'**Et-cet-er-a, et-cet-er-a.**' What do you think?" Dad grinned, rubbing his naked scalp. "Do I make a cool Yul?"

He was referring to *The King and I*, which the family had seen at the drive-in theater the summer before last; but this hospital room was no royal palace. It wasn't even as good as the room Dad had been in when he'd come here the first time—not by half. Dad's hair was gone all right, even his eyebrows; and his skin had a waxy cast; but as disturbing as these changes were, what unsettled TK more was how gaunt he was. His size and strength had diminished dramatically. It was as though the machines tethered with tubes and wires to his arms were actually draining away his life force and somehow his body was being used to run the devices, not the other way around. TK felt torn. He wanted to go to his father and hug him, and at the same time he was eager to flee; to speak softly, yet also to shout at the injustice of it all. When a nurse came in, Mom drew TK back to let the woman tend to Dad. Perhaps feeling his tension, Mom whispered, "Hold your tongue." *Pinch your tongue and say, "My father works at the shipyard" five times, fast. My father works at the "shityard," no, the graveyard, works in those big steel coffins . . . it isn't the cough that carries you off, it's the coffin they carry you off in . . . The shityard the shityard the shit . . .* But Mom needn't have worried; TK didn't dare talk for fear that he would break down completely.

Later, when the two of them were sitting in the hospital cafeteria, poking at their meals (chicken croquettes, mashed potatoes, and peas doused with a gluey sauce) he said, "Dad isn't going to make it, is he?"

He was prepared for the stiff-upper-lip denial that stoics like his mother always gave (Yes, Dad *would* die, someday—as everyone had to die *some*day), but she surprised him. Setting down her fork, she took a pack of cigarettes from her purse. She hadn't smoked in years, not since TK was a child; but she had started again in the past month. She would go through a carton of Raleighs a week, putting the empty packs into a drawer in the kitchen counter, evidently intending one day to clip the coupons and get free gifts. With shaking fingers she struck a match and inhaled. Water gleamed in her eyes, tears that she hadn't allowed herself to cry because she was being strong for all of them; but now the tears let go and streamed down her cheeks, falling fast from her chin onto her hands, which had begun to tremble so that the cigarette zigzagged smoke. And in his own desperation TK realized that it was his turn to be strong, not angry, not now. He pushed back his chair and went around to his mother. Gently he took the cigarette from her, mashed it out in an ashtray there on the cafeteria table, then put his arms around her and hugged her.

Clam Man lately found his youngest worker digging double tides, getting a phone call that TK would be out in one of the coves at some absurd predawn hour, or occasionally after dark, and although TK would likely be the only digger there, the man never quibbled. Dutifully he would show up in his truck and buy the clams, dealing out crisp bills into TK's hand.

TK was doing it for the money, certainly, putting in time before winter came and the mud froze, as it sometimes did; but he had a growing sense that he needed to step up and take on more responsibility for his family. There was something about being out there on the flats. Even with other diggers present, you were essentially alone, working your own inspiration, bent over, forking back the mud, plucking the clams, dropping them in the bucket, and when the bucket heaped, emptying it into one of the burlap sacks. You trailed a winding line of upturned mud, flanked by the parallel lines of your boot prints as you worked backward against the pull of the moon, and the tide ebbed and began to flow. It was at such times that TK sensed that his mother and father needed him, needed the extra money, and that the labor was necessary to keep his own mind from spinning away—the way it seemed, more and more, Mom's mind was doing.

He would return from school and find her, this woman who had always been a diligent and unflagging homemaker, the true north in the family's compass, still in her bathrobe and pin curlers, sitting hollow-eyed at the kitchen table, drinking coffee from the Niagara Falls mug they'd bought on a family vacation there when TK was ten, and smoking a chain of Raleighs, breakfast dishes stacked in the sink. It was small wonder that he found himself preoccupied at school. At best, studying was a scattershot exercise these days. The one exception was writing his column. He'd heard nothing further from JAVA or the administration, but he scarcely noticed. Some nights he would sit up past 1:00 A.M. pecking away at the Olivetti until the letters on the page began to blur and his fingers grew too sluggish to strike the keys. Then, finally, he would switch off the duck decoy lamp, lie down, and surrender to exhaustion.

Though even in sleep, sometimes, there was no rest.

One night in mid-October he came twisting up out of a dream, full of a terror he could not name or understand, gasping into a darkness that crowded close around him. It wasn't the dizzying, bed-spinning sensation he'd had last April vacation after staying out with a few of his football teammates, sharing a quart of Tango and a lukewarm case of Schlitz on the beach. He'd come lurching home after midnight, had to throw one leg over the side of the bed and plant a foot on the floor to steady the room, which wallowed around him like the ship in that Poe story about the Maelstrom he'd read in Longchamp's class. Next morning he found Mom in the bathroom with a mop and pail, cleaning up where he'd evidently puked the night before (though he had no recollection of it; nor had she ever mentioned it). No, this was different, frightening. It had started as one of the flight dreams, only this time he came to the end of a tunnel and in the dark behind him the footsteps of his pursuers slowed from a sprint to a jog, and now to a purposeful walk, as whoever was back there realized TK had reached a dead end. With dread turning to terror, he stared at the wall ahead of him . . . *and saw a door*. Sheathed in metal, it was low in the wall, and he had the wild thought that the footsteps weren't behind him, but *ahead* of him—on the other side of that door! Now a freakish hand—or *paw*, with three triangular pads—was pressing hard at the door, which had become suddenly pliable, more like a sheet of vinyl foam than a steel door. Awful hissing, sloshing sounds pulsed through it.

Then, hyperventilating, damp with sweat, flesh crawling, heart drumming wildly, he woke.

"Hey, TK, check this."

Brain was examining a notice posted on the bulletin board in the school's main lobby. JAVA had been busy, TK saw. The petition they'd circulated hadn't garnered very many signatures apparently and was in limbo for the moment, but now they had compiled a list of books and presented it to the administration with a request that the books be removed from the school library shelves. TK scanned the titles.

> *Of Mice and Men*
> *From Here to Eternity*
> *The Catcher in the Rye*
> *Peyton Place*
> *The Doors of Perception*

There were others, too, twenty-some titles in all, included because of "objectionable content." TK had read only a few of the books, but now he was curious about the others. Were they books you read in college? Absent from the list was *Lady Chatterley's Lover*—the *town* library didn't even have a copy of that!—though a well-thumbed paperback edition had made the rounds in the locker room last year. *Ulysses* was there, but aside from Longchamp, who'd talked about it a few times in class, who around there had ever read *that*? TK certainly couldn't picture Regina St. Claire or Chad Long venturing through James Joyce's tricky minefield of a novel. Which meant the list was probably put together by somebody else, by adults. TK said this.

"You need to mention that," Brain declared.

"I just did."

"To the vice principal, I mean. Tell Pop Sterns."

More students had clustered, rubbernecking to view the list of books. TK could feel their body heat. No one said a word. He felt his own growing irritation. "Do you agree with this?" he said. "Should these books be taken off the school shelves?"

There was a confused exchange of glances, some muttering; still no one spoke up.

"Write about it," Brain went on.

TK rounded on him, his voice rising. "Me?"

"You've got your column. People read it. This is an outrage."

"I'm the only one sticking his neck out—and it keeps getting chopped off."

Brain tried a soft laugh. "Yeah, but . . ."

"But *nothing*. I'm not gonna do it. I don't have time, *goddammit!*"

It startled everyone, TK included. He almost never swore. Brain's face colored to the roots of his red hair. He cleared his throat and mumbled, "See you later," then he backed away, bumping into other kids, and skulked off.

After school, perhaps as some kind of atonement, TK went to the gymnasium where a group of student volunteers were decorating for tomorrow evening's dance. Brain sometimes took care of putting colored gels over the spotlights, but he wasn't there today. Penny was, and TK joined her and a crew of other kids, hanging crepe paper and inflating balloons. Later, he and Penny waited together for the late buses. JAVA's proposed book ban didn't come up, for which he was grateful. The dance was the safer topic of conversation, and when she asked if he was planning to go, he told her that he would be visiting his father in the hospital, as he and his mom did most evenings, and then there was a low tide at 7:45 and he was hoping to dig clams.

Penny was nodding. "Those things are important. More important than a dance," she said, and meant it. He liked that about her: there were no concealed meanings.

"Actually . . . I *want* to go to the dance," he said, "I just don't know what time."

Did her face seem to brighten? The buses rolled up then. He stood there, feeling awkward and abashed, all but digging a toe into the sidewalk. "Well . . . I guess I'll see you there," he said.

Walking to his bus he thought how ridiculous he was. He could dig clams in a blazing sun, run sprints on a track, and yet he couldn't ask a girl a simple question? Ask *this* girl, whom he really liked? A crow was perched on a maple branch along the school drive, and as TK passed, the bird seemed to mock: *Smooth, lover boy.*

"Beat it," TK hissed.

No, I mean it. Way to go, pal. What a romantic.

TK made an abrupt scatting motion. "Scram!"

The crow flapped to a higher perch where, if anything, it squawked louder. *You sure got a way with the ladies there, laddie.*

TK actually looked around for a pebble to peg at the crow, and then he caught himself. What was he doing taking out his frustration on a bird? He drew a slow breath and let it out. He turned and started back. Penny was still standing by the bus, waiting behind some other kids to board. "Did you forget something?" she asked sincerely.

His heart was beating fast and felt so feather-light in his chest he thought it would flutter away before his eyes, but somehow he got the words out. "It might be late when I get there tomorrow night, and maybe you'll be all booked up—but I was wondering if . . . I mean I was *hoping* . . . could I have the last dance?"

She looked at him, her eyes turning the dark emerald hue he'd sometimes noticed when she was serious, or angry. *Haw, haw, taunted the crow, shoulda kept your mouth shut, fool. Now you've put your foot in it.* Then Penny's eyes softened, and she smiled. "I'd like that."

Instant relief. He grinned, probably like an idiot, but he didn't care. "Okay then. See you."

He had to restrain himself from skipping down the sidewalk to his bus.

The crow didn't make a sound.

At 9:42 that evening, TK's father died.

TWO

scissors
cut paper

11 TK

The several days leading up to the funeral felt unreal. Dr. McGowan gave Mom a prescription for something to calm her, though even with it she seemed to be on a rising and falling course of emotions. But TK moved through the daytime half asleep and the night half awake. He did not go to school. He'd read someplace that in the casinos in Las Vegas there were no clocks or windows so that gamblers couldn't tell whether it was night or day; all that existed was now. Lovell's Funeral Home on Sea Street had something of that feel, and while he knew that there were scheduled hours when people who had known his dad could come and pay their respects, his sense of time had become surreal. The people who did come might have been figures on a carousel, moving past in a blur, with a murmur of condolences. If Rod Serling had stepped from amid the bright baskets of flowers decorating the drape-hung room and declared that TK had crossed over into that realm of substance and shadow, a dimension beyond space and time, he would have accepted it.

At Mom's request (he didn't know what his father might've wanted) the body was arranged in an open casket, and people hovered near saying, "How well he looks . . . how *real*." For his part, TK kept silent. The body on view in the pleated crème satin interior of the casket bore no likeness to the vigorous man his dad had been. The suit was stiff, the face puffy, the hair silken. It was as though no sun had ever browned the skin, no frown ever creased the brow, no beard ever stubbled the cheeks that had sandpapered TK's own when he was a boy and he and Dad roughhoused together.

Even the hands weren't Dad's. Thomas Knowles's hands were thick-fingered from his labors; these were manicured and waxy, protruding from starched white shirt cuffs and joined over his breast like bunches of early parsnips. In fuzzier moments, brought on no doubt by the lack of sleep (and the overpowering sweet stench of flowers), TK began to half imagine that in place of the actual body the funeral people had wheeled out a mannequin, that they had a selection of such in a concealed room and trotted out each accordingly ("We need a middle-aged workingman—bring dummy number five!"). At this idea a ghastly urge to laugh would rise in him, prompting him to tighten his jaw and look around for something to distract him until the compulsion subsided.

While he didn't recognize it then, TK was being schooled in a couple of the truths of adulthood: that life had no truck with death, and gone was gone.

The minister would pick up the same theme a day later in his eulogy, taking as his text the resurrected Christ's appearing to his own mother to ask, "Why seek ye the living among the dead?" But for now the sense of the surreal ruled.

People arrived, lingered, and left—relatives and neighbors and family friends, folks his parents knew from church and other organizations. Men who had worked with his father at the shipyard came: union brothers in mismatched slacks and suit coat combinations, their calloused palms offered in oddly limp handshakes, as though, without rivet guns and sledgehammers, they weren't quite sure what to do with their hands. People introduced themselves to TK and mentioned some link to his dad, offering well-meaning words and then moving on, so that as soon as they passed TK had already lost any sense of who they were. Earlier a few of the clam diggers came, including Artie Dewitt reeking of Jade East and gazing around as if he were checking out the crowd for a girl to spirit away in the T-Bird. Miss Mutterperl came, and Mom seemed genuinely moved that a teacher had taken the trouble to attend. Brain and Croz and a few other friends came. Nothing was said about the dance.

Toward the end of the visiting hours, when the flow of people had ebbed and only a few relatives remained, Mom touched TK's shoulder and indicated a deeply tanned older man standing quietly alone by the casket in a black suit and tie. It took TK a moment to recognize Sid Yarrow. TK introduced him to Mom, and after expressing condolences Clam Man drew TK aside and gripped his shoulder with a strong, freckled hand. "I'm sure that your father, may he rest in peace, was a fine man. Take your memories and make them his immortality." Clam Man's grip held firm. Over the heavy scent of cut flowers, the faint aroma of mothballs came from his suit. "You hear what I'm saying to you, boy?"

Mr. Yarrow was Jewish, and TK wondered if that meant he didn't believe in heaven, though he honestly didn't know. What he did know was that he found comfort in the man's presence, that after the parade of people going through, the old man's simple words steadied him, assured him he could get through this.

"Thank you for coming, sir. I'll see you tomorrow."

"Take some time off, boy. The clams aren't going nowhere."

"No, I'll be there."

Just then, Mom appeared. Her expression was pinched. "You're making my son *work*?" she hissed with barely suppressed anger.

"No, Mom—that isn't what's happening."

She paid no attention. "Is that all you think about? Money? Shame on you, sir. *Shame!*"

"Mom!"

Mr. Yarrow cast a quick glance at TK, silencing him. "Mrs.

Knowles," he said quietly, "I am sorry for your loss. May God bless you."

He left, Mom looking stern and then confused as TK managed to explain, and finally just looking sad once more. At the very end of the evening TK spotted Penny. Apparently, she had just come in and was standing in the archway, looking around uncertainly. Seeing him, she gave a small wave and he went over.

12 Tom

Driving across the bridge, Tom saw the shipyard, weed-grown and ghosted; the old rail tracks bushy with saplings, the gigantic superstructures in place, whether because they were simply easier to leave behind than to dismantle and move, or out of some stubborn belief that the glory days of U.S. shipbuilding would return and boats would be launched here again, he couldn't say. Something about the place, lying there in its abandonment, gave him a chill, and he turned back to the road. But soon he was recalling a seventeen-year-old version of himself trying to handle business after his dad died.

There'd been a day early in November 1963 when, arriving home from school, TK found his mother in the living room, fountain pen in hand, holding a sheaf of papers on her lap. On the coffee table sat a fedora. From the wing chair, a man rose. He was short and stout, wearing a suit in the same brown as the hat on the table. TK eyed him.

"Here's my son. Thomas, Junior. This is Mr. Porter, from the shipyard. He's with the office of personnel. Have I got that right, Mr. Porter?"

"That's correct." He handed TK a card with P. ALBERT PORTER embossed in black letters on the ivory card stock, KEYSTONE STEEL. TK shook the man's hand, which was soft and dry.

"As I was saying, Mr. Porter," Mom went on, "what is a waiver?"

TK reached for the papers she was holding, and she passed them to him. They appeared to be some sort of official document, he saw, from Keystone Steel.

"It basically means that you and your son will get your husband's pension and will continue to be covered by health insurance."

"Well, that's a relief then," Mom said. She was still holding the fountain pen.

"And in exchange . . ." TK was still scanning the last page, "we agree to hold the company free from 'indemnity.' "

Mom's expression grew quizzical. "What does *that* mean?"

Porter donned rimless spectacles, stepped alongside TK, and peered at the small print. "Hmm . . . Yes," he said, as if he'd never paid it much attention before. "That's a standard disclaimer. It means you don't intend to bring legal proceedings against Keystone Steel, its subcontractors, or the people who hire Keystone."

"Why would anyone do that?" TK asked.

"Well, that's just it." Porter took the papers and gave a knowing smile, as though there were something the three of them were in on together. "There's *no* reason; but an indemnity clause is a formality that companies observe. As a matter of procedure, don't you know? We live in a litigious society."

TK knew that word from Longchamp's vocabulary drills. It meant that people liked to sue. He still wasn't clear why someone would even think about suing the company, and he said so. P. Albert Porter unhooked his glasses and put them in a small leather case and slipped it into his inside pocket. "My aim, of course, Thomas, and Mrs. Knowles, is to see that there's no lapse in the health benefit payments. It generally takes five weeks to get the pension payouts in motion, but I'm going to see if I can't speed that up." He handed the papers to Mom once more. "Signing this will help that cause."

But now it was Mom who hesitated, saying she would most likely sign it but that she'd like a day or two to read the document over. Mr. Porter didn't appear happy with the idea, though he didn't try to dissuade her. He replaced the fountain pen in his pocket. "Please just bear in mind that the sooner we get the paperwork processed, the sooner you'll begin collecting the pension." Porter reminded TK of the salesman who sometimes came around the neighborhood, selling all kinds of things out of the trunk of his old Chrysler: shoes and kitchenware and cheap novelties ("for the kiddos," he liked to say). He tended to show up when the men were at work, as if he knew the women were an easier sell. At times, though, when he had shown his wares and there didn't seem to be anything that Mom wanted and she said so, he would adopt a wheedling tone, and although he never came right out and *begged* her to buy something, he did look pained. Mr. P. Albert Porter seemed to wear that look now. "We'd hoped to get the pension settled before the Veterans Day holiday," he said. "Mr. Knowles was in the Navy, I note."

"He was in the South Pacific, on a cruiser."

Porter nodded, as if this were an interesting detail. Mom was resolute about not signing yet, and he didn't push it.

"Armistice Day," TK said as Mr. Porter picked up his hat.

"Beg pardon?"

"November eleventh. We call it Veterans Day, but it's really Armistice Day, the day World War One ended, supposed to commemorate the end of *all* wars."

"He's correct." Porter addressed himself to Mom, adult to adult. "Regrettably, we know how that naïve idea turned out."

The way most naïve ideas tended to, Tom thought, giving a final glance at the bleak abandonment of the shipyard, like the idea that the American machine could roll on forever, building ships and cars and steel, keeping men employed, holding families together. On his way back to the house, he stopped by the Atlantic Diner for a coffee and discovered Brain just finishing his lunch break. "I tried to call you," Brain said, pulling a tattered painter's cap onto his tangle of hair. "I spoke with your mom."

"What's up?"

"Got to get back to work. Swing by the old school later—where you dropped me off the other night. There's something I want to show you."

"Can't you just tell me?" Tom was aware of all he still had to attend to before his flight back to California, but Brain insisted that he really had to see it, so Tom promised he'd try to get away later.

Penny brought coffee. "Does he come here often?" Tom asked.

"Paul?" She'd always called Brain by his given name. "He's in for lunch a few times a week. We get a lot of regulars. Mary Agnes's husband, the mayor, drops in. He says this is the real town hall. Mike and Maureen come by. Or *used* to," she amended.

"Still the local fun spot, huh?"

Penny smiled. "Probably the same songs on the jukebox, too." Her hair was in a bun and she had a rosy glow from her labors, and he was struck again by how pretty she was.

"And Miss Mutterperl?" he said, glancing around for an ashtray before realizing there wasn't one. "Does she ever come in?"

"The teacher?" Penny looked quizzical. "I haven't seen her in years. Probably not since we left high school."

Tom explained how he'd seen her—or thought he had—then told of his visit with Mike.

When he got to his mother's house, there was a message to call his agent in L.A. Tom knew from the tone of Randy Wilson's voice that the news wasn't good.

"The script get shot down?" Tom asked preemptively.

"Actually, no. I haven't heard a word about that yet, so maybe that's the good news. This is something else."

Putting it off until late that afternoon, Tom dialed Tamara's number. Randy, probably not convinced it was part of an agent's job description to serve as romance counselor, had merely suggested that Tom call her. He reached her at the day spa where, between occasional modeling jobs, she worked as a receptionist. She seemed a little surprised to hear from him, but said she was glad he'd called. She wanted Tom to hear it from her that she'd been out a few times with a Russian émigré documentary filmmaker who'd recently been given a directing deal, and, well, he'd offered her some acting work, and they'd become involved romantically. "It isn't anything *serious*," she insisted, "but . . . you know." And he did.

"It's okay," he said after she'd explained that she wanted to give this new relationship a chance. Tamara was a comely young woman, good to have on one's arm when he attended parties; and yet had he felt anything more special for her than for any of her predecessors? The answer was no. "Good luck."

"You, too."

He drove over to the old high school building where Brain met him in back. But his former friend was in no hurry to reveal anything. Talking the whole time about what nice weather they were having and how he expected an Indian summer, Brain jingled a ring of keys, selecting one, and used it to unlock a basement door. He pushed it open, flicked a switch, and a tray of fluorescent tubes plinked on overhead, revealing a low-ceilinged space cramped by ranks of dusty typewriters, Dictaphones, hand-cranked adding machines—equipment that might have come out of a secretarial pool, circa 1960.

"Watch your head."

Brain led the way through aisles of more castoff equipment— TVs on wheeled carts, a Gestetner mimeograph duplicator, several filmstrip projectors. Everything was jacketed with dust. The basement was like a mausoleum for low technology. Tom had the feeling that if you dug deep enough you'd find hornbooks and desks with inkwells.

"Here we are." Brain was jingling keys again, opening an inner door. He led Tom to a corner and switched on a vintage lava lamp.

On a long workbench fashioned from several old wooden doors sat an array of laser projectors, tape machines, and video monitors. It was the gear Brain had used at the reunion. "This stuff isn't cast-off," Tom said.

"Better believe it isn't. This is five grand worth of goodies."

Brain turned on one of the computers and busied himself at the keyboard. Looking around, Tom saw there was still a fair amount of clutter: tools and electronic components, as well as tech manuals and several desktop computers that looked as if they had been cannibalized for parts. In an odd way, the place was a latter-day version of Brain's father's home TV repair shop.

"Okay, here's what I want you to see." On a monitor, groups of their classmates appeared, as they had been last Saturday night. "It's the video Larry Blake shot."

Tom groaned; but Brain fast-forwarded through much of it (there was the deejay in his black beret inviting Russ Rigden to hum the *Bonanza* theme song, in reply to some now forgotten trivia question). The video came, at length, to the old black-and-white film projections on the wall of the VFW hall, and Brain returned the tape to normal speed. Tom had the sense, as he'd had on the night of the reunion, of looking through a small window, watching the past roll by. The distinctive, raunchy strains of "The Stroll" began and teenage couples formed their lines.

Once the holograms had taken form, like everyone else at the reunion, Larry Blake gave them his full attention, capturing the scene as it had occurred, minute by minute. There went Dee Richards and Mary Agnes Blanchard (now Kinney) and Dennis Daley, along with the images of people who existed only in their past form—Ray Sevigny, for one, KIA in the Mekong Delta in 1966. And there stood Tom Knowles, forty-eight, inveterate skeptic, last to move forward to approach himself at seventeen—shy TK, who, finally, with the air of someone screwing his courage to the sticking point, began walking toward the cluster of wallflowers on the opposite side of the gym, going to one girl in the group, saying something to her. Whatever he said (obviously it was brief), the girl responded, and he led her onto the busy dance floor, and now, in this basement workshop, Tom bent close, full of curiosity. "Who is she?" he asked. "Do you know?"

Brain said nothing. On the sound track there was the rumble of thunder. The video continued, and soon there was the sequence of events that had ended the show: a gust of wind, the door flying open, a scattering of cups and napkins; then Brain, in a panic, slipping and going down . . . and then the moment when electricity surged into Tom. With a grunt, Brain rewound the tape and started it again.

"What're you doing?"

No answer. Brain's focus had become total, and Tom, realizing it was useless to persist, shut up and watched. Inside the cone of glass of the lava lamp, a deformed lump of wax glowed with green iridescence like an alien homunculus. He had begun to feel strangely vulnerable, the way he imagined that boy there on the screen must've been feeling, leading a girl to the dance floor—not with a sense of macho triumph, no, he would've been frightened, wondering: *Am I up to this?* He was no dancer.

As the video reached the part where the thunder began ominously to rumble, Brain slowed the projection to a frame-by-frame advance. Perhaps sensing Tom stirring beside him, Brain stilled him with a "Shh." Then, on the sound track, a boom of thunder. *"There!"* The word hissed through Brain's teeth. "Did you catch it?"

Catch what? All Tom saw was a blur.

Brain rewound the tape and again played the last of the preceding sequence: the people as they had been Saturday night, approaching their holographic images. At the thunder crash, as the lights flickered, Tom's teenage image seemed to intensify while the image of him at the reunion simultaneously dimmed.

"Is that what you're talking about? That brightening and fading?"

"When I watched this earlier today, I didn't catch it at first."

"It's just a trick of light. Right?"

"Is it?"

"You were there, Brain. Did you see that actually occur?"

"No, though at the moment, I think every eye went straight to you. Larry Blake's did, obviously."

"Sure, and the camcorder caused what we're seeing here—because of the electrical storm."

"The result of the power sag," said Brain.

"What else? It's not anything that was actually going down there."

"Uh huh." Brain was nodding. "That's what I figured, too. At first. But listen. Hear the music? The Platters, 1959, 'Smoke Gets in Your Eyes.' It's not affected."

And it wasn't. The song continued to play without a break.

In the corner of the workshop the lava lamp had warmed up, and the blob of wax shape-shifted in slow silence, like a misshapen moon. "So . . ." Tom let out a breath, "if it wasn't a power sag, what *was* it?"

"Try this. What we see is what was actually going down?"

It was Tom's turn to be puzzled. Brain froze the frame. "Suppose the jolt of electricity activated something in your *brain*, and what we're seeing is the actual charging of one image and the simultaneous *dis*charging of the other?"

"That's a reach, even for you."

"Hang on—"

"You hang on, Brain. For your information, that 'image' standing there is *me*. Okay? It's this one here"—Tom touched the hologram on the monitor—"that's the image. Younger, quicker, hornier, to be sure—but still an image." His voice had risen, and he realized all at once that this was scaring him, this talk of his mind being affected. "So how about earlier, when I went outside for a smoke—there was a cop out there, a security guard, smoking a cigar—maybe he busted me."

"My idea is wiggy," Brain admitted. "I know."

"Maybe aliens took me, put in surgical implants. Or how about—?" He shut up. *How about something growing inside of me*, was what he'd been about to say, thinking all at once of his father's cancer. "Definitely a trick of light," he said finally.

"Caused by the power sag, when the lightning struck. Okay," Brain said agreeably, and shut off the video deck. "I'll buy it."

"Good. Now, I'm leaving."

"*If*," Brain qualified, forefinger raised, "you can offer an explanation for one other thing."

"Well?"

"Larry Blake's camcorder was on battery mode. It wasn't plugged in."

13 TK

"You want to hire a lawyer?" Mom blurted. "And sue Keystone Steel?"

TK didn't know a thing about lawyers beyond what he'd seen on *Perry Mason*, and he guessed that was mostly made-up. Still, hiring one was his idea. Mom was flatly opposed, wanting to sign the paperwork that Mr. Porter had brought and get it turned in. "We don't have money to be wasting on any lawyer—and that's what it'd be!" she insisted. "*Wasting.* They use lawyer math—'two-thirds for me, one-third for you.' Win or lose, it's the same." But TK produced the money for a retainer, one hundred dollars in cash. She looked at the bills in his hand. "Did you withdraw that from your savings?"

He hesitated on the brink of a lie, then told the truth. "Mr. Yarrow gave it to me."

She frowned suspiciously. "Why would he do that?"

"It's an advance. I'm going to work for it."

She argued against his taking money and insisted they'd be "poking at a hornet's nest," but TK held firm and finally she gave in. An acquaintance had recommended Newt Cromwell. He didn't look like Raymond Burr. He was a bony man with a high forehead and watery brown eyes, which he fixed first on Mom and then on TK as he got them seated in maroon leather chairs, a decorative theme that seemed repeated in the shelf of weighty-looking law books that lined one wall of his office. He sat with his fingers tented under his chin, listening as Mom explained why they were there.

"Let me see if I have this straight," he said, smiling uncertainly. "You want to bring suit against Keystone Steel so as to learn more about your husband's death."

"That's right."

"Weren't the medical records made available to you, Mrs. Knowles?"

"Well . . . yes."

"But the doctor was the company's doctor," TK spoke up.

"Doctors are doctors." Cromwell went on addressing Mom. "They've no reason not to be completely candid. Did you request a second opinion when your husband was ill?"

"No," she said softly.

"Did your husband voice concern about the competence of the physicians, or the rationale behind his treatment?"

"No."

"Did anyone else mention a problem?"

She shook her head.

"Well . . . I honestly don't believe there's merit to initiating legal proceedings. In my opinion I think you'd be wasting your time and money, not to mention stirring up what I'm sure are painful memories. It just doesn't—"

"Sir, are you saying we can't do it?" TK slid forward in the leather chair.

"No. You can, of course. You've a right. I wouldn't recommend it, that's all."

Mom took this quietly. "I see. Well, perhaps you're right then."

"I still think we should," TK said.

This time, the attorney addressed him. "Son, you understand that in taking on Keystone Steel you'd have the added matter of dealing with the federal government."

"What's the government got to do with it?" Mom asked. A new look of uncertainty crossed her face.

Newt Cromwell smiled patiently. "Who do you think orders those ships? Keystone Steel is the contractor, but they work for the U.S. Navy. Name Keystone as a defendant in litigation, and you've pretty much got Uncle Sam, too."

TK hadn't connected the two before, but it made sense—as did something else now, too. Of *course* the company reps wouldn't be keen on the idea of a real Armistice Day. If wars ever did cease once and for all, who'd need all those ships? "Okay, then," he said, "we'll sue both."

The lawyer chuckled. "That's what I was getting at. You can't."

"Come along, Thomas," his mother said, rising.

TK stayed in his chair. Sunlight and the shadows from the moving trees outside dappled the office walls. "Why not?"

"You *can't* sue the government. Don't they teach you this stuff in school? They're *us*, for goodness' sake. We're all on the same side."

The attorney walked them to the outer door and put a bony hand on TK's shoulder. "Take my advice, son. Cherish your dad's memory, and let him rest in peace."

And let Keystone Steel rust in pieces, TK thought bitterly as they went out.

14 Tom

"Everything's approved." Monica Kim gave her bright, efficient smile. "Your mother will become a resident of Elm Hill Estate on Friday."

She explained the details, breaking it all down for Tom, who had come today without his mother. Lately, any mention of the impending move and its attendant transition only raised Mom's anxiety level. When the phone rang, Monica Kim answered, listened a moment, then handed the receiver to Tom.

"I know your time is short," Mike Burke said, "so I figured I'd better get to it."

"Get to what? How'd you know where to find me?"

"Your mother told me."

Which begged the question: how did *she* know. But, of course, she would. "Well?"

"You still into what we talked about, guy?"

"What we talked about . . . We talked about a lot of things."

"If so, cruise by *mi casa* when you get done paying your thirty pieces of silver."

"What's that supposed to mean?"

But Mike Burke had hung up.

"It occurred to me you might want to take a stroll down memory lane." Mike Burke was driving, one hand on the wheel, his beefy left arm cocked in the open window of the truck. There was a bottle of beer between his legs; the six-pack it had come from sat on the floor at Tom's feet. "I know a way past the gate. Sure you don't want a pop?"

Tom hadn't brought up the Judas reference, and now he had an urge to say let's forget the whole thing. He had lots to do. And what was the point in any of this, really? Yet for reasons he wasn't clear about (though he sensed they were somehow linked to having seen, or *thought* he'd seen, Audrey Mutterperl) he *was* curious to see the shipyard.

The sky, which had been clear earlier, was beginning to clump with gray clouds by the time Mike unlocked a gate in the chain-link fence that surrounded the vast abandoned property that had been the Keystone Steel shipbuilding facility. Mike admitted that he'd previously cut away the existing lock and replaced it with his own. He refastened the gate behind them. The broken asphalt had gone to weeds, which brushed at their pants legs and hid the tracks of rusting railroad spurs that threatened to snag Mike's cane and send him sprawling. As it was, he walked with a limp and twice had to stop to catch his breath. The third time he stopped he pointed with the cane at a long, two-story brick building. It stood out among the surrounding structures, which were also brick, but whose large windows—mostly broken now, boarded up—said those places had been craft shops, where shipbuilders had worked their special trades. The building Mike indicated had smaller windows, most still intact, and had the look of a place that had housed offices.

"That was the admin center. I got in there, too, found some old papers and stuff the company left behind when they decamped, but anything important was long gone."

Mike propped the cane before him and leaned on it with both hands. "Can you dig it? This place was once like a world unto itself. With its own citizens and a railroad and round-the-clock action."

"And some dark secrets."

"You're thinking like a cop," Mike said approvingly. "Though I guess that's how writers think, too, huh? Ideas just flow."

"Yeah. Like water from a cleft rock. Actually, I'm just picking up on your vibe."

"Like I said before, I got this notion that when this place closed, it took secrets with it." But, as before, he didn't elaborate on what those secrets might have been.

15 TK

On a golden Tuesday in mid-October, TK skipped school to dig a late-morning tide. He knew that the good weather would not last, that November would come, with December crowding close and cold behind it, and the mud would start to freeze and that would put crimps on the digging and slow the cash flow. He should be looking for another part-time job to get him through the winter and to help at home with money. Mr. Porter from the shipyard had been right about health insurance continuing, but the payments from Dad's pension had yet to begin. TK also should be thinking about applying to college, as he'd told Blinky Keenan he would. Today, however, these thoughts were nothing more than whispers at the edges of his mind.

There was a sense of wonder being out here on the lap of the sea, this self-contained clam digger's world, which had a balance as carefully calibrated as a farmer's. Knowing which shellfish to take was important, being sure to leave the small ones that were the seeds for future crops. There was a quality of mystery here as well, of never knowing exactly what might come up in the next forkful of mud you turned. Clams, you hoped, of course, but there were also burrowing sandworms that but for the thick rubber gloves a digger wore could bite and draw blood, and scary-looking spider crabs, harmless enough, but they never failed to send a chill along TK's spine. There were *strange* things, too. One day, TK had taken hold of an odd grub-white worm, fleshy feeling, even through the gloves, and big around as a carpenter's pencil, and he had pulled it squirming from the mud, close to six feet of it, and tossed it down, frightened somehow. It had still been wriggling as it vanished down a seagull's throat.

He sometimes thought of the tidal flats when he began a column for the *Echo*: the notion that everything lay there below the surface and his task was to uncover it and draw it out, the good with the bad, the usual with the odd. And it was the latter that he found himself thinking of now, here alone on the flats: the dreams that had come more and more often lately. And the shipyard sounds. And what about the penchant he seemed to have for coining new words and expressions . . . words and phrases that somehow *seemed* familiar, yet no one claimed to have heard before.

So absorbed was he in these thoughts, he didn't realize he wasn't alone until he glanced up and saw a car drawn in next to the Rambler, partly hidden by it. A man was coming down the slope of beach toward him. The angle of sun was such that TK made out only a silhouette, and his first thought was that it was the shellfish warden, come to check his permit. Technically there was supposed to be a master digger on site, too, though the rule wasn't strictly enforced. The five-gallon bucket TK used to hold the clams was heaped, so he lifted it and started up the beach to where he had his burlap sacks, three of them already full, with still another hour of digging before the tide came.

As TK neared he saw that the man was holding a nightstick, which he was slapping casually into the palm of his other hand. *Whap.* And then he recognized the truant officer. His felt a little barb of fear. "Cut classes today, huh?" said Frank Ripley.

TK set the bucket down. "My mother gave me permission," he said, his voice hoarse with the lie. Mom paid little attention to what TK did anymore; and yet he thought it likely she'd vouch for him, if it came to that. "I'm caught up on my schoolwork." And that was a lie, too. The drum of his heart kicked up a few beats.

Officer Ripley went on whapping the stick into his palm with the same slow rhythm. He looked at the clams. " 'Yessir, yessir, three bags full.' You've done good this morning."

TK didn't know what to say to that. He fought back a rising sense of alarm.

"You'll earn some money."

"I'm pretty much done. I could . . . still make it back for afternoon classes."

"Money from the Clam Man, huh?" Ripley went on, riding his own train of thought. "What's he pay you?"

"Fi . . ."—TK's voice wanted to squeak—"five dollars a rack."

"And he sells 'em for what?" *Whap.*

TK had no idea. "It's a fair price."

"Is it?" *Whap . . . whap . . .*

TK's heart beat harder, a painful throb he could feel against his ribs. He was afraid of the truant officer. He knew the stories about him, about how Ripley would rough up kids, gut-spear them with his nightstick, threaten them with worse if they told anyone. "He's got to get the clams chlorinated," TK went on, feeling some impulse to explain. "And then deal with restaurants."

The truant officer tipped his head back in a silent laugh. "If there's a buck to be made, you can be sure there's a kike in the middle of it."

TK swallowed again. "Don't talk like that." His throat felt as if it were filled with sand.

"What? That he's a gold-grubbing Jew? It's fact." *Whap.* "Show me where there's money and you'll find kikes." *Whap.* "Not doing the work themself, but you can be damn sure they got their hooks in the dough."

TK was suddenly thinking about the note in his dad's lunch box. *Nigger's pal.* He swallowed hard at the thickness in his throat. "That's just prejudice. I'm not listening to you."

The nightstick paused, and TK thought: *I should run. I won't make much speed, what with the mud and these hip boots, and if Ripley swings that stick it won't be like trying to hit a Mike Burke curve, yet, if I don't at least try . . .*

Just then a blue Plymouth station wagon appeared, drawing into the little clearing at the top of the beach. At the sound of the tires crunching on rocks and broken shells, Ripley turned and saw it, too. TK recognized the car as belonging to one of the other diggers. He let out a breath of relief. Ripley turned back. With a final spank of the nightstick into his palm, he fitted it through a loop of his belt. "I keep files on everything," he said cryptically. Turning, he started up the beach. After a few strides he stopped and looked back. "One other thing about that Jew. He's a Communist."

On the day before Halloween, the afternoon sunlight fell in mild beams in Picknell Square, and the shop windows on the west-facing side of Bridge Street—O'Keefe's Pharmacy, DeSantis's barbershop, Jacobs' Hardware, Kresge's—glowed with it. In the window of the Weybridge Savings Bank the rays seemed to set fire to a tall glass jar filled to the top with candy corn. Beneath the jar a neatly lettered sign asked: HOW MUCH DOES THE JAR HOLD? The prize for the best guess was a $25 Savings Bond (plus the candy), and this afternoon the winner was to be announced, and maybe this accounted for the busier than usual bustle of activity in the square, TK mused. About sixty people were gathered before the podium that the Chamber of Commerce had set up.

Both Brain Mclain and Bob Crosley had submitted entries. TK had been with them the day earlier that month when Croz was first to spot the jar. "Wow!" he'd cried. "That much candy'd last me a year! There's gotta be ten thousand in there. What do you guess, Brain?"

Brain gave a dismissive little spurt of breath. "I wouldn't guess."

"What, you don't want to try for the prize?"

"The Savings Bond would be nice. But I'm not going to guess."

"Then how else you gonna win? If you don't guess, you don't get a shot."

"First off," said Brain with exaggerated patience, "a guess has no basis in reality. Ten thousand? You pulled that outta your butt."

"One thousand, then. I'm just sayin'."

"What I'd do, I'd get the dimensions of that jar, or one like it. Then I'd figure out the volume in cubic inches. Next I'd determine how many candy corns fit in one cubic inch. I'd do the math, and I'd have a reasonable estimate, not a wild guess."

Croz was frowning. "Too much work. I'm gonna say one thousand."

"How about a little bet," TK proposed, "to make it interesting. You guess, Croz; Brain, you calculate."

"Ah, mathematics versus ignorance," said Brain.

"Count this, Brain." Croz showed his middle finger.

"Is that your I.Q. or your sperm count?"

"Why don't you both bid," TK went on, "and we show up when they announce the number and see who's closer? Loser buys ice cream."

"What about you?"

"I'm the witness, and that entitles me to ice cream either way."

That's what they agreed to do. Now the day had come for the winner to be announced. In the crowd, TK spotted Penny with Mary Agnes Blanchard moving through the throng of people on the sidewalk. Penny was wearing her new glasses, the round wire frames that TK had helped her pick out. They made her look more mature and pretty in a kind of intellectual way, he decided. Especially since she was carrying her book bag, obviously having come straight from school. He waited for the girls.

"Hi," Penny said.

"Don't tell me," TK said, "you two put in a number."

"She didn't," Mary Agnes said at once, "*I* did." Penny smiled; she looked happy to see him. She had on the green cardigan sweater with white reindeer on the front, and a matching green ribbon in her hair. "I didn't even know about that till Mary Agnes mentioned it. No. I came to see—"

"I multiplied my age by thirty-one," Mary Agnes explained, "the day of Halloween, and got five hundred and twenty-seven."

"Not very scientific," Croz sniffed. "I said one thousand even. It's a big jar."

"You weren't in school today," Penny said to TK.

"I went over to the Sears, Roebuck catalogue store to apply for a job. They're hiring part-time help for the holidays."

"You missed a vocab quiz," said Mary Agnes. "And Longchamp doesn't give makeups. Though maybe if *you* ask him . . ."

"Why would he change his system for me?"

She clicked her tongue. "Longchamp is a fairy. You didn't know that? Why do you think he wears those silly ascots? That's a signal to let other queers know."

"Know what?" Croz asked.

"That they're queer."

"Seriously? Is that true?"

"It's common knowledge. And I think Miss Mutterperl's probably a dyke." TK sent a sharp glance at Mary Agnes, who shrugged.

"Anyway, it's no big deal. When you think of it, most English teachers are a little light in the loafers."

Penny rolled her eyes and came around to where TK stood, and they fell into step, heading toward the little platform that had been set up on the sidewalk in front of the bank. Mary Agnes joined some other kids. "I found out she was coming over and I hooked a ride," Penny confided. "I really came to see Kennedy."

TK stopped in his tracks. "Kennedy?"

Penny looked as surprised as he was. "You don't know?"

Was this another joke? Was President Kennedy a queer, too?

"Remember when you said no one's ever seen a real politician?"

He felt chagrined. He well remembered his rant. He was sorry she did.

Penny dug in her book bag and drew out a copy of that day's Adams Point *Eagle* and unfolded it for him to see a front-page storyline: KENNEDY TO VISIT.

The president was coming? Why hadn't he heard about it? Then he read closer. It was *Edward* Kennedy—Ted—the youngest of the brothers, who had been elected to the U.S. Senate last November. He was visiting with voters in his home state this week, including a stop today in Weybridge. That explained why things were busier than usual.

They joined the crowd in front of the bank, and from the makeshift reviewing stand the bank president, a man with silver hair and a pink face, announced the contest results. "The actual number of candy corns in the jar is seven hundred and thirty-six."

Mary Agnes bobbed with excitement. "I'm close . . . I'm close," she whispered.

Croz began counting on his fingers.

"The winner," the bank president resumed, "with a guess of seven hundred and sixty is . . . *Paul Mclain*! Congratulations, Paul. If you're here, come claim your prize."

To applause (and a slug on the arm from Croz), Brain went up and was presented with a U.S. Savings Bond, along with a big bag of

Halloween candy. He passed the candy around and invited people to help themselves. TK dug a handful, too, but before he could eat any, Penny announced that Senator Kennedy had arrived. Sure enough, there he was getting out of a shiny blue Buick that had drawn to the curb. Kennedy climbed out of the passenger side, brushing at his thatch of brown hair and smiling the familiar toothy Kennedy smile. Shaking hands with well-wishers, he moved through the crowd toward the platform. "Let's get closer," Penny said.

TK tried to keep up, sidestepping through the crush of people, gently pushing, but there were more people here than he'd imagined, all eager to see Kennedy, and now TK found himself hemmed in. He could just see Penny through the bobbing heads and waving arms. Then, all at once, he felt himself growing queasy. His skin was clammy and he was light-headed. "Penny," he called.

She had already reached the front of the crowd, yet somehow she either heard him or chose that moment to look back. His legs were rubbery and he had a sudden panicked thought that he might collapse. Without hesitating, Penny turned, reaching toward him, and took his hand. She drew him the last few feet forward and he was beside her. At just that moment the senator passed where they stood. Kennedy shook Penny's hand, then reached for TK's. TK buckled with a sharp cramp. He swung abruptly away, bumped through the press of people, and broke free. He lurched toward the alley between the bank and Kresge's, and got there just in time to hurl his lunch into a patch of sumac.

After, he leaned against a brick wall, recovering. Must've been the candy. Yet . . . He felt in his pocket; the candy was there. He hadn't eaten a single piece.

He was in a corridor, running hard. Whatever was back there was moving this way, coming *fast*. He could hear it, some kind of clawed feet clicking on the tiled floor, scrabbling as it skidded around corners. He took one more turn, skidding himself, lunged ahead, and saw to his shock that the corridor ended. There was a wall there, and in the wall was a closed door. He slid to a stop, his ragged breath seeming to catch up to him.

He approached the door. And then he saw the hands.

Two of them this time, like paws, pressing from the other side of the metal-sheathed door. They were more insistent than they'd ever been. He froze, trying to keep as motionless and quiet as he could—maybe whatever was back there pursuing him wouldn't find this stretch of corridor. Even so, the tiny thread of a whimper escaped his lips. The pressure on the other side of the door grew, the outline of the hands actually visible in the metal. With heroic effort—

TK pushed up from his bed, cutting off the next part of the dream. His breath was coming in gulps. The bedside clock hands stood at 1:17 a.m. He drew off the tangle of bedclothes and stood. Weak-kneed, he moved in a crouch to the window and looked out.

Eerily moonlit, a coastal fog had cat-footed in, silent and fey, cutting off all sound and any view of even the closest features in the yard, so that he had the perception, improbable as it seemed, that the apple trees, the rail fence with the shrubs, the flagstone walk—all those familiar landmarks—did not exist. He had a tingling sense of certainty that just beyond the screen of fog lay something else, something decidedly dangerous.

For a moment he crouched, frozen with an icy sense of terror. Then he spooked. He dove back to his bed and flailed in the dark for the decoy lamp. With light, reason returned. When he felt calm, he padded to the window again. The fog was gone. Moonlight bathed the lawn. Edgewater Road was empty save for Mr. Shannihan's Edsel parked under a maple tree, from which, as TK looked, a single yellow leaf let go and wee-wawed silently to the ground.

Barefoot, wearing only pajama bottoms, he went down the hall, past his parents' bedroom (where his mother slept alone now; though some nights she fell asleep on the davenport downstairs, where he might find her after midnight, TV screen alight with the test pattern that signaled the end of the programming day). He used the bathroom and got a drink of water. His face in the mirror looked blurred. Back in his room, he glanced at his desk. Still in the platen of the Olivetti was the Curb Feelers column he had started that evening before going to bed.

Taking Pop Sterns's vague cue, TK had decided to write about something uncontroversial. Centered at the top of the page, he had typed PRESIDENT KENNEDY, then had gone on for a couple of paragraphs about the man's Boston birth and some rewarmed hash about PT-109; and then he had stalled. What was there to say about the president that hadn't already been said a hundredfold, said much better than *he* was able to? He was surprised therefore to see, after several blank spaces, more words: JKF IS AT RISK, with a row of hyphens crossing out the last two words, and after them, replacing them, the words IN DANGER.

He stared at the line, uncomprehending.

Had he been so tired he couldn't remember having written it? What did it mean? He had no clue.

He reached to turn the roller and felt a sudden twinge at the back of his neck. He withdrew his hand and sat on the edge of the bed. The pain held on. He'd dug a late-afternoon tide; had he lifted something the wrong way? He gripped the sore spot and squeezed, kneading the muscles. When the ache began to lessen, he looked at the sheet of paper again. JFK IS AT RISK . . . IN DANGER. He drew it out of the roller, crumpled it, and tossed in the wastebasket. Turning off the light, he lay down.

He switched on the little transistor radio on the nightstand. He didn't bother to put the earpiece in, but he kept the volume low, not wanting to disturb his mother—not that it would anyway; the pills that Dr. McGowan had given her knocked her out.

Too late for Woo-Woo Ginsburg and the *Night Train* show. TK thumbed the tuning wheel past WMEX, WBZ, and WEZE, past stringy arrangements of Percy Faith's Orchestra and André Kostelanetz, and picked up a fragment of music that stopped him. He thumbed back, fine-tuning.

"... *saw her yesterday-yay* ..." The signal was weak, so he brought the radio nearer, excited by the guitars and the driving drumbeat. He'd never heard the song before, but he was spellbound. He shut his eyes, the better to focus on the music: "She Loves You." The image of extended, groping hands and whatever else had caused his panic was gone, and he felt the last trace of tension draining from his body, found himself drifting down into the music and sleep.

16 Tom

"I've got a possible explanation," said Brain.

Tom looked at him doubtfully. They were sitting on stools at the counter at the Atlantic Diner. "That makes one of us."

"That night at the reunion—um ... how do I say this? Well ... I think you might've become involved in another dimension."

"Involved in another dimension. Uh huh. I should've known."

Brain was wearing baggy jeans and his lime green Chuck Taylors. He spun a quarter circle on his stool to face Tom. "I'm serious."

Another of Brain's cracked ideas, what they used to call "Brain Storms" when they were kids. Tom stifled a laugh but did give a small grin. Brain took on a forgive-them-they-know-not-what-they-do expression, and Tom's grin subsided.

"It would explain some things," Brain went on, using his fingers to tally what those things might be. "For instance, the fact that you don't remember anything from the brief time you were unconscious. The physical changes, like the tingling sensations, or why you don't need reading glasses all of a sudden. And that running catch that I heard about from at least five people who were at the softball game. And," he added, "it could account for the dreams. You said yourself that they started after that night."

"And you offered a perfectly plausible explanation."

"That your coming back to Weybridge is stirring up old memories. Sure, and as a general rule it's wise always to go with the simplest explanation. Occam's razor. And I would go with that, *except* for what I showed you on the film shot at the reunion, which wasn't linked to any power sag—*and*, I believe it is possible."

"What? That I was sucked into some kind of time warp?"

"Another dimension, I said. Not the same thing. It's as if you'd reached escape velocity to some other space-time, and now there's a past and a present bumping up against each other."

"That's it? That's your explanation?"

"In a nutshell."

"Spin on this, pal." Tom flipped him a bird.

"Craziness, right?"

"Lunacy."

"Okay," Brain admitted. "But it might be explicable in terms of physics."

"Don't tell me. Your old MIT mind game—string theory."

"Voilà."

"Very cool. And you've already covered your ass. You said no one knows squat about it. So I'm stuck, huh? Trapped in the ozone?" And this time Tom wasn't able to restrain a laugh.

Then Brain laughed, too. "I believe I said *almost* no one."

17 TK

TK's name being called over the P.A. system was becoming a more frequent event as fall term moved into November. He wasn't like some kids, who seemed to get called daily for violation of school rules: perennial detention rats like Steve Allison, Craig McDonald, Kenny Nicholas, and the notorious Butch Tracy (though Tracy was gone now, quit, TK had heard; good riddance). Still, he found himself having to report to the office more often these days. This morning it had been a question about an excuse note he'd brought for missing school the day he'd gone to Sears to put in an application for seasonal work. It was true; the note was a forgery, though not because his mother hadn't agreed to write one. It was just that she had not been awake yet when he set off for school the next day. He'd considered telling Sterns this but worried that it would raise questions about Mom and things at home since Dad's death (questions that Miss Mutterperl and Blinky Keenan had already raised but fortunately hadn't pressed). So he admitted the note was a fake and took detention.

But now he decided he might as well get something for his trouble. He stopped in a shadowy stretch of hall and used a pencil to change the time on the hall pass from 10:05 to 10:15. Now he had permission to be out of class for ten more minutes. As he passed a window he happened to glance outside and saw the truant officer driving away. Ripley had been turning up in odd places lately, and this set TK to wondering. Had the man been here for the purpose of checking on *him*? It was possible, though there were other explanations, of course—TK was hardly the only truant in school, and certainly not a chronic one at that; yet . . .

Looking around to be sure he wasn't seen, he cut down a cross corridor. The chem lab was on the second floor. Mr. Morrisette, one of the instructors, had made Brain a lab assistant, which meant setting up the laboratory for the day's lessons, laying out whatever equipment was needed, and cleaning up afterward. The job also gave Brain access to a locked closet where supplies were kept, and sometimes he took advantage of this. Like the time he'd ignited a strip of magnesium. The metal flared, making the lenses of his glasses gleam with white light, and he'd basked in the attention from the group of girls who'd clustered around him for the spectacle; but it was short-lived, and when the bell rang they gathered their books and hurried off. "I don't know why they bother to carry books," Brain remarked soberly in their wake. "They spend more time on a trip to the girls' room to apply lipstick than they spend all year studying."

Brain was alone in the laboratory now, fitting rubber hoses onto the jets of Bunsen burners. He looked up as TK appeared.

"What're you doing here? Aren't you supposed to be in class?" Then, something dawning: "I heard your name called—you didn't get . . ."

"Bounced?" TK shook his head. "It was a misunderstanding. Listen . . ." he spoke in a lowered voice, "what're you doing to-night?"

"I've got rocket club after school . . ."

And I have a date with Room 309, thought TK. "Later, though. You still have Wilhelm Reich?"

"Wil—?" Brain's eyes widened with surprise. "My *bicycle*?"

"I've got a mission for us."

When TK got home after detention there was a message that Sears, Roebuck had called and wanted him to come for an interview. He called back to confirm, then drove over to the catalogue store in Weybridge Landing. The sales manager was on the floor working a middle-aged couple who were looking at freezers. TK wandered around the store, which consisted mainly of the big showroom with its array of kitchen and laundry appliances and home electronics. He lingered in the area where a dozen or more TV sets were on, each tuned to *The Price Is Right*, where Bill Cullen was joshing with Don Pardo. TK watched a few minutes of the show, absently comparing the quality of the various black and white images, though his mind was on trying to guess what questions he might be asked in a job interview, and what he might say in response. Finally, the sales manager came over.

"Knowles, right?"

TK came to attention. "Yes, sir."

"Al Lake."

They shook hands. Mr. Lake had thinning blond hair and wore a white short-sleeve shirt, brown slacks, and a black clip-on tie. He couldn't have been much past thirty-five, but a potbelly gave him a swayback posture. His most prominent feature, however, the thing that got TK's attention, was a parade of big white teeth. TK could almost *hear* him smile. "C'mon in back," he said.

He led TK through a door into an area with a concrete floor. The space overhead was just unfinished structural girders and electrical wiring. "This is the nerve center," Al Lake said, moving to a corner desk cluttered with paper. TK's eyes went to a wall calendar for a trucking company, the November picture showing a chestnut-haired woman holding out a cornucopia that just concealed her large bare breasts. The caption read: "Won't you share our bounty?"

Al Lake picked up a clipboard, clamped to which was the application TK had filled out a few weeks ago. Lake gave it brief attention. "Between now and Christmas," he said, "it gets *busy* around here. You dig? I'm talking nucking futz."

TK blinked. "Yes, sir."

"I'm looking to put on a few good workers." The grin was probably standard equipment for a salesman, TK thought, though it seemed a bit facetious. "You're on your feet. There's lifting involved, picking items from the shelves in there, packing orders, loading, unloading trucks. Some of the merchandise is small, but there's big-ticket stuff—refrigerators, stereos. You look physically fit, but tell me, why should I hire you?"

Why? *Because clamming is about ready to die for the winter and money's going to dry up like a keg at a house party.* "I'm reliable, sir."

"Big deal. Everyone says that."

"I mean it."

"I'll be straight with you. I've had bum luck with high school kids. They talk a good game, but something comes up, they call in sick with more headaches than my wife."

TK didn't know how to respond. He'd never had a job interview before. With clam digging you applied for a permit and just went and did it, showing up day after day, proving yourself on the flats. If you didn't get the clams, you gave up. Here was the sales manager at Sears telling him he probably wasn't going to get the job, and TK didn't have a response. Lake glanced at his watch, then crossed his arms, like a TV lawyer resting his case. Out of nowhere TK thought of something that Miss Mutterperl told the *Echo* staff—told it often enough that it had finally made sense to him.

"I can do the job, Mr. Lake," he said, keeping his voice firm, "and if you give me the chance, I will. I get my teeth into something, I don't let go. I won't call in sick, and I won't punch in late. But I know the work is seasonal, and you probably don't want to wait to find out if that's true, so rather than me just telling you that, I'll *show* you."

Lake uncrossed his arms. "Yeah? How?"

"If I don't prove my worth to you the very first day, you can fire me and Sears won't owe me a dime."

When Mom asked him how the job interview went, TK told her he was going to start working Monday after school.

At 7:20 that evening TK was at the town library, a notebook open on the large mahogany table before him. He opened volume 8 of the *World Book Encyclopedia* and found an entry titled "John Birch Society," which he read with interest and began jotting in his notebook.

"Hi, TK."

He looked up and saw Mary Agnes Blanchard, who worked part-time as a library aide, shelving books. "What're you writing?"

"Just . . . stuff." Trying to be casual about it, he moved his hand to cover the page.

Giving up, she indicated the stack of books. "Finished with these?"

"I'll put them back."

"I don't mind. It's my job."

Brain arrived five minutes later and slid into the seat across the table, red-faced and out of breath.

"I had to patch a flat tire on Wilhelm. It's been ages since I rode it."

"Were you able to get what I asked you about?" TK asked.

He motioned outside with his head. "In my basket. What're you doing? Homework?"

TK slid over a pamphlet he'd taken from DeSantis's barbershop, like the one his father had torn up. This was titled: THE ENEMY ARE AMONG US and asked: DO YOU KNOW WHERE? It was about Communists who lived undercover while holding prominent positions in the news media, college classrooms, Hollywood, and even the government. TK leaned across the table and lowered his voice in case Mary Agnes was lurking in one of the nearby aisles. "I'm pretty sure Officer Ripley is a member."

"The truant officer is a *commie*?" Brain looked dumbstruck.

"A member of the John Birch Society. What do you know about them?"

"Not much. My mom and I ran into a lady outside Stop & Shop who was ranting about 'Impeach Earl Warren' and the 'Red Menace,' saying how we were nuts not to bomb Russia before they bombed us. She was a member." Brain frowned. "You sure about Ripley?"

"He may not be as extreme as the lady you saw, but he leaves these things around. I'm just connecting dots."

Brain gave the pamphlet a sour glance but left it alone. "So what's this mission?" He, too, spoke quietly, though most likely because of where they were; to Brain libraries were sacred places.

"To uncover Ripley's secret life."

"*Us* investigate *him*? Are you crazy?"

"I knew you'd want in."

"Like fun. The guy's a frickin' cop."

"Truant officer," TK pointed out.

"Even worse. He could get us in bad trouble."

"I thought we'd spin over to where he lives. On bikes we'll be invisible."

Brain was staring in disbelief. "Walk up to his door and talk to him. Sure."

"He won't be home; I already checked. He's working a PTA meeting." In addition to being the town's truant officer, Frank Ripley was an auxiliary cop, and tonight he was detailed to the Athens elementary school for traffic duty.

"What about his wife? His kids?"

"I checked that, too. He's not married."

"So if no one's home . . . ?"

"We poke around, see what we can find."

" 'We,' right. And what're you gonna do if we find he's dirty? Write an exposé in the *Echo*? With interviews from guys he's poked in the nuts with his nightstick?"

"Uh uh, this is pure curiosity."

"Well, I'm not that curious. Not about him, anyway. Thanks just the same."

"All right. I just thought you'd like to know what's going on in town."

"Forget it. I know all I need to about this place. The one remaining fact I want to know is that I'm *gone*. And that means I've got to get a scholarship—which means *grades*, buddy. I need to be *study*ing." He rose.

TK shrugged. "I'll just have to get by without you."

"The term grades are almost—" Brain broke off. "What *do* you need me for?"

"You brought along what I asked you to. What'd you think I had in mind?"

"I don't know. Why don't you tell me?"

"You were going to rocket club. I thought some air support might come in handy. In case."

"In case of what?"

"Whatever might happen. When in doubt, blow something up.

Isn't that what you rocketeers say? But it makes no difference now. I can't do it by myself."

Brain groaned and shook his head. "You're a dog turd, you know it?"

They pedaled through the town following the weak gleam of their battery-powered bike headlights, the wind cool in their hair. Before leaving home that evening, TK had found a telephone number and address for Francis Ripley in the South Shore directory. Now he drew over to a booth. He dialed the number and let it ring. No answer. He gave Brain a high sign and they rode on.

Brain was puffing to keep up when they got out on the neck, past the beach. They located the address. It was on a narrow road, a dark ranch with an attached garage and a wire fence along the front of the property. TK had anticipated a fence, but the bright lights he had envisioned weren't there. The house sat in a pocket of shadows behind shrubs. Wisely, he had brought a flashlight. He and Brain pedaled slowly past, headlights off now, turned, and came back. They dismounted and TK instructed Brain to stay off the road, behind some bushes. "You keep watch, I'll do reconnaissance."

"You don't need any firepower, then," Brain said. He sounded disappointed.

"Stay alert."

A third thing TK had anticipated was a guard dog, though so far the property was quiet. Behind the house, a stockade fence enclosed the entire backyard. Stuffing the flashlight into his jacket pocket, TK boosted himself up onto the fence. Raising first one, then the other leg carefully over the pointed pickets, he dropped onto the other side, landing on his sneakered feet on a concrete apron that surrounded a swimming pool. The pool had been drained for winter. At the back of the enclosed yard stood a thatch-roofed lanai, with stools fashioned from wharf pilings. Ripley had apparently caught the Polynesian bug, that campy fervor that had begun a few years back with people watching *Adventures in Paradise* and listening to the exotic sounds of Martin Denny on the hi-fi. The Knowleses' next door neighbors used to have folks over to stand at their out-door bamboo bar and drink mai tais and Singapore Slings while pineapple-marinated steak seared fragrantly on the hibachi, causing young TK's stomach to churn with hunger, even as neighborhood women in clingy tropical print dresses made his loins stir where he watched from his bedroom window. How many times had he over-heard the neighborhood men in their Honolulu shirts joke about getting "lei'd"? By contrast, TK's parents' idea of a big time in "poor man's paradise" (Dad's term) was Nepco franks and Zar-Ex punch and a few bottles of Haffenreffer beer. Here, though, was a pool, (a pair of life rings made ghostly O's on the back fence, one labeled HMS TITANIC and the other LUSITANIA—yuk yuk) and several large carved tiki heads with menacing faces set amid an under-growth of ferns. It had never occurred to TK that Ripley would have any friends to invite over, let alone be a fun guy; but now, see-ing this put a different face on the truant officer, made him seem halfway normal, with even a warped sense of humor.

But Ripley hadn't been funny that day in the clam cove, with his "Commie Jew" remarks and his nightstick routine. Not by a long shot. Why had he been there? How had he even known TK was digging? And the only answers TK could find were the obvious: either Ripley had spies, or he had followed him. But why? Because he'd learned that TK had taken a pamphlet from the barbershop? No, that was far-fetched. And then TK found the more probable, more disturbing explanation. As part of his job, Ripley spent time at the high school. Would he have seen issues of the *Echo*, perhaps read Curb Feelers? Had he been one of the objectors Pop Sterns was referring to in the argument with Ms. Mutterperl that Penny had overheard?

TK recalled a face he'd seen beyond the pebbled glass of Sterns's office door one day when the vice principal had braced him in the hall for being tardy . . . a blurred face, but one that, he was suddenly convinced, had been Frank Ripley's. This thought added to his apprehension at being here now; but it also gave him a reason.

His eyes had adjusted to the darkness, so he left the flashlight in his pocket. Bypassing the empty swimming pool, he went first to the lanai, which was a kind of shed and pool house, padlocked, then to the house and tried the back door. Locked.

Next he tried a window, then another. Both secure. He looked at his watch; the radium dial showed that only a couple of minutes had passed. But he couldn't just leave. Not yet. The recon was incomplete.

The third window was unlocked, but the sill was higher than he had anticipated. He tore one knee of his dungarees, skinned his elbow—and probably put scuff marks on the side of the house!—but he was in. He stood in the dimness, listening. His heart beat steadily in his chest. Nearby, the refrigerator motor hummed softly. Otherwise, the house was silent. He lit the flashlight.

He was in a dining nook adjacent to the kitchen: a small table, two chairs, a corner china cabinet—nothing that said "secret life." With careful steps, he moved deeper into the house, going from back to front, from linoleum tile to shag carpet. The image that he'd briefly formed of Frank Ripley as fun guy didn't hold up. The house was as drab as TK's own . . . drabber. Bland furnishings, cheap decor, wall prints of sad clowns. No hint of wild bachelorhood. TK's friend Croz liked to imagine that one day he'd have his own pad, with bookshelves full of *Playboy* and *MAD* magazines, a refrigerator crammed with beer, a hi-fi set with rock-and-roll playing at full volume, the door always open to friends. Croz would've considered the truant officer's place Dullsville.

TK stole along a narrow hallway past the bathroom to the bedrooms. There were two of them, one obviously Ripley's: double-size bed made, dresser top bare except for a bottle of Lectric Shave and a tube of Brylcreem. He flashed the light around, considering the closet and dresser drawers, but the idea of going through them seemed more violation than he was up to for the moment.

The other, smaller room held a twin bed with a bare mattress. Stacked under the window were several cardboard cartons and TK discovered that they held pamphlets of the kind that Ripley liked to leave at the barbershop and presumably other places as well. One of the pamphlets promoted the banning of books. He stared at it, read the same list of titles as on the JAVA petition at school. He experienced a dizzying spin, followed by a jab of anger. He shone the light around and was startled to find something else.

In the corner next to the cartons was a copy of the *Echo*. No— not just one copy, he realized as he went nearer. There were *bundles* of them, still tied in the string as when they came from the printer. There must have been a hundred copies each of the last three issues. What were they doing here? As he pondered this, a sizzle of sound from outside caught his attention. He switched off the flashlight and bent to peer out past the edge of Venetian blinds. A streak of fire climbed up into the sky. What the—?

Brain's rocket!

Damn. He'd missed it . . . a dark-colored car had pulled into the driveway. TK bolted from the bedroom. An escape plan hadn't occurred to him. He considered that he ought to go out the way he'd come in, through the dining nook window, but that would leave him still confined within the stockade fence. No, better to exit through a door; but which one? What door would whoever had just arrived be coming through? He hurried along the short hallway.

Footsteps on the porch, a key scraping at the back-door lock. Ripley.

He'd have to try the front door, but to get there he'd have to pass the dining nook, and now the back door was swinging open. A kitchen light went on. He froze. Where to go? He opened the nearest inside door and ducked into the bathroom. He hesitated, and then stepped into the tub. Quickly, as quietly as he could manage, he drew the plastic shower curtain across the opening. In the house were the sounds of a person coming in, closing the door, depositing keys on a table or counter.

TK was shaking. What was he going to do? Wait till the man came in here? Maybe he'd want to shower after his detail. At the very least, he'd use the toilet, the sink. What to do? Even if Ripley didn't find him—most unlikely!—would TK have to sweat it out here till the cop went to sleep? Then what? Trickles of perspiration rolled down his forehead and out of his armpits. His elbow, where he'd skinned it getting in, had begun to sting.

Footsteps came this way, the bathroom light went on and the door swung open. TK could see through a gap in the curtain. Reflected in the mirror, he saw Frank Ripley. The man was in his uniform. On his utility belt were a gun and his billy club. TK swallowed back his rising terror. *Should I just step out and surrender?*

And maybe get shot? Or clubbed? Oh, God, what to do? His knees were knocking together.

At that instant, a doorbell rang. Ripley mumbled a low curse and went out, leaving on the light. TK heard the front door open. He stepped out of the bathtub. His face in the mirror was gray.

From elsewhere a muffled voice said: "I'm terribly sorry, sir . . ."

Brain!

"I don't mean to bother you . . . but—"

"What is it?" Ripley demanded.

"I was launching a rocket—"

"*What?*"

"—and I think the nose cone came down in your yard."

"What the fuck are you—?"

"It's for a merit badge. Rocketry. For my Eagle Scout project." Brain was improvising. His voice was high but oddly firm. TK was in the hallway now. "We've got to stay ahead of those godless Russians, sir."

From here at the edge of the hallway, it was like listening to a radio drama—*Duke Drake, G-Man.*

"Find your nose cone, then get your tubby ass off my property, you fat shit! *What's* your name? Why aren't you at home?"

Ripley stepped out onto the front stoop, and TK didn't waste time listening for the rest. He scooted through the kitchen, bumping painfully against the edge of a chair as he went, and fled out the back door. He was waiting for Brain by their bicycles when Brain reappeared, flushed and sweating, carrying his rocket, its nose cone intact.

"Holy crow!" cried Brain. "I thought we were sincerely doomed."

"That was quick thinking. Your rocketry merit badge, huh?"

"Yes, sir! Scout's honor."

Brain was exultant and TK didn't want to spoil his mood of triumph, so he said nothing about what he had discovered inside Frank Ripley's house. They laughed as they pedaled home in the dark; but when TK remembered the stacks of the school newspaper in the truant officer's spare bedroom, their laughter had a brittle sound.

18 Tom

"This is the place?" Tom asked.

"Yep," Brain confirmed.

Tom was underwhelmed. Ahead stood a tattered-looking Brazilian storefront restaurant. Brain had said only that they were meeting his former professor, Sir Solomon Buckley, for lunch near the scientist's MIT office in Cambridge.

"And that's him." Brain pointed.

Shambling along the sidewalk, puffing a pipe, came a pudgy old man in Bermuda shorts, black rubber sandals with white sox, and a T-shirt that read ASK ME ABOUT MY GRANDKIDS. More disappointment. *This* was Brain's mentor? Winner of the Nobel Prize? Knight of the British realm? He looked two paychecks away from a homeless shelter. Brain made the introductions, Buckley giving forth with a Bronx cheer when his former student addressed him as "Sir Solomon." "Just first name, please." They shook hands, Tom still sizing up the man. What had he been expecting? An Einstein lookalike? Someone in tweeds and an argyle tie to go with the Scots burr Tom heard in his voice? The pipe, at least, fit: a big rust-colored meerschaum with the face of some kind of Indian fakir carved into it. Buckley knocked sparking ashes from the bowl, and they went into the restaurant. The tantalizing aromas belied the worn exterior. The fare was set up buffet style, and they each selected from trays of vegetables, beans, rice, sauces, and grilled meats. The food was weighed and they were given a slip to pay when they were through eating.

"So," the physicist addressed Tom with a lift of thick eyebrows over inquisitive gray eyes when they'd settled at a corner table, "you're interested in the strings."

"That's right. For a screenplay. Just enough science to satisfy the average ticket buyer." The cover story Brain had concocted and fed his old professor on the phone was that Tom was researching a science fiction film.

"Our friend here says you've had some success out there in Hollywood."

Tom wasn't about to reveal that with his last go at anything approaching sci-fi (a good enough story idea to start) he'd fought to get his writing credit removed from the final product, which after everyone on the project had insisted on putting his or her creative stamp on it had ended up a soulless crapfest. "Some," he answered simply.

They talked and ate. Buckley suggested that they begin with the notion that the universe arises from the "music of vibrating strings, membranes and blobs in multiple dimensions"—his words. His excitement was evident at once, his hands starting to flutter like eager birds. "Our known universe may be trapped on a nine-dimensional subdivision of a larger ten-dimensional universe, kept there by gravity. And that may be only the beginning. There may be other universes beyond that."

"Okay . . ." Tom said tentatively.

String theory, according to Dr. Buckley, was first supposed in the early 1970s (Buckley himself was one of the early theorists), but for the next twenty years most physicists dismissed the idea as so much theoretical navel gazing, as untestable as determining the weight of the soul. "Still . . ." Buckley went on with a wistful smile, "we were attracted to the idea because it resolved some big gaps between the macrocosm and the microcosm.

"String theory suggests that the building blocks of nature aren't particles, but rather vibrating strands of some fundamental, unknown 'stuff.' Imprecise? Yes, I know. But if it's *right*, if the theory is true, it could answer nearly every remaining question in physics. Think of it!" Buckley paused to wipe a drip of red pimento sauce from his chin.

"Of course, it calls for nothing less than an ontological earthquake! A seismic shifting of the bedrock we've built our entire epistemological paradigm on, with a resultant merging of dimensions, including time. It means letting go of what we've always perceived as solid, immutable structures." He rapped sharply on the Formica tabletop.

One evening a year or so back, Tom had listened to Stephen Hawking on PBS attempting to explain black holes. Tom stuck with it for a few minutes, already lost, but intrigued by the strange but brilliant scientist with the buzzing voice and big brain—then he'd grabbed the channel changer and switched to a Lakers game. He had the feeling now of a man who has jumped onto a fast-moving flatbed truck careening down a twisty mountain road and has to hang on or be flung off. He was clinging by his mental fingernails. Brain attempted a rescue. "An image might help Tom visualize it."

"Ah, of course. What would it look like?" Buckley mused. "Well . . . suppose we take a sheet of plastic wrap . . ." And he did, picking up the transparent film that had sealed the top of a dish of flan. "Crush it." He did. "Then let it be."

Their eyes fixed on the ball of tightly crumpled polyethylene wrap there on the table. For a moment, it just sat, as inert and shiny as a little meteorite; then, slowly, it began to expand outward with a whisper-soft crackling, losing its spherical shape.

Buckley did the play-by-play. "The potential energy I stored in it by compressing it and distorting its form is working to try to restore that form. Contained within are all sorts of little air chambers, with varying amounts of light, and separated from each other by membranes of the plastic wrap. Imagine that all of what we see around us, all that we consider to be the *world*, were happening in one of those spaces, with its own dimensions of height, width, breadth. Yet just beyond the thin walls is another space, and another, and another, and what's occurring in each of them could be identical to, similar to, or totally unlike what's occurring in ours. All those spaces, all those times . . ."

"All those stories," Tom murmured.

The old physicist was watching him. "You're a writer. Would you need new words to tell them? Expressions of time not invented yet?"

Tom found himself going from doubtful to incredulous as he felt the solid ground being pulled from beneath him. Brain was nodding jubilantly. "And suppose there's an occasional small break in a separating wall."

"It could account for some things," Buckley agreed. "Like those occasional inexplicable vanishings of people or objects that we hear of. Maybe that's what the Bermuda Triangle is about." He smiled to show that he was mostly joking about this; but he seemed open to possibilities, too. "We might posit the perception of déjà vu as being something other than how we've tended to explain it, which I've never been quite satisfied with.

"Time is a useful enough concept in its way; but we've made a god of it, forever thinking in terms of the calendar or the clock, of present, past, future, early or late, of age, life spans . . . measuring ourselves against it, until it's become a Procrustean bed. But the space-time continuum is far more nimble. If we were willing to revisit the dynamic of change, I think we could eliminate the concept of death, for instance. I'd propose we try something else, more in keeping with what we now know. 'Time is but the stream I go a-fishing in. Its sandy bottom slips away to reveal the stars . . . ' "

"*Walden,*" said Tom.

"I think old Henry's got something there."

"Speaking of which," Brain said, "I'm going to get some more chow."

As Brain went to the buffet, Buckley began extolling the virtues of the place to Tom. "If all restaurants were like this—take only what you'll eat, eat what you take, pay after, no doggie bags, Americans wouldn't be such fatties. I see that our friend there has lost weight. When I knew him last he was . . . ample."

"So, is it possible," Tom began hesitantly, "that a past and a present, that . . . separate realities . . ." He knit his fingers experimentally, fashioning his own graphic illustration.

"Let's throw in a future, too."

". . . could mingle?"

"Ah, yes, we mustn't forget the moviegoer. All right, enough of the head, let's get to the heart of this." Buckley slid his chair closer, pushing aside the remnants of their meal, clearing a little oasis on the tabletop, and planting his hands there. In a lowered voice, he said, "Pick an age, any age. A year of your life."

"Any one?'

"One you associate with interesting times."

Tom was feeling as if he had walked into the middle of a strange movie; but he couldn't leave now. Brain, who had returned, shrugged. "All right," Tom ventured. "Uh . . . seventeen."

"Seventeen," Buckley echoed. "No longer sweet sixteen, not yet the age of maturity. Very good. Now, think of one season in that year that made it interesting . . ."

A little less hesitation. "Summer."

"Now, this is crucial." Buckley raised a finger. "Think back to that summer and select one event . . . one moment that stands apart."

"Does it have to really have happened?"

"That's up to you."

Tom closed his eyes, shutting out the surrounding hubbub of

the busy little restaurant. One moment . . . Dad falling ill, Mom struggling to cope, his own getting ready for senior year . . .

"When you have it, don't tell me what it is. Just think of it."

Okay. He had it. Late summer, really. September, after classes had started, but warm still. Football practice had ended early that day, and as he was driving from the school parking lot he saw a girl waiting for a bus. Penny. This would've been several weeks after that night he'd seen her at the drive-in theater, and he hadn't seen her after that . . . but now, there she was. On an impulse he stopped and offered her a ride home. But they hadn't driven over to South Weybridge where she lived; no, the warm sunshine had got them talking about the beach.

Mostly deserted, lifeguards long gone, floats and buoy lines hauled in for the season and stored, bathhouse closed . . . a lonely quality there, a kind of melancholy, yet both admitted that this was their favorite time of the year at the beach for just that reason. They got out and set off walking.

"All right," Tom said, his eyes still shut.

"Good," said Buckley. "There's a bonny lass in the picture, what?"

"Yes."

"How'd you know that?" Brain asked.

Buckley chuckled. "I was young once, too."

Tom concentrated. He and Penny talking some, not a lot, and though this was the first they'd ever spent any time together, it was comfortable just being there in the silence. They walked the entire length of the beach, way out to the neck, a mile or more.

"Time of day?" Buckley asked.

"Late afternoon . . ." Tom said.

They beachcombed and skipped stones. They took off their shoes, and on the way back, walking more slowly now, they saw that an early moon had begun to rise . . .

"You're walking with this lassie," Buckley resumed, almost as though he were witness to Tom's thoughts. "And she's with you. I mean you're *really* together."

214

He and Penny Griffin strolled, not holding hands, no direct contact between them, and yet, in the rhythms of walking there, barefoot at the very edge of the sea, their arms would brush together every once in a while, neither trying to make it more, yet neither drawing back from that occasional touch, either.

"All the old worries—will I measure up? Does she think I'm a hopeless twit?—gone. She fancies you, you fancy her."

Was that part true? And he realized . . . yes, it was true. That was how he felt, without realizing it.

"And you know you're going to kiss her."

Had he *ever* known that back then? He didn't think so, but it sounded good.

"You pause, an arm around each other's waist, and then . . ." Buckley puckered his lips and gave a soft, zesty smack, such that Tom had the distinct idea that the man was reliving a cherished memory of his own. "All around you, time races on its merry way; but you're so now-fixed, that *your* time slows. Quite nearly stops. Ever had that perception?"

"I guess," said Tom.

"Forever after, it's there, in the synapses of the brain, as memory. Now, imagine that in the moment of that event's occurring, one reality sheared off . . ." He speared his left hand toward the wall. "Went through that little break in the membrane wall and into another space completely. *You*, meanwhile"—Buckley clamped his right hand on Tom's forearm—"went on in *this* space . . . this dimension, this reality—and here you are. But in this other reality"—he wiggled his left hand—"it's still that warm summer evening, with that young woman, who has not changed by so much as a single cell . . ."

Tom gave a nervous laugh and shot a look at Brain, who was sober faced. "But . . . that's not really possible, right? To put a knot in the string, and keep the moment there?"

Buckley let go of Tom's arm and sat back. His eyes, which had been dancing, seemed to settle. His smile faded. He didn't answer right away. Sitting there in the cool shadows, his unlit pipe at hand, his eyes half shut, he might have been Ahab, ruminating on the fate of the *Pequod* and her doomed crew. At last he said, "The human eye can see approximately six thousand stars in the night sky. Reasonable estimates are that there are a hundred billion galaxies in the universe, times a hundred billion stars per galaxy, each single star with its own potential solar system. Can anything be called impossible?"

A moment later, Buckley's watch alarm sounded. "I've got a dissertation committee meeting. You want chaos theory, try arranging six people's calendars so you can all sit face-to-face and help crank the sausage grinder to churn out yet another student with pompous-sounding initials after his name. And yet you think, maybe this one's the person who'll discover the cure for cancer."

"Or be the next Sir Solomon Buckley," said Brain.

The old man laughed. "Now *that's* impossible."

Tom insisted on paying the bill. As he signed the charge slip, he asked, "But if other dimensions do exist, where are they?"

Buckley reached for Tom's MasterCard. "May I?" He tilted the card in the beam from the recessed spotlight overhead, moving it slightly as they looked on. "What have we got?" It was the issuing company's familiar eagle logo flapping its wings in 3-D. "To the touch, this card is two-dimensional. Our senses are presenting us with that experience. Yet we can see there's a third dimension here, another experience. Both true. A crude illustration," he said, handing back Tom's card, "but perhaps enough for the moviegoer. The answer to your question is"—he moved his hand in an arc—"here."

On the sidewalk, Tom lit a cigarette and Buckley struck a match and fired his meerschaum, the tobacco smoke swirling fragrantly around them. The physicist couldn't seem to pass up an opportunity to elucidate ideas. "Do you fully understand the mechanics of an automobile?" he asked. "Yet we keep riding in them, because they work. String theory is like that. No one has actually seen the proof, but it explains all sorts of things, solves mysteries, so we use it. Remember, science itself is but a frame we've fashioned to put around this exquisite and ever-changing chaos that we call, for lack of a better term, home. But imagine a dimension where things did not change, or changed at an infinitely different rate. Another home. Reality would cease to have meaning . . . or least *our* meaning of it. And maybe we could forever kiss that lovely woman."

"I'd be hung up on forever foreplay," Brain said.

The old scientist stood motionless a moment, as though caught in that other place; then he gave a yip of laughter. "Must run. I'm late." He gripped Brain's hand. "It's wonderful to see you again, my dear old friend. Be well. And you," he said, taking Tom's hand, a glint in his eye, "when you finish that screenplay and sell it to Hollywood, should you need someone to play the crackpot scientist . . ."

"By the way, sir," Brain said, "how *are* your grandkids?"

Buckley looked flummoxed. "Grandkids? I don't ha—" Then light dawned. "Oh—this shirt. I just found it in my drawer and put it on. Perhaps it's mine in another life." He winked.

On the ride back in crossway traffic, Brain couldn't contain his enthusiasm about the visit. It *was* heady stuff, Tom had to admit; yet as they got closer to Weybridge, he found himself preoccupied with a more immediate reality. In the morning he was bringing Mom over to Elm Hill Estate to stay.

He and his mother had a quiet dinner together, and then she said she wanted to be well rested for tomorrow and went off to bed. He turned in early himself, but he didn't find sleep. So this was it, the end of something, her final night in the house. He'd stay on another couple of nights while he wrapped up the last of her affairs, and then he'd be gone from here, too. That had been the plan, after all: in, out, gone.

Riding back from MIT that afternoon, he had found himself in

217

the role of doubter. "So you think in another reality, D. B. Cooper could be in Tahiti living the life of Riley, instead of being a silk-shrouded sack of bones hanging from a Douglas fir?" he'd challenged Brain, but as he lay there now, he wondered otherwise. Had he really been asking if seventeen-year-old TK Knowles might be somewhere right now? Still in high school? Maybe living in this house, sleeping in this room?

Kissing Penny Griffin?

Crazyass nonsense. Right?

The small drum in his chest began to beat. Was it possible to tie a knot in the string? Could he keep Dad from . . . ?

He wedged that idea away.

Or to prevent Mom's . . . ?

He shut his eyes tighter, breathed to slow the thudding of his heart, and listened to the night sounds—crickets, the hushed passing of an occasional car in the street. Nothing from the shipyard; thank God for that, at least. He lay there, vague and cryptic ideas swirling in his head like the smoke from Solomon Buckley's old meerschaum. Crazyass nonsense. Right?

Eventually, he slept.

19 TK

" 'Thou still un—' How d'you say that word again?"

"Un*ravished*," Longchamp repeated patiently. Why did he bother to make these clowns recite poetry, TK wondered. They butchered it every time.

"Yeah, whatever," the student went on, " '. . . bride of queerness—' "

" '*Quiet*ness.' "

218

" '. . . bride of quietness, Thou foster-child of silence and slow time . . . ' "

Slow time . . . Boy, the poet had that right. TK twisted his neck and stole a peek at the clock on the back wall of the lecture hall. Ten more minutes of this torture, one more class to go, then off to Sears, not the most fascinating job in the world, but at least he was getting paid for putting in his time, and the time there did go pretty fast. Not like here.

Even the teacher's patience ran thin, or maybe he just decided that the poet's words deserved better. Longchamp took over for the struggling student. " 'Heard melodies are sweet, but those unheard are sweeter; therefore ye soft pipes, play on . . .' "

TK hadn't forgotten his challenge to Al Lake that if Sears hired him and he couldn't hack it, Lake could fire him and wouldn't owe him a dime. TK had held up his end. He worked afternoons and all day Saturday and received his check each week. The part of the work he liked best was unloading the trucks when they came in, especially the big box items—TVs, kitchen appliances—and as the holidays approached, things were getting busier. Al Lake, despite his smile, was proving to be a bit of a dick, continually reminding TK and the other stock boys that he, Lake, was the one wearing the white shirt and tie and that if he told them to do something, and how to do it, then by God and sonny Jesus that was the way it had better be done, because the business of America was business, and *he* understood that.

> "Fair youth, beneath the trees, thou canst not leave
> Thy song, nor ever can those trees be bare;
> Bold Lover, never, never canst thou kiss . . ."

TK drew his attention back to Longchamp, who was holding the literature book pressed to his chest and was reciting the poem by heart. It was not the dramatic, hammy thing he'd once done with that "Caliban upon Setebos" poem (TK had liked that a *lot*);

no, this time Longchamp was just saying the words slowly, but his voice sounded as if he were really speaking his own thoughts, that's how natural he sounded. The rest of the students, even some of those who ordinarily would be noisily clapping their textbooks shut at this point, zipping up book bags, shuffling feet in preparation for blasting out of there when the bell rang, were mostly quiet.

> *"Though winning near the goal—yet, do not grieve;*
> *She cannot fade, though thou hast not thy bliss,*
> *For ever will thou love, and she be fair!"*

Longchamp stopped. He was at the end of only the second stanza, TK saw with a look at his own book. There wouldn't be time to finish the rest today; but the teacher gazed at his class a moment, then said, "Those may be the saddest and yet most tenderly hopeful lines in all of English literature. Why?"

Before he was even aware of intending to, TK raised his hand.

"Ah, Mr. Knowles . . ." said Longchamp wryly. "Welcome back from the foggy realm of wherever you've been today—and for the past few weeks."

TK felt his cheeks warm but he didn't shut down. Longchamp had it right. TK had been elsewhere. He rose. "What do you mean by calling those lines sad but hopeful? Is that what you're asking?"

"Quite," Longchamp agreed. "Or put another way, what is the poet Keats—dead by the age of twenty-six, poor youth—expressing?"

And TK told it. The poet was describing the figures painted on the outside of an ancient Greek vase, and among them were a young woman and the young man who was leaning toward her as though to kiss her—not quite there, so they'd never share that kiss, but neither would they fade or grow old or die . . . preserved as they were for all time . . . "Yet do not grieve . . . for ever wilt thou love, and she be fair . . ." Or so TK answered in words to that effect, and Longchamp nodded his approval, looking at him with an odd and curious glance, as if he, Longchamp, were wondering that someone young could grasp what John Keats's lines really, truly meant.

But TK was pretty sure he had.

20 Tom

Goal achieved, Tom thought, and yet as he drove out through the gate of Elm Hill Estate Elder Residence his emotions were mixed. For her part, Mom seemed to have accepted the move. Since the decision to have her sell her house and get into assisted living, she had gone, by degrees, from resistant to resigned to cooperative, and finally, this morning, to almost eager. Monica Kim had greeted them and escorted them to the room where Mom would be living. Tom had spent the morning with her, and in the dining hall at noon Mom discovered that there were residents at Elm Hill whom she already knew. She assured Tom that she would be fine and insisted that he go about taking care of what he needed to do. He told her that he would be back that evening.

Later that afternoon, having talked with Stan Jarvis and made final arrangements for the sale of the house, Tom went over to the Sand Trap, where Brain had told him former shipyard workers sometimes congregated. The bar was quiet, and it wasn't hard to pick them out: a half dozen weathered men sitting at a table in the corner, looking as if they had time on their hands. Tom took his beer and went over. "Excuse me; did you gentlemen work at the yard?"

A skinny, red-faced man with a shock of crisp white hair, who seemed to have been holding court, beamed. "Indeed we did."

"My dad worked there, too. I don't know if you knew him. Tom Knowles?"

"Tommy Knowles! Sure. God rest him. Tommy taught me the ropes—literally, I'm talking. I was a rigger. Jimmy Cogan." The white-haired man shook hands and introduced others, the names coming too fast for Tom to process. Cogan pushed out a chair. "Sit down. Jesus, I remember Tommy like yesterday. The one thing I *can't* remember is him ever cursing. Mother of God, for the rest of us in that gang the talk was enough to make a sailor blush. But not Tommy Knowles. And not on account of he was a Holy Roller, your old man. He just . . . didn't." Jimmy Cogan paused and his eyes danced with sudden mischievous relish. "Except once." And he told it.

"We're lugging this big-ass block and tackle, him and me— thing must've weighed three hundred pounds—and I dropped my end too soon, and he lost *his* grip, and didn't it land smack on his foot, steel-toed boot be damned. Well, your dad's face goes white as chalk, and he lets out a string of language so thick you could've pulled your way along it to Southie. It was like every blue word he'd never said had been corked up inside, just waitin'. And the thing is, soon as it was said?" Cogan snapped his fingers. "Never heard another swear out of him. Ha. So you're his boy?"

Around the table there were other brief, remembered stories. Tom was surprised and touched that after all these years his father was held in such high regard by the men he'd worked with.

"Is your mom still living?" Jimmy Cogan asked.

Tom said she was. He made no mention of Elm Hill Estate.

"The shipyard was a widow maker," muttered a bald, burly man.

"True enough," said Jimmy Cogan, "but you'd have thought they were right up there with the saints to hear my wife tell it. She'd light a candle for Keystone Steel at mass. The phony bastards."

"Phony in what way?" Tom asked.

Shrugs, down-turned mouths; but no one spoke up—and Tom understood. It was a yardbird's version of *omertà*. Even after all these years, people were reluctant to speak ill of the company that had signed their paychecks. Across the room a furtive figure ducked in and made his way to the bar. He wore a raw silk sport coat, his brown hair obviously tinted, his face deeply tanned; but it was the expression on the face that struck Tom. It was a lost, haunted look, and vaguely familiar.

"I'll tell you one," Jimmy Cogan spoke up. "OSHA would visit, and the inspections were supposed to be a surprise, y'know? To find things like they really were. But Keystone was always one jump ahead." He drew closer to the table. "The company must've had someone inside that they were greasing. When the inspectors'd come, the bosses would be all 'Gee, looks like you caught us with our pants down.' Which was shite, of course, because the inspectors never found squat."

"Didn't they ever talk directly to workers?"

"Sure they did," said the burly guy, "but they were escorted by company men."

"Even when they weren't," Cogan went on, "we knew to stay clammed. If the Feds found violations, they coulda shut us down."

Tom took a drink of beer. "What violations might they have found?"

"Hypothetically?"

"Sure."

"You know, safety, storage of materials. Hell, all kinds. But the point is they didn't."

"What about . . . workers getting sick?"

It was subtle, but Tom felt it. Faces tightened, eyes got evasive. The burly man sent him a hooded glance. Even Jimmy Cogan grew distant. "Caused by exposure to asbestos, for example," Tom pressed on.

From the TV over the bar a babble of voices and music was audible in the silence. The man with the silk sport coat had drunk up and gone. Finally, Jimmy Cogan sighed. "*Grave*stone Steel is what we called the company on the sly. In public though? No one said 'boo' for fear of losing the work—or later, the pension." He showed his dentures in a quick, cheerless grin. "I guess you could say they're buying our drinks right now. How about it? Another?" Tom said he had to go but insisted that the round was on him.

On his way out, he spoke to the barman. "The guy who was just here . . . in the sport coat . . ."

"Art Dewitt."

For an instant, he was surprised; and then not. The barman parked his cigarette and whiffed smoke from the side of his mouth. "The guy's what, fifty-nine? Sixty? He works for a landscaping crew, spends all his money on clothes, snatch, and his car."

"The 'fifty-seven *T-Bird*?"

"A new Riv. And a new broad in it every time I see him. I don't envy him though. It's like when he was eighteen his selector switch got turned to 'pussy,' and it's stuck there. Poor bastard can't change it."

"How you doing?" Brain asked when Tom picked him up outside the high school at 5:30. He was referring to Tom's having taken his mother to Elm Hill.

"I'm okay," he said.

Brain looked at him. "You sure you're up for this?"

"Let's do it."

Brain nodded. "Head over to the old school annex and go around the back."

The entrance in the rear of the old high school was a formidable-looking steel door. Brain produced a key ring. There must've been thirty or more keys on it, which he jingled the way an Apache warrior might display a stringer of cavalry scalps, as a sign of power and access to secret places. He began to search for a particular key. Around them in the golden light of late afternoon, shadows were lengthening, and the wind cartwheeled dry leaves into a corner, where they spun a moment, as colorful as confetti, before settling into a drift. The Escape was the only vehicle in the parking lot.

Brain had telephoned that morning, sounding excited. He had been up all night with an idea. "Oh, great, another Brain storm." Tom sighed. No, he was serious. He'd thought of ways to test whether the theory they'd hatched in Cambridge had any basis in reality. He knew Tom was going to be spending the day with his mother, but when Tom was ready—no rush at all, Brain insisted—could they meet so Brain could share his idea?

So here they were.

Brain found the key he was after, poked it into the lock, and swung open the heavy door. They stepped inside and went down a short flight of concrete steps. They were in the annex basement, Tom realized, under the old gymnasium. He could almost imagine the drub of a basketball being bounced overhead, the stamp of feet. To the right, in the space behind a low door that hung open, stood a neat phalanx of large, dusty, olive-brown cans with faded yellow writing on the sides and the unmistakable Civil Defense logo. Water canisters. He gaped. "Those've got to be decades old. Does anyone know they're still here?"

"Or care?" muttered Brain. "Though if they haven't all leaked dry, the water's probably better than what comes out of the town taps these days. C'mon."

Tom gave a backward look at the cans, untouched after all these years, as though awaiting some new bogeyman to rekindle Cold War fears; then he turned and followed Brain.

The line of overhead lamps didn't extend into the concrete tunnel beyond, and Tom was given over to a sudden sense of having moved back in time. He half expected to see torches burning. The tunnel was long and vaulted, lighted only by a series of narrow windows, mounted high on the basement walls and covered with heavy wire. On one side, the wall gave way to a storage area. There in the dimness he could make out disused gym equipment: a set of parallel bars, a vaulting horse, several misshapen medicine balls capped with dust (there amid the cobwebs the balls might have been the egg sacs of some monstrous spider). Ahead stood a map on a stainless-steel tripod base: Africa, he saw, the "Dark Continent," with countries that didn't exist anymore—Rhodesia and Tanganyika, names as quaint-sounding now as Zanzibar and Timbuktu.

Driving over here, Brain had offered his latest idea. A way of testing the hypothesis of an alternate reality, he argued, would be to put together another holographic show and reenact the experience of the night at the reunion.

"Hold on . . . is this going to be like *Frankenstein*? Are we going to go up to the castle and wait for an electrical storm?"

"One step at a time. First we've got to get some more films."

"What's wrong with the ones you used the first time?"

"Unfortunately, they got destroyed that night."

Brain had originally got the idea for his hologram show while he was cataloguing old game films for the school's sports archive. He'd found the footage of the dance down here in this basement.

They came to a wire door and Brain used another key, opened another lock. Beyond was a dim series of alcoves that resembled the catacombs under an ancient church. Stacked in some of the alcoves were cardboard boxes and storage crates.

"End of the line," Brain said. "This is where we search."

Following Brain's lead, Tom began to go through the boxes. It was a dusty, laborsome process, moving cartons, tearing open taped lids, peering in. And the boxes contained practically everything: little plastic cylinders of filmstrips ("Tenth Grade Hygiene," "Amazing Amphibians," "Nathaniel Hawthorne's Salem"), mimeographed study guides for long-forgotten tests, yellowed sports programs—but no films. Every once in a while Tom or Brain gave in to a sneeze.

When Tom realized that they had worked their way through several of the alcoves, he stepped over to a wire-grated window, his chin level with the sill. There was enough light to see his watch: 6:45. Outside, the light was a deeper gold now, the shadows bluer as they stretched across the asphalt. A month ago the sun would have still been high at this time; he'd forgotten how perceptibly New England days hurried toward change once fall came. At the left of what he could see, beyond a Cyclone fence and no longer screened by the thinning trees, he could make out the rear of the VFW hall. A dozen or so vehicles sat in the lot, the troops mustering for the afternoon libations, the potions and elixirs that would open the gates and let the ghosts out. At the right he could see the side of the old school building he and Brain were in, the facing wall bearded with ivy. The leaves were turning red with the season, and as the wind shook them, he had the impression that the building was a living, breathing entity, that the moving ivy was its lungs. It was a distinctly unpleasant image, and he felt an inexplicable shimmer of anxiety. He was glad to turn back to the dim basement.

Brain was still occupied with rummaging. He appeared to have gone through most of the cartons in his area of the search. Visible in the fading shafts of daylight, dust was settling in slow billows. "Maybe we should call it a day," Tom said. "It doesn't look promising."

"We're here. There isn't much more. I'll go through the rest of these boxes, you check out that last bastion in there. If we don't find anything . . ." Brain let the idea trail away. Reluctantly, Tom agreed, if only to satisfy both of them that no more films survived.

The "last bastion" was home to a defunct coal-burning furnace, a hulking cast-iron monster that seemed to expand into the darkness with branching, cobweb-festooned ductwork. It lurked in the shadows like an asylum inmate's conception of Shiva. Beyond, something caught Tom's eye. Going nearer he saw the sign from some long-forgotten pep rally: Weybridge vs. Brockton. The Thanksgiving Day game, one of the classic rivalries in eastern Massachusetts. The sign had to be ancient—the two towns hadn't played in the same league for years.

Words from the old song came to him. *Give a cheer, give a cheer, for the kids who drink the beer, in the cel-lars of old Weybridge High.*

Were these the fabled cellars, then? He seemed to think he'd been here once before, long ago, but it was only the vaguest impression, like a puff of breath on a windowpane.

"Anything?" Brain's voice echoed from the other part of the basement.

Beyond the nearest window, the light outside was fast fading now, the gold taking on a dusky cast.

Cheer, cheer for old Weybridge High . . . wake up the echoes . . .

"No," he answered.

And now something else came to him . . .

A dance, upstairs in the gymnasium. He's with someone, though in the dim light he can't make out who she is. Little Anthony and the Imperials are singing "On the Outside Looking In." TK—for that's who he is all at once—draws his partner close, but she pulls back. It's Penny Griffin. Uh oh, has he overdone it, hugging her tight like that? But no, she doesn't leave; she keeps one arm across his back, and with her other hand she removes her glasses, holding them for one uncertain moment, then, in a spontaneous gesture, she slips them into his inside jacket pocket. It's a small intimacy, the kind of thing a real girlfriend would do; then she lays her cheek against his and he holds her near, closes his eyes . . .

"Hey." Brain's voice rose from another part of the basement. "Come see this."

When Tom got to the other side of the furnace, Brain was bent over a banker's box that he'd just hauled into the light. Its sides were bulging, and the top, which lay beside it on the floor, was so dust-covered it looked as if it were clad with gray velvet. Before Tom could ask what it held, there was a sound of the wire door creaking open, then footsteps moving their way. He and Brain exchanged a glance and turned toward the arched doorway. In a moment, a beam of light cut the dust-choked air and a watchman appeared holding a six-cell flashlight. "What're you doing here?" he demanded.

"I work for the school department," Brain said. "Sometimes I work late."

The guard, who looked to be around thirty, with a barrel chest and fat, hairy arms, eyed them suspiciously. "That's irregardless. No one's supposed to be here after hours."

"We're almost through."

"Hey, do I look like the complaint department? I do what I'm told, okay? You got a problem, take it up with my supervisor. Let's move it."

"Sure," Brain said equably, "we're good."

The guard flashed his light into the dark corners, as if he half expected to see the glint of hastily stashed bottles of booze in there, or perhaps party girls in French maid getups waiting for the "all clear" signal. When he turned back, he seemed disappointed. He consulted his wristwatch and made a note on a clipboard, and as he did, Tom saw Brain slip a flat round metal container from the banker's box into his pocket. When the three of them got outside, day had turned into dusk.

Mom was sitting in a padded chair in her room doing the *Herald* crossword puzzle when Tom showed up at Elm Hill. She gave him the detailed account of her day, though he sensed it was perfunctory; he didn't hear any real engagement. When he asked her about this, she just said she was tired, there had been a lot of stimulation. He told her he'd seen Jimmy Cogan and some of the others Dad had known at the shipyard, and she perked up a little. He took a chance.

"After Dad died, when you talked with the Keystone officials, did they ever speculate about what might've caused his cancer?"

"Did I talk to them?" She seemed uncertain.

"You spoke with them about insurance and Dad's pension, right?"

"I spoke with the doctors, of course. And, well, you're right . . . later, there was a man . . ." She furrowed her brow, trying to remember.

"Mr. Porter," Tom said.

"He helped us get the papers signed."

"But did he or anyone else ever suggest a direct cause for the cancer?"

She went into deep thought again, and suddenly she seemed old and stooped and frail. "No," she said at last.

"Did they mention other instances of shipyard workers getting cancer?"

"Not that I recall."

When Tom got back to the house, Brain called. "How's tomorrow night for the laser show? Say seven o'clock, my office at the school?"

"I'll be there."

$\overline{21}$ TK

Among reasons to stay off detention, Room 309 was definitely one. It was on the top floor, at the far end of a corridor where routine high school traffic seldom went. The only other rooms at that end were a janitor's closet and a book storage room. The hallway ceiling was scabrous from old roof leaks, and the warped wood floor had a yellow gleam under decades of wax. Three-oh-nine had the usual classroom decor—the flag hanging from a wall staff at the front, a thick-framed portrait of George Washington (the one that looked as if Martha had gone overboard trying to eliminate the ring around George's collar and bleached away the bottom front of his coat as well)—but the room had touches all its own. Like the wall clock, whose face had been pasted with so many generations of spitballs that they'd left a residue on the glass that obscured time. High windows looked out upon a flat roof where vents brought up the smells of the cafeteria: Dutch

Cleanser and Easy-Off at this point in the afternoon, but a lingering, greasy redolence of whatever meal had been served a few hours earlier, too.

On that Wednesday afternoon in early November, TK found himself taking a seat, along with twenty or so other detainees. He had left the house behind schedule that morning and jogged halfway, slowing from time to time to walk because he didn't want to get to school sweaty. But he was sweating anyway as Sterns backed him against the bulletin board in the main lobby. The charge was more of the vice principal's Mickey Mouse enforcement of the rules since TK had actually arrived *ahead* of some other students, who'd been even tardier, but that made no difference; he was the one caught. Worse, as far as Sterns was concerned, was that TK's shirt wasn't ironed that day (or the last several days, for that matter), strictly verboten in WHS's unwritten dress code. TK might have contested the charges, noting that the rules were selectively enforced, but he was already on such thin ice with Sterns lately it had just seemed simpler to take the detention. He handed his pink slip to the monitor, Mr. Morrisette, who checked off TK's name on a list and waved him to a seat.

Like everything else in 309, the furniture was timeworn, the desktops carved with names and obscenities. "Mobby Dick is a venrial disease," some illiterate scholar had etched on the desk TK took. As he settled in, a paper airplane sailed past, skidded off a chair, and hit the floor. "You planning to work for Boeing?" Morrisette called wearily to someone at the back of the room. TK took out a notebook and his U.S. history text.

Some monitors liked to assign work to the students in their charge, usually mental gymnastics (counting backward on paper from 1000, or writing repetitions of "I will not . . ." and the offense they were there for); others had students memorize some verse from Emerson or Franklin, meant to be inspirational ("Experience keeps a dear school, but a fool will learn in no other"), but any spark the words might possess began to flicker after the twentieth iteration and was gone by the hundredth. Sometimes, a monitor would add incentive—"Finish the assignment, let me check it, and you can go," although this was a carrot dangled on a pretty long stick, since it was near to impossible to get the task done in less than the hour-length period. The best circumstance was a monitor who didn't care what you did as long as you kept quiet. That was the case today. Morrisette, a craggy old warhorse with a rumple of white hair, sat with a blue pencil, going through a stack of chemistry tests, raising his face occasionally to tell someone to shut up. TK had his notebook open to a blank page (there were a lot of them these days) and after several moments of idle thought, he began to write. *I didn't think to ask for a rain check last time. Maybe it's too late, but if not and if you haven't already made other plans for the dance, would you consider going with me?"*

He read it over, imagining Penny Griffin reading it.

Too wordy; too tentative. He didn't like the "maybe it's too late," the "if you haven't already." He wasn't crazy about that "consider going . . ." either. He scribbled out the note and turned to a fresh page. "Penny, do you want a ride to the dance?" Better, more direct. He glanced up when Dee Richards walked into the room. Everyone else in 309 glanced up as well; somebody wolf whistled. "Can it," Morrisette barked, but even he was looking at Dee.

She had on a short black skirt, black nylons, and a tight pink sleeveless sweater (and if *that* wasn't against the unwritten dress code, what was?; though he doubted that was why she was here). Morrisette waved her to a seat. Paying no attention to anyone else in the room, Dee took a desk two places ahead of TK, in the next row. When the eddy caused by her entrance quieted, people went back to sleeping or studying or whatever they'd been doing. TK reread his note to Penny, tore it out, folded it, and tucked it in his shirt pocket to finish later. There was homework to do; his grades were on a skid. He had a history quiz to prep for and a vocab worksheet, plus his next Curb Feelers to write.

Drifting fragrantly past the handful of empty seats between

them, Dee Richards's perfume was overcoming the rancid smells from the vents on the cafeteria roof. It was definitely not the White Shoulders his mom used. He peeked at her—and speaking of shoulders: at the edge of Dee's tight pink sweater, one bra strap had slipped ever-so-slightly and showed starkly white against the smooth tanned curve of her shoulder. Something in his chest tickled.

On summer days, when he wasn't digging clams, TK would sometimes go to the beach and sit along the seawall. It was where plans were made, dates set up, gossip spread, secrets shared, and for the kids who gathered there, it was their turf: a strip of sand, a margin of time, which it was possible to believe would stretch on without limit and that they would always be young. Dee was one of the crowd who came there to play whist and listen to WMEX on transistor radios, and rub Johnson's baby oil onto themselves. She was also one of the few girls who wore a two-piece swimsuit, and on occasion, as she lay on her stomach on her beach towel, she unhooked the back of her suit top to get an even tan.

The tickle moved down to TK's belly.

Dee was no stranger to detention, either. Smoking in the girls' room and skipping out after lunch were among her infractions. She wasn't "bad" in the real sense of the word and was unfailingly polite to teachers—she was a minister's daughter, after all—and yet she tested, and certainly sometimes crossed, boundaries. Interestingly, this never tarnished her reputation. In her own way, Dee was popular: not like one of the bouncy cheerleaders or the good-natured class jokers, but a long way from the true bad girls (one could only *imagine* what they did). She seemed to have what most girls wanted—and most boys, too. As TK had told Brain recently, she was "a fox."

Brain smiled vaguely (he'd had a crush on Dee for years). "You mean sly?"

"No . . . a fox. Foxy. Attractive."

"Never heard the word used like that before."

Neither had TK, for that matter (not even from Artie Dewitt, who had a slew of colorful terms for girls), but the word had occurred to him and it fit. He had found that happening lately, found himself coining phrases. Just the other day, talking with Mom about Sterns, he'd complained that the vice principal liked "'laying his power trip on me.' Pulls rank," he explained, seeing Mom's confusion. And yet he'd liked the way he'd first expressed it. It sounded . . . fresh. And wasn't that something Miss Mutterperl urged, for writing, at least? Try to make your language sound newly minted?

Watching Dee Richards now from his vantage point several seats behind her he didn't ponder what words described her; he was content just to sit and look. For her part, Dee was oblivious of him and everyone else in the room. She had her pocketbook open on the desk and was peering into it.

TK occasionally wondered what lay in the depths of those big handbags girls carried, and the thought recurred now. Hmm . . . could that be the topic for a column? To fathom the depths? He'd have to do a little research, quiz some girls, but it had possibilities. He tucked the idea away for future consideration.

Dee took out a fat black wallet and set her bag on the floor. When she unsnapped the wallet it fairly sprang open with its compressed contents. She began to flip through little Lucite sleeves of photographs. She appeared to be doing a quick inventory. By craning his neck slightly, TK was able to see that some shots were of girlfriends, taken in the photo booth at Kresge's, but many were snaps of boys. He sensed she was looking for one in particular. Noting that Mr. Morrisette was still absorbed in marking tests, TK slipped from his chair and crept to the next seat, so that now he was only one desk behind Dee, across the aisle in the next row. As she fingered through the snapshots, she came to one and sat back to gaze at it. It was a photograph of Ray Sevigny.

TK thought of the pair of them, Dee and Ray, back on an August night at the drive-in theater. Already eighteen, with a cool car, Ray was a senior in the trade program, a tough, good-looking kid who lived over in the Pines, a neighborhood of project houses near Whittle's Pond. TK had known him casually in junior high school, when both were on the track team. Whip-fast, Ray Sevigny consistently won the fifty-yard dash, never mind that when practice, or a meet, was over for the day the first thing he did once he left school grounds was light up a butt. He hadn't gone out for sports in high school. His speed these days seemed to be focused on getting from zero to sixty in his hot rod Merc, and from first to second to third, and probably even home, with girls.

Dee had slipped the photograph out of its plastic sleeve and was holding it in her ringed fingers, bending close, as if making a detailed study. Ray Sevigny's dark shiny hair was combed back on the sides from a pompadour prow. He wore a black sport jacket over a white collarless shirt, with a little string tie, like James Garner wore in *Maverick* on TV. TK felt a little jolt run through his left side, like an electric current. He jerked and sat up straighter in the chair.

And felt it again.

What was *that*? He twisted to look at the chair back, expecting to see that a splinter had jabbed him; but the old wood was shiny-smooth with wear. He glanced up, wondering: Had anyone seen him react? People were as they'd been a moment before. Dee was still looking at Ray Sevigny's portrait. She held it slightly farther away, considering it from a new angle. TK thought he could make out writing across the bottom, the letters as pale as a trace drawing, but legible. "Deceased."

He caught his breath. His stomach squirmed. Perhaps peripherally aware of him, Dee turned and caught him watching. She drew the photo to her. "What are you looking at?" she demanded in a harsh whisper.

"No-nothing."

"Keep your eyes to yourself."

If she knew who he was, she didn't show it. To her he was probably just another detention rat. He wanted to fidget under her gaze. Swallowing, he managed to say, "Is that Ray Sevigny's senior portrait?"

Dee was still frowning but mention of the topic seemed to appease her a bit. "He just gave it to me."

The portraits had been taken during the summer. Kids were getting the proofs back already (TK thought his own made him look like Wally Cleaver). "Can I . . . can I see it?" he heard himself ask.

Dee's gaze probed a moment, then she sent a glance toward Morrisette (still at work), held the photo, and handed it over tentatively. "Don't smudge it."

TK looked at the picture. There *was* writing across the bottom. "Hey Hot Stuff," it read, and Ray's signature. Nothing more. TK wasn't sure if he kept his expression neutral. He was feeling a strange sensation once more . . . no words this time. Images: green leaves, sun-flicker, swirling motion. Then (and this shook him) something came flooding in to blur the face he was staring at—the way the residue of spit balls blurred the face of the clock—something like . . . dirt.

"Hey, give me that!" Dee said.

A few kids sitting nearby looked up. TK's face warmed. His hand trembling, he passed the portrait back. Dee wiped at a corner, as if for imagined cooties, then slid the photo carefully back into its protective plastic sleeve.

Route 3-A was the business strip that ran through Adams Point, across the bridge into North Weybridge, and then through Bingham and on down the coast, eventually to Cape Cod. In the Weybridge stretch, the road passed Chinese restaurants, pizzerias, secondhand shops, a marine supply, and, near the bridge, Jim Mulligan's auto body, where Ray Sevigny worked afternoons after school. TK drove past and saw several guys in the lot standing around a cherry red Wildcat. He parked on the street. Getting out, he remembered he was still wearing his tie; he yanked it off and tossed it back into his car.

The men by the Buick had cigarettes dangling, and TK could imagine them talking in low, fraternal tones about gear ratios, Hurst shifters, and four-barrel Holley carburetors. He approached, not sure what he would say or, suddenly, why he was even here. One of the men looked up. He was the oldest by more than a few years, dressed in faded blue coveralls with "Mully" stitched in orange over the breast pocket, and TK realized he was Jim Mulligan. He was a legendary figure around town, having some claim to being the toughest guy in Weybridge. (It was a running debate and there were a number of candidates—Red Goodwin, Clem Donovan, and Herc Decoste were other names—though oddly enough none of them, including Mulligan, ever took a side in the discussions, and in fact, in TK's experience, they all seemed like pretty mellow guys.) Talking to Mully were two men TK didn't know, along with a broad, monkeylike guy with greased hair and a pack of L&Ms rolled in the sleeve of his T-shirt, whom TK did recognize. Butch Tracy was a loudmouth troublemaker who'd quit school just ahead of being expelled. Addressing himself to Jim Mulligan, TK said, "Um . . . is Ray Sevigny around?"

Tracy was suddenly cracking up with laughter. "Those your wheels? Jesus."

TK turned, wondering if his car was blocking something.

"A slushbox Rambler? Holy shit," Tracy hooted. "If I was you, I'd take it home and hide it. *If* it can make the trip."

Mulligan ignored Tracy. "In there," he said agreeably enough, indicating a garage bay. Inside, TK saw, was Ray Sevigny's black '49 Merc, the hood raised.

Butch Tracy hawked up something from deep in his throat and spat it sideways in a gob. "Hey, Ray! Some dipstick here wants to see ya."

TK stepped around him and walked to the garage. Ray Sevigny, his white T-shirt seeming to glow in the gloom of the bay, was elbow-deep in the Merc's engine compartment, one eye squinted shut against the rise of smoke from a cigarette in his mouth. On the side of his neck, like a dark hickey, was a smudge of grease. He flicked a look at TK (recognition? TK wondered) and then turned his attention back to what he was doing, pulling on a socket wrench, veins standing out on his lean biceps. Hanging from the garage walls were the assorted pretzel shapes of exhaust pipes, the figure-eights of fan belts, and the dark O's of new tires, which lent their rubber aroma to the mingled smells of oil, B.O., and the soapy tang of degreaser. Suddenly TK felt the ridiculousness of his being here. What was he going to say? *I was staring at Dee Richards's bra strap in detention today and I happened to see your senior portrait and . . .*

Abruptly, the strain on Ray Sevigny's arm ceased. He gave the ratchet several quick, clicking turns and extracted a spark plug. Straightening, he turned to TK—and TK's jaw wanted to drop. Inked in red on the inside of Sevigny's forearm was a skull, and above it, in a curving gold ribbon, *Death Before Dishonor* and under that the letters *USMC*. It looked brand-new.

TK stared. Oblivious, Ray Sevigny inserted a new Champion spark plug, tightened it, and reattached the distributor wire. He got into the car, turned on the engine, which started with a throaty roar, and backed out of the bay, the hood still up. Under the hood he made one final adjustment, then shut off the motor and brought down the hood with a firm slam. He stepped back. "So what's up?"

TK was still transfixed by the tattoo. "What'll Pop Sterns say when he sees that?"

There were rules, even in the trade school—no tattoos. Some guys had homemade designs they'd done with the tip of a sewing needle and India ink, but those were usually in places you could conceal under a shirt. Sevigny turned his arm and looked at the image. "Sterns blows," he said calmly.

TK forced a laugh. "Agreed, but he's still the warden, and we're still inmates."

"You mean *you* are, crud." Butch Tracy had drifted over. "Scrape off."

TK ignored him; his business was with Ray Sevigny. Ray dropped the stub of his cigarette onto the grease-packed asphalt, stepped on it. "Three more days, I'm gone."

"Gone?" TK said; though the tattoo already told him where. "You'd graduate this year. Why not stay till then?"

"Who're you, my old lady?"

"I think Dee sent him," Tracy chimed in. "This's got pussy tracks all over it." Going to a falsetto, he said, " 'Oh, Ray, please don't go away and leave me all alone. I'll do anything if you stay.' "

"Shut up," Sevigny said without heat and to TK, "You got a big nose, man, or what? What is this shit?"

What it is *is I saw your picture in Dee's wallet, with your Tony Curtis curl and Bret Maverick string tie and "Hey Hot Stuff" written across the bottom (though what it had really said—or what I saw—was "Deceased" . . .)* TK cleared his throat, which had become constricted. "Do you know about . . . Indochina?"

Sevigny's eyes narrowed. He seemed genuinely perplexed.

"What the hell you yappin' about?" snapped Tracy. "One Hung Low's? Where the chicken's so rare, you can still hear it meow?"

What *was* he talking about? Indochina? It was strange-sounding, utterly unreal. Where had he heard about it in the first place? From an issue of *Life* magazine at the barbershop? A newsreel at the Rialto? He swallowed, his mouth gone suddenly as dry as math paper. "It's this place . . . over in Asia." Was it? Was he even sure of that? "A war. You could get hurt, or . . . killed."

The punch came so fast TK had no time to brace. Tracy hit him low in the stomach. In a dazzle of light, he doubled over. Pain spiked out in sharp, broken spokes, piercing up into his chest, jabbing down into his balls. He felt like he'd been gored. He tried to straighten but couldn't. It was as if his gut muscles had clenched around the blow, holding the imprint of Butch Tracy's fist. Through a red mist of pain he saw Ray Sevigny yank Tracy roughly back, all the while looking at TK with a strange mix of anger and confusion. He said nothing.

Tracy, however, seemed to be jazzed on the thrill of sudden violence. He danced forward, his hands flexed. "A person can get killed right *here*, queer bait, sayin' shit like you done. I oughta

239

stomp you inta the sidewalk myself." He bobbed there menacingly a moment—as if half expecting TK might mount a counterattack, or that Ray would clap his back approvingly; but Sevigny had already walked around and climbed into his car.

TK was able to straighten a little, and that's when he saw the fold of paper on the ground and realized it was the note he'd had in his pocket. It had fallen out when he'd bent over. Before TK could reach for it, Tracy snatched it up. He unfolded it. "'Penny,'" he read. "Ooohh, who's Penny? 'Do you want a ride to the dance?'" He looked at TK, a leer curling his small, mean mouth. "You're gonna give her a *ride*, huh? Sure."

"Gimme that."

"So who is she? She got nice tits? A round ass?"

TK made a grab for the note, but Tracy pulled it away. He brought it to his mouth, as if it were a handkerchief, and hawked into it and dropped the note to the ground. He turned and, discovering that Ray had left, hurried after him. The two other guys who'd been talking with Jim Mulligan had already climbed into Ray Sevigny's Mercury. Butch Tracy was consigned to the backseat. The V8 rumbled to life. TK still couldn't manage to stand all the way up. He wanted to shout after them, curse them out, and tell them what worthless pieces of crap they were, but he couldn't quite get his breath. The Merc lurched out of the yard with a little spurt of gravel and dirt. As it passed, Tracy pressed his pale butt cheeks against the back window and mooned him.

Jim Mulligan appeared. "Y'okay? What happened?"

TK forced himself to straighten, despite the lingering ache in his stomach. He shook his head, clearing it. "Misunderstanding."

The man looked doubtful but said nothing; after a moment he turned and went into his garage. On the greasy pavement lay the crumpled note TK had written to Penny, wet with the green gob of Tracy's loogie. He left the note there.

22 Tom

In the town hall lobby, Tom consulted the locator. Weybridge had expanded over the years, with jobs and functions that didn't exist when he'd lived here; though there was still a shellfish warden. How much did a clamming permit cost these days? What was the going rate per rack? He wondered if Sid Yarrow was still around; he'd be in his nineties now. The mayor had a suite on the second floor.

That morning, Tom telephoned, gave his name, and asked to speak with the mayor. The wait was short. "Hey, how are you?" Fred Kinney greeted him amiably. "Mary Agnes has told me about you."

"It's nice to be known in the seats of power."

"I wouldn't mind changing seats for a while. I'm in a meeting with the state DEQ about this water treatment plant. They send these guys in pinstripes—" he lowered his voice confidentially, "they oughta be *jail* stripes. What do you call ten lawyers tied to a railroad track?"

"I don't know, I just—"

"A good start." The man's laugh was so dry it was hard to imagine a smile with it.

"Mr. Mayor, is there a statute of limitation in negligent death cases?"

The silence on the line told Tom he had Kinney's attention. "We're taking a five-minute break."

Tom gave an abbreviated version of what he'd begun to believe: that shipyard workers back in the days when his dad had worked there were exposed to asbestos and some had become sick, even died. But when pressed for details, Keystone Steel, the yard's owner, knowing of the hazards, had systematically denied any connection. If true, this meant that the company, even now, might be open to litigation. Also, though Tom kept this point to himself, it suggested that the company's doctors lied when they claimed that Tom's father was the first case of lung cancer they'd seen. "I think," he concluded, "that the company may have conspired in a cover-up."

"That's quite a claim," the mayor said. "We're talking a long time ago."

Tom considered that he might have another go at getting Jimmy Cogan and some of the other retired yardbirds to remember; but he didn't have time to wait. His visit here was coming to an end. "If you want to pursue it, I've got what you need."

"Look, Tom—may I call you Tom?" The man's voice had dropped, ominous-sounding somehow. "I'm up to my neck here with this water treatment proposal, but what you're saying is important. I want us to talk. Can we do that? Can we meet?"

There was no one in the reception area now, the workers having left for lunch. Fred Kinney's corner office had large windows that overlooked Commerce Street in front and side views across a lawn to the pine grove and the town's roll of honor. The mayor was on his feet and moving around his desk, ready with a handshake and a smile. "Good to meet you. I've heard Mary Agnes toot your horn for years. I don't think I've ever known a real writer."

He was medium height, wiry, with crisp gray hair. His rolled shirtsleeves revealed sinewy forearms, an old tattoo fading on one. "I flunked out after tenth grade. I've always been one for practical things. Business courses, math . . . those were the only subjects that made any sense to me. I went to junior college nights." Fred Kinney brushed down his shirtsleeves and buttoned the cuffs. "We won't get settled here. You had lunch yet?"

The country club was a short drive away on a rolling expanse of land on the Bingham side of town. Tom had known kids who caddied or worked greens but never anyone who'd actually belonged to the club; and yet he understood it was where business was conducted, sweetheart deals made, sons and daughters betrothed, futures decided.

"There's a very good kitchen here," Kinney explained, "and great margaritas, if you're into that sort of thing."

On a patio set up for al fresco dining, a three-piece band was playing "The Girl from Ipanema." Kinney stopped and greeted several parties of diners: quick handshakes, quicker words, then on to a corner table reserved for him. Beyond a screen of nylon mesh lay clay tennis courts, where a game of doubles was in progress, the crisp *pok . . . pok* of volleys audible, and from farther away came the sound of sprinklers where they threw long rooster tails of water on the fairways and made rainbows. "They're getting ready for a gala wedding reception here this weekend. In fact, the bride's an old classmate of yours. Diana Richards." The mayor gave a wry smile and lowered his voice. "Dee is still a piece of work. She gets a little frisky at times, according to my sources. She's marrying the district attorney. You know Ben Grasso?"

"No, I don't."

"He's a hardnose; good to have in our corner. In fact, as it happens, I thought your claim was sufficiently serious to bring Ben in for our talk. I hope you don't mind?" He broke off as a man approached. "Speak of the devil. Ben Grasso, Tom Knowles. 'TK,' I guess it was back in the day when our better halves were his classmates."

"The author," Grasso said without elaboration.

Tom offered his hand. Grasso wasn't tall, though like his gaze, his handshake had steel in it. Probably recommended equipment for a person whose clients were kept behind bars.

"Good you could make it, Ben," continued the mayor when they'd settled into chairs. "Tom, why don't you take it from the top?"

Tom replayed it for Grasso, who reserved comment until he'd finished. "So you think the company's apparent resistance to release information suggests it may have conspired to cover it up?"

"I've had former workers tell me that the company used to deceive OSHA inspectors about working conditions. I think it may have been systematic policy."

"What prompted you to pursue this?" Ben Grasso asked.

"Curiosity at first." Tom didn't mention having seen the findings that Mike Burke had put together, or either of their meetings. There was no need to link Mike to it; not, at least, until he'd had a chance to talk with him again. Instead, Tom said he had found the newspapers in his mother's attic.

"But you have no hard proof of anything," Kinney said.

"No. I was away when much of this was going on."

The mayor steepled fingers at his chin. "From time to time someone gets a whiff of an old case—'Ah, foul corruption in a small town.' A few years back, a TV producer from one of those reality crime shows contacted us about an unsolved murder from the 1950s. I referred him to the town's legal counsel, yadda yadda—nothing ever came of it, thank God. That's not the kind of attention Weybridge needs." He gave his quick grin.

The food arrived. It was, as Kinney had promised, delicious. The shipyard deaths, as a topic of discussion, were sidetracked. "You notice the decor?" Kinney asked Tom. The inner wall of the patio was hung with vintage photographs, blown up to poster size, of the shipyard in its boom times. "According to local lore there was an inspector in those days whose job it was to examine the welds and joints. If they passed inspection, he signified it by chalking his name on the nearest bulkhead. His particular trademark was to add a little drawing."

Kilroy. Tom knew the story, and the little peering-over-a-wall face, but he let Kinney tell it. "Men who went overseas remembered seeing that here, and it was simple to draw, so they began putting it in all sorts of places. Legend has it there was one chalked in Hitler's toilet. After a while no one even knew what the sign meant anymore, but on it went—'Kilroy Was Here.'" He grinned. "And to think it started right here."

"The town's got a glorious past," Tom granted, and Kinney didn't miss the note of impatience.

"I know; emphasis on the *past*." He nodded, as if no one grasped that better than he. "But here's the thing we're up against, Tom," he went on, taking a more politic approach. "The town's in a budget crunch, as you've probably heard. We've got wolves nipping at our balls. One of the saving graces is that Keystone Steel keeps paying rent on that property, has since the yard quit building ships. Even closed, just sitting there, it still provides a hefty chunk of the tax base for the town, helps pay for schools, infrastructure. This proposed water treatment plant? That alone is going to cost more money than what the entire town budget was back in the late sixties."

"I guess I'm a little dense," Tom said, his impatience growing. "I'm not getting the connection. You've got that white elephant over there, and . . . ?"

"What you're suggesting here—OSHA violations, asbestos, sickness, deaths. If that were to result in some kind of probe, or class action lawsuits? We're looking at heavy consequences."

"I think we're talking about criminal activity of a damned serious kind."

The mayor gave a little laugh. "That's quite a leap. It's creative, and it's interesting." Grasso was frowning. "But are you maybe connecting dots where there aren't many to connect? I mean, that's what you do, right?"

"I don't follow you."

"Look at your profession, for Christ's sake."

"What's that got to do with this?" Tom was trying to stay calm.

"What it's got to do with is you write TV shows, movies. Pretty bizarre ones, from what Mary Agnes says. I can't judge. I don't have time for fiction, or any of that made-up crap, because what *I* do is work my tail off." He rapped the table, as if to assert that it was real. The skin around his eyes had paled and gone tight. "I've been elected by the citizens to run a town—a town, I might add, that you left behind. I honor that trust. People *live* here, friend. They pay taxes and send their kids to school and retire here. Budgets are squeezed tighter than a dog's butt in tick season. I have to scramble just to keep it all going."

"Understood, Mayor, but what's—"

"Like giving that brain-fried friend of yours a work space in order for him to jury-rig equipment so teachers can go on using it. One of the few things keeping the ink black is Keystone paying big rent on that 'white elephant,' as you so creatively put it. Paying, when they could be putting their goddamn Republican minds to work figuring out how to *avoid* paying. Well, I didn't go to MIT. I've got a junior college education, but by Jesus I know where my loyalties lie."

Tom's heart was thudding, like the drum in Kinney's voice. The man liked to pretend he was just a working guy, with his humble roots and his gibes about the "pinstripes," but he was a player, and he liked the good life. His contempt for Tom was clear, but all at once Tom didn't care; he wasn't here to make friends. Keeping a rein on his own anger, he said, "The fact is, these are two separate things. We're talking about possible crimes having been committed, about a cover-up going on for years. The company should've disclosed to workers what they already suspected."

"And what was that?"

"The link between asbestos and lung cancer. It can't be coincidence that workers died of lung diseases. That should've raised red flags."

Kinney's scowl deepened. "Speculation."

"It's more than that."

"Show me one scrap of proof."

"My father worked at the yard for years, then got lung cancer and died. Keystone paid his medical and funeral costs and got my mother to sign papers. They said it was to release his pension. *I* think it was hush money."

Ben Grasso, who was the only one who'd kept cool, sat forward. "So this is personal?"

Silence. Fred Kinney had tipped his hand; and now Tom had, too.

Beyond the screens, the *pok-pok* sounds of the tennis match had ceased. There was the muted murmur of conversation, the clink of table and glassware, and from the cool, green fairways the *wssshh* of the sprinklers. At a nearby table, a white-haired man puffed a fragrant cigar. This was a nice world, one that a person like Kinney wasn't normally invited to be part of. But here he was. He'd risen to it, and he liked the view from here. Tom realized something else now, too: that there was no official record of a meeting; this was just an informal social gathering, for all anyone could claim, to discuss golf handicaps, mixed doubles partners, or who was screwing whom. In the parking lot, Fred Kinney said, "I'm going to take this Keystone business under advisement. But on another point, make note. I've spoken with the school superintendent about Mr. Mclain's access to the basement annex. He had no right to use those films for that show of his."

The holograms. Of course the mayor would know about that; not for nothing had his wife been the class gossip. "He didn't steal them," Tom protested. "He discovered them. They've been sitting there for years."

"I've got a security guard's report that shows that on at least two occasions Mclain was on the premises after hours, and on one he was with another person." Kinney raised a hand in a halting gesture. "I'm not going to debate technicalities with you. The point is, those materials belong to the town. They've been reclaimed for evaluation. As for Mclain, his keys won't do him any good now. The locks have been changed."

$\overline{23}$ TK

The Pines had been a government housing project slapped up in the early 1940s for the families of shipyard workers who'd been recruited in the war effort. Small, prefabbed units crowded into what once had been pine woods at the east end of Whittle's Pond, they were now dilapidated rental housing, the yards crisscrossed with clotheslines, a few derelict cars and castoff appliances, and this time of day, with school out, small bands of ragged kids playing in the street. TK found the address he was looking for. The air had turned cold and his breath smoked as he walked across patchy lawn to the front door. *I'd be safe and warm if I was in L.A.* Where did *that* come from? TV? A dream? He'd never been to California.

He knocked.

TK hadn't seen Ray Sevigny around for a week or more, and on this gray Wednesday afternoon he had finally gone to Jim Mulligan's body shop. There he spotted Ray's Merc parked in one of the bays. Printed across the car's windshield in white was: MUST SELL '49 MERC XLNT COND. $1,300. And a phone number. Dizzily, TK stared at the words and numbers swimming there against the rolled and pleated black and red Naugahyde of the front seat. In the office he found Jim Mulligan.

"Ray Sevigny is selling his car?"

If Mulligan caught the anxiety in TK's voice, he didn't show it. "Should've come by earlier," he said. "That cretin Butch Tracy bought it this morning. What a waste."

But TK wasn't worrying about who bought the car. "Has Ray already gone then?"

"He's probably saluting about now. Or will be soon. You might still catch him. You know the Pines?"

TK could hear music playing in the house. He knocked louder.

Last night he had spent an hour in the library, reading some stuff, mostly an entry in the *World Book Encyclopedia*, volume 19, V–W (probably one of the volumes Brain had searched half a dozen years ago, looking for words . . . "vagina;" "venereal disease" . . .) thinking that maybe he was imagining all this. He found an entry for "Vietnam." He had copied parts of it into a notebook and torn out the pages; he had the pages folded in his shirt pocket now.

The door opened. A thin woman in black Capri pants and a loose, satiny blouse stood there. Her dark hair hung in a ponytail. Ray Sevigny's mother? She almost didn't look old enough; she was certainly younger than TK's mother. He had never pictured Ray as having parents, somehow; or *needing* them. TK introduced himself and asked if Ray was there.

She seemed barely interested. "Were you at the party last night?"

"Party?"

"Ray's going-away party."

"Oh . . . no. I know him from school."

She motioned him in. Without comment she walked through the living room and TK followed. A large wall mirror added an illusion of space to the room, but even so the house seemed cramped. He smelled smoke, though it wasn't from tobacco, more like burning rope. The music was jazz. TK couldn't envision his own mother listening to it. Within was a tiny kitchen where, next to the door, stood an olive drab duffel bag, nearly busting at the seams. There was a shelf collection of ceramic figurines and a starburst wall clock in a brass finish, showing 4:35.

"Out there." The woman nodded toward the backyard. Beyond the trees that gave the area its name, Whittle's Pond was visible. Ray was standing beside a rusted barrel, the air above the opening wrinkly with the heat from a fire. He was taking papers from a cardboard box and dropping them into the barrel. "There's someone here to see you," the woman called.

Someone. Had she forgotten TK's name already? Ray didn't appear to hear her. TK went out.

Ray Sevigny was wearing pegged slacks and a black short-sleeved shirt with pink panels in the front, dressed as he might be for a date; not for outdoor weather. The tattoo was vivid on his forearm. DEATH BEFORE DISHONOR. USMC. TK approached warily, the punch he'd taken the last time still fresh in his mind. Ray glanced up then and saw him. He frowned questioningly. TK nodded hello. "When are you supposed to report?"

"That again." Ray tossed another handful of papers into the barrel. Sparks rose in a quick red spiral. "I've got to be in Boston in a couple hours."

TK felt a shimmer of alarm. "Can't you put it off?"

Ray looked at him incredulously. "Why are you here?"

"Say that you have to finish school. Or get out altogether if you can. Is that possible? There must be a way." A slightly frantic note had invaded TK's voice. "You haven't been sworn in or anything yet, have you?" He had no idea how military enlistment worked, though he imagined there was some sort of ceremony.

Ray spat at the barrel; the saliva hit the side with a crisp sizzle. "I got no time for this. I got stuff to do." But he didn't say it with much energy, as though his mind really was elsewhere and TK's being here or not was a matter of complete indifference to him.

"Have you ever heard of a place called Vietnam?" TK persisted. Ray Sevigny's frown gave TK his answer. "It's this skinny little country in Southeast Asia." TK shaped it with his hands and realized that seen from a distance he might've been talking about a woman. "There's been war going on there practically forever." TK thought of the notes he'd jotted last night at the library but left them in his pocket.

Sevigny picked up the carton and upended it over the mouth of the barrel, letting the last of its contents flutter out. School papers, TK saw; old quizzes and compositions, discarded book covers, a few car magazines, a pen and ink drawing of a Big Daddy Roth figure.

Ray tossed the carton aside. "What's this got to do with anything?"

"The U.S. is getting involved. A little bit at a time, but it's happening."

"How would you know that?"

"I just . . . do. And when the fighting gets bad, Marines are going to be in the thick of it."

Ray leaned over the barrel, jabbing at the fire with a pine branch. Sparks swirled away like hornets from a hive that's been disturbed. "Well, that's the whole point, isn't it? Why the hell d'you think I joined? To spit-shine boots? Have some crummy NCO bark at me? Shit, if that was it, I might as well just stay here."

TK's mouth was dry. "I think it's going to be really bad."

Sevigny scowled. Then, as though TK's report were a minor annoyance, certainly not something worth his energy and emotion, he turned away from the fire. In the adjoining yard an old Chrysler convertible sat on blocks, its roof torn and sagging with the leaves and pine needles of several seasons. Beyond, a cluster of birch trees stood at the edge of the clearing. In the fading light, their leaves darkening, the branches looked as if they were full of blackbirds waiting to swoop. "That's what you want, too, ain't it?"

TK looked at him, not comprehending.

"To get the hell out?"

TK drew a quick breath, which felt feather-light in his chest, barely enough to form words. "I'm saying there could be a *war*."

Ray turned, his dark eyes flashing. "Don't bullshit me. I've seen it."

TK stared at him unbelieving. Was he saying that he'd experienced what TK had? That he, too, had a sense of impending doom?

"In those articles you write. It's in there."

Ray Sevigny read his columns? Now TK was thoroughly confused.

"That stuff you write about—the tricks the football coaches pull, the school's back-asswards way of doing stuff, the stupid rules. I read your column and I laugh. I mean, man, you nail it. I think to myself, this guy *gets* it. Up to a point."

"What . . . point?" TK asked tentatively.

"You never say what to *do* about it. You're like someone who's been nailed up in this little box." Ray picked up the carton, like a weird show-and-tell. "What he's really saying is, 'Lemme the fuck outta here!' "

They weren't talking about the same thing. TK's face felt like a hot mask, his skin baked tight by the heat from the fire. He glanced toward where the birches stood out palely against the coming dark. If there was a way to retreat right now, to turn and walk away, he might have—but there wasn't. Sevigny ripped at the carton, tearing out the ends. He shoved the flattened cardboard into the barrel. "And I say," he went on, "there's a guy wants out as bad as I do."

Was that true? No, it couldn't be. He wasn't like Ray Sevigny. Sevigny could rebuild a carburetor, and unsnap Dee Richards's bra, and drink a half pint of whiskey and not chuck it up, but did that stuff matter? Finishing school was what was important, right? Sure there were little annoyances, but they weren't talking about the same things. TK didn't live in the projects, didn't have a zero future. Anyway, this wasn't about Tom Knowles right now.

Ray's mother appeared on the back stoop. She had put on makeup and a short black denim jacket with rhinestone snaps, and her hair was brushed out now, shiny and dark. He'd never seen his own mom look like that. She looked as if she were ready for a night on the town, though she didn't seem very happy. "Time to go." She snapped open a small purse. "You drive." She took out a set of keys and threw them to Ray in a long underhand toss. Ray caught the keys. "Don't forget your duffel bag. I'll be in the car." Without another word she walked around the house, slightly wobbly in spiked ankle-high boots. Suddenly, TK had an odd awareness that the burning aroma he'd smelled in the house was marijuana; though he was equally sure he had never smelled marijuana before. He stepped to block Ray's path. "Guys are going to get *killed*, Ray."

Sevigny stopped, his jaw set, dark eyes fiery with something that might've been anger. TK braced, uncertain of what would happen, knowing only that he had no choice but to let it. The two of them stood there, locked in static tension, like those mechanical boxers in the game in the penny arcade at Nantasket, drop a coin and *biff! bam! bop!* He and Ray Sevigny were unalike in so many ways—yet each in his way was a son of this town and maybe more alike than either would ever have guessed. TK knew that if push came to shove, it would be a battle, but in the end, TK's own summer muscles and fitness notwithstanding, Ray Sevigny could take him, knew, too, that there was nothing he could do or say that would make Sevigny change his mind. TK reached into his pocket and pulled out the pages he'd copied last night at the library—facts and details about the long history of Vietnam. He held them above the dwindling flames and dropped them into the barrel. Ray glanced at them but didn't ask what they were. Then, unexpectedly, Ray's eyes softened, the strain in his face melted, and TK saw something he hadn't credited before but that the girls who'd been with the guy obviously had. It wasn't just toughness in Ray Sevigny, he had this other side, too . . . a gentle side that, for reasons TK hadn't seen, Ray wasn't afraid of showing, and because he wasn't afraid of it, it made him courageous. It was something that pricks like Butch Tracy, with all their mouth and posturing, wouldn't understand in a million years.

"Look," Sevigny said quietly, "I got nothing against you, okay? I like that stuff you write, but tonight I'm getting on a bus in Boston and I'm heading for boot camp. You dig? I don't want to go out of here leaving enemies. I'd rather find 'em somewheres else."

And a year from now, maybe a little more, you're going to be dead, TK thought woefully. Do *you* dig? Dead. Gone. It was a terrible thing even to *think,* let alone to say. He had no basis for such a statement, no possible way to back it up; except that, somehow, he believed with utter conviction that it was true. But he couldn't voice it. Left with this helplessness, he shook Ray Sevigny's hand. Two weeks later, in the *Eagle,* there was a photo of a tightly smiling Pvt. Ray Sevigny, in dress uniform, hair shorn, and the cutline, "Local Man Trains at Parris Island."

24 Tom

The neon clock on the front of the Atlantic Diner read 7:09 P.M. when Tom drove into the lot. The smell of the sea was strong in the air. He saw Penny standing inside the restaurant's entry, talking with a man with a shaved head and goatee. The man indicated his watch and began making sharp hand gestures, like someone lecturing a child. Tom felt an instant and instinctive dislike for him. After a moment, the man left, got into a van, and drove away. As Tom headed for the door, Penny came outside, shivering slightly in a thin cotton jacket. Quickly, she motioned for him to get back into the Escape, and she climbed in on the passenger side.

"Was that your husband?" Tom asked.

Penny looked startled, then nodded. "I had Alan drop me off. I told him I was filling in for another waitress."

Before Tom could ask another question—like why was she here? Where was Brain?—she said, "Paul called. There's been a change of plans. The mayor has had the old school annex sealed, so Paul's moving the location. He's going to do the laser projection at his house."

He was surprised. Did she know what this was about? Had Brain told her everything? "I don't even know where he lives."

"I do."

And that was another surprise.

"Paul asked me to come. He'll meet us there."

"What about—?"

"Alan?" Penny glanced at the diner, alight in the coming dusk. "He'll be here to pick me up at eleven."

As Tom shifted into reverse, he jumped at a knock on the hood. Mary Agnes Kinney stepped over the curbing and came around to his window as he lowered it. Her brow was ribbed with tension. "Mary Agnes . . . I didn't see you there."

"I'm asking you to stop whatever it is you're doing." She glanced past Tom at Penny. "I know you're in this, too."

Penny and Tom exchanged a look.

"No point denying it," the woman went on.

Tom shut off the engine. "What are you saying?" Penny asked.

Mary Agnes cut her attention back to Tom. "You should go back to California. Let this alone."

"Let what alone?" he asked.

"I'm begging you, go back."

"Mary Agnes, I don't—"

"Oh, I should've seen it that night at the reunion. Everything out of your mouth was twisted somehow, mocking. It's as if you came back to laugh at us. It's what you're doing now, too, isn't it. You came back to ruin us."

Tom stared at her, confounded. Had she been drinking?

"I believe you hate this town, hate everything it stands for. Because *you* failed." She pointed at him. "I know about the negativism you preach, all that 'nothing good can come of this town.'"

It took him a moment to realize that she was talking about Brain's 'No Wey' idea from long ago. How did she even know about that? Why was it coming up now? All at once there were tears in her eyes. She blinked them back, and her expression grew pained. "You couldn't take this, so you're determined to destroy it. You've got poor Paul Mclain all stirred up and confused, and he's going to be in trouble with the school department. He could lose his job!" Her voice had risen, her hands fluttering, pale in the dark like large moths. "And what went on between you and Dee Richards? She's engaged to be married. Why can't you just go back where you came from and write your depressing books and your dirty movies! And *you*!" she flared, rounding on Penny, pointing. "My God, look at what you've become! You couldn't keep your own child safe! You let poor Tina—"

"Mary Agnes!" Penny cried.

The woman brought a hand to her cheek as if she had been slapped. "Well, I'm . . . I'm not . . ." she mumbled, sounding disoriented. "It *is* too late." She turned, almost stumbling over the curb, and fled.

Tom shoved open his door to climb out. Penny's hand on his arm stopped him. "I want to talk to her," he said.

"Let her go."

"She's got everything wrong. About you, especially. And Brain."

"I know. But that's what she's feeling right now." Penny's voice was contrastingly calm, as though somehow she had not been party to what just went down.

Tom shut his door. "One thing she said, though, is true. That night after the reunion . . . I *was* with Dee Richards." He looked at Penny, who nodded. "You know?"

"No, but I wondered if something might've happened. Dee is . . . Dee. She has a reputation. She would've seen you as a trophy of some sort."

"No. I can't put it on her."

"Don't worry about it. We're all adults."

He considered explaining that the evening was a blur, that he remembered nothing of it, but what would that prove? Or change? "I know I'm a little cynical," he said instead, "but am I really that negative?"

Penny shook her head. "No. Oh, I thought you were when you first arrived. But I see through that. In fact, I'm beginning to think that you may be the only person around here who isn't negative."

He wasn't sure what she meant. She glanced out and gestured at the diner and the encircling parking lot, half full of cars. Beyond, just a smudge of rouge remained in the sky as night descended and lights along the Bridge Street drag came on. "Many of us have this notion of Weybridge, this mental map . . . but it's a map drawn up so long ago, in our youth. Those of us who've stayed here still navigate by it. We've accepted things and have just chalked them up to

256

'that's the way life is.' Now you're asking us to rethink things, to redraw the map."

"Penny, I never—"

"Wait, hear me out. This isn't easy. In fact, it's . . . scary." Penny shivered and clutched her arms across her chest. She looked vulnerable in her thin jacket. "It strikes me all at once that maybe we're caught between then and now, trying to find a way to keep the past in our lives, and a part of us is stranded back there, searching for a way to let the future in."

Tom winced as though reacting to some throb of inner pain, though outwardly there was no physical counterpart. "Then help me with this," he said.

"With what you told the mayor? About Keystone Steel? That's what's got Mary Agnes hysterical, right?"

"Probably."

Penny was watching him intently. "You heard what she said. She connects me with this, too. And she's the type to use it."

"You really think she would?"

"I don't want to find out. I can't jeopardize my work. Here at the diner I don't worry about, but what I do at the hospital—I can't lose that. Mayor Kinney's got a strange sense of ownership for this town. You need to be careful, too. You don't want to get on his bad side."

"I'm not worried about him."

"Whatever you're planning with Paul tonight—and I don't claim to know; he didn't say much; I think he just wants me along for support—but whatever it is, I get the idea that it could be dangerous." Her eyes were suddenly full of worry. "Am I right?"

"I don't know."

Abruptly, Penny sat forward in the seat. "So why do it? For what, Tom? Speculation that's decades old? Nothing you can even prove? Is that what this is?" Anguish had come into her voice; she heard it, too, and sat back slightly. "Those children you met when we went apple picking, Vivian and the others, they're so dear to me,

I can't even begin to tell you. They need me, and I realize that . . . that I need them. They've replaced Tina, replaced even Alan. And I can't fail them. In a way, they're . . . they're . . ." Her eyes brimmed suddenly with tears, and she broke off.

He was struck, as he had been before, by how youthful she looked. Partly it was the failing light, but of all the people from his past whom he'd encountered in this trip, she had moved forward through time the most gracefully. He waited for her to complete her thought, and in a constricted voice, she said, "They're all I've got."

"I hope you're not buying into what Mary Agnes said. About your daughter," he said gently. "You weren't to blame for anything."

"No, but . . . I'm scared. I'm hanging on by my fingernails." She broke down then and the tears came.

He put a hand on her shoulder, but unlike the one other time he'd touched her, the night of the reunion, she didn't stiffen and pull away. Facing him, she was half-lit by the diner's lights, and he saw that his notion that she'd somehow escaped the stamp of time wasn't accurate. There were lines at the edges of her eyes and the corners of her mouth, but she was lovely still. She found tissues in her jacket pocket and wiped her tears.

"Penny, what you said about looking for a new map, for a way to let the future in . . . there may be a chance to find out."

"That's not fair."

"No, it isn't. None of this is. Your daughter dying, my dad busting his ass for years, then being shafted by the company he served. Or those children who get ill. Let's throw in an idealistic president gunned down in his prime, or the kids we knew in school whose names are etched on that war memorial. Even Mary Agnes, consumed by fear. Not fair? You can say *that* again." His voice had risen; he struggled to lower it. "But now we've got an opportunity to maybe, *maybe*, make it just a little less unfair, and so the question is, what are we going to do about it."

"You're back to Paul's idea, aren't you. His lasers and holograms? His idea about some . . . alternate past?"

So Brain had shared his wild theory. It was just as well. It was laughable anyhow. He knew it. All of this was crazy, and he was crazy for even being here contemplating it. Farther down Bridge Street, the fog lights on the bridge had come on, flaring like vaporous yellow moons. He craved a cigarette. He felt he should apologize to Penny for having gone off on her like that, and yet he knew that she understood. "Hey, what would've happened if . . . ?" He let the idea trail off. Outside, in the gathering dark, the diner gleamed, patrons visible beyond the curved glass like passengers on an ocean liner. He had a sudden wish to be in there among them.

"If what?" she asked.

If the Colonel made chicken this good . . . He shook his head.

"Tell me."

He let out a breath. "If that night at the dance, the fall of our senior year . . . what if I'd gotten to you and we'd danced? Could it . . . have changed things?"

"Tom, don't. You can't possibly—"

"Not just us; changed *everything*. Could destiny have been different? The war averted . . . those kids we knew gone on and lived full lives and be here with us now?"

"You're talking crazy," Penny said, and yet she was looking at him with an insistency that seemed to contradict her words.

"Am I? I'm not so sure. Because lately I've begun to think that—"

Something chirped, startling them both. His phone? Hers. A look of alarm flashed across her face. Penny put a finger to her lips, warning Tom to be silent, and then took the call. "Marilyn? What's—?" She listened a moment. "Oh, no," she said. "Please no." She looked at him. "It's a nurse I know at the hospital. Mike Burke has been in a terrible accident. Hit by a car."

Tom's heart clenched.

"A priest is there," Penny echoed. And to the nurse, gathering herself now: "Does anyone know how to reach Mike's wife? Someone should contact Mo."

THREE

paper
covers
rock

$\overline{25}$ TK

Whatever Dee Richards's reaction to Ray Sevigny's departure might have been, she didn't say, at least not that TK ever heard. Then Brain reported that the minister's daughter had a new man in her life.

"You're kidding," TK said when he heard this, but he knew Brain wasn't.

"I saw them together in the T-Bird."

"Maybe they're just friends." But TK knew that wasn't true either. Artie Dewitt didn't have girls for friends.

"That damned Don Juan and his Four-F club," Brain said wretchedly. "He was probably just waitin' for Ray to leave. Sevigny is a prince compared to that crummy snake. I wouldn't trust him with *any* girl."

"Dee isn't just any girl," TK pointed out. "I don't think she'd let someone get away with anything." *That she didn't* want *them to get away with*, he added to himself.

"Where's he digging clams these days? I want to get into his glove box and prick holes in all his Frenchies."

TK argued that wasn't wise (whether or not rubbers entered

into the equation where Dewitt and Dee Richards were concerned) and finally convinced Brain to wait and see what happened. But TK didn't have a lot of energy to spend worrying about what might be going on in the love lives of other people; he was too busy trying to cope with the growing difficulty of his own life. Alfred E. Newman's *MAD* magazine philosophy to the contrary, he found it impossible not to worry. Most nights he was lucky if he got a few hours' sleep.

One morning, running late again because Mom wouldn't get up, and certain that Pop Sterns would be lying in wait for him, TK tried to start the Rambler, but an overnight freeze had sapped the aging battery. He flung open the car door, grabbed his books, and loped toward Sea Street, his breath steaming over his shoulder like a ragged scarf. Each time a vehicle came along, he turned, trotting backward, and stuck out his thumb, but no one was picking up hitchers that day. As he neared the colonial cemetery in the Heights, he heard the rumble of glass-packs and then, rounding the corner, scattering leaves in its wake, came Ray Sevigny's Merc. He still couldn't bring himself to think of the car as anything but Ray's, hanging on to that image (as Butch Tracy must've, too; beyond BUTCH pin-striped on the driver's door, with a little skull and crossbones insignia beneath, Tracy had done nothing to the car). TK hadn't seen him in weeks, other than the occasional glimpse of him speeding recklessly by. He sped by now, too; oblivious to TK's upraised thumb.

Suddenly the brake lights went on and the Merc stopped. Ready to set aside old grudges, TK loped toward the car. As he reached for the door handle, the car screeched off, leaving him choking in a cloud of smoke. When TK got to school fifteen minutes later, heart still pounding, reeking of scorched rubber, Sterns was waiting with a detention slip.

26 Tom

It took a while to locate the neighborhood. He hadn't been to Brain's place before, and he imagined what he would find: an empty refrigerator, a full sink, and more books than Brain would ever have time to organize and shelve, though he probably had read them all. Beyond that, Tom didn't care to speculate.

He and Penny had gone directly to the hospital, but Mike was in emergency surgery. After a doctor came out and explained that the injuries were serious, Penny said she'd stay, and Tom went to the Burkes' house to find a way to contact Mike's wife in Nevada. He located a phone number taped to the wall and called and after several disconnects reached Mo Burke. "Oh, my God, is he—?" No, Tom tried to reassure her. She was going to call the hospital directly. Now Tom wanted to get word to Brain about the accident. Holograms would have to wait.

Brain's neighborhood lay above a lonely tidal cove that, in Tom's memory, was perpetually closed to shell fishing because of contaminants from the soap factory and the shipyard. The homes were run-down cottages, mostly, clumped together on small lots. Brain's address was one of the larger houses on the dead-end street, but as Tom started for the door, he discovered that Brain's address was actually located in the rear, behind the main house, in a tiny outbuilding. The structure looked to have been a garage converted to living space. Lights were on inside. He approached on the crushed shell walk. Out over the tidal basin, the night clouds had thickened, and the moon bedded behind them cast a greenish light, like something oozing out of an infected wound.

Despite the heavy air, he felt cold. His longing for the balmy evenings of Southern California was becoming palpable. He stepped over to a small window and peered through. The room inside was a jumble of wall shelves cluttered with papers and books. Set up on a table was the equipment Brain had used the night of the reunion. Something rustled in the bushes behind him, and Tom felt a flicker of sudden dread. After the shipyard closed, the population of rats that had occupied the dank piers, feeding off the leavings of the vast workforce of men, had soon found themselves facing starvation. The more venturesome rats had made their way across the tidal cove to neighborhoods here. He'd seen them on occasion, late at night, crossing a street, sleek and wet-furred, pausing to cast a red-eyed glare at an intruder before scuttling into shadows. He wedged the image away. When there was still no response to his knocking, he tried the knob and was surprised to find the door unlocked.

"Anyone here?" he called in that standard and illogical greeting of the uninvited. He stepped inside.

Where he saw Brain. He was crouched in a corner. He had his back to the wall, his sweating face knotted, his eyes large orbs of fright, his nostrils flared as he breathed rapid, shallow breaths. Tom had a sudden memory of him one time when Brain was a small, frightened boy in hand-me-down corduroy pants and a Davy Crockett T-shirt, facing a whipping from his father.

"It's okay, man. It's Tom."

"Yuh-yuh-you scared me."

It was mutual; Brain was scaring him now. He reached to offer a hand, but Brain recoiled, and Tom stepped back, giving him some space. The sour odor of fear came off him. Had he already heard about Mike's accident? Or had the mayor stripped him of his job? He seemed like a man standing very close to the line that divided the sane from the mad. His terrified eyes groped for Tom's. "Wh . . . where's Penny?"

So he didn't know about the accident. Tom told what he knew.

Slowly, as though succumbing to great fatigue, Brain shifted his feet and legs until he was sitting on the floor, his back still wedged into the corner—*almost as though he were attempting to push through*

266

the spaces in the atoms and disappear. Tom dialed the number for Penny's cell phone and got her at the hospital. Mike was still in the ER; Mo Burke had called and was catching the first flight back.

"Does anyone know what happened?" Tom asked her.

"It was a hit-and-run."

A wave of cold washed over him. "Penny, I'm worried about Paul."

"I'll call you right back."

He started to give her the phone number, but she'd already hung up. Brain hadn't moved. Tom went into the kitchen and got him a glass of water and set it on the floor within reach. In the bathroom there were various medications in the cabinet, but nothing that told him what to do. As he shut the cabinet, his phone rang.

"Tom?" a male voice said. "It's David Simkin—Penny's doctor friend. She just called. What can you tell me?"

"Well?" Tom asked twenty minutes later as Dr. Simkin folded his stethoscope.

"He's had an episode."

"Episode?"

"It's medicalese for 'we don't rightly know,'" admitted Simkin, zipping his backpack. He was a lean, handsome man, a hint of the Jersey shore in his voice. "It could've been a panic attack, or some kind of fugue state. His heart rate and blood pressure are up. He claims he didn't take any meds. To be on the safe side, I'm going to get an ambulance and admit him. We should know more after some tests. I have one question for you, though. You say he was like this before he heard that his friend had been struck by a car. Do you know of anything that might've keyed him up?"

Anything? What about what we'd planned for tonight? What about weird ideas about other dimensions? A proper answer to the question would require some while to frame, starting with a more-than-passing knowledge of Weybridge's past, and the culture of the class of 1964, facts about what fathers did for work, toss in $E=mc^2$ and the A-BOM . . . and while you're at it, give a cheer for the kids who drink the . . .

"No," Tom said earnestly, "nothing I can think of."

An ambulance was soon pulling into the driveway, the lights strobing around the book-lined room. Dr. Simkin and the EMTs got Brain into it almost quickly enough to beat the arrival of a small crowd of onlookers, who stood around briefly and dispersed once the ambulance left. Tom started to go back inside to close up the house, when his phone rang again. "Penny?" he said at once.

"Well, good," his agent said with a chuckle, "I can tell you're already cool with the Tamara split."

Tom let out a breath that he didn't know he'd been holding. "And the bad news?"

Randy laughed, and Tom realized how good it sounded. His body was rigid with the tensions of the past few hours. "This you're gonna love, brah. Ready? Warner's just green-lighted the film."

It took him a moment to process this. "You're *serious*?"

"How soon can you get here?"

Tom called the airport. As he locked the door to Brain's pad and headed for his car, Penny arrived. Mike was undergoing emergency surgery, she said; his condition was still touch and go.

"Are you going back to the hospital now?"

"Alan thinks I am. He called and I told him I was. I've thought about what you said. About following through."

Tom frowned uncertainly.

"On what you found out about Keystone . . ."

"Forget what I said. I'm sorry I pressured you. And forget all this—what Brain had cooked up here, with the lasers and the holograms. I have."

"He was doing that for you. Trying to be a friend."

"Yeah, well. I'm not a reliable friend. Hospitalization and bed rest are what he needs right now. Tests. I heard Dr. Simkin. Thanks for sending him, by the way. He'll get Brain the help he needs."

"I'm sure he will, but vindication might be just as important."

They were standing outside, and he tried to read her expression, but it was half-shadowed in the light from the door fixture. "Yeah, I've been a big help to him. To him and Mike both."

"You didn't cause Mike's accident. And you certainly aren't responsible for Paul's condition. It's a mental illness. It's been diagnosed and treated before, but things don't magically go away. Maybe we've all been in denial about Paul, chalking his quirks up to eccentricity, because he's smart. 'That's just Brain; he's always had these kooky ideas.' Okay, but he's our *friend*, too. I know you didn't mean what you said before—about you not having friends here."

"Didn't I?"

"And friendship has requirements."

"Then let's leave him be so he can get well. He's done fine all these years without me around. He'll be okay again once I'm gone."

Penny tipped her head, and the lamplight lit her face fully now. "Gone?" She looked surprised, uncertain. "What about . . . ?"

"I've accomplished what I came for. My mother is settled, the house is sold, and I just found out—I sold my screenplay."

Penny seemed suddenly off-balance, as if the crushed shell walkway had trembled under her. "Oh. So you can't continue with this anyway."

"I've caused more hassle here than any of it's worth. There's no way of proving anything. The records are gone. Fred Kinney's determined to make it all go away. And maybe it needs to. *I* need to. Things'll be a lot better here with me out of the picture."

Penny blew out a breath, and when she spoke, her voice had dropped almost to a whisper. "Well, I guess I knew going into this that I shouldn't really expect anything."

He swallowed. "It's just that—"

She silenced him with a raised hand. "You don't have to explain. You've been honest with me all along. I was the one not being honest. I see that now. Hell, I've been lying to my husband."

"Penny—"

"Congratulations on your success. Your movie." She mustered a wan smile. "If you let me know when it comes out, I'll go see it. I don't go to many movies, my work schedule and all, but maybe I could ask Alan, and . . ." She broke off, frowning at some distant point, and for an instant her face looked so stricken he thought it might crumple, but then she drew a steadying breath and stood straighter.

"Hey," he said, "you all right?"

"I am now. I don't know what I was thinking." She walked toward the street.

He went with her, something dawning. "Are you going to pursue this?"

"When I told you tonight how some of us here are stuck with old maps—I need to be wrong about that."

"You don't have to prove it. I can tell you that."

"Thank you, but right now, Tom, I'm not sure you're the best witness."

"Look, I'm not staying. I've already called the airline about leaving tonight. They have me on standby. Staying was never in the plan, and it's not negotiable."

She stopped walking and faced him. "So, why tell me?"

"My life is out there, in California."

"I know." Her gaze didn't waver; he felt it, palpable, like an accusation, though perhaps that was just his projection. Restless under it, he went on: "What's here? Brain maybe slipping back into psychosis? Mike drinking and going noplace—now this? And what about—?" He almost said her marriage; he let it alone. "Am I supposed to wait around to pick up people when they've crashed and burned?"

"People? I thought we were talking about friends."

"*Were* friends. Once upon a time."

"I forgot. So stick with your Hollywood friendships. You told me about those."

"At least out there your problems are your own. You deal with them yourself, you don't go whining to other people."

270

"Then go back, really. Because you wouldn't belong here."

"Damn straight."

"I mean it. You've done the right things. Hey, you achieved escape velocity. Who else can say that? Others tried, you *did* it. You can leave with your head high."

She went to her car. In the tidal cove beyond the dead-end street, a low bank of fog had gathered. He wanted to call her back, to explain, but what else was there to say? She opened the door. The hell with her. "You can just say I'm chicken, Penny. That I've *always* been chicken."

Abruptly, she turned and came back so fast he thought she would charge right into him. But she stopped two feet from him. "That's crap. Whoever you are now, you didn't used to be. You've changed. You're not TK. You're someone else."

"You've got that right. TK was a dumb kid who got pushed around and finally had the sense to get out."

"No. You're wrong. Naïve, okay. We all were. But pushed around? No. You thought not playing football messed things up for you. And your dad dying. Those were hard, yet you were honorable, you got through. So the rest of it? That's who you are now, Tom. That kid, TK—he was different."

"Oh, hot shit. How?"

"He just was."

"That's not very convincing."

"He wasn't bitter, for one thing. He wasn't cynical, or snide . . ." She sought for more words, but the anger or the fight was gone. "He was strong," she said simply, "and . . . sincere." This time she went straight to her car, started it, and drove away.

27 TK

A steeple bell was tolling five as TK climbed out of the subway at Park Street. The clocks had been set back last weekend, and already the sky was deepening, city lights coming on.

The old and shabby Boston he remembered was being torn away in favor of the new and modern, a tug of war between the city's Brahmin past and what the politicians spoke of as its shining future. Perhaps no place was feeling it more than Scollay Square, with its burlesque houses, tattoo parlors, and dive bars. It had changed even since the last time he'd been here, a year ago, with some members of the football team, all trying to look older as they went into the Old Howard Casino, standing tall in their letter jackets, prepared to add several years to their ages if questioned at the door; but there was none of that. The man with the cauliflower ears and mashed nose at the gate passed them through with a toothless grin, and TK realized that they weren't the first group of teenage boys to go to a striptease show. Nor had they been disappointed. Sure, they discovered how much of it was tease, but they'd soon entered into the fun of the succession of acts—the baggy pants comics, and the exotic-looking (though unexpectedly older) women who never quite got down to the altogether, but certainly showed enough flesh to widen the eyes of a group of horny adolescents.

TK glanced fleetingly in the direction of Old Howard's glittering marquee, tatty now, many of the bulbs burned out. Already, construction scaffolding was sprouting close by and the wrecking ball was near. He shut his eyes against a gust of wind that swirled grit, old newspapers, and leaves, then set course for the Federal Building.

There were lights glowing in some of the windows, but not

many. In the lobby he shed his topcoat and straightened his tie. A mustached man in a government security services uniform directed him to the third floor. There, in the reception area of Senator Kennedy's office, a slender Negro woman in a brown tweed skirt and a cream-colored blazer looked up from her typing as TK walked in. "Mr. Knowles?"

"Yes, ma'am."

She rose and came to greet him. She was tall and athletic-looking and reminded him of Wilma Rudolph, the great sprinter who had won three gold medals at the Rome Olympics a few summers ago. "Hang your coat there if you like." She had an engaging smile and a soft Southern accent. He put his coat on a hook by the door. "So you write for your high school newspaper," she said.

"Yes, ma'am." It had been his entré on the telephone: He wanted to interview Kennedy. Now, all of a sudden, he realized he hadn't brought a notepad. Did she notice?

"The senator likes to meet with citizens. Can I get you a soda?"

"No, thank you."

"Well, please have a seat. He'll be with you shortly."

TK took one of the dark blue leather chairs. The woman returned to her desk and the quick clatter of the electric type-writer resumed. Actually, he thought he would like something to drink, his throat was dry, but he was too shy to say he'd changed his mind.

The outer office was narrow, with a high plaster ceiling with decorative molding, two of its walls given over to a gallery of framed photographs. Beyond the room's lone window the sky was darkening with coming night. TK sat, fidgeting, no longer sure why he was here. Which was one more question on a growing list of things he wasn't sure about. On the subway train, on the long clank-ing run from Fields Corner, he had gone over in his mind what he wanted to say to the senator, but now he discovered that the words had deserted him. It was like having studied for a Latin test, sure that he knew the declensions and conjugations, but realizing, as Ma

Casey passed out the mimeographed test paper, that his mind was as empty as an old soup can.

"Are you worried about something?"

The senator's aide was looking up, smiling kindly.

"Me?" *Who do you think, dummy? There's no one else in the room.* "No," he added quickly. "Not at all."

"It shouldn't be much longer."

Too restless to sit, he rose and went over to look at the photographs. Mostly black and whites, they showed the Kennedy family over years and generations. There were pictures taken at the Hyannisport compound, of touch football games on the lawn, of big holiday dinners; photos from the president's inauguration: top-hatted dignitaries, their breath smoking in the January cold. There were group photos of the brothers and sisters, wives and husbands, skiing and at the beach, photos of President Kennedy among crowds of people, smiling and shaking hands.

The photo that held TK's interest was of the brothers on a sailboat, taken on a summer afternoon, the three looking windblown and happy, their gazes fixed on a distant horizon. Young, suntanned, and handsome, they glowed with promise. He jumped at a tap on his shoulder.

"I guess you didn't hear me." The aide smiled. "The senator will see you now."

She ushered him back past her desk and through an open door, announced him, then stepped out and drew the door shut. The inner office was plush, lighted softly by table lamps. Windows looked out onto the tops of floodlit trees. There was no view of the old Howard Casino burlesque house, though TK wondered fleetingly if the young Ted Kennedy had gone there in his prep school days? On a narrow table sat a football, on which was printed: HARVARD 13—YALE 9 1954. The senator, in a tuxedo and a black bow tie, was standing and reading something in a manila folder, which he set down now and moved around the desk, flashing the broad, familiar smile, offering a large hand, whose firm grip prompted TK to grip harder himself. "Mr. Knowles. Good to see you."

"Thank you for seeing me, sir. I mean, Senator." He felt his cheeks warm.

"What do they call you?"

He started to say TK but thought: was that what the senator might also be called? Anyway, it suddenly sounded juvenile. "I'm Thomas, Junior—but I go by Tom."

"Well, then, Tom. Thank you for coming."

There were chairs in the room, chairs where important people had no doubt sat, but Kennedy remained standing, and TK was aware of the value of time here. The senator's evening garb was obviously not for this occasion. He jettisoned his idea of mentioning having seen Kennedy just a week ago outside the Weybridge Savings Bank, an occasion that had sent TK rushing into an alley to throw up. He got right to the point. "I'm worried about the president. I think he might be in danger."

Senator Kennedy's manner lost some of its casualness. "Uh . . . sit down, Tom." TK did, and Kennedy sat, too, his stiff white shirt-front buckling over his cummerbund. "Go on."

TK's necktie felt like a noose. He felt his purpose fading. With no credentials, his sole link to being here was tenuous at best. Outside dusk had settled deeper on the city. He had the sensation all at once of being cooped up, in need of physical action. He wished he had brought a pad to write on. Absurdly, he wondered if the conversation would go better if they took that game ball there and went out into the corridor and passed it back and forth. "Well, it's just . . . a feeling."

"A feeling," the senator repeated.

. . . *one that might not mean diddly, and yet it was like* . . . He swallowed, suddenly lost. He thought of a day he'd been riding in the car with Dad—TK might've been fifteen, in a quiet despair that, despite what all the songs claimed, he didn't have a sweetheart or a lover, didn't, in fact, have a clue as to what he was supposed to feel.

Dad must've sensed some different quality to his son's silence (companionable quiet was common between them), so he asked, glancing over once or twice, then back at the road: "Something bothering you, son?" TK had said, "How do you know when . . . when you're in love?" and after the briefest hesitation, Dad said, "You just know." It seemed a cheat, not at all what he'd hoped to learn; he felt disappointed. It was one more question his father didn't have a real answer to. Yet, TK had filed the response away. *You just know*. He had something close to that now, about this and about being here— a *knowing*—and looking at the photographs had confirmed it. "I guess it's . . . from the way the president is right out there with the people . . . *among* them."

"I see. Well, the president believes that elected leaders need to be accessible to the people they represent. It's a democratic idea."

"I understand, but . . . but I mean, if someone were to . . . you know, try to hurt him."

Kennedy's face darkened momentarily, a look somewhere between perplexity and anger. "Uh, wait here a moment, will you, Tom?"

The senator went out of the room, shutting the door behind him. TK wished he had said nothing, wished he hadn't even come. Was it possible just to leave? A moment later Kennedy returned, accompanied by a tall, dark-haired man in a blue suit. He looked about the senator's age, though his face had a harder look, his brown eyes scrutinizing.

"Tom," Kennedy said, "this is Agent Reynolds. He works for the Secret Service."

TK swallowed. The man waved TK back down and took a chair himself. Senator Kennedy remained standing.

"Did I do something wrong?" TK asked, glancing from Kennedy to Agent Reynolds. He was a little breathless.

"No, son, not as far as I can tell, but it's the job of the Secret Service to make sure that everything goes smoothly. So there aren't any misunderstandings. When you were speaking with the senator just now, about the president," (the words were spoken in a low, conversational way, but the man was watching him with hawklike interest) "was there something particular you had in mind?"

Had there been? Should he mention his reaction when he'd seen Kennedy in Weybridge and had to run into an alley? Or what about the crazy dreams . . . or the line on the sheet of paper in his type-writer: JFK IS IN DANGER? "No," he said, then felt compelled to add, "I saw newsreels of the president . . . I guess I was just . . ." Just what? He cleared his throat. "We studied Abraham Lincoln and then Archduke Ferdinand and I . . . well, I really *like* the president."

Later, riding home on the MTA, he recalled all this, how the agent had asked him a few more questions and finally had smiled and said, "We all like the president, Tom, and you can be assured that we're going to take good care of him."

The senator had added, "There are some parts of the coun-try . . . certain places where some people aren't quite ready for change. There's a very human tendency to, uh . . . to want to go back . . . to a past that while it was good for some folks, wasn't nec-essarily good for all. You understand that."

"I think so, yes."

"Most folks are good people; some just need time to grow. Occasionally, there are people whose intentions aren't good, people who might try to hurt others, might want to hurt the president. So we just like to keep an eye on them. But if the time ever came where our leaders can't freely move among the people they represent . . . well, I hope I'm not alive to see it. That would be a dark day for America."

On his way out the nice receptionist had said she noticed TK's interest in the photographs, and she asked if he'd like to have his picture taken—which they did sometimes, "to encourage future voters"—and TK agreed. Now he wondered: would his picture hang there on the wall? Or would it be stashed away in some secret government file?

28 Tom

Tom watched Penny make a U-turn on the dead-end street and drive off. As he got into the Escape, his cell phone rang. It was a reservations agent from United, calling to say that they had a cancellation on the red-eye to Los Angeles, scheduled for an 11:50 departure. He said he'd take it.

It was just before nine when he got over to Elm Hill. His mother was already asleep for the night, and he considered asking the attendant to wake her so that he could say good-bye; but he thought about what Monica Kim had told him, how sometimes it was good to let a parent settle in for a while before visiting. Instead he wrote a short note, explaining that some writing business had come up suddenly and needed tending to but that he would call her tomorrow. Back at the house he quickly packed. He called Jarvis and Eaton Real Estate and left a message asking Stan Jarvis to arrange for a local attorney to represent Tom at the closing. Then it was time to head to the airport.

Fog was moving in off the water, lapping at the shore. As he drove across the bridge, the blinking red warning lights atop the old gantries at the shipyard were just visible. A foghorn moaned out beyond the mouth of the river. He wondered if flights would be delayed. In Adams Point he approached the "NO. WEY." sign, and then it was behind him, Boston ahead. He felt as if a load had been lifted from his shoulders. Still, he found himself thinking of the place where he lived all those years ago . . . thinking about his mother, this woman who had changed his diapers, and later sponged his vomit from the bathroom floor on one green-gilled morning after a monumental night of vodka with his high school friends. His mother, who had never failed to wait up for him when he came home as an adolescent and then as a young man, later in each case; but no matter how late, never responding with

278

a reproachful word or an accusing glare. Most often she was ready with a sleepy smile and a "How was it?" wanting to share his evening, impervious to his laconic or loutish or sometimes tipsy reply, as if she understood that some parental vigil was over, for that night, at least. He tried to remember when she had stopped keeping that vigil. After Dad got sick? Perhaps never; he honestly couldn't recall.

What of the time when he wound up in sick bay at Fort Dix after a virulent respiratory infection spread through the barracks, and he'd weakly phoned to tell her. She proposed driving right down to see him, had been ready to travel alone, in an aging car, to New Jersey to be with him. Of course he told her not to bother, that he'd be well again soon (and was), but the fact remained that she'd been willing, that to come to him in his need was her first impulse. When had he ever been so selfless with this woman? With anyone, for that matter, he thought unhappily. Here was this aged woman, who had never done anything worse than to love her wayward son, and who was guilty now of nothing more than living. It didn't matter, young or old, all of us were under the sentence of time, and like a sudden blow Tom realized that he didn't want to leave her here, didn't want her to die alone, among strangers—for no other reason than she was his mother and he loved her.

He'd have to act quickly. He'd contact Elm Hill, though that could wait till morning. Other things couldn't. With the fog drifting languidly in the streets, he turned around and headed back to Weybridge.

29 TK

A big pep banner hung in the main lobby. Weybridge vs. Brockton was a Turkey Day rivalry going back to the 1920s. Still over a week away, the game (and that evening's rally) was nevertheless the hot topic of conversation in the halls and cafeteria.

TK felt a twinge of regret at all that might have been, but he had more pressing concerns at the moment. He was scheduled to take a term final in U.S. History last period, but where was his textbook? He hurried to his locker between classes to look for it; he was pretty sure he'd brought it, yet the book wasn't there. This was happening too often these days. He felt scattered and confused—and frustrated. He banged the locker door shut.

"My ears!"

He nearly dropped the combination lock. He turned to see Penny standing there.

"I'm joking," she said, though her expression didn't seem full of fun at the moment. She was out of breath. "Tom, there was some guy asking about you."

"What guy?"

She flinched at a sharpness in his voice. "He wore a dark suit, had a little ID thing . . . not a badge. He said he's a federal agent." Her look grew uncertain. "He asked if we could talk a moment."

"When was this?"

"Last period. He pulled me out of homeroom. He called me 'Miss.' He was so formal. 'Miss, do you know Thomas Knowles? How long have you known this individual?' Like you had no name. It frightened me. TK—what's going on?"

"What did you say?"

"I wasn't going to lie. I said of course I know you. I said we're friends."

"I meant . . ." He glanced at other students passing in the hall-way. "Did he ask you anything else?"

"He wanted to know if you get in trouble, who you associate with. That's just how he said it, too—'associate with.' Who talks like that?"

Just then the hallway loudspeaker squawked. "Thomas Knowles, please report to the vice principal's office. Thomas Knowles."

Penny's forehead crinkled with fresh concern. "Oh, Tom, are you . . ."

"Am I what?"

"Doing anything you shouldn't?"

He frowned.

"Okay. I just don't want you in trouble. He also said . . . don't tell you that anyone was asking."

But she had. She was frightened, yet she had come to him. "Thank you."

"For what? Disobeying?"

TK exhaled and managed a smile, a weak smile, but at least it was genuine. "For saying we're friends."

She clutched his hand in a quick squeeze, and then hurried off.

He opened his hand and saw a tiny square of paper. Lettered on it were a phone number and the message: "If you need to talk, anytime, call. P." Standing a little taller, he put the note in his shirt pocket, straightened his tie, and headed for Sterns's office.

When he reported, the vice principal's secretary handed him his U.S. History book; a student had found it in the boys' room. No mention about a man in a dark suit, and TK didn't ask. The less he had to deal with Sterns the better.

When he got home that afternoon he found his mother sitting at the kitchen table, working with scissors. The Formica tabletop was littered with empty Raleigh cigarette packs. She'd finally gotten around to clipping the coupons from them, which was more pressing apparently than getting out of her bathrobe or preparing supper. She looked up as he came in. "Thomas?" It was what she had taken to calling him since Dad died. "I need to know something."

His heart missed a beat. Was she going to say that a man from the government had come here asking questions? He waited.

"Look through this catalogue when you get a minute. Do you think I should get the sunburst clock or a nice set of pewter candlestick holders for the mantel?"

I think you should quit smoking so much. I think you ought to get

dressed and brush your hair. I think you should cook some supper for us.
"All right," he said.

Supper would have tasted good. He had skipped lunch to cram for the history test and he was starved, but he'd grab something on the way to the pep rally. He hurried through his homework (as he always did lately, completing the rock-bottom minimum of what was required). The only assignment he gave anything more than the barest attention to was the vocabulary worksheet for Longchamp's class. As usual, it included twenty words; among them tonight were "melee," "miscreant," and "poignant." At 6:30 he took a shower, put on fresh chinos and a flannel shirt. He took a twenty-dollar bill hidden in a sock in his top drawer. Mom had finished her coupon clipping and had evidently gotten a second wind; she was organizing the boxes in the cereal cupboard, alphabetically, from what he could see (Alpha-Bits, Bran Buds, Cheerios . . .). He told her where he was going.

"Good for you," she said. "You work hard. You can use some pep."

He sent a sidelong glance at the little pill bottle on the kitchen counter. *And what about you?* She'd gotten Dr. McGowan to write a prescription for Dexedrine.

"Better take your winter coat," she said. "It's supposed to get chilly."

"I'm fine. I won't be outside." He had his letter jacket in the car. What he didn't have in the car was enough gas for the evening if he intended to take Penny out afterward, but he'd get some later; right now he opted for human fuel. At Varsity Pizza he got two slices of pepperoni pizza and a Pepsi, which he scarfed, then headed for the school.

The event was being held in the gym, the only place big enough for the crowd that turned out for the pre-Brockton game rally. Miss Mutterperl was one of the chaperones; Mr. Morrisette was there, too, and a few of the other teachers. Unsnapping his letter jacket, TK climbed up into the wooden bleachers and joined some kids he knew.

There were brief words of welcome from the principal and the athletic director, then the lights dimmed and a spotlight illuminated the doorway that opened to a corridor that led to the boys' locker room. As the band struck up a fanfare, TK felt an ominous sinking sensation. A year ago, he was back there in the tunnel, standing eager and expectant with the other members of the varsity team.

On the gym floor now, the cheerleaders were chanting, their pom-poms waving like green and white sea anemones. "Grogan! Grogan! He's our man, if he can't do it, *Jarvis* can . . ."

All around, kids were holding up squares of poster board that they'd decorated and emblazoned with the names and uniform numbers of team members. Over the sea of raised signs and wildly pumping arms, TK watched as, one by one, players loped from the spotlighted doorway.

". . . if he can't do it, Sweeney can!"

To the swelling cheers of the crowd and the clashing of cymbals, the players ran out onto the hardwood and took up a stand in the center of the gym, a growing line of them there in the gleam of the lights, like young gods of autumn.

"Burke! Burke! He's our man . . ."

And big tall Mike loped out, cheeks ruddy, his butch cut gleaming . . . and *don't do it, Mike, don't play anymore, give it up* . . . TK looked around: where had *that* thought come from? Jealousy, he decided somberly. Jealousy toward Mike, toward all of them, because they'd stuck with the game, endured for the season, and he hadn't. Disgusted with himself for having these feelings, he made his way back down the ziggurat of wooden treads and risers and headed for the far end of the gym, toward darkness. When all the players had been introduced, the lights went up, and the MC said over the frenzied cheering: "Ladies and gentlemen . . . the 1963 Weybridge High School football team!"

The noise reached a crescendo, crepe streamers floated to the floor, balloons rose. TK felt a sudden spasm in his gut, like a miniature version of Tracy's punch that day at the auto shop. He bent over slightly, a worry crowding in on him. This wasn't jealousy; this was physical pain. From gulping Pepsi and pizza? He glanced around. That was when he spotted Penny Griffin. She was standing on the other side of the gym. She had on her reindeer sweater and a pleated skirt and saddle shoes and she was holding a WHS pennant. She saw him then, too, and waved. He wanted to wave back, but his stomach was still tight. Penny waved again, and then she pointed with the pennant. He looked where she was pointing.

By the doorway leading into the gym from the outside, there seemed to be a commotion. People were gathering, and someone was on hands and knees on the floor. For a moment, TK thought someone had lost a contact lens, but then he realized that the kid on the floor had been knocked down. Mr. Morrisette and a man in a dark suit were talking, but TK was pretty sure they weren't exchanging chemistry formulas.

TK looked back toward Penny, but she was gone, and then he saw her making her way through the press of people at this end of the gym, most of them still waving their signs and pennants. TK pushed away from the wall and moved to meet Penny. The pain he'd felt was gone, and he moved through the ring of students until he and Penny met near the doorway where the football team had come in. Penny said something to him, but over the noise of the band and the crowd, he couldn't hear it. She took hold of his arm and stood on tiptoe to speak in his ear, and this time he heard her. "That man in the dark suit . . . he's the one who was asking me about you."

The man was no longer talking with Mr. Morrisette; the chem teacher was helping up the student who had gone down. The man was now speaking with a lean-faced man who had joined him beneath one of the basketball nets on the side of the gym. As TK and Penny watched, a third man joined them; he had a blond crew cut, and like the other two he wore a suit with skinny lapels, a white shirt, and a skinny tie.

"Government men?" Some of the noise was subsiding, but TK spoke directly into Penny's ear.

"That's what the one told me." Penny sounded a little breathless.

"They sure know how to blend in with a bunch of high school students."

"What're they doing here?"

The men conferred, and the first one motioned the other two toward the entryways. The line of football players, still standing in the center of the floor, was breaking up, the guys moving to greet friends and family in the crowd. TK didn't see what happened, but all at once a scuffle broke out (no, a *melee*; the word from tonight's vocab worksheet). Apparently some players had gotten in the way of one of the suited men, and the man was shoving them back. Mike Burke tried to step in, reaching to grip the man's arm, but the man grabbed Mike in a come-along hold and flung him into the bottom row of bleacher seats, where Mike went down in a tangle. The man stood gazing around, and TK realized that he was surveying the crowd, looking for something, or some*one*. TK was pretty sure who.

"I've got to talk to them," he announced and started toward the floor.

Penny clutched his arm. "No," she cried. "Don't."

Now TK saw that the man had spotted him. He brought something like a small phone to his mouth and spoke into it. The two men who'd been guarding the doors held units to their ears. They lowered them and started moving his way.

"Come on," Penny coaxed, "we should leave."

TK sent a final glance toward the confusion on the gym floor. They hurried through a cluster of students. As they reached the doorway that the football players had recently come through, Miss Mutterperl was there, barring his path. Without a word, she motioned Penny to stop. TK and Penny exchanged a look. He nodded and, reluctantly, he thought, Penny stayed put. Miss Mutterperl took TK's arm and hurried him through the doorway. Still without a word, the teacher led him along the corridor, down a flight of steps, but going in the opposite direction from the boys' locker room.

He faltered. That was forbidden territory, the girls' side of the building; but her tug was insistent. She led him to the door of the girls' locker room, where she stopped.

"What's going on?" he asked.

"I recognize one of those men. He was asking about you today."

"Why? What did I do?" He was scared now.

She shook her head. "You did nothing." Unfallen tears had troughed in her lower lids, giving her eyes a fervent light. She clenched her hands in front of her, determined that he should hear her out. "TK, the forces of conformity are so strong, so powerful on all of you. Grinding and grinding, like big millstones . . . making everything into one smooth, bland, faceless consistency. Which is the way it's got to be, I suppose. No one wants lumps in the batter . . ."

He had no idea what she was talking about; still, he wanted to respond, to say *some*thing, but words failed him and he only stared. Then the sharp, metallic sounds of lockers being yanked open came to them from the boys' side, one locker after another, the noise amplified in the connecting corridor, and he had an image of mechanical monsters moving this way on jointed legs. The voices, though, were very human:

"He can't have gotten far."

"Check the showers. I'll go this way."

Miss Mutterperl grabbed his arm. He felt her grip through his jacket sleeve, an almost convulsive clutching, as if her hand were trying to keep itself from trembling as much as it was gripping him. She led him into the girls' locker room, past a series of small individual shower stalls, each equipped with its own privacy curtain and a tiny wooden bench for undressing—details he noted in passing. The only illumination was from a night bulb and the red glow cast by an exit sign over a door at the end, which is where Miss Mutterperl led him. Then, abruptly she released his arm. He looked at her. From the expression on her face it was clear that she was as afraid as he was. He wanted to say something to comfort and reassure her, even to thank her for being a good teacher. But before he could speak, she reached and pushed open the exit door. An alarm began to sound. "Go!" she said tersely.

And he did.

The exit from the girls' locker room took him into another branch of the basement, a hallway he'd never been in before. He hurried along it to a set of double doors but quickly saw that the way was barred, the doors chained shut. To his right was a flight of steps. Up would take him back to the gym, where the rally was still going on; he could hear the pep band playing; down . . . he didn't know.

He went down. He took the stairs two at a time, holding on to the pipe railing because the worn terrazzo treads were slippery. He descended to a subbasement corridor that was lit by small lamps mounted in thick glass jars screwed into the top of the wall at intervals along the way. He kept moving, hoping he was headed toward some escape. He rounded a corner and bumped into a pull-down map on a tripod (Africa, he saw). It teetered and he had to grab it to steady it, then he veered past it and went on. Mutedly, more indistinct but still audible, were the sounds of the band . . . the *oom*pah, and the bass drum (*"Give a cheer, give a cheer . . ."*) and then he saw another set of doors, wire-reinforced glass, shadowy on the other side, and he stopped. His breath was coming fast and shallow. He eased open the door. Darkness. Lost. He had no idea where he was or how to get out (*". . . in the cellars of Old Weybridge High . . ."*) and the idea came: Why not just go back and confront the men in the suits? They were government agents, after all. The government was good, right? *Of* the people, *for* the people . . . What was there to fear? The only thing to fear is—

There was a screech of metal at a distance behind him, and then a clattering *snap* as something rolled up like a giant window shade. He froze. The map! Someone cursed, and then the whole map stand crashed over.

TK scooted through the door.

When it had swung shut he was nearly blind. He put up his hands to shield his face, and he started forward. He shuffled one foot ahead, then the other. From somewhere he could hear a furnace roaring and old steam pipes clanking and hissing. Slowly, his vision began to come back; but at each sliding step his sense of dread grew. Where would this take him? What would he find?

A light fried his eyeballs.

"Gotcha!"

The voice was familiar, but TK had no time to reflect on this, or anything else as something speared into his gut. Swirled into a vortex of pain, he went down.

He lay in a fetal curl, gasping like a boated fish. A flashlight still shone in the dark, casting weird, moving shadows.

"Can't breathe?" someone barked. "You *better*. You got some talking to do."

The speaker rolled TK onto his stomach, wrenched his arms behind him so sharply TK yelped in pain. The man snapped on handcuffs. TK could hear the man breathing from effort as he seized TK under the arms and began to tug. He was dragged a short distance, over a threshold, and dropped onto another floor. A light went on and TK saw he was in a closet crowded with mops and pails. The man—TK still hadn't seen his face—hoisted him up enough to loop the handcuffs around the faucet of a heavy porcelain and steel utility sink. Then, leaning so close that TK could smell his sweat, he said, "You got one chance."

TK looked at Frank Ripley.

"What're the Feds doin' in town?"

"I . . . I don't know."

"The hell you don't. You *called* them." Ripley speared him in the kidneys with his nightstick. He grabbed a fistful of TK's hair and twisted his head around. "Don't horse with me! I'll rough you up good!"

Tears had sprung to TK's eyes. "Please. I—"

Ripley hit him again. "Enemies are taking over the country." He hit him once more. Ripley's face was blotched and veined. Sweat ran from his forehead, glistened in his thick eyebrows. When he spoke again, his voice seemed to come from far away. "I want answers."

A dazzle of panic forced itself through the wooziness settling over TK's mind. It occurred to him that no one else knew he was here. He thought of the stories about kids being caught by the truant officer, menaced, beaten. Was this where Ripley took them? There were rusty smears on the drab concrete walls. Bloodstains?

"People wanna *kill* me," Ripley snarled.

"Who . . . who'd try to do that?" TK was trying to sound reasonable, trying not to cry. Ripley yanked his hair, sending pain lacing through his scalp.

"The fuckin' commies! The yids!" he hissed, spraying spittle. "Because I speak the truth. They gang-banged Joe McCarthy 'cause he had the guts to tell the truth! He was stealing freedom, the pinkos say. Bullshit. Freedom ain't what people need. They need a strong leader, someone with the balls to stamp down hard on the crazies who'd hand the country over to the Reds." His breath was coming hard and fast. "So *talk*!"

"About what? I—I don't—"

Ripley hammered the back of TK's head, banging his face against the sink edge. He felt his lip split open, tasted blood. He struggled against the handcuffs, but it was futile.

Ripley moved back, and TK could see that he wore street clothes, though he had a handgun tucked into his belt. He hunted briefly on a shelf and found a sink stopper, which he plugged into the drain hole. He turned on the taps. Water started to gush into the sink. As the level rose, Ripley picked up a big bottle of Lestoil, uncapped it, and poured the contents into the water. The water began to foam, and the reek of pine solvent filled the air, stinging TK's eyes. Ripley removed his gun and reached to set it on a shelf, out of the way. Suddenly he jerked back with a shriek. TK looked and saw a large gray spider on the shelf.

"Goddamn creepy things!" Using his gun like a hammer, Ripley smashed the spider to pulp. "Damn!" Gingerly, he set the gun on a lower shelf.

A new possibility forced itself on TK. Was the man truly crazy? He *looked* crazy. The salt taste of blood filled TK's mouth, and mingled with the strong pine scent, it made his gorge rise. He swallowed hard.

When the sink was three-quarters full, Ripley shut off the taps. With an abrupt motion, he grabbed TK by the neck and shoved his head down. Water splashed. TK wrung his eyes shut but felt the water burning in his sinuses, searing his cut lip. Ripley held him there for a moment, then yanked him back.

"What do you want?" TK gasped.

Ripley repeated the process several times. Each time he held TK's head under longer. TK had to fight a spiraling panic that he'd drown . . . then he'd be yanked up coughing, water and snot streaming from his nose, eyes blurred. A dark, smoky ribbon of blood moved through the sink water.

"Last chance," Ripley said.

Words were impossible. Ripley shoved him under. This time TK didn't have enough air. His lungs were on fire. His cheeks bulged. He'd swallowed water, the harsh solvent raw in his throat. He'd have to exhale, could already hear the bubbles gurgling past his ear and knew that when he'd vented all his air he would breathe in water and drown—*in a janitors closet, in a damn sink!*

Then, suddenly, the downward force let go. He was jerked upright.

Dizzied, he caught a glimpse of Ripley: eyes agape, face rigid, except for his Adam's apple, which bobbled wildly. TK blinked several times before he saw the other man. The man yanked Ripley back, slammed him against the utility shelves, sending bottles and cleaning supplies scattering. TK struggled to sit up.

It was the man in the dark suit. He thrust the barrel of a revolver under Ripley's chin hard enough to clap Ripley's jaw shut with an audible click.

"Rules say I'm not supposed to draw my weapon unless I mean to use it," said the man, "and I'm nothing if not fussy about rules." He cocked back the hammer.

TK froze. Ripley's face was quivering like an unbaked blob of bread dough. He was wide-eyed and gibbering, making loose, gooey sounds in his throat that frightened TK even more than if they'd been words.

"This place needs some decoration," Dark Suit went on, "so the only question is, which of these walls do you want your brain splattered on? That one? Or—"

"Whatever he's told you about me," Ripley blubbered, "it's—it's—a lie."

"About *you*?"

"—a filthy lie."

"You dumb shit, what makes you think *any* of this has to do with you? You've got a gnat's understanding of the world."

"—I . . . I . . ."

With a sharp, crisp sound, Dark Suit squeezed the trigger.

The gun dry-fired, but right then Ripley did something that TK had read about characters doing in stories in magazines like *Peril* and *Real Male* at DeSantis's barbershop. Even with the overpowering reek of pine solvent the odor was unmistakable. Ripley's sphincters had let go. The truant officer had soiled himself.

Dark Suit lowered his gun and stepped back, and Ripley sagged to the floor. The man put his gun into a shoulder holster under his suit coat. "The keys," he ordered. Mechanically, Ripley obeyed. The man took the keys. He unlocked the handcuffs and pulled TK to his feet. "Let's go."

TK thought to ask where, but Dark Suit was already out the

door. In the corridor, he was joined by one of the other men who'd been upstairs at the rally. Were they both government agents? The second man produced a walkie-talkie. "Okay," he spoke into it, "we've got him. Put me through."

"Wha-what's going on?" TK asked.

No one paid any attention to him. In the janitor's closet behind him, Ripley was sitting on the floor, shoulders sagging, face slack, eyes unfocused. TK wanted to go punch him, kick him. Then, all at once, TK's eyes were streaming tears.

"We've got the kid," the man said into the walkie-talkie. "We're bringing him in."

The kid. The damn crybaby kid. Bringing him in. TK sniffled and wiped at his face. In *where*? What was happening? Who *were* these men? Suddenly he saw the gun there on the bottom shelf. Ripley's. He shook off his self-pity. Without a conscious thought, he picked up the gun, and shoved it into his jacket pocket. That scumbag Ripley might be the truant officer, but this wasn't his school! And these other guys, going around bracing his friends, asking questions. They could *all* go take a flying leap. This isn't their school. It's *mine!*—and if anyone knows his way around here, it should be *me*.

He stepped out of the closet, bolted past the two men, and ran.

"Hey! Get him!"

He was awed by the mazelike vastness of the place. Corridors seemed to go on and on before branching into other tunnels, each one yawning off into darkness. He kept moving, ducking to avoid overhead pipes and ventilation ducts, keeping to the lighted portion, though "lighted" was an overstatement; the bulbs were intermittent, encased in wire cages and casting a weak yellow glow. His footfalls echoed in the narrow spaces, and he was glad for the conditioning he'd done all summer, but even so he was breathing hard. Bile soured his mouth, forcing him to swallow it back.

The basement was the domain of janitors and the men who worked on the furnace. He'd never been down here before; and yet, it was as if he *had*, for with each turn he made, each choice, he was able to keep going, encountering no locked doors, no dead ends. Far behind he heard his pursuers, heard the crackle of a walkie-talkie, saw the occasional bobble of a flashlight beam. As he rounded the next corner, his heart was banging at his ribs. The water he'd swallowed sloshed in his belly, nauseating him. He was light-headed, woozy. He slowed. Now the voices from behind were closer.

"Go that way, I'll go this!"

"I think I heard him."

"We'll get the son of a—"

Gun, TK suddenly thought. He was holding Ripley's gun. Should he ditch it? If they saw him with it would they shoot him? He rounded yet another turn and slid to a stop. The tunnel was at an end. Ahead stood a metal-sheathed door. Affixed to it was a sign. FALLOUT SHELTER. He stared at the familiar three inverted yellow triangles. Like the print from a three-toed paw . . .

Behind him the sounds of his pursuers were closer. He hesitated only a second. He pulled at the door and it swung open without resistance. Just inside, illuminated by the faint glow from the light without, stood stacks of cylindrical brown canisters. Water. This was a cache for civil defense supplies, for use in the event of nuclear attack. He peered into the narrow space, and there, behind the canisters, was another door. A loading door. TK wedged in past the cans, almost knocking over a stack, but he steadied them just in time. The inner door was secured with a barrel bolt lock. He hammered at the bolt with the palm of his hand. Hammered again. It slid free. He pushed open the door and found himself looking into the night.

From far off, over the rooftops of the school, came a wail of sirens. The air was cool on his damp forehead. He was in the back of the high school annex, where trucks came for deliveries. Beyond was the patch of woods that he had looked out on from the detention room; to the left would be the parking lot, night lit by a few outside lamps. He started in that direction, then stopped, his gut seized by a painful cramp. Reflexively, he bent over and retched.

It was over in three spasms. There wasn't much cargo to heave overboard: some bits of undigested pizza in a Pepsi sauce. He coughed out a last thin gruel, coughed out most of his fear and disgust, too. It didn't take away the brackish taste of acid, but he felt better. He wiped a hand across his mouth. There was a streak of blood on his palm from where his lip still bled. Nevertheless, he felt purged. His pursuers would be here any moment. He pulled the gun from his pocket so that it wouldn't fall out, and holding it he started off in a stumbling run, unsure of any destination, without a plan. He hurried around the corner of the school building.

And almost ran smack into someone.

"Tom—!"

Penny.

Stay back, he wanted to tell her, *turn around and leave at once*, but she gave him a look of such tender concern that he almost reached for her, wanting only to hold her and be held by her . . .

"You're soaking wet, and you've cut your lip. Tom . . . are you sick?"

She became aware of the gun in his hand. Her eyes went wide.

What TK saw next was a dark Fairlane parked in back, the lights out, engine running. A spot of orange bloomed in the shadows behind the steering wheel, then it arced out the driver's side window and hit the pavement with a little splash of sparks. Then TK did what he realized he should have done at the very first. He gave Penny a shove. "Get away from me!" he cried.

30 Tom

It was going on 10:00 P.M. when he got back to Edgewater Road. As he sat in the driveway, he put on the mirror light and reached for his cell phone, and as he did he saw the manila folder on the seat. He'd forgotten about it. It was the material on the shipyard that Mike had put together. He'd seen the folder at the Burkes' house when he'd gone there earlier to find a contact number for Mo, and he had grabbed it. Mike was effectively done with the case; Mo would be back soon. So maybe it had just been a temporary distraction for Mike; for Tom, too. Something to keep their minds off other woes. Mike had plenty else to deal with now.

So do I.

Tom flipped through the contents. Pages of notes in Mike's handwriting. Photocopies of Keystone documents on yard safety, worker reports. He went through them perfunctorily. There was nothing he needed to know. More paper to get rid of. The last sheet was a typewritten list. He held it close to the mirror light. It was a tally of the names of men who had worked security details at the yard, ten or so names, none of them familiar.

Except one.

He stepped outside and dialed Penny's number; his heart was drumming a little faster now. He thought—that's odd. Had he left the side door to the garage open?

"Penny," he said when she answered.

"Tom?"

"It's me. Listen—"

"Tom, I've found something. An old file cabinet. It's from—"

"Where are you?"

"I don't know why, but I felt I had to come here. And now . . ."

"Where *are* you?"

"At Officer Ripley's house."

"Get away from there."

"No one's here. These files are from—"

"Did you hear what I said? Get *out*. He could be back any minute. Come here to my mother's house. We have to talk."

Silence.

"Penny?"

Silence.

"Penny!"

The signal was gone.

"He *will* be back," a voice said from nearby. "But he's here right now."

Tom looked up, startled as a man emerged from the shadows of the garage. Not Ripley. Who are *you?* was the question that rose to mind; but he knew. He recognized him from the diner.

"You blow into town and next thing she's lying to me. What the *hell* d'you think you're doing? I saw her looking in her old yearbook. I *heard* you just now!" Penny's husband's voice sounded near hysteria. "Are you *fucking* her?"

Alan raised his right arm high, and there was no missing what he held in his hand. He must've taken the clam fork from the garage. Tom lifted his own hand with the cell phone. (Was he thinking it would make everything clear? That he might urge the man to call Penny and straighten this out?) Alan swung the rusted fork.

The points spiked into Tom's left shoulder and upper chest. The phone clattered across the driveway. Tom gaped after it in strange wonder; then his knees buckled and he collapsed. Pain came almost at once; the irony took a little longer. He was going to die by means of the tool he'd once used to make his living.

Alan stepped near. Tom looked up at him. A moan escaped the man. He hesitated, moaned again, then dropped the clam fork and fled in a wobbling run. Tom had the vague thought to call out to him, to explain to him that he was wrong about his wife, that Penny was faithful . . . but he had all he could do to stay conscious.

He almost managed it.

31 TK

At his shove, Penny took an awkward, stumbling, backward step, her expression full of puzzlement and wounded surprise. "Tom—what's wrong?"

"Just go," he whispered harshly.

The push had been meant as a ploy, a warning. If the men who were after him thought she was there to help him, she could be in trouble, too, but Penny stood where she was. He looked at the dark Fairlane parked in the lot, engine running, and now she did, too. "Go back inside," he said. "Please. I'm getting out of here."

"Going where? You're soaking wet, and it's cold. And get rid of *that*."

It was the first acknowledgment either had made of the gun. He put Ripley's revolver back into his jacket pocket. He didn't try to explain. "I have to get to my car."

"Take me with you."

"*What?*"

"Maybe if we're together . . . or if . . ." She was improvising now, as frightened as he was. "Maybe they won't do anything."

Might that be true? If they . . . No. Out of the question. He couldn't allow it. "Go," he said. She looked hurt. Her shoulders sagged. "Penny, go back inside."

"Miss Mutterperl will ask."

"Say nothing. I'll be okay."

"Take some money, at least." She unsnapped her purse.

"I can't."

"What? Take money from a girl?" She was pushing a crumpled five-dollar bill at him. "Don't be a jerk. Remember what you wrote in Curb Feelers?"

His split lip stung, but he had to smile. She was throwing his words back at him. "All right. A loan." He took the five.

"I'll get a ride home with someone else."

This last was like the unexpected lash of a whip. He'd wanted to be the one, and here he was pushing her away. He felt a bleak helplessness at the absurdity of all of this. Her eyes had a glint of tears. He opened his mouth to speak, but there were no words. And then something happened that took him utterly by surprise. Penny kissed him—a light pressure on his cut lip; just for an instant—then she turned and darted back toward the school.

He got to his car. Inside he locked the doors. At the driveway exit, where school buses departed each afternoon, he paused. His sense of relief vanished. The government sedan was rounding the corner of the building. He faltered for an instant, then stomped the pedal. As he sped down Commerce Street, reason was telling him to go to the police station, report everything. Emotion was saying otherwise. The aftershock of what had just happened was setting in. He began to tremble. He clenched the wheel for fear of losing control. He scanned his mirrors. No sign of the sedan. He couldn't go home; someone might be there waiting. So where? Dari-Twirl? The diner? Drive up to the Crow's Nest to think?

His eye went to the gas gauge. The needle was on the peg. Boss, man, really boss. He'd had the chance to feed the tank earlier, but he'd chosen his stomach instead. Nice move, Bowels. So step one was clear. The Esso station in the Heights would be open. He'd go there, put a tiger in his tank, then figure out what to do next.

32 Tom

On the third try Tom managed to get to his feet. With uncertain fingers, he peeled back his shirt and undershirt and saw four small, ugly punctures, two in his shoulder, two in the meat of his chest. There was a slow ooze of blood. The sight of it freaked him a little. Hell, it freaked him a lot. He couldn't tell how deeply the tines of the clam fork had penetrated. The wounds looked superficial; he had taken something off the blow with his own arm. He found the cell phone lying at the edge of the driveway. It looked like a large bug that had been squashed. He thought of going into the house but then remembered that phone service had been shut off. His hands were shaking as he dug the car keys from his pocket.

He drove as fast as he dared, through scarves of fog drifting across the windshield. The muscles in his upper body were stiffening. Should he go to the hospital? Or find a booth and call the cops? The pain was tolerable, a dull ache, mostly. Still, he was light-headed. To get his mind off the wound, to give his head some ballast, he switched on the radio.

"If you're driving south of the city later this evening, folks, go easy. It's going to be pea soup."

No lie. The fog was growing dense. He poked one of the presets.

"That was Fabian, for all you kids out there, singing 'Turn Me Loose.' Gone from the charts, but not from our hearts. Solid gold because you dug it!"

Tom glanced at the radio. Because we *dug* it? Fabian? Where'd they find that mossback deejay? There was a goose honk and then a bell clanging . . . radio sounds riding a faint memory, and then a musical jingle began . . . *"Out on Route One in Saugus, come dressed just as you are . . ."*

He frowned in mystification.

"Adventure where the service is tops and you never get out of your car." (Laughter.) *"Tell them—"* (Goose honk.) *"Woo-Woo Ginsburg sent you."* (Double goose honk.)

WMEX? AM? That station had gone off the air decades ago. Was Arnie Ginsburg still around? And Adventure Car Hop? There was no chance that place was still operating . . . was there?

"Here's Jimmy Clanton and 'Just a Dream.' "

Tom turned the volume louder and got:

". . . more hits from the eighties and nineties coming your way in sixty seconds."

The digital dial showed an FM signal. He lowered the sound and actually smiled with relief. Just a dream. Yeah, that's pretty close. Or a *prank*. Some wiseacre short-wave op messing with the broadcast signal, sitting in his radio shack, squeezing the rubber bulb of a goose horn, clanging a dinner bell. Ha ha. Good one. Guy had had him going . . .

But the explanation dribbled away. The ham operators he'd known were serious, heavy-browed types, do-gooders, not pranksters, not into mischief. And besides, the wave frequencies weren't the same. But what, then? No way could he bring himself to believe that he'd been hearing Arnie Ginsburg and the *Night Train* show. And who listened to music on the AM dial? The stress of the past few days was getting to him. Tonight's attack. He slowed down, a good idea anyway in this fog, and he tried to slow his heart.

A woman's voice said, "This song goes out to TK . . ." Tom gawked at the radio. The AM signal light glowed. ". . . who didn't get that last dance . . ." He knew the voice. Miss Mutterperl's— sounding as it had thirty years ago.

Then the Platters began to sing "Smoke Gets in Your Eyes."

33 TK

A November wind spanked the trees, sweeping gusts of leaves across the road ahead. TK cupped a palm over his mouth and nostrils and huffed into it. Lestoil-and-puke. God, Penny Griffin had *kissed* him on this mouth. What a treat for her. Like making out with a fresh-scrubbed toilet bowl. Yet, remembering the kiss, the brief softness of Penny's lips, he couldn't help but smile.

A truck bucketed out of a side street and into the road ahead, a newspaper delivery truck (*Boston Traveler/*"Travel the World with Us"). TK slowed. He wanted to pass, but tromping the gas pedal would gulp up whatever little fuel remained. Another couple blocks and he'd be across the railroad track and into the Heights. The Esso wasn't far beyond. At the next corner, the truck braked and a bundle of bound newspapers flew out the door, like a depth charge from a navy destroyer. Papers for the morning delivery kids. Suddenly TK heard a sound that startled him. The whistle of an approaching train. He felt a small flutter of panic. The truck lurched into motion again. Hurry, man.

This time of night any train would be a freight, and likely to be a long one. If he didn't get through the crossing ahead of it, he'd have to wait, or circle all the way down East Street to Elm Hill and back—and no gas stations that way.

The truck braked again. More newspapers went out. The train whistle sounded louder now, nearer. Impulsively, TK spun the wheel hard left, hit the juice, and passed. He bounded toward the crossing. He'd make it.

And right then the motor sputtered and died. Momentum carried him up a short incline, right alongside the old wooden X with the faded warning to STOP, LOOK & LISTEN, and that's where the Rambler stopped. Red lights began to flash. A bell clanged.

He shifted to park; turned the key. *WRRR . . . wrrr . . .* The engine wouldn't catch. He pumped the pedal, praying for one last spurt of fuel. *Wrrrr-wrrrrr-wrrrr.* The guard arm was descending. He flung open the door and jumped out. With the delivery truck driver shouting curses at him, TK put his shoulder to the Rambler's doorpost and managed to push the car across the tracks to the other side, down the short decline. But that was it.

He stood by the dead car in a bitter, helpless frustration. It was all collapsing . . . nothing was working out right. For the second time tonight, his eyes burned with tears. He'd have to leave the car here, walk down to the Heights, borrow a gas can, buy half a gallon of gas if the Esso was still open.

Far away, from back in the direction of the high school, came the faint, frenzied beeping of car horns. The pep rally ending. Soon, a convoy of cars full of hepped-up kids would be parading through the streets of town. Were any of them even the least bit aware of what had happened? Hell, was he? *Give a cheer, give a cheer, for the kids who drink the . . .*

What about Penny? Was she going home? Or was she in the Fairlane, handcuffed and being grilled by the men in suits? He'd better go back . . .

The train's air horn jarred him. In the near distance, through the autumn-bare trees, he could see the glare of the locomotive's head-lamp, like a probing eye. With a creaking and screeching, the slow-moving train approached.

It was a freight, as he'd guessed—a long one from what he could see; out of Boston or Portland or Bangor, perhaps, rolling south. Not sure what else to do, he stood there by the Rambler and watched tank cars and boxcars and flatcars rumble past. *Travel the World with Us.* He stood there as though hypnotized. And then, in an instant, more impulse than plan, a notion came to him. Some of the boxcars had their doors open.

He didn't waste time wondering if he could even do it. He opened the Rambler's door, leaned in and grabbed his letter jacket, slammed the door shut. He pulled on the jacket and loped toward the train. He ran alongside the next open boxcar, gaining speed, and jumped.

He got his head and shoulders in. The floor was rough planks and packing straw that tore at his palms. For a terrified instant he was sure his legs would whack against the post that held the flashing warning lights. Then he scrambled forward. Even so, the post nicked the heel of his trailing foot, nearly knocked off his shoe— and then he was in.

He crawled over packing straw and stood up, spraddle-legged for balance in the rocking car. Steadying himself on the slatted metal wall, he edged back to the door. The train was through Weybridge Heights and starting to pick up speed. Freight cars parked in a siding seemed to blur past. DO NOT HUMP read a sign on one, and he managed a wan smile. *Okay, I won't.*

But Artie Dewitt might try it.

His grin got a little wider. Sure, put the boxcar into the T-Bird. Don Juan's latest conquest. *You want big? Oh, ho, have I got BIG!*

But his jollity was short-lived. As the train got beyond the siding, the locomotive continued to gain speed and soon was racing along, and he realized that, for better or worse, he was committed.

Night wind whipped through the slatted walls and brought a chilled edge. His shirt was still wet, and he shivered. Should've listened to his mother. *Better wear your winter coat, it's November after all. And if you should decide to hop a freight train, rolling along to points unknown . . . well, you just never know.*

He snapped up his letter jacket. Not the warmest of coats, but it cut some of the wind. *I'd be safe and warm, if I was in L.A.* That again. What was that? If I was in L.A.? A song? Mind noise; he'd never been west of Niagara Falls. And right now . . . ? He had no idea where he was going. He settled back in the packing straw, his back against a wall, and let his mind fray out.

Sometime later he heard rustling nearby and felt the nape of his neck prickle. Was someone else in here? He hadn't checked. Was it possible? Is that why the door was open? Afraid to move from his corner, he kept still but peered into the darkness, eyes strained wide. The rustling came again, nearer. Not a person, no. A rat? A snake? He drew farther into his corner.

Whatever it was was moving toward him. He remembered the gun. He tugged it from his jacket pocket. He pointed it, not at all sure how to work it. Suddenly there was a thrash of wings. Birds flapped up and fluttered to the far end of the boxcar. TK let out a breath of relief. Pigeons. He could make out their shapes in dim moonlight, four or five of them, huddled together with their feathers puffed. He laughed.

Where was he now? Kingston? Plymouth? It was hard to say since the view zipping by was mostly of low trees and swamplands and occasional quick glimpses of backyards. Somewhere he passed an orchard, the ripe fruit visible as small moony shines on the low trees, the air briefly fragrant with apple, and then the heavy smell of diesel exhaust returned.

Some of his panic began to subside. It was just a train, after all. Sooner or later it would take him *some*where. He even began to see the adventure in all this. Would any of the kids there at the pep rally tonight believe it? Heck, they wouldn't even have an *inkling*. "See," he could picture Ben Longchamp saying proudly, "vocabulary comes in handy, can even save your life." Sure, but there was nothing *bucolic* about the landscape, thought the *miscreant* as he *absconded* in his *fugue* . . .

Since TK could not seem to get his mind off the chilly night air and all the aches from his flight and escape, his worry about his mom, about Penny, he tried using these things to come up with a plan . . .

But he couldn't. He hadn't had a plan to start with and he certainly didn't have one now. He went over and managed to shut the door; it didn't help much, given that the sides of the car were slatted, but the wind lessened some. Back in his corner he tried to get comfortable, seeking, like the pigeons at the other end, the warmth that all living things sought come November. He drew his head down turtlelike into his jacket, and he discovered that he could conjure the faintest scent of Penny—a clean after-shower smell, the rinse she'd used on her hair . . . and some sweet floral perfume. Was it coming from him? From that one brief contact she'd made with him behind the school? He shut his eyes and tried to imagine her lips on his own . . . the wince of pain the kiss brought to his cut, and yet the incredible, unexpected softness of that brief contact . . . and sitting in the cold, with the rocking, pulsing movement of the train, he felt inconceivably happy.

At least, he told himself, the train was headed south, which might mean Providence or New Haven, where it wouldn't be any warmer than this, but it could also mean New York City, Philadelphia, Washington, Baltimore . . . no, Baltimore first, *then* Washington . . . and he grew sleepy, lulled by the motion and speed of the train . . . Charleston . . . Savannah . . . and on down the eastern seaboard, through towns and cities, summoning names, picturing them on the map in his mind, coming at last to Miami (though why stop there? Did the train run all the way to Key West? Hemingway used to live in Key West), and he would occasionally glance past the slats at the moving moonlit landscape, like a landscape in a dream, and perhaps it was.

He came fully awake, half frozen and stiff, and realized that the train had stopped. Or *mostly* stopped. He was jarred by a spasmodic jerking, which was accompanied by a series of booming rumbles, like approaching thunder. He sat up and glanced at his watch. More than six hours had passed. He dragged the door partway open, blinked, and saw that the sky was paling in the east. He could make out distant buildings. The train was moving in slow fits and starts through a large freight yard. On sidings, lineups of boxcars were being assembled—he guessed they were being humped, and he managed a faint smile, though his cheeks felt like cold taffy. Long chains of DuPont tank cars came into view. Then a sign drifted past. WILMINGTON. *Delaware?* When the train seemed to have stopped for good, he looked around to be sure he wasn't seen, then he climbed out and stood there a moment among cinders and weeds. Beyond rows of idle train cars loomed the outlines of a city, still slumberous but waking.

It was chilly, but he guessed it would be some warmer once the sun was fully up. He took a leak, and then set off to see if there was anyplace where he might get a cup of coffee and breakfast. As he walked around the end of a tank car, he stopped. About a hundred feet away, half a dozen figures were standing around a barrel fire, dancing foot to foot, warming themselves. They were little more than silhouettes, but from the fire-glow on their rough, shadowed faces, he guessed they were hobos. One, a squat figure in a long heavy coat, was talking animatedly, gesturing with his arms. Long hair fell from a pointed cap so that he looked like a troll. The troll shoved a long stick into the barrel and sparks flew up like a swarm of hatching fireflies. He stepped away from the others, looking now in TK's direction. And although the other men didn't lift their attention from the fire, the troll watched him, and something in his intent watching made TK afraid.

TK ducked back the way he'd come. Another freight train was moving through the yard. He hesitated, and then saw that the troll had followed him. Spooked, TK climbed into a freight car. He was getting to be an old hand at this. He withdrew deeper into the protection of the car; and in a moment the train began picking up speed. As it did, he went to the open door and looked back. The man with the pointed hat was running after the train, but he seemed to be moving in slow motion, growing smaller and more distant, and then TK lost all sight of him.

34 Tom

He was out on the neck, though he could not remember having decided to come here. He drove slowly, moving with a sense of dead reckoning, the once familiar streets made strange by darkness, fog, and time. He had not been here since his days of clamming in the tidal coves. He found the street, and then the house. It sat lightless, quiet. He parked and got out. For the moment, the ache in his chest and shoulder had subsided. Penny's car was nowhere to be seen, and probably that was a good thing. She had listened to him and left.

The fog swirled around him, and he shivered a little. Not bothering with the house yet, he went to the high fence surrounding the backyard, lifted the latch, and passed through. Time seemed to collapse. He was here as he'd been on that night long ago, when he and Brain rode their bicycles out.

The swimming pool was gone, filled in; but proof of its existence remained. The lanai still stood in a corner of the yard, and a pair of life rings hung on the back fence, two chalky O's in the dark. A line of ersatz wharf pilings marked a weed-grown path to and from the house. As he stood there reconnoitering something stirred in the back of his mind, the vaguest impression, then it was gone.

He looked down the path to a rear gate, which hung ajar.

Using his good arm, he drew open the back gate. Beyond was a path that ran a short distance through marsh grass to a low finger-pier that reached out into the cove. Tied on the side of the pier closest to him, afloat in the slack tide and just visible in the drifting fog, was a runabout with an outboard motor and a canvas top. On the pier lay a squarish bundle wrapped in plastic.

Forcing himself, he made his way to the pier and started out. As he got nearer he saw that the bundle was in an old shower curtain, bound with rope. His heart was suddenly heavy in his chest. *Get out of here. Go find help, come back with somebody else* . . . Tom stooped beside the bundle. The plastic was opaque and covered with dust and cobwebs. He felt his rationality skidding away, like a car on a sudden patch of black ice. Around him, the marsh grass stirred in a soft wind. He hesitated, then looked closer and saw that the bundle contained paper, files.

"I should've got rid of that stuff long ago."

He spun at the voice, and a white-haired man stepped onto the pier behind him. Tom rose, too. "After you stopped working as a security man at the shipyard," Tom said.

Frank Ripley seemed not to hear him. "And then I just forgot it was even here. Seems everyone else had forgotten, too. Then here she comes poking. Shit. Like you."

35 TK

TK awakened to a rough shaking of his arm, and to an image that made him think it had seeped up out of a bad dream. The railroad yard hobo, the troll in the pointed hat, was crouched over him. TK yelped, but the man clamped a hard palm across his mouth. Frantically, TK tried to scoot away, but he was already wedged into a corner of the boxcar. In a panic he began shuffling a hand around in the straw.

"Lookin' for this?" The troll held up Ripley's gun. He took his hand from TK's mouth and sat back. He had a sour odor of sweat and wine and piss. TK swallowed hard but couldn't speak. "I tried to signal you back there in Wilmin'ton."

"What do you want?" TK managed, just holding on to his voice.

"To warn ya. There's yard bulls ahead."

Yard bulls? In one of the Hemingway stories TK had seen the words. Sadistic railroad guards who looked for guys riding freights, and when they found one . . . The troll pushed to his feet now. Moving in a crabwalk to counter the rocking motion of the car, he made his way toward the door and hauled it open. The train was slowing. "C'mon," he called over his shoulder, "this's your last chance to get off before the siding."

TK wasn't sure whether to trust the man. It could be some kind of trick to lure him off the train. "I don't know. I might take my chances."

"They grab you, it ain't gonna be pretty. If you're lucky, you'll do thirty days for vag. If you're *lucky*. And if I was you, I'd get ridda this." He tossed the gun to TK; then, grabbing hold of one side of the door frame, the man vaulted out.

A minute later, TK did likewise. He chose a slope thick with high grass, which helped some, but even so, the impact was jarring and knocked the wind out of him. When he stood up, he was alone; no sign of the troll. Brushing straw from his clothes, he set off in the direction the train had been going. During sleep, his mind must've been working on the rudiments of a plan, for now one suggested itself. If he could get to Washington, D.C., perhaps he could some-how find out who the federal agents were, could learn what the *hell* was going on.

The walk into the city took about twenty minutes, and to his surprise he discovered he was in Baltimore. There was probably passenger rail service to Washington, but he'd had it with trains, even as a paying rider. The thought of what he'd done made his knees weak. He stood on a busy street and waved futilely at a few cabs, which fled past, ghostly in the pale morning; finally, one stopped. "Washington, D.C.," he said, when he'd climbed in, "as fast as you can."

The driver, a Negro wearing a tweed cap with a union button pinned to one side, turned, frowning. "Did the president die?"

TK's jaw wanted to drop. *"What?"*

*"Some*body high and mighty musta kicked off, to put *you* in charge. Jump in my hack and start dishin' orders."

Chagrined, TK tried again. "Sorry. I didn't mean . . . Can you *please* take me to Washington?"

It seemed to mollify the driver some, but his expression remained skeptical. "For one thing, it's forty miles. And quiet as it's kept, you don't look as though you got the bread."

"What would that cost?"

The man screwed up one eye, rubbed his cheek. "I'd give you a flat rate. Say . . . twinny-fi' bucks."

TK tried to imagine what the fare might be if he chose to stay on the meter, but he had no way of knowing. He envisioned the bills in his wallet. Twenty-five dollars was five racks of clams, a couple tides' worth. He considered trying to haggle with the driver, but he didn't know how to do that. "Okay," he said.

"In advance."

He'd heard stories about cabbies taking advantage of unwitting riders, though the man had an honest face, if a gruff manner. "Fifteen now," he said, surprising himself, "the rest when we get there."

The man chuckled. "Fair enough."

TK had dozed, but now he sat up abruptly and looked out. "Where are we?"

The cabbie glanced across his shoulder. "Just comin' in."

Beyond the windows, huge stone buildings rose against sweeps of trees and lawn. None of the buildings was very high, but they were massive. Last year he'd taken civics with assistant football coach Leo Dunphy, whose teaching method was to sit at his desk and tell the students to do their homework for their other courses, and if anyone wanted to they could read one of the fat history texts he kept on a shelf at the back of the room—no one took that option; the books had dust on them as thick as Bigelow carpets—but the classroom walls were decorated with travel posters of the nation's capital. In the distance now he saw the spire of the Washington Monument.

What he saw next brought him forward in his seat. The long grassy mall leading to the spire held a vast crowd of people. There must've been a hundred thousand or more, many of them carrying signs, though at this distance he couldn't make out what the signs said. In one section of the mall tents were set up—hundreds of tents, in all shapes and sizes, and most of the people in that section were Negroes. He stared as the cab drove past. "Do people camp here?" he asked.

The driver angled his head. "Say what?"

"On the lawn back there—can you pitch a tent?"

The man snorted. "That's gub'ment land."

"But all those . . ." TK turned to look back, and he felt a jolt of utter bewilderment. The tents, the vast crowd, the signs . . . gone. The mall was empty. The morning sun was burning off the clouds, and the Washington Monument was doubled in a long, calm pool of water, shining like a dagger. TK shut up. He considered asking the driver to take him to the White House, but thought better of it. Stay anonymous, he told himself. Why have even one person who can connect you with being here? He paid the remaining fare and got out at the next corner. With the large green W on the right breast of his jacket and "Weybridge High" across the back he'd be a walking commercial. By trial and error, he located a Trailways bus station, rented a locker for a quarter, and stored the jacket. He used the restroom to clean up, and then set off.

At the White House, people were lined up for tours. He had no definite plan yet; maybe it'd be enough to get into the place and be told that the president was in his office safely working. He paid a dollar and joined one of the lines behind a troop of Brownies. The line worked toward an information counter where several older women sat greeting the next people in line. Slowly, since he'd arrived in the city, a belt of pain had been cinching itself around his stomach. Several times he had an impulse to bolt from the line and find the nearest bathroom, but he resisted, and each time the pain subsided. The Brownies went as a group with their leader, and then it was TK's turn. He moved to the far right, to a white-haired woman. "Hello," she greeted with a kindly smile.

"H . . . hello . . ." TK stammered. "Is the president in?"

"I'm sorry, the president and first lady are traveling this week, but he does like to hear from people. Where are you from, young man?"

"Uh . . . Wisconsin."

"Wonderful. Delicious cheese there. Would you like to leave a message?"

"A message?"

"You can write to him," she explained. "People do it all the time. That's what this is for." She patted a wooden box that sat at her elbow. It was about the size of one of the racks that Sid Yarrow used for clams, only instead of being open on top, this had a cover, with a mail slot in it. "There's paper right here."

He took the half-sized sheet she offered—ivory-colored, with an image of the White House embossed on it—and went to a long side table where there were pens in pen stands, like in a bank. The Brownies were already there, scribbling away. One small girl, a southpaw, had her hand turned in that awkward, almost crippled-looking way that lefties have, a pink dab of tongue protruding from her mouth, her face a study in concentration. TK looked at his blank paper. It seemed a mirror of his mind. He hadn't foreseen any of this. He drew a steadying breath and began to write. "Dear Mr. President, if you're reading this I'm glad, because it means I'm wrong, and these bad feelings I've been having that something awful is going to happen are wrong, too." With cross outs and hesitations, he went on in this vein for another few lines, before he realized it was a hopeless ramble. Anyone reading it would be convinced he was a nut. He glanced around. The Brownies had gone. Other visitors were writing quick greetings of their own. He could hear the soft scratching of pens. Slowly, so as not to be conspicuous, he crumpled his sheet and pushed it into his pants pocket. He asked for another sheet, which the woman gave him. He wrote: "Good luck, Mr. President." He signed it, "Sincerely, Thomas Knowles Jr., North Weybridge, Mass."

The white-haired woman smiled and put it into the wooden box without a glance. "I'll be sure he gets it, dear," she said.

With his feelings teetering between the brief exhilaration of having made it here and taken some action to a sense that he hadn't really accomplished anything at all, TK walked around Washington for a time. The belt of pain loosened some but didn't go away entirely. At the big grassy mall, he wondered about the huge crowd of people he'd seen—or obviously imagined. What had been written on the signs they'd been carrying?

He got directions to a public library branch and used the card catalogue. Although it took some time, he located what he wanted: a list of U.S. newspapers, along with addresses, circulation figures, and contact information. Mainly on the basis of recognizing the newspapers' names, and because he wanted sizable dailies in various parts of the country, he selected *The Washington Post, The New York Times, The Atlanta Constitution*, the *Chicago Sun-Times*, the *Dallas News*, the *Los Angeles Times*, and the *Kansas City Star* (where Hemingway had once been a correspondent). On a whim, he added one more: the *Adams Point Eagle*. In a stationer's he bought plain white notepaper, envelopes, and a Scripto ballpoint pen. He fed a quarter and a nickel into a postage machine and got ten first-class stamps. He wrote the identical letter eight times, printing it in block capitals, varying only the addresses. His hand was cramping when he finished. He stamped and sealed the envelopes. Handling them by the edges so as not to leave fingerprints, he mailed them in three separate batches at mailboxes he passed.

He wandered around the city awhile longer and found himself

on a street corner, watching a traffic light go through its cycles and feeling that his time here was coming to an end. He made his phone call at three o'clock. On the sixth ring, just as he was about to hang up, a female voice answered.

"Is this . . . the Griffin residence?" he asked haltingly.

"Tom?"

"Penny? I didn't recognize—"

"Where are you?"

"A long way off. I'm in—" He stopped, instinctively aware that it might be better not to say. "Penny, are you okay? Since last night I mean?"

"I'm fine. But I'm worried about you."

"I'm okay, really. I need to ask a favor. Can you telephone my mother?"

"Of course."

"Tell her we spoke, that I'm okay. Say I'm on a field trip and I meant to call."

"Will she believe it?"

"Maybe."

"All right. Do you want me to tell school anything?"

Yeah, he thought. There's plenty I want you to tell them. Starting with Pop Sterns. But that would have to wait; and he'd have to do it himself. "No, that's all." He hesitated, then said, "Thanks for last night, for . . . being a friend."

"When will you be back?"

"I'm not sure yet."

"Oh."

"I'll call you."

"All right. Tom—"

"Yeah?"

"Good luck."

He walked to the Trailways bus terminal, reclaimed his jacket from the locker, and bought a ticket to Boston.

36 Tom

Frank Ripley had not changed as much as some people in Weybridge had, though enough that Tom hadn't recognized him smoking a cigar on the VFW porch the night of the reunion, or at the country club just that afternoon. He still had a gun. It was pointed at Tom. Funny, as many times as Tom had written about such a situation in fiction, it had never happened to him in fact. He was scared.

"The past," Ripley mused. His voice was raspy with age. "Better to have left the past right where it was. Except we can't any longer." He motioned with the gun for Tom to step over to the boat.

Tom did. He peered down into the covered cockpit and by the glow of a dock light he saw Penny. She sat against the gunwale, bound hands and feet with rope, a strip of duct tape across her mouth. She looked up at him, wide-eyed.

Tom turned on Ripley, who kept his gun leveled on Tom's chest. "She isn't part of this." But *he* was beginning to understand. The former cop and truant officer, moonlighting as a security guard at the shipyard, had brought company worker files here, maybe under instruction, perhaps on his own. Tom was pretty sure that the files would reveal a trail of deception and a cover-up of asbestos-related health problems, even deaths. He looked at the bundle sitting there on the pier, shrouded in plastic.

"It should've stayed hidden," Ripley murmured. "*Would've.* I'd more or less forgotten it was even out there. Put it in the boat." He motioned at the bundle. "We'll take a ride."

And only you will come back, Tom thought, the dialogue forcing itself on him:

The way it'll go down, I'll have to shoot you. The rest won't be a problem. Some weight, some rope.

That'll be the end of it.

I'm tired. I've worked my ass off for years. Time for all this to be over.

Did you get to Mike Burke?

Burke? Big-shot athlete in his day; wound up batting zero. I've kept an eye on him. I was watching him the night of the reunion.

Tom cleared his throat. "Does the mayor know about this?"

Ripley frowned. "That shallow dope? He's in his own fantasyland. He thinks he invented this town."

Tom glanced down at Penny. She was watching him so intently that he had the idea she was reading his thoughts. He looked away, processing this; then back, just a quick glance.

"Let's do it," Ripley said.

Tom bent and put his hands underneath the bundle of files. The plastic shower curtain rattled crisply and gave off an odor of must. His chest and shoulder ached. With Ripley standing by, Tom moved the bundle to the edge of the dock. Ripley pushed it with his foot and it dropped into the boat with a thud.

"Get the bowline."

Suppose I refuse?

Then I shoot you right here.

Her, too?

There's no one around to hear it.

Tom moved to the bow. The night around them was blind, and except for the intermittent moan of a foghorn off in the channel toward Germantown it was dumb, too. As he bent to loosen the line, at the corner of his vision, he saw movement. A large spider crab was scuttling up the seaweed bearding the nearest piling. Harmless but ugly. Tom suppressed a shudder. *Ripley is scared of spiders.* Tom blinked. Where'd that come from?

"Untie the goddamn line."

Tom knelt, his back to Ripley, and began to loosen the rope.

The thought came again, as insistent as it was irrational: *He's afraid of spiders.*

Carefully, Tom reached one hand into the water and gripped the crab's rough shell. For an instant, the crab resisted, then released its hold on the seaweed and came away, wriggling long stick legs. Tom rose, turning, and lofted the crab into Frank Ripley's face.

Ripley shrieked. He batted at the crab with his gun, and Tom straight-armed him. Ripley stumbled. One foot stepped off the edge of the pier, managed to find the plastic-wrapped bundle behind him, but slipped. Arms pinwheeling, he fell. His head slammed against the gunwale. He bounded off and splashed into the water facedown. Tom watched him for a moment, but the man's only movement was a slight bobbing on the tide.

"Penny," he cried and went to her.

37 TK

"**Come on**, you guys, let's put it out for Sears!"

Al Lake was pinging around the sales floor, trying to rev up his crew; what he was mostly doing, though, was getting on everyone's nerves. He and the music. The store had been playing Christmas carols pretty much nonstop since early November, string-heavy arrangements from the likes of the Ray Conniff Singers, and Percy Faith and his Orchestra. One of the other stock boys, a dark, angular kid name Augie, who'd been there a week longer than TK, said, "Gee, Mr. Lake, can we do something about the music?"

"Something wrong with it?"

"Well, you know . . ."

"You want some of that 'Jingle Bell Rock' crap, that what you're saying? 'Rockin' Around the Christmas Tree'?"

Be fine with me, TK thought. Or that new one by the Beach Boys he liked, "Little St. Nick," but he wasn't going to get into it with Al Lake. Augie, however, seemed to consider the challenge a moment before withering. "This is okay, I guess."

Customers and sales staff alike were busy. With little more than a month till Christmas, catalogue shopping was brisk. TK and the other warehouse boys on duty that Friday were filling the orders (or hanging decorations, as TK was presently doing, suspending foil snowflakes in the big windows).

At two o'clock, he was sent on break. As strictly seasonal help, and low in the pecking order, he didn't have much choice about his schedule. He drew on his loden coat, working the wooden toggles into their loops, the day having grown rainy raw out there. He wasn't hungry yet, but he'd go to the sub shop next door and get a Coke, which might help keep him awake. As he stepped into the parking lot, preoccupied, a green Simca braked with a screech a foot from him. The driver, a moon-faced woman in a gold kerchief, leaned on the horn. TK stepped back and she bucked past with a shrill volley of unseasonal greetings. Absently, as if he'd forgotten why he was even out here, he turned and went back into the showroom.

He walked over to the television display section. Of the twenty or so demonstrator sets there, about two-thirds were turned on. *I've Got a Secret* was in progress (Al Lake insisted that all demonstrator models be tuned to the same channel, for comparison purposes— "So customers can see what horse they're buying"). The first set was a twenty-one-inch Motorola console model in a blond wood cabinet. Henry Morgan and Betsy Palmer were cracking up at some joke. TK raised the volume. Impelled by something he didn't even think about, he went to the next set, an Admiral, and the next, a Zenith, and did the same.

Augie drifted over. "Man, what gives?"

TK turned to the next set.

"You better cool it. Lake is on the rag."

TK continued along the row of demonstrator sets (a Westinghouse, a Magnavox, another Admiral), raising the volume, which began blotting out some choir (was it the Mormon Tabernacle?) singing "O Come, All Ye Faithful" on the store PA system.

When Al Lake hollered, "Hey!" Augie sent TK a sidelong I-told-you-so glance and drifted away. Lake excused himself from a customer and stalked over.

"Knowles!"

TK paid no attention. He was on the next row of TVs, turning on the ones that were off. He was reaching toward an RCA tabletop model when Al Lake grabbed the sleeve of his coat and yanked him around hard enough that one of the toggle buttons popped off. "What the hell d'you think you're doing?" Lake demanded.

By now there were a dozen or more sets going at high volume. With the babble of sounds, the TV host seemed to be pissed off, shouting questions at a contestant. The video images were identical in their content, all black and white, but some were crisp, others softer, the grays more muted; one was downright fuzzy.

Lake let go of TK's sleeve and poked a finger into his chest. "Punch out! You're fired!" He bent to the nearest set and snapped it off. As the picture was sucked into a small glowing center, he reached for the next TV in line, the blond wood Motorola, and shut that off, too, sliding the console door shut with an emphatic clack. He bent to the third set . . . and stopped.

The picture on the screen, on every screen that was still active, went to a test pattern. There was a blare of music, and a determined voice said, "We interrupt programming to bring you a special bulletin."

Walter Cronkite appeared, looking slightly shaken, as though the studio camera had caught him before he was ready. But his voice was firm when he said, "In Dallas, at approximately"—he plucked off heavy-framed eyeglasses and glanced at a row of clocks mounted on the studio wall behind him—"one o'clock Central Standard time . . ." He replaced his glasses and faced the viewers, "there occurred what was apparently an assassination attempt on the president."

319

Over the Christmas song still issuing from ceiling speakers there was a collective sound of breath being suddenly held. From across the showroom floor, people converged. Salesmen and customers, phone operators, stock boys and clerks stood facing the ring of TV screens. Augie slid open the door to the twenty-one-inch Motorola that Al Lake had peremptorily shut off and turned it back on.

"It appears," Walter Cronkite resumed, "that the president and his party, including Texas governor John Connolly, were unhurt. The Secret Service has diverted the motorcade to an undisclosed location. Dallas police, meanwhile, have sealed off the area of Dealey Plaza and reportedly have taken several suspects into custody. Early reports say that there may have been advanced warning of a plot. Again, repeating . . . at approximately one o'clock Central time . . ."

People pushed in close to the TVs, every eye, every ear taking in the details, the reassurances that President and Mrs. Kennedy and Governor Connolly and his wife were safe, that suspects were in custody. For one instant, TK looked up and saw Al Lake give him an odd, quizzical look, before they both turned back to the screens.

38 Tom

What?

You're going to make me say it again, aren't you, girl. All right, I will. I'm coming back here.

What about Los Angeles?

It's not home.

But your career, your movie . . .

Tom played the dialogue, inventing it the way he did, speaking the parts aloud. Imagining the action, too. Imagining Penny with him.

And there she was, for real, waiting by the war memorial near the old high school. She waved as he reached the top of the rise.

"Sorry I'm late," Tom said. "I was at my mother's."

"How is she?"

"Glad to be back in her own home, I think."

Penny held his gaze. "And how are you?"

"I'm fine. Dr. Simkin says I'm on the mend."

"Good. I'm sorry about what happened."

"It's past."

I'm considering new options. I think I'll start digging again.

Come on, no offense, fella, but aren't you a little old for digging clams?

But she knew what he meant. He wanted to learn all that had gone on at the shipyard. He wanted to think about people, and connect with their stories. He wanted to know more about Brain, and his slow recovery that still lay ahead; and Audrey Mutterperl, and Ben Longchamp. About young Mike Burke's being scouted by the Washington Senators, a team that didn't even exist anymore. And about Ray Sevigny, and Croz and the A-BOM and Blinky Keenan and Pop Sterns. About Frank Ripley.

And about you, too, girl.

The dialogue went on in his head. It wouldn't play out so fluently in reality; it never did; there was always that gulf between the energy of thought and the labor of words, but he hoped some parts of the big story would hold true. He'd work at it. There was no rush. For now there were improvements to make on the house on Edgewater Road so that Mom would be more comfortable there. In due course he would get to other things. But as he had not done for a long while, not for years, he felt there was time now. The stories, and the people and places that they were about, they weren't going anywhere. Memory tended to deepen with time.

He remembered a conversation with Brain, probably thirty years ago. A question: What happens when something doesn't quite achieve escape velocity? And Brain's reply: Eventually, gravity takes hold and brings it back to earth. Tom felt he was reentering the world at its very heart.

He felt forgiving of others and of himself. He did not know if or how Penny figured in any of this, and for now it was okay not to know. She had her own life, and whatever she decided, he would accept. He was happy to be her friend. He didn't have answers, but he was hopeful, and when you had hope, you could act.

"Shall we walk?" Penny said.

"Let's."

They started down the slope, their footsteps kicking through the vivid drifts of leaves, and for just a moment he shut his eyes and breathed in the mingled aromas of deep autumn and of the ever-constant, forever-changing Atlantic. He had been away a long time.